PRAISE FOR THE BOOKS OF KAREN McQUESTION

"I was riveted to the page and on occasion brought to tears. A book you don't want to miss."

—Barbara Taylor Sissel, bestselling author of *Faultlines* and *The Truth We Bury* on *Half a Heart*

"Karen McQuestion just keeps getting better! *Hello Love* is an enchanting, impossible-to-put-down novel about big hearts and second chances."

—Claire Cook, *USA Today* bestselling author of *Must Love Dogs*

"An emotional and engaging novel about family . . ."

—Delia Ephron on *A Scattered Life*

"McQuestion writes with a sharp eye and a sure voice, and as a reader, I was willing to go wherever she wanted to take me. After I finished the book, I thought about how I might describe it to a friend, and I settled on . . . 'You should read this. It's good.'"

—Carolyn Parkhurst on *A Scattered Life*

"The plot is fast paced and easy to dive into, making this a quick and exciting read."

—*School Library Journal* on *From a Distant Star*

"I devoured it in one sitting!"

—*New York Times* bestselling author Lesley Kagen on *Edgewood*

"At first glance *Favorite* is a story of a girl and her family learning to cope with loss. But at some point it morphs into a psychological thriller. It's an unexpected but welcome turn that will leave readers on the edge of their seats."

—Jessica Harrison, *Cracking the Cover*

"This story featuring a strong protagonist who has mastered the art of being the new girl will appeal to girls who are fans of this genre."

—*School Library Journal* on *Life on Hold*

"This is an adventure that is sure to appeal to both boys and girls, and I can't wait to read it to my students."

—Stacy Romanjuk, fourth-grade teacher at Hart Ransom School in Modesto, California, on *Secrets of the Magic Ring*

"An imaginative fable about two witches that should excite young readers."

—*Kirkus Reviews* on *Grimm House*

Dovetail

OTHER TITLES BY KAREN McQUESTION

FOR ADULTS

A Scattered Life

Easily Amused

The Long Way Home

Hello Love

Half a Heart

Good Man, Dalton

FOR YOUNG ADULTS

Favorite

Life on Hold

From a Distant Star

The Edgewood Series

Edgewood (Book One)

Wanderlust (Book Two)

Absolution (Book Three)

Revelation (Book Four)

FOR CHILDREN

Celia and the Fairies

Secrets of the Magic Ring

Grimm House

Prince and Popper

FOR WRITERS

Write That Novel! You Know You Want To . . .

Dovetail

A Novel

KAREN
McQUESTION

LAKE UNION
PUBLISHING

This is a work of fiction. Names, characters, organizations, places, events, and incidents are either products of the author's imagination or are used fictitiously.

Published by Lake Union Publishing, Seattle

www.apub.com

ISBN-13: 9781542042376
ISBN-10: 1542042372

Cover design by Shasti O'Leary Soudant

Printed in the United States of America

For Barbara Ostrop, who translates my books into German, making them better in the process.

We don't actually fear death, we fear that no one will notice our absence, that we will disappear without a trace.

—T. S. Eliot

CHAPTER ONE

Pearl ~ 1983

Time has a way of evening things out. I was beautiful once, turning heads and garnering admiring glances, but now I would not stand out in a group of my peers.

If you saw me in public, picking up prescriptions at the drugstore or sitting in the waiting room at one of my many doctors' appointments, you wouldn't give me a second glance. If you thought about me at all, you might think I looked like a nice white-haired grandma. Or, if you're a mean-spirited type, you'd peg me as a broken-down old hag, one who'd lived a bit too long. One foot in the grave.

And you wouldn't be wrong either way.

If you read a brief summary of my life, nothing would seem out of the ordinary. It would go like this: Born to an upper-middle-class family in a small town in Wisconsin in 1899, the second of seven daughters, Pearl married young and had one son. Upon the death of her husband, a World War I veteran, she was widowed in her forties and never remarried. After her husband's death came a succession of office jobs, none of them noteworthy, but because she made some good investments in the stock market, she accrued enough to build a nice nest egg. When her father passed away, she moved back into her childhood home and spent most of her elder years living there until poor health forced her into an old folks' home.

Phrased like that, it sounds like a very small, uneventful life. I guess in a way it has been. Honestly, I had planned for more. I was going to travel the world and have big adventures. So much for that.

Getting old sneaks up on you. People see you differently. Weaker. They use the word *frail* and rush to your side to help you over curbs and such. Others see you as a problem just for existing. I understand that and will not be offended if you're wondering why God takes youngsters and leaves old-timers like me behind. I have often wondered the same thing myself. My body has long since worn out, held together now by spit and baling wire, my bones creaky, my joints complaining with every move.

I have regrets, many, many regrets. One night, while lying in bed, I realized that I'd broken each of the Ten Commandments at least once. It was a horrifying thought, made all the worse by realizing there's nothing that can be done about it. What's done is done. You can't unring the bell. You can bet I would, if given a chance.

I find myself praying every day, something I never did much of before. Fear is what drives me. I don't want to go to hell, if there even is such a place. And I know I'm not a shoo-in for heaven; this worries me.

You'd think after so many years, I would be as wise as an old owl, but if anything, the opposite is true. The more I learn, the less I understand, and the more uncertain I become. And maybe that's just the way it should be—the afterlife as a mystery known only to God.

I do know one thing. I am the only one left who knows the truth about the final moments in the life of Alice Louise Bennett. She was my sister, only eighteen months older. The two of us were as different as the night sky and the morning sunrise. Alice was the one with a heart of gold. My father called her Ally-bird because she sang like a nightingale. She loved everyone in our family, but I always thought I was her favorite. She was the best of all of us.

There has to be a reason why I'm still around. Lately, I've been thinking that it may be to seek redemption. To that end, I'm on a quest to change my ways, to repair some of the damage I've done. When I meet my Maker and he says, "Pearl, what do you have to say for yourself?" I want to be able to say that at the end, I tried. Better late than never. The effort has to count for something.

Alice died at the tender age of nineteen. She would have lived much longer if not for me and my foolish pride. Her death was a great loss.

After she left this earth, nothing was ever the same again.

I miss her still.

CHAPTER TWO

1983

Joe was in group therapy when he got the news that someone had come to sign him out and he would soon be leaving the facility. This was a surprise. Just that morning, Dr. Jensen had told him he was nowhere near ready to be discharged from the Trendale Psychiatric Treatment Center. The good doctor, his face serious, had said, "In my professional opinion, you are still in need of a lot of help, the kind you can only get right here."

"I'm legally an adult," Joe said. "I can check myself out, right?" It made sense. He was twenty-two—old enough to vote, drink, and drive. He should be able to make decisions about his own health.

Dr. Jensen shook his head. "Not if you're deemed to be a risk to yourself or others."

"But I'm not. A risk, I mean." It was ludicrous that his sanity was in question. Joe wasn't a drug user or an alcoholic. He'd never had hallucinations. Sure, two of his recurring nightmares were violent, but he himself was not prone to violence. Even as a kid, he'd avoided schoolyard fights. He didn't have it in him.

"I understand that's your take on it, but it's really my call." The doctor clapped a friendly hand on his shoulder. "I know it's difficult, but we'll get there, Joe. Patience, son. Patience."

Defeating words meant to be encouraging. Joe wasn't in prison, technically, but it felt like it. The doors were locked; his mail, both incoming and outgoing, was read by the staff, and they listened in on his phone calls. So many times he regretted having confided in his father in the first place. That had been a mistake. His dad had told his stepmom, who'd become insane with worrying. If he were being perfectly honest about it, she had good reason. On more than one occasion, he'd woken the entire family with his screaming. After a while, bedtime began to make him anxious, so he'd started staying up late, throwing back a few beers in the hope it would mute the dreams. Even the guys at work noticed the mornings he'd staggered onto the jobsite exhausted, bags under his eyes. The worst of it came the night he'd sleepwalked into his sister's room, waking her up and mumbling in a way that scared her. Knowing that he'd done that terrified him as much as it did the rest of the family.

He'd lived with his family for only a month at that point, having moved home after his landlord sold the building to a developer who was converting the place into condominiums. Joe wasn't planning on staying with his folks for more than a month or two, just long enough to get another apartment. And that's how it would have gone down, if not for the dreams and his stepmother's fears.

The next thing he knew, they'd driven him north to Wisconsin and had him checked into the treatment center, something he'd reluctantly agreed to just to placate them. The white coats at the center promised him help, but in three months, all he'd gotten was a lot of talk and an array of pills. At least the pills helped dull the nightmares, but they weren't really a solution. He was ready to call himself as cured as he would ever be, then head home to deal with it on his own, but each time he brought up the subject, Dr. Jensen said he wasn't ready. "You're holding back, Joe. If you want us to help, you need to open up."

Learning he could walk out of Trendale that very day was like hearing that the governor had unexpectedly pardoned him.

When it happened, he was one of eight people sitting on hard plastic chairs arranged in a circle. The TV across the room was still on, a leftover from the previous group, "Current Events," which consisted of watching the five o'clock news and discussing it afterward. Joe's group was called "Open Discussion," leaving the topic open to the staff member who would be moderating.

Joe found the images on the TV screen distracting. Even without the sound, he knew the words to the Sony Walkman commercial and mentally inserted them: "Sony introduces the only cassette player as small as a cassette case. The incredible-sounding Super Walkman!" The banner at the bottom of the screen said, "Coming this September!" The new one looked cool, but he wasn't about to replace the one he had back in his room. He'd packed only a few cassettes, not realizing he'd be gone for so long. Joan Jett & the Blackhearts. Fleetwood Mac. Hall and Oates. Before coming to Trendale, he'd used his Walkman every day, but they'd discouraged it here, saying he was using it as a buffer to keep from dealing with real life. He missed having his music with him all the time.

The Trendale Psychiatric Treatment Center was a big believer in schedules, something that kept him occupied from the time he woke up until lights out. Sleep schedule. Meal schedule. Exercise schedule and, of course, therapy schedule. He attended a lot of therapy discussion sessions as well as a regular one-on-one appointment with Dr. Jensen. And tucked between the regularly scheduled activities were music therapy and art therapy.

The staff seemed to believe that their therapy, combined with the right medication, could cure anyone. Joe was proving to be a challenge, but they assured him they wouldn't be giving up on him anytime soon.

He tried, really he did. Joe had discussed every event in his life in detail, with a special focus on his mother's death and his father's remarriage, since Dr. Jensen thought the disturbing images that came to him in the night stemmed from childhood trauma. While it was true his mother had died in a car accident when he was a toddler and his father had remarried when he was in first grade, neither event struck him as being overly traumatic. He'd been home with his father at the time of the accident and didn't remember his mother at all. Shortly after her death, he and his father had moved in with his aunt Betsy, who had been kind and nurturing. Nothing traumatic there. They'd lived with her for two years until his dad had met and married his stepmother. Joe had adjusted well to the new family dynamic. It helped that his stepmom was a sweet woman who loved his dad, cared about Joe, and was a good cook. And after she'd given birth to his little sister, Linda, they'd come together as a real family. From then on, she was his mom. There was no trauma that he could recall, no matter how hard he tried.

On the day he was sprung free, Nurse Fletcher was leading the group, starting them off with the topic of "Progress," which was really just a sneaky way of getting them to talk about their problems and how they were faring. One by one, they went around the circle, explaining the events that had brought them here and talking about how Trendale had helped improve things. It could have been a commercial for the place.

When Joe had first arrived at the facility, his philosophy had been to downplay his symptoms, hoping to sound sane and reasonable, all the quicker to go home. *No problem here! Just a few bad dreams!* He'd glossed over the lack of sleep, made light of how he sometimes woke up in a cold sweat, screaming, his heart pounding, the memory of the dream as vivid as anything he'd experienced in real life. Making light of his situation had backfired in a big way. When Dr. Jensen told Joe one of the therapists had labeled him uncooperative, Joe adjusted accordingly, using more descriptive words and making sure to be expressive, using gestures and talking about his *feelings*, but they still viewed him suspiciously. He suspected his status had been changed from *uncooperative* to *holding back*.

If there was a way to satisfy them, he couldn't figure it out.

This particular evening, he listened intently to each of his fellow patients, nodding sympathetically at their litany of woes. When it came to his turn, Joe took a deep breath and summarized the situation as it had happened at home. "It started out when my parents were concerned about the dreams I'd been having," he said.

"Your parents were concerned?" Nurse Fletcher raised one eyebrow.

"I was concerned too, of course." He looked around the room, taking note of all the expressions. Most of the others had heard his story many times before and were clearly bored. The newest patient, a doughy-faced woman in her forties with a tendency to swear like a sailor, looked only slightly more interested. "The dreams were vivid and had auditory, visual, and olfactory components." He was proud of this additional information, the wording of which he'd stolen from one of the doctors. "A physical exam and blood tests did not show a biological reason for my problems." Finding that out had proved reassuring, until he realized that since there was no biological underpinning, he was now officially a head case. "Two of the dreams leave me feeling sad and depressed, and two are frightening."

The new woman broke in. "What is it about them that's sad and frightening?"

Even though he knew the answer, Joe took a moment to appear as if he were seriously considering her question. Finally, he spoke. "They didn't feel like dreams. They seemed real. Like I was there."

She scowled. "That's no big deal. All dreams feel like they're real when you're in them."

Nurse Fletcher cleared her throat and said, "This group is about respect. We don't disparage the experiences of others here."

"Sorry." Her head dropped, and her gaze went to the floor.

"Don't worry about it," Joe said.

The door, which was slightly ajar already, flew open, and one of the aides stuck her head into the room. It was Frieda, a favorite among the patients, known for her cheery disposition and sympathetic glances. "Joe Arneson? Someone is here for you."

Nurse Fletcher stood, all the better to show who was in charge. "He's in a therapy session right now."

Frieda said, "It's his grandmother. Come to check him out and take him home."

"Check him out?"

"Yeah. It's his dad's mother. She says he's being held here illegally, and she's threatening to call the authorities."

"Very well then." Nurse Fletcher gestured impatiently to Joe to leave. "You may go."

Joe rose to his feet, puzzled. There was no way someone had come to check him out, and especially not his dad's mother, who'd died before he was born. Following Frieda down the hall, he squelched the urge to tell her there must have been some mix-up. Maybe he could take advantage of the confusion and slip out the door before they figured out this woman wasn't connected to him at all.

"She's a feisty one, your granny," Frieda shot back, walking quickly. "Said if we couldn't produce you packed and ready to go in fifteen minutes, she'd leave and come back with the police. She brought her attorney with her."

"Sounds about right."

Frieda stopped now, gesturing down the hall toward his room. "Better get scootin' then and get your things together. Dr. Jensen don't want no trouble."

"Yes, ma'am."

She waited while Joe gathered up his few possessions and stuffed them in his duffel bag. He took one last look at the room: twin beds bolted to the floor, dressers built into the cement block wall, and a clock over the door, the incessant ticking enough to make a person insane if they weren't already. His roommate, Clarence, was not in the room, probably pacing the hallways near the dining room. Poor Clarence.

Nice guy but so troubled. Clarence had routines he couldn't seem to stop doing, no matter how much talk therapy he participated in. He'd had electroconvulsive therapy and had lost some memory. The staff said it was likely to come back over time, but the loss troubled him, and sometimes at night, Joe heard him crying. The only things that helped were the pills the nurses doled out each evening. As much as Joe wanted to leave, Clarence wanted to stay. He liked the routine. He said it made him feel safe.

Joe spoke to the empty room. "Goodbye and good luck, Clarence." He hoisted his duffel bag off his bed and went out in the hall where Frieda stood, waiting to take him to meet the woman claiming to be his grandmother.

CHAPTER THREE

1983

Pearl didn't know what to expect at Trendale, so she came prepared to fight. Paperwork and legal expertise were her weapons of choice, and to that end, she brought Howard, her old friend and former attorney. Well, maybe not former. He still *was* her attorney, even though he was no longer practicing. Nothing wrong with his mind, although his body had definitely seen better days. The same age as Pearl, he walked with the trepidation of a baby who'd just learned to move upright. He always seemed just on the verge of toppling over and probably would have without his cane. She'd urged him to dress in his finest for the trip, and when he walked out, the sight of him attired in his Sunday best made her smile. Even at his age, he cut a fine figure in a suit, his bow tie only slightly askew.

Pearl had run the scenario past him weeks earlier, and Howard had advised her to bring proof of her family ties. She already had a copy of her son's birth certificate, and getting a copy of her grandson's proved to be easy, if not immediate. After she'd gotten his home address from the private investigator she'd hired, she'd called the courthouse in her grandson's county of birth. The nice lady who'd answered the phone had mailed her a form, which she'd filled out and mailed back with a check.

Three weeks later, the birth certificate had arrived. When she opened the envelope, she regarded it with amazement. Her grandson, Joseph Allan Arneson, son of her son, William John Arneson. She counted backward; the current year, 1983, minus Joe's birthdate meant he was twenty-two, nearly twenty-three. For more than two decades, he'd been alive and she'd never set eyes on him. Well, that was about to change. After being disconnected from family for so long, it was good to have confirmation that she really did have people. Right in her hand, she held the legal documents that proved the generational flow, mother to son, and then from that son to *his* son, her grandson. The fact that she'd never met Joe was beside the point. He was blood, and she needed him. Selfish? Maybe a little, but she was too old and too tired to dwell on such thoughts. If the boy didn't want to go with her, that would be her answer, and a disappointing answer it would be too, but she had to try. She'd had no luck with his father; perhaps the son would be more open.

When Joe walked confidently into the lobby, his duffel bag slung over one shoulder, it all came together. Her plan was working, everything falling into place. She grinned at the sight of him, not even caring if she looked like a dotty old lady, leaning forward on her walker. She hadn't been prepared for him to look like such an adult. He could have passed for much older than his age. He was a handsome man, reminiscent in appearance of both her husband and her uncles on her mother's side. Something else was familiar about him too, the way he walked, the half smile he gave her in return to her own, like he wasn't sure what game was being played but he was happy to go along with it. He didn't look like he belonged in a mental hospital, that was for sure.

Dr. Jensen spoke first. "Joe, I was explaining to your grandmother that this is an inopportune time for you to be leaving treatment. I feel—and I think you do too—that we are on the cusp of a breakthrough. If you can assure your grandmother that you're fine, perhaps she can come back tomorrow during visiting hours. That will give us all time to think this through."

Pearl moved the walker aside and took a step forward. "Come here, you," she said to Joe, her arms extended. "Give your old granny a hug." He walked into her arms and leaned in for an embrace. She whispered, "Let's get the hell out of here." When they pulled apart, he nodded in agreement.

"The risk of leaving now," Dr. Jensen said, appealing to Howard, as if he had any say in the matter, "is that all of Joe's progress could become undone. It would be a shame for that to happen, after all the hard work he's done in therapy." His tone was sincere, but Pearl wasn't having any of it. From the looks of the boy, he wasn't buying it either.

Howard, always agreeable, nodded gravely, the wobbly skin below his chin betraying his age. Most of the time, Howard looked the same as he ever did to Pearl. It was only when going through old photos that Pearl was forced to admit that time had done a number on both of them. Sometimes she couldn't believe how the years had ravaged her. She stared in the mirror in the morning, wondering how in the world she'd gotten so old. Luckily, nature had chipped away at her eyesight while simultaneously stealing her former beauty, the only blessing in the whole process.

Pearl cleared her throat and said, "I think that's a risk Joe is willing to take. Am I right?"

"Absolutely. I've been wanting to leave for weeks." Joe boosted the duffel bag higher over his shoulder. A sign of readiness. She was glad to hear that his voice was strong. No hesitation, no reluctance to go against the wishes of the so-called professional. His father had always been a bit weak, too worried about what other people thought. She could tell already that Joe was able to make a stand.

"I think it's a mistake," Dr. Jensen said, his voice louder, "and I know the boy's parents would agree."

"Not a boy," Joe said, objecting. "I'm legally an adult. So it's not up to them."

"Do you have everything?" Pearl asked her grandson. The duffel bag hardly looked sufficient, but what did she know? She was an old lady who'd acquired a lifetime of things. Young people just starting out hadn't yet gotten a chance to be burdened with so much stuff, most of it not necessary, and some of it painful reminders of the past.

He nodded.

"Well, then, there's no need to tarry. Let's go." This last bit was directed at Howard, who was shaking the doctor's hand as if this were a social call and not a rescue mission. "Howard!" It came out like a reprimand, but Howard was so used to her ways, he didn't mind. He was a good egg.

When they got to the double front doors, the woman at the desk called out, "Goodbye, Joe. Good luck."

"Thanks." He didn't look back. The sound of a buzzer accompanied the release of the front doors. Howard, always the gentleman, held the door for her, then Joe did the same for Howard, deferring to the older man's age and the use of his cane. Her grandson had manners, then, always a good thing.

As they walked to the parking lot, Joe let out an audible sigh. They were almost to the car when he stopped and held up a hand. "I'm sorry to tell you this," he said, "but I think there's been some mistake." A lone unseen bird chirped off in the distance.

"Oh?" Pearl leaned against the car, her bulky purse hanging from the crook of her arm. "Did you forget something?"

"No, I . . ." He ran his hand over his shaggy dark hair. "I don't know why you claimed me as your grandson, but I'm afraid there's been a mistake. I'm sorry to have to tell you I'm not related to you. My name is Joe Arneson."

His confession amused Pearl. "I know your name," she said. "Arneson is my name too. I'm Pearl Arneson. Your father is my son."

"*My* father?" He squinted, puzzling it out.

"Your father is Bill Arneson, is he not?"

"Yes, that's his name." The duffel bag dropped to the pavement. "But maybe we're talking about a different Bill Arneson? My dad's mother died a long time ago. Before I was born."

"Good news," she said, rifling through her large purse. "Not so dead after all." She pulled out the two birth certificates that proved their shared lineage and thrust them toward him. "I'm not surprised he told you that. Bill always did have a flair for the dramatic." *And a sense of righteous indignation,* she thought. He was probably still mulling over all her wrongs decades after the fact. As if he were so perfect.

Joe took what seemed like an exceedingly long time to read over the birth certificates. She could almost see the wheels turning and the gears locking into place as he made the connection. Mother to son, son to son, grandmother to grandson. Howard motioned toward the car, and she waved her permission for him to get behind the wheel. Standing was difficult for him.

Joe looked up and met her eyes. "So why would he say you were dead?"

Pearl grimaced. "We had, shall we say, a falling-out." A mosquito buzzed around her face, and she brushed it away.

"A falling-out?"

"Yes. I'm sure you love your father very much, but he can be a bit of a stick-in-the-mud. Likes to hold grudges. That kind of thing. It's not a very interesting story, but I can tell you later, after we get home. You do want to leave here, right?"

"Right." He handed the paperwork back to her, and she stuck it into the middle compartment of her purse.

"And you don't have any other way of leaving. No trains or buses around here." She glanced around the parking lot ringed by trees. On the drive in, they'd passed a whole lot of nothing. Just one small rural town after another, with farm fields and woods in between. "You could hitchhike, I suppose, although it's getting dark."

He put two fingers to his chin, a familiar mannerism. "How did you even know I was here? Did my dad tell you?"

"Ha!" She spat out the sound. "Don't go giving him the credit. It was me who saved your butt. This was all me." She pointed to herself. "It was meant to be, I tell you. I phoned your house, trying once again to talk some sense into your father. He's a stubborn man, but I had planned on apologizing this time just to placate him." This was not the truth, but it served her purposes. "As it turned out, he wasn't home, but I had a nice conversation with your sister, Linda. I didn't even know I had a granddaughter, if you can believe that, but I found her to be a lovely girl with very nice telephone manners." She grinned. "It didn't take me but a minute to get the truth from her. She told me that Bill and his wife had stuck you in here. And for what? A few bad dreams? I couldn't believe it! No one in our family has ever suffered from any sort of mental deficiency. It's an outrage. It was then I devised a plan to spring you. No one treats my grandson that way!"

She'd expected admiration for her cleverness, the way she'd tracked him down and gone to so much trouble to help him. Praise for how resourceful she'd been. Appreciation for all her efforts. Clearly, that wasn't forthcoming, but she would have been happy with even a little gratitude. A thank-you would have gone a long way.

Instead, he said, "Is Linda okay? I haven't talked to her in weeks."

Pearl waved her hand. "She's fine. If you just get in the car, we'll be at my house in no time at all. You can call her from there and talk to her yourself."

"Maybe there's a phone booth down the road I could use?"

"There's nothing down the road, believe me. Just get in the car." She saw the hesitation on his face. "Please, Joe? It's getting dark, and

Howard's eyesight isn't the best, so we really should get going. We're just two old codgers who wouldn't hurt a fly. We're not going to hold you against your will. Just come to the house, and we can sort out the details later, okay?" Off in the distance, the chirping of insects broke the silence. "If you want, you can stay for the summer. I have a project I could use some help with. I'd pay you a good wage." She tried to read his face. Had she broached the idea of staying for the summer too soon?

"I can't believe I have a grandmother I didn't know about."

So he was still stuck on that. "Yes, I'm sure that was a shock to find out," Pearl said. "I'm guessing there's a lot you don't know about your father's side of the family. If you come with me now, I can show you lots of family photos. The family home is about two hours north of here, in a charming little town called Pullman." She gave him a forced smile. "You might find it illuminating. It is your history, part of who you are."

Joe vacillated. He'd never heard his dad mention a town called Pullman, but then again, his father had always been evasive when talking about his childhood. Once Linda had asked where he grew up, and he'd answered, "Nowheresville, Wisconsin." They'd laughed then, but he wondered why no one had ever pressed the issue. Probably because they'd sensed he didn't want to talk about it.

Pearl tapped her foot impatiently. "Would it help if I showed you some identification?" She rummaged through her purse and handed him her driver's license. She fixed her eyes on him as he read it over.

After a minute, he handed it back to her. "Looks official," he said.

"That's because it *is* official." She tucked it back into her wallet. "I know this is a lot to take in. I'm sorry for that, but you should know I can't make you do anything. Stay here, or go with me. It's up to you."

Joe lifted the bag to his shoulder. She was making progress. "Okay, I'll go to your house. But I'm not saying I'll stay."

"Whatever you want," Pearl said smoothly. "It will be entirely your choice. It's not like I can force you to stay, after all."

"I'll want to call home as soon as we get there to let my folks know where I am," Joe said, as if this was conditional.

"Of course. I understand that you wouldn't want them to worry." She reached over and opened the back door to the car and gestured for him to get in. "As soon as we get there, you can call."

CHAPTER FOUR

1916

"Pearl! Pearl!" Alice called out as she dashed up the stairwell. Pearl had snuck away for a midafternoon nap and was now curled up on top of the coverlet of the bed she shared with Alice. Her eyes were closed, her mind envisioning the day she'd be strolling down the avenues of Paris, France, dressed in the latest fashion, getting admiring glances from every man who crossed her path. Goodbye to Pullman, Wisconsin. Once Pearl made her debut to the world, she'd never look back.

Alice burst through the door. "Pearl, you lazy thing! Come with me." She gave her sister's shoulder a nudge. "You're missing all the excitement. You have to come see what Father is making out in the barn."

"Oh, Alice," Pearl groaned. "I was right in the middle of the loveliest daydream."

"You shouldn't be lying down in the middle of the day anyway. Unless you're sick?" Alice rested a hand on her forehead.

"Sick of doing chores. Does that count?"

"No, it does not." Alice took both of Pearl's hands and pulled her to her feet.

Pearl reluctantly followed her down the stairs. "Can't you just tell me?"

"No. You have to see it for yourself."

The girls walked from the house to the barn, with Alice in the lead, nearly giddy with excitement. She spun around, walking backward for a moment to talk. "It's so beautiful, Pearl. Wait till you see." Pushing open the barn door, she led Pearl past the empty stalls, the ones that housed their cow and two horses at night, and went straight to the corner of the barn that served as their father's woodworking shop. They found him kneeling in front of a chest, holding a drill steady with one hand, turning the crank with the other. Little Daisy stood next to him, watching with wide eyes.

Hearing the girls, he set down the drill and grinned. "What do you think, Pearl?"

She circled around and then paused to lean in closer. As far as she could tell, there was nothing extraordinary about this box. "What is it?"

Daisy piped up. "It's a hope chest for Alice."

"Isn't it gorgeous?" Alice said, clasping her hands together. "Father has been working on it on the sly, but I caught him at it today."

Their father laughed. "Do you know how hard it is to keep a secret in a house full of seven girls? I had a feeling one of you would find out before I finished."

Alice ran her hand over the top. "It's made from solid oak and lined with cedar to keep out the moths. Father is going to carve the top with whatever kind of picture I want. I have an idea to show songbirds with a heart in the middle." She traced a heart with her fingertip.

Their father nodded. "That would be pretty, and just right for you, my little Ally-bird. I'm no artist, but if you draw it on paper, I'll do the best I can."

"He's going to put brass hinges on it and a brass latch." Alice gave her father a sunny smile.

"A hope chest?" Pearl said, frowning. "But isn't that for when you get married? I thought you didn't want to marry Frank."

"I don't want to marry Frank, but that doesn't mean I'm not going to marry *someone*." Daisy lifted her arms, and Alice scooped her up. "And someday I'll have a little petunia of my own, and I'll be glad to have a chest full of fancy linens and blankets and candle holders." She rested her forehead against Daisy's, and the little girl patted her cheek.

"But if not Frank, then who?" Pearl wondered. "Who would you marry?" And more importantly, she thought, who would actually want to marry Alice? Plain Alice with her straight brown hair and the freckles that crossed from her cheeks over the bridge of her nose. When she smiled or sang, she could almost pass for pretty, but still, she was nothing out of the ordinary. And she was such a stick-in-the-mud considering she was only a year and a half older than Pearl. Boys liked girls like Pearl, girls who complimented them and laughed at their jokes. Alice was so serious, thinking everything through. She didn't even try to curry their favor.

In Pearl's opinion, Frank wasn't such a bad beau. The son of a prosperous farmer, he kept coming around with gifts and flowers, even though Alice never encouraged him. He wasn't all that smart, but he sure was sweet on Alice, and that had to count for something.

Their father spoke. "Any man would be lucky to have your sister as a wife. She's done quite well for this household, hasn't she?" His wide smile showed his pride.

Pearl supposed he was thinking of her cooking and baking and cleaning. Grudgingly, she had to admit Alice had a talent for household duties. And she had more patience with the younger girls than Pearl ever did. Alice could settle a squabble and treat hurt feelings like she was born to it. She was just the person to go to with a physical injury too. There wasn't a scrape or cut that didn't feel better after she'd cleaned it and wrapped it. Her caring hands soothed burns and softened bumps. Those were the kinds of problems that made Pearl want to flee and never return.

Alice said, "And there's going to be a secret drawer built right into the base where I can store letters and documents." She met Daisy's eyes. "Out of reach of little hands. Father said he'll make it so no one will ever know it's there."

Pearl took a step back to get a broader view. "What kind of documents would you have?"

Father said, "Her marriage license, and then later, when the babies come, she'll have birth certificates . . ."

"Father!" Alice blushed and hurriedly changed the subject. "Tell Pearl what you told me. About the joints that hold it together." She set Daisy down and ran her fingers over the corner of the chest. She looked up at Pearl. "They're called dovetail joints. Dovetail. Doesn't that sound beautiful?"

"I guess."

Their father said, "The sides of the hope chest are connected using dovetail joints. The edges are cut in a pattern, so one side slides into the other. Wide tails and narrow pins are what they're called. It works almost like this." He clasped his hands together, fingers interwoven. "Once the two pieces are glued together, the place where they're joined is stronger than the wood itself. Your mother always thought it was perfect for a hope chest, because when a couple is married, they are stronger together than they were when separate." As so often happened when he mentioned their mother, emotion overcame him. "It's very difficult to break the connected pieces once they're locked in place. A dovetail joint can stand the test of time." He paused to look away, then pulled a handkerchief out of his pocket to dab at his eyes.

Pearl came behind him and wrapped her arms around his shoulders. "We miss her too, you know."

"I know, darlin'." He blew his nose, then folded the cloth and stuffed it back in his pocket. "Your mother loved that it was called a dovetail."

"Because it sounds like *love tale*," Alice said, filling in the rest. "And when he's done with my hope chest, he's going to make one for you, Pearl."

"For me?"

"Yes. I'll do one for each of you girls. Your mother always regretted never having one." Father turned toward Pearl with a smile. "So you better start thinking about what design you'd like on yours."

"I will," she promised, but in the back of her mind, she wondered what in the world she would want with a hope chest. She had many plans for her future, but collecting linens was not among them.

CHAPTER FIVE

1983

When the car jolted to a stop, it sucked Joe out of a disturbing dream. Instinctively he clutched his chest to try to quell the pounding of his heart, but it was no use. Emotionally he was still in the grip of his subconscious, his body drenched with sweat. How had this happened? He must have somehow drifted off, the rhythm of the car's wheels lulling him into sleep. His mouth automatically formed the words *It was only a dream*, a phrase suggested by Dr. Jensen, who said his body would eventually believe his mind. It never worked.

Even after opening his eyes, it took some time to put together where he was and to identify the two elderly people staring back at him from the front seat. He squinted as if to make what he saw come into focus. Slowly, it came to him. The woman, his supposed grandmother. The old guy, her attorney and friend. And the inside of a car headed to some town called Pullman. The car was pulled over to the side of the road now, and he had their full attention.

The old woman spoke up. "You okay, Joe?"

"Sure. Why do you ask?" He held his breath, waiting for the reply. The dream he'd just had was the worst of them all. He thought of it as the Death Dream. The beginning of the dream was wonderful.

He was with a woman, and they were madly in love. He'd never felt that kind of love in real life, hadn't known it was possible to feel that connected to another human being. But the joy of being with her was ruined when they were interrupted by an angry man waving a gun. At the end of the dream, he held the woman and watched in horror as she died in his arms. The dream was devastating, and he always woke up feeling as if his heart had been ripped open. He could never see the woman's face, but he knew he loved her more than life itself. When he'd told Dr. Jensen that particular detail, the good doctor had asked, "Why do you think you loved her?"

He'd shrugged and said, "Just a feeling I have," but it was more of a certainty than a feeling. The real feeling of love made the raw terror of the dream even more horrifying. The dream was so real that he could feel the humid night air and the touch of her fingers against his cheek.

It should have been a relief to be awakened from the horror of the dream, but instead he woke up feeling like he'd abandoned the woman he loved.

He sat up and stretched. The car was idling, the radio playing a song about two kids named Jack and Diane. The contrast between this contemporary pop song and Howard, the aged attorney, didn't escape him. Joe would have pegged him as a Big Band–era guy, not a fan of John Cougar. The lyrics said something about life going on even after the thrill of living was gone. That part fit anyway.

Judging from the alarmed expressions of the two oldsters staring at him from the front seat, they were ready to take him back to Trendale. He cleared his throat and gave a nervous chuckle. "Was I crying out, by any chance?"

Pearl frowned, her eyebrows knitting together. "You were making some god-awful noises. There were words too, but the only one I could make out was *no*."

"It didn't sound like your voice," Howard said, his voice accusatory. Joe could see him as an attorney now, cornering someone on the witness stand by stating something emphatically, practically daring them to contradict him. "It sounded like someone else."

Joe raised his hands like a magician. *No tricks here. Nothing in my hands; nothing up my sleeves.* "I'm the only one here, so it had to be my voice."

Howard said, "It sounded deeper than your voice. And raspy, like you had a cold."

Joe nodded. "I know what you're saying. I've heard this before. I was having one of my troubling dreams. It's one of the reasons I was at Trendale."

There were four dreams in all. Even the nicer ones had a tinge of foreboding, and he'd always wake up with a sense of dread. He knew every dream by heart, every detail, every word uttered. As part of his therapy, Dr. Jensen had him write them all down, thinking that the transference of words to paper would lessen the dreams' power over his subconscious. It didn't. A few weeks later, he handed Joe a pen and a yellow pad, telling him to describe each dream again. Joe filled four pages with details, writing down everything he'd experienced. If Dr. Jensen was surprised that this version exactly matched what Joe had written down the first time, he didn't let on.

Getting no response, Joe added, "I'm sorry if I scared you."

Pearl shrugged. "I don't scare that easily, so don't you worry about that. I just hated to see you so distraught." She turned to Howard. "Show's over. Let's get going."

Howard steered the car off the side of the road and continued down the highway. Under his breath he muttered, "Not that anyone asked, but I found it scary."

Joe rubbed his eyes and watched the landscape rush by. "Are we getting close?" He was starting to wonder what he'd signed up for. They could be taking him anywhere.

Pearl said, "Very close. Just a few more minutes and we'll be home."

Home. Maybe it was because of the intensity of the dream that his imagination headed into overdrive. It occurred to him that the birth certificates might be forgeries. What if this old couple was crazy and would hold him captive? And do what with him? he wondered. Ask for ransom, make him an indentured servant, use him for scientific experiments? What if they were part of a cult and were recruiting members? No one knew where he was going, he realized with alarm. Did the folks at Trendale even ask the old lady for ID? They must have, he reasoned. They were such sticklers for protocol and documentation at the facility; they would absolutely verify her story. For safety reasons, he made a mental note to be more attentive. Randomly falling asleep was not an option. If anything struck him as wrong, anything at all, he was bolting. It didn't matter that he didn't know precisely where they were going. He would walk or hitchhike, and once he found a phone, he'd call a friend or his folks to come and get him.

He kept alert, watching for landmarks, relieved when he saw a sign welcoming them to Pullman. So that part of her story had been correct anyway. Maybe the rest was true too. He was eager to talk to his father. He had so many questions.

When they pulled off the highway, they passed through a quaint downtown—shops, a barbershop, a bank, a few restaurants. Cars were parked at an angle in front of a row of businesses. Only a few places were open: a pub and two restaurants. The others had **Closed** signs in their front windows. They drove past side streets lined with small, tidy houses. Nowheresville, Wisconsin.

A few blocks more and they'd passed all the way through Pullman's downtown area and were back on a country road. "Blink and you'd miss it," Pearl said wryly.

The day's light was fading, and Howard was now leaning toward the windshield, as if trying to see the road better. The car made such sharp turns that Joe's upper half swayed with the curvature of the road. Howard turned the steering wheel right onto one road and then left onto another, finally entering a frontage road marked with a sign that read **Stone Lake Road.**

"There's a lake?" Joe wondered.

"Indeed. There used to be a mill too, back in my day. A gristmill using power from the nearby Bark River. The mill was owned and operated by my father, your great-grandfather," Pearl said. "But that was a long time ago. Everything changes."

The road circled the lake, which was barely visible through the trees. Finally, Howard pulled onto a drive toward a large two-story house, dove gray with white trim. A porch ran along the front of the house with a small balcony over the front door. The trim along the peak was ornate, with swirls and curlicues. The decorative molding above the windows resembled curved top hats. It was once, Joe decided, a grand home, although now it would benefit from a new coat of paint. The yard was also in need of work. The shrubbery in front was overgrown, and the lawn was weedy and bare in spots.

"This is your house?" Joe asked incredulously. "And my father grew up here?"

"I grew up here and moved back after my father died. Your dad spent a lot of time in this house when he was growing up, but he never lived here."

"It's quite a house."

She nodded. "It's Gothic Revival, a style not very common in this area." Her voice was full of pride. "My grandfather built it. For many years, there was always a tire swing on the branch of that oak tree." She pointed. "And of course, if you go down that hill, you'll find the lake."

They got out of the car, Joe with his duffel slung over one shoulder. He couldn't take his eyes off the house. It was the size of an apartment building. A mansion compared to his own house.

Pearl swung her legs out of the car, waiting while Howard brought her the walker, which had been folded up in the back seat next to Joe.

She unfolded the side pieces and rose to a standing position, shutting the door behind her.

Joe followed Pearl and Howard inside, which seemed to take forever, Howard with his cane and the old lady leaning on her walker. Shuffle, move, shuffle, move. Once inside, Pearl flipped on a light switch, and the front hall came into full view. To the left was a sitting room, with furniture covered by white sheets. A large arched opening on the far side of that room led to a space defined by a hanging light fixture. A dining room perhaps? A small study sat to the right. A rolltop desk was open, with papers and pens covering the surface. In the middle, a hallway stretched into darkness. Joe could tell the place was once impressive, but years of neglect were evident in the faded wallpaper, dusty baseboards, and cobwebs in the corners.

"You said I could call my folks?" Joe said.

"Of course." Pearl crooked a finger, beckoning him to follow, then shuffled down the hall, turning on lights as she went. Each light switch made a loud click, like she'd thrown on the lights at a stadium. Along the way they passed a staircase and another room on the right. When they turned left into the kitchen, he saw that one side of the room opened into the space he'd guessed was a dining room. They seemed to have come full circle.

Pearl pointed to an old rotary-dial phone sitting in an alcove. A fabric cord dropped down to a plug above the baseboard. He dialed and listened as it rang at his house.

Pearl raised a finger and whispered, "I have to go check on Howard," then made her way back down the hall, one pronounced step at a time.

His sister answered, using the wording required by their mother. "Arneson residence, Linda speaking." He smiled. Such a little lady.

"Linda, this is Joe."

"Joe!" He heard the excitement and love in her voice and suddenly missed her terribly. "Oh my gosh, I can't believe it's you. I've been missing you so much."

"I miss you too."

"Are you coming home?"

"I hope so. Can you go get Dad?"

He heard the receiver clunk as she dropped it to the counter and went to get their father. A minute later, his dad was on the line, and Joe was giving him an update.

The conversation didn't go the way he'd hoped. It would have helped if Trendale had called his house to lay the groundwork, but that hadn't happened. "Let me get this straight," his father said, exasperated. "A woman shows up at Trendale saying she's your grandmother, and you just walked right out and left with her? Have you lost your mind?"

"So she's not your mother?" Joe asked. "Because she has paperwork that's pretty convincing. Birth certificates. And she showed me her driver's license too."

"Pearl Arneson is my mother, yes, at least legally, but we haven't been on speaking terms for a long, long time. And I'm not planning on changing that anytime soon."

"Why? What happened?"

A heavy sigh. "It's not important anymore."

Joe knew that impatient tone. He just didn't want to talk about it. Sweeping away painful memories was his father's way of dealing with things. Or in this case, not dealing with them. Joe said, "Do you want to talk to her?"

"No, I don't want to talk to her." The impatience notched up to irritation.

Joe knew he better get to the point. "I'm at her house now. On Stone Lake Road? Can you drive up tomorrow and pick me up?" He knew enough not to ask him to come tonight.

There was a noticeable pause, and then his father said, "Just a minute."

Down the hall, Joe heard Howard saying something to Pearl about having to get back to the home. In his other ear, he heard the muffled sounds of his father explaining things to his mother. His dad must have covered the receiver with the flat of his hand.

After a long pause, he heard the fumble of the receiver and his father's voice. "What's the number there, Joe? I'll call you tomorrow."

Joe leaned over and read what was printed on the card in the middle of the dial. "Hopkins 4–3695."

"The same one as always, then."

"I guess."

"Tell you what, Joe." He paused, and Joe imagined the weary look on his face and the way he pinched the bridge of his nose when dealing with something uncomfortable. "I have to think this through. I'll call you in the morning, and we'll talk then."

"Okay."

Disappointed but not surprised, Joe said goodbye and hung up. Pearl appeared in the doorway a moment later. "So," she said, "how did that go?"

"As it turns out, I won't be able to leave until tomorrow."

"I see."

"If that's okay?"

"It's more than okay. I would love it if you'd stay. As I said, I have a project that I could use some help with. It would take most of the summer, and I have to hire someone. If I'm giving someone large sums of money, I'd just as soon give it to my grandson."

Grandson. The word came so easily out of her mouth, but it struck him as so odd to hear from a woman he'd just met. She gave him an expectant look. He said, "That's nice of you to think of me, but I have to get back home. I have things to do." Truthfully, he didn't have anything to go back to—no job, no girlfriend—but he wasn't going to admit that. From her skeptical expression, she knew that already. Maybe she'd pried that information from Linda during their phone conversation. Linda knew not to be rude to an adult, even on the phone. If she was asked a question, she would most likely answer it.

"One night, then," she said finally. "Lock up after I leave, and make yourself at home. One of the bedrooms upstairs, the second door on the left, was recently cleaned and has fresh bedding. The rest of the place is a bit of a mess, I'm sorry to say, but it beats sleeping outside."

"Wait. You're not going to be here?" He should have felt relieved at finding out he wouldn't have to stay with a stranger, even if they were related, but he wasn't. This house was enormous and in disrepair. If he were someone who frightened easily, he might think of ghosts. More important, he wanted her to stick around so they could talk about the schism with his father. What would cause a man to break ties with his own mother? He couldn't even imagine.

"No." She shook her head. "I don't live here anymore."

"What?"

"They made me move out." She harrumphed. "It's a long story, but I was getting my medication mixed up and wound up in the hospital. Then my doctor filed a report with the county, and there was an *investigation*." She put the last word in finger quotes. "A bunch of busybodies. You wouldn't believe the brouhaha when I wouldn't let a visiting nurse come to my house. It was like end-times in Pullman. I finally took charge and decided to move into Pine Ridge Hollow, where Howard lives, before they got some court-appointed person to take away my rights."

"So Pine Ridge Hollow is an apartment complex?"

"An old folks' home." She frowned. "They like the residents to be back before dark unless you let them know in advance."

Joe pondered this. "Are you going to get in trouble?"

"Ack." She flapped a hand dismissively. "They have so many rules, but as you know, rules are meant to be broken. What are they going to do, say I can't have my pudding for dessert?"

"Pearl!" Howard called from the next room, his voice thin and anxious. "We better get back. I already missed my evening medications."

"And they're a little hung up on the medications," she said. "They dole them out like Tic Tacs. And then they give you the tiniest little paper cup of water. Bunch of cheapskates."

"They did that at Trendale too," Joe said, remembering the disposable cups that held only a sip and a half. Like someone might overdose on water.

"Did they watch to make sure you swallowed the pill?"

"Yes, they did."

She sighed. "I hate that."

"I hated that too." He met her eyes, and for the first time, he felt like maybe there was a family connection. They'd bonded over having medication dispensed.

From down the hall: "Pearlie!"

"I have to go," she said. "You'll be fine here. I'll come back tomorrow about nine. If you need me, dial the operator. Her name is Nellie. Ask for Pine Ridge Hollow. She'll know how to put the call through." She gave him an appraising look. "But you seem like a capable young man, so I doubt that will be necessary."

"Okay."

"Oh, and I put some food in the refrigerator earlier today. There's also some canned soup."

"Thank you."

"Pearl!"

"I'm coming, Howard. Hold your horses." And down the hallway she went, her walker leading the way.

CHAPTER SIX

1916

Pearl thought that even if she lived to be a hundred, she wouldn't forget the day John Lawrence came to stay with the family. Little did she know that his arrival would mark the beginning of the end, her life changing in so many ways, and none of them good. All she knew was that John Lawrence—an eligible young bachelor—was being delivered right to her doorstep. Even though she didn't know what he looked like, the idea made her shiver with anticipation.

She'd known all the young men in their small town since they were practically infants, and they were essentially the only men she knew. Not being allowed to venture far from home, Pearl rarely met new people. Occasionally, someone in town would have a relative come to visit, which was always of interest, but having a young man come *live* with them was an event like no other. As far as she was concerned, it was the most exciting thing to happen in Pullman, Wisconsin, in a long time, maybe for years. Absolutely nothing ever changed for the better in Pullman unless you counted a new picture at the Victory Theater. Pearl and her five younger sisters had seen all the pictures, many times. Their oldest sister, Alice, was the pianist on Saturday nights, and so the owner, Mr. Kramer, let them in for free as long as they sat in the back and were very quiet.

The day John was set to arrive happened to be the twins' birthday. Mae and Maude had turned nine that day and were so excited, Pearl could barely stand to be in the same room with them. Pearl, at seventeen, didn't think she'd ever acted so silly, the way they skipped around the kitchen, getting in the way of Alice, who was trying to get a cake in the oven. A year and a half older than Pearl, Alice had a sweet disposition but was as dull as an old maid. By necessity, she'd taken over the household after the birth of little Daisy. At first they'd thought their mother just needed time to regain her strength, but when the baby was six months old, their mother had gotten influenza and a croupy cough, and it grew worse from there. Their mother, so beloved, faded before their eyes, finally becoming delirious with fever. For weeks, Alice tended to her, and the doctor visited daily, but nothing seemed to help. Even as much as they saw her struggle and weaken, it was a horrible shock when she died, the younger girls sobbing and wandering listlessly around the house, their father stoic but shattered. No one smiled until one day when they heard Alice singing a lullaby to the baby and little Daisy gurgling in delight.

Alice kept the household together. Ever since then, she was always on the move, going from the garden to the clothesline to the kitchen, never stopping, never resting. Even when all of them were eating, Alice buzzed around the table, filling milk glasses and making sure the serving dishes were being passed around. Her life was over before she'd ever gotten a chance to live it up, poor thing, but it didn't seem to dampen her spirits. As she bustled around the house, she sang: folk tunes, church music, and little ditties she made up to amuse the younger girls. "My little Ally-bird," their father called her. Alice's voice lightened their moods every single day.

After their mother's death, Alice never had time to talk to Pearl anymore, unless Pearl wanted to follow her around when she was cleaning out the horses' stalls, beating the rugs, or milking the cow, which Pearl definitely did not. She missed the days when she and Alice had time to sprawl on their beds, leafing through *Motion Picture Magazine*, copies of which Pearl had gotten from old Mrs. Donohue. Of course, it was mostly Pearl who marveled at the pictures and read bits aloud while Alice looked on, her fingers flying as she worked on her latest knitting project, but even so, they had done it together.

Today Mae and Maude skipped around the table, laughing and singing as Alice poured batter into the buttered pans. They were identical except for their hair. Mae always had a single braid going down her back, while Maude had two pigtails. One time they'd tried switching, but halfway through the morning both had complained that their heads felt crooked, so they had Alice braid their hair once again, putting them to rights. "I wouldn't do it," Pearl said. "Put your foot down for once, Alice. It was their idea. Make them keep it that way, at least until the end of the day."

Alice didn't listen. Her hands flew through Mae's hair, weaving the strands so fast, it would be hard to follow how it was done. She shrugged. "I don't mind. It only takes but a minute." When she was through tying a ribbon at the end of the braid, she kissed the top of Mae's head. "Finished. Now you're right as rain, my little chick." Next, Maude settled into the chair, and Alice deftly parted her hair and braided both sides so that the twins' identities were restored in no time at all. A kiss atop the second twin's head, and then she ushered the two of them out the door to collect eggs.

Alice was the one who assigned the chores. Summertime was particularly busy. Helen and Emma, who were thirteen and eleven, helped with the laundry and split logs for firewood. Mae and Maude scrubbed floors, collected eggs, and helped beat the rugs. All of them worked in the garden, dusted, and cleaned, both in the house and in the barn. On Saturday nights, they took turns hauling water from the pump to the stove to heat it for the family's weekly bath. Even Daisy, who was three years old, did her part, feeding the chickens, dusting, and following Alice around like a little duckling following its mother.

Pearl pitched in when she could, but she was not the housekeeping type. She hated getting her hands dirty and had no patience for scrubbing pots and running wet clothes through the wringer. Hanging laundry and gardening was out of the question. The hot sun gave her a headache. She was just not put on this earth for domestic duties, something that became apparent when she burned the chicken and the soup pot boiled over when she'd been entrusted with cooking. Sighing, Alice had said she'd do it herself from now on. Pearl had wrapped her arms around her sister's waist and rested her cheek against her shoulder. "Someday I'll be rich, and you can come live with me in my mansion where my servants will do all the work. We'll be ladies of leisure and have rooms full of fur coats and silk ball gowns, and a chest full of diamond jewelry."

Alice smiled. "Oh, Pearl, you do spin such stories! I am quite sure I would get bored living that way. Besides, if you were that rich, wouldn't you want to use the money to do some good?"

Pearl considered the idea. "I could send out food baskets at Christmas, I guess. Isn't that what rich people do?"

Alice shook her head. "You could do so much more than that. So many people struggle, and if you were rich, you could be their saving grace. I've always believed that God gives people money to see what they will do with it."

"I'd do lots with it, and I'd let you help me, Alice," Pearl declared. "When I'm a famous film actress, I'll make so much money that I can do whatever I want."

Alice laughed. "Don't let Father hear you talk like that." They both knew he wouldn't approve of having a daughter who was an actress. He wasn't even happy about Alice playing the piano at the theater, but the owner of the theater was a friend, and the family needed the money for doctors' bills. Besides, he'd said, "I know I can trust Alice to conduct herself as a lady, no matter where she is." He'd glanced at Pearl, his eyes narrowing. She got the definite impression he didn't feel the same way about his second daughter.

Pearl wanted a big life to match her big dreams. She was impatient with wanting to see what else was out there. Someday she planned to visit all the big cities and take in all they had to offer. Paris. New York. Rome. While her time was wasting away here, excitement awaited elsewhere, and it was all going on without her. The thought made her want to cry. She was missing so much.

Alice did not share her discontent. She said she didn't even have time to think of other places. Today she moved faster than usual, spinning like a top to get the house prepared for their guest. She had an old kerchief tied around her head to keep her hair back and one of their mother's aprons wrapped around her middle, covering most of her front. When Pearl sat down, plopping herself into a kitchen chair with a cup of cold water straight from the pump, Alice paused to dump a pile of carrots, onions, and potatoes on the table in front of her. She took a cutting board their father had made in his shop and set it next to the vegetables.

"Why don't you make yourself useful? Cut these up for the stew." She rummaged in a drawer and handed Pearl a knife. "And you two," she said, pointing to Mae and Maude, "go on down the road and invite Mrs. Donohue and Howie for dinner. Tell them we'll eat at six."

Pearl sighed loudly before reluctantly chopping. "Why do they have to come?"

Howie was an orphan whom Mrs. Donohue had taken in ten years earlier, when he was only eight. She told everyone he was a distant relation, but the truth of it was, there were no family ties between them. She was an old widow with no children. Howie was a strong young man who could read the newspaper out loud to her and handle the heavier of the household chores. Together, life was made easier for each of them. Mrs. Donohue often said, "This boy is such a blessing. An angel sent straight from God." Her words of praise made Howie squirm even as he looked secretly pleased.

Alice wiped her hands on her apron. "Because they are our closest neighbors and good friends." She added, "It is the very least we can do."

Pearl knew she referred to the visit right after their mother had died. Mrs. Donohue, hearing the news, had Howie bring over a tied handkerchief wrapped around something the size of a large onion. When Father had unwrapped it, all seven of his girls gathered around him, he'd found it filled with silver dollars and a note saying she would be offended if they did not accept this small token. It had been the family's saving grace.

Pearl had not been planning on spending the afternoon working in the hot kitchen, but Alice never let up. When she was done with the chopping, there was silver to polish and linen napkins to iron. "I don't have time for this busywork," she grumbled, running the iron back and forth over the linen. "I need to get ready."

"Ready for what?" Alice leaned over the table, pressing a measuring cup onto rolled-out dough to make biscuits. There was a smudge of flour on her cheek.

"For John's arrival," Pearl said, with a toss of her head. Her hair was her crowning glory. Besides Daisy, she was the only one who had their mother's blonde locks. If she worked on it, she could get her hair to fall into curls like Mary Pickford. The previous night, she'd slept with her damp hair rolled into rags, but in the heat of the day, her curls were drooping already. "I'm calling dibs on him, just so you know." Not that she was worried. Her sister had Frank, not that Alice was even interested in him. Many times she'd sent him away, giving excuses that fooled no one. Still, Frank continued to come calling. Pearl thought he'd wear her down eventually.

Daisy climbed up on a chair next to Alice to watch her work. Alice said, "You and John have my blessing. Remember, though, he's only staying the summer. Don't let him break your heart."

Pearl laughed at the thought. Boys flocked around her, and even the old men in town followed her with their eyes. If anyone was going to get a broken heart, it wouldn't be her. John Lawrence better watch out. She would steal *his* heart. It was as good as done.

When the afternoon sun crested and all of them felt the familiar pang of hunger that came just prior to dinner, the clip-clop of her father's horse-drawn wagon paused as it came to a stop right by the front porch. Pearl ran upstairs to fetch a hand mirror to check her appearance, pinching her cheeks to give them a bloom of color and dabbing her perspiring forehead with a cloth. Her hair had wilted, but it was just as well. Her father would have disapproved of her having her hair down, so she pinned it up, then waited until her father and John entered the house, watching through a window as Helen and Emma led the horse and wagon to the barn.

When she heard the men's voices in the kitchen, she sauntered into the room, ready to make an entrance. Her father stood next to a young man with thick dark hair neatly parted to one side; he held his hat by the brim. His skin had the healthy cast of a man who worked outdoors. His hair was black and wavy, smoothed down on top, the sides closely shaved. John Lawrence was handsome, she decided, with the sharp good looks of an actor in a moving picture. It didn't hurt that he wore a suit as if he were going to Sunday service. It might have been buttoned up this morning, but the train trip and the heat of the day had done its worst, and now his suit coat was open, revealing a vest underneath. At the sight of her, her father said, "John, this is my second daughter, Pearl."

"I'm pleased to make your acquaintance, miss," he said, smiling in her direction.

Pearl dipped her knee into a slight curtsy, something that usually charmed the local boys, but John's attention was already back to Alice, and he was asking her how she'd managed to cook such a sumptuous meal all by herself. "I don't think I'm deserving of such a feast."

Alice blushed. "We're so happy you could come and help Father at the mill. We wanted to welcome you with our best to show our appreciation."

"I thank you for it," he said.

"She didn't do it all by herself," Pearl interjected, wanting to set the record straight. "I chopped the vegetables."

Alice said, "That's true. She did all that and more. I couldn't have done half of it without Pearl." She slung an arm around her sister's shoulder and pulled her close, their faces aligned, Alice's glistening with a sheen from cooking over a hot stove, the kerchief still securely around her head, and Pearl's freshly powdered, her hair swept up, some tendrils escaping to trail over her shoulders.

Dear Alice. Always willing to give Pearl just what she needed. John gave Pearl an appraising look, as if he now saw her with new eyes. He leaned forward slightly, a bow in response to her earlier curtsy. "Well, then, I guess my gratitude goes to you as well, Miss Pearl."

CHAPTER SEVEN

1983

Joe watched from the front window as Howard and Pearl climbed into the sedan. Pearl didn't look nearly as formidable from this distance. Her hard-backed posture seemed less imposing as he watched her navigating her way into the front seat, lifting one leg at a time. Once the door slammed shut, they were off, the car surging forward. Joe speculated that Howard really wanted to get back before there was trouble. As the taillights faded in the distance, he stepped away, letting the curtain drop back into place.

The empty house had an air of abandonment, the silence quieter than he'd ever known. He'd hated Trendale, the constant noise, the flickering fluorescent lights, the way he was always accountable. He could never get away from their watchful eyes. The staff monitored his eating habits, his energy level, his mood. It was exhausting trying to anticipate what they wanted from him, but he kept doing it, hoping at some point he'd fulfill their requirements so he could leave. Now, having left, he felt a bit empty.

Was it a mistake to leave? No, he decided. Being here was weird, and finding out the grandmother he'd thought was dead was alive was weirder still, but he could handle it.

It was only for a night.

Having Pearl ditch him had thrown him for a loop. He didn't have a good sense of where Pullman was exactly, and not knowing was a little troubling, but the house had a working phone and supposedly some food in the fridge. In the morning, he'd talk to his dad and know more.

Joe thought about his friends back home. Most of them had gone to college, including his high school girlfriend, who he'd heard was now engaged. Their lives had taken such divergent paths. He'd dated other women, but nothing ever came of any of it. One of them, Darlene, said he always seemed distracted, like he was trying to remember something or his mind was elsewhere. He didn't know what she meant, but after that, he'd tried to be more attentive. Still, things had fizzled between them. Relationships were so much work.

He had better luck with guy friends. One of his buddies, Wayne, had gotten Joe a job at the construction company where he was employed. Joe had picked up a lot of carpentry skills on the job and was glad to get a paycheck during this terrible economy. A lot of guys weren't so fortunate. The job market was bleak, and it was nearly impossible to find anything at all. Now that he was out of Trendale, he'd have to go begging to see if they'd take him back. Likely he'd been replaced a long time ago. The fact that he'd left without giving notice was not in his favor either. It was doubtful that they'd give him another chance.

Joe was sure to find something, though. Even if it meant flipping burgers at McDonald's. He shuddered at the thought, then put it out of his mind. That was a problem for another day.

He walked around the house, turning on lights in each room. The place was huge, but each room was modest in size, no bigger than the rooms at his own family's house. The tall ceilings and large windows gave the illusion of more space; the illumination from the hanging light fixtures cast creepy shadows.

Some of the rooms were completely empty of furniture; others were furnished, with each piece covered in a sheet or blanket. The bookcases were, for the most part, empty, but there were still paintings and framed family photos on the walls. It was as if someone had started packing up the house to move but had gotten interrupted and never quite finished. Joe stopped in the hallway to inspect a photo of two young parents and a little boy. The woman sat ramrod-straight, wearing a high-collared blouse and a long pleated skirt. With a start, Joe realized the woman was Pearl in her younger days, which meant the father in the picture was his grandfather and the little boy, a toddler dressed in a sailor suit, his own father.

Now that he thought about it, he'd never seen a photo of his father as a child.

Joe took the framed photo off the wall and flipped it over, but there was nothing written on the back. Turning it back around, he examined each face. Pearl had been a stunner back in the day. Hollywood glamorous. Even in the black-and-white photo, it was easy to see her white hair had once been golden blonde. Her husband too was good-looking, broad-shouldered, tall, and clean-shaven, with slicked-back hair. The boy, his own father, sat on Pearl's lap, his hand wrapped around one of her fingers. The man, his father's father, stood behind them, one hand on his wife's shoulder. He looked proud, Joe thought. Both the father and the son gazed adoringly at Pearl, but she looked straight ahead at the camera, her chin tipped upward, her lips curved into a satisfied smile.

Whatever happened to this family? They looked happy enough when this picture had been taken, but later on something had gone terribly wrong.

Joe had lost his mother but had known only love from all the mother figures in his life. How did this permanent rift start? He'd ask Pearl about it the next morning, and if she wouldn't talk, he'd question his dad. He wasn't going to push it until he was home, but he hoped his father would trust him enough to let him know the truth of the matter. If he didn't find out, he'd always wonder.

He wandered some more, taking note of other family photos. He had no clue who most of them were, but there was one of a large family, parents with four daughters, taken in the front yard with the house in the background. One of older girls was almost certainly Pearl. Were the others her sisters? He shook his head. So many questions.

In the kitchen, he checked the cabinets and the fridge, glad to see eggs, juice, coffee, and milk for breakfast. He wasn't hungry at the moment but knew tomorrow he'd be ready for a meal.

By the time he'd gone through the house, it had gotten late. His body was still on Trendale time—medication at nine thirty, lights out at ten, and not a peep after that. When he felt his eyelids drooping, he decided to get some sleep.

He debated for a moment, then decided that leaving some lights on downstairs would be reassuring to him. Not that he was afraid, but it would be a good deterrent to some would-be thief who might think the house was vacant. Plus, it helped guide the way. Just as Pearl had said, the second door on the left upstairs led to a room that was cleaner than the rest of the house. The sheets and blankets smelled fresh too, like fabric softener. He found a nearby bathroom, washed up for the night, and brushed his teeth.

Stripping down to his briefs, Joe slipped between the sheets and turned off the bedside lamp. He'd been afraid that he wouldn't be able to sleep at all without the nighttime pills he'd gotten at Trendale, so he was glad when a wave of fatigue washed over him. There was something rewarding about the feeling of drifting off to sleep, particularly after a long day. And it had been a long day, at least emotionally.

Joe dreamed.

Again, it wasn't the shapeless nonsense of most dreams but a scene unfolding sequentially as experienced by someone who was there. He used the word *dream* when describing it only because he didn't know what else to call it. There were some similarities. He experienced it during the night while he slept, like a dream. Also, he had no control over what unfolded. But there were differences too. More vivid than a memory and more real than a dream, it felt like he was there, thrust into the situation, hearing and seeing and smelling and feeling all of it. All of it. He had no choice in the matter. He never knew he was dreaming at the time he was experiencing it, just that he'd been thrust inexplicably into someone else's life. He was another man, or at least that was the sense he got, and when he was this other person, he wasn't Joe Arneson anymore. When he woke up, it was always with a shock at finding himself transported to a different body.

The dream he had that night started off on a positive note. For the most part, the emotion he felt during it was one of joy. He saw a young woman sitting at a piano, playing dramatic, vibrant music. Others were in the room in his peripheral view, but he couldn't have said who they were or how many there were. He had eyes only for her. Her hands fluttered over the keys like the wings of a bird. She wore a simple blue dress, and her hair was swept up, revealing the back of her neck. Oh, the music! She played with a passion, pouring her soul onto the keyboard, the music swelling, and his own mood swelled with it. Above and behind her, there was a flickering of light, something that puzzled him when he thought about this dream later. What was that? The pulse of light was large and erratic and had the attention of everyone else in the room.

Joe was along for the ride as an unidentified man. He walked down an incline to join her, surprising her by sitting next to her on the bench. She gave him a quirk of her lips, a small brief smile, but kept playing. He was so close now that he could see the sweep of her hair as it was pulled back and pinned in place. Again, he noticed the graceful arch of her neck above her collar. He had to fight the urge to kiss it; he sensed they didn't know each other well and that kissing her around other people would be shameful in some way.

Her hair was a warm golden brown. It was frustratingly hard to get a good look at her face. Her hands were small, but that didn't stop her fingers from moving deftly up and down the keyboard. She leaned into the piano, pressing with a fury, the music building and building and then softening. Above them, the lights quivered, casting moonbeams over her. The people behind them gasped. He leaned in cautiously, wanting to inhale her, all of her, aware that this was his moment, that he could physically connect with her while everyone else was distracted. All he wanted was a touch, and an innocent one at that—the brush of his hand on her arm or his knee against hers. He would have settled for one brief moment of connection.

It wasn't destined to be.

Just as he leaned in, he was jerked backward by someone gripping the collar of his shirt, yanking so hard that he was thrown to the floor with a force that took his breath away. The room swam above him, the flickering lights outlining a figure leaning over him in a menacing way. In the dim light above the man's head, he could make out what appeared to be a crystal chandelier mounted on the ceiling.

He couldn't see a face. What he heard was a threatening voice saying, "Keep your disgusting hands off her!"

When Joe woke, the words were still ringing in his ears, and his heart raced as if he'd faced real danger. At Trendale, he'd had discussions about this particular dream, with Dr. Jensen suggesting that he had the power to change the outcome.

"This is your mind creating these images, Joe. Next time, you can be ready for this guy. You know when he's going to knock you down. Turn before that happens, and stand up." Dr. Jensen chuckled. "At least make it a fair fight."

Everything the doctor had said made sense, but nothing he suggested ever worked. Some part of Joe wondered if he really was mentally ill, destined to have these awful dreams dog him for the rest of his life. He wasn't sure his heart could take it.

Lying in bed, Joe mentally re-created the good parts of the experience, remembering the sight of the woman's hands and the back of her neck. Her thick upswept hair. And the way she played the piano with such passion, her hands running over the keys, her right knee bobbing in time.

He could vividly recall the urgent feeling of being drawn to her side, closer and closer. An emotion had overwhelmed him, and even now, out of the dream, it stayed with him. Joe had never been in love, so he couldn't speak to that, but longing? He knew longing, knew it well, and sitting on that piano bench, he'd felt the ache of it all the way through.

As he fell back asleep, the woman was still on his mind. He'd been so close, so very close. If only he could have seen her face.

CHAPTER EIGHT

1983

As promised, Pearl arrived at the house at nine the next morning. This time she was alone. Joe watched as she pulled up the circular drive in the old sedan, accidentally driving onto the lawn a few times before correcting and veering back onto the pavement.

By that point, Joe had already showered, eaten some breakfast, and made some phone calls—initially to his father and then to his friend Wayne. After that, he'd tried a few other friends. No one could help him.

He'd been hoping his father would drive to Pullman to pick him up, or at the very least, tell him he was welcome to come back home again. Instead, his father informed him that neither was going to happen. "I talked to Dr. Jensen this morning," his dad said in a brisk manner. "Since your condition hasn't responded to medication, he thinks you'd be an excellent candidate for electroconvulsive therapy. They've had terrific results on patients who—"

"Stop right there," Joe said. "Electroshock therapy? No, no way. Not happening. Absolutely not."

"Joe," his father said. "I had my doubts too at first until it was explained to me. Believe me, Dr. Jensen has your best interests at heart. It's an extreme therapy, but yours is an extreme case. You've said yourself that none of the talk therapy or medication made a bit of difference. I'll come up today and drive you back to Trendale, and Dr. Jensen can explain it to you himself."

Joe knew better than that. Once he was inside the facility, there would be no turning back. He still remembered the feeling of being locked up, unable to leave. Having his long-lost grandmother show up was a lucky break. Nothing like that was likely to happen again.

"How about I come home and get some sort of outpatient treatment?" he said. "There has to be a doctor in the area who will see me."

"I'm sure there is." His father sighed. "But I think we're beyond outpatient, don't you?" His father had a habit of voicing his opinion as a question. It was damn annoying.

"I don't feel like I'm beyond anything," Joe argued. "Being in my own home will provide me with the security and family support I didn't have at Trendale." He'd picked up some of the staff lingo and now used it to his advantage, lobbing it back as a defense.

The conversation went back and forth then, with Joe downplaying his nighttime terrors and making a case for coming home to deal with his problems and his father insisting he needed to be back at Trendale getting professional help. "It's the only way."

Finally, Joe said, "Are you saying I absolutely can't come home?"

"I'm saying you can't come home *yet*." The emphasis on the last word was exaggerated. "Not until you finish your treatment plan at Trendale."

What his father didn't seem to understand was that the treatment plan was nothing official. Dr. Jensen had been stymied by Joe's issues and now was just making stabs in the dark. The doctor had messed around in Joe's head long enough. Joe wasn't going to be his lab rat anymore. "I won't be doing that."

"Then I'm sorry, son, you can't come home. It's not just about you and me. I have Linda and your mother to think about."

"What about them?"

"When you cry out at night, it terrifies them, and I find it disturbing as well. You've never heard it, so you'll have to trust me on this. The voice doesn't sound like you."

Joe said, "I can't control that. You know I'd never hurt Linda or Mom. The idea is ridiculous." He got his father to agree that Joe himself was not violent, but still, he could tell that wouldn't sway him.

His dad said, "Nothing else has worked. The electroconvulsive therapy is worth a try. It could be the answer."

"Or it could be a big mistake."

His father kept on arguing its merits as if Joe hadn't even spoken. By the end of the conversation, they each knew the other wasn't going to yield. There was no compromise between allowing an electric current to pass through his brain and leaving his brain just as it was. He did manage to say, "Thanks for telling me your thoughts, Dad. Give Mom and Linda my love."

"I will. Let me know what you decide to do. I'm open to helping if you change your mind, and if you're smart, you will."

He sounded so smug that Joe knew his father was counting on him to have no other options. He'd wait for Joe to call back, asking for forgiveness and saying he'd try the electroconvulsive therapy. What he didn't know was that Joe would sleep in a ditch before going back to Trendale. It was never going to happen. No way, no how. There had to be a better answer. If it took the rest of his life, he'd find it.

He called Wayne next, catching him right before he was out the door to work. He'd written Wayne a letter shortly after being checked in at Trendale, but that was where they'd last left off. Now he explained everything that had happened since then, including being rescued by the grandmother he'd thought was dead. Wayne listened, fascinated. When Joe asked if there was any way he could get his old job back, Wayne laughed. "You gotta be kidding me, Joe. Do you know how pissed off the boss was when you just didn't show up? He couldn't believe you bailed on him after he took a chance hiring you with no experience."

"Did you explain what happened?"

"Yeah, but it didn't help. He said he didn't want some psycho working for him anyway."

Joe chewed on this for a bit. Being labeled a mental case did not fit with being a good employee. People usually covered up that kind of information. Certainly no one would reveal it to a boss or prospective employer. The part he *wanted* to explain was that being pulled off to a psychiatric facility was not his idea. Leaving on short notice was not the way he'd have done things. He'd gotten swept up by his father's insistence and his mom's worry. He exhaled.

"Okay, so I'll have to get another job." Unspoken was that he couldn't use his old one as a reference, because who knew what they'd say about him? It would be hard to explain the gap in his employment history.

"You'll find something," Wayne said. "I'll ask around. If I hear anything, I'll let you know." Joe knew he would. Wayne was a great guy and a good friend.

"In the meantime, can I crash on your couch? Just until I get a job? I've got some money saved. I can pay you rent." First, he'd have to get home and make a withdrawal from his bank. But he was good for it. He wouldn't expect Wayne to let him stay for free.

Wayne cleared his throat. "Stay with me? On the couch. For how long?"

"Just until I get a job, and then I'll get my own place. Maybe a month?"

"A month."

"Or maybe less. It's hard to say. You know I'm a hard worker. I'll take anything at this point."

He heard a long pause on Wayne's end. "See, I don't think that's going to work out. I just moved in with Debbie, and our place is tiny, like, really small. And we have her two cats, and the landlord wouldn't like us having another person here." His voice trailed off, getting quieter. "And we only have parking for two cars. It's not that I don't want to help you out . . ."

Joe got the impression Debbie was lurking in the background, probably frantically shaking her head. He said, "It's okay. I get it. I just thought I'd ask."

Wayne wrapped up the conversation quickly. He was sorry, but he had to leave for work. Joe understood.

Then Joe called a few other friends. All of them were glad to hear from him, but none could let him live with them, however temporarily. Ruefully, he realized that he'd spent a small fortune on long-distance calls, all for nothing. He'd have to pay his grandmother back. She would have a coronary when the bill came if he didn't warn her in advance. Long distance was expensive.

When Pearl arrived, she went straight to the kitchen. She still used the walker but moved a little more quickly today, even setting it aside as she brewed some coffee, then gestured for him to join her at the kitchen table. Sipping from a mug, she made small talk, asking how he'd slept.

"I slept well, thanks," he said, then got straight to what was on his mind. "I want to hear about this summer job you were talking about last night. What does it involve?"

CHAPTER NINE

1983

This had been her hope all along, but until that moment, she wasn't sure if he'd go for it. A smile tugged at her lips, but Pearl didn't let it get too far. She thought about the expression the kids used. *Playing it cool.* That's what they called it. Outwardly, she tried to appear cool as a cucumber. Inside, though, she was jumping for joy. Joe was staying for the summer, or at least entertaining the idea.

Pearl said, "Why do you ask? Do you know someone who might be interested?"

"I might be."

She didn't let it go at that, instead feigning innocence and asking why the change of heart. "Last night you seemed so certain you'd be going home today." When he told her of his father's insistence on electroshock therapy, she was irate on his behalf.

"That Bill," she said. "We've had our differences, but I never would have thought he'd let some quack shoot electricity through his own son's brain. How horrible. It's like torture."

She saw her mistake then, the look on Joe's face when she spoke negatively of his father.

He said, "He wants me to do it because he thinks it will help. It's not that he doesn't care. Just the opposite." The boy was loyal. That was admirable.

"Of course." Pearl spoke soothingly. "He just doesn't know what else to do." That did the trick. The boy's face relaxed. She took a sip of her coffee. "So now you're thinking you might stay?"

"Maybe. What would I have to do?"

"It's very simple, really, but time-consuming." She waved a hand around the kitchen. "You'll need to empty this house and get it ready to sell."

"You're selling it?"

She nodded. "I have no choice. First of all, I no longer live here, and it's pointless for it to sit empty. But even more important, the truth of the matter, Joe, is that I'm dying."

The word landed right where she thought it might. His mouth dropped open slightly, incredulous. "Dying? But you look just fine."

"Why, thank you. I expect I look fine to you because we've just met, but I assure you it's true. I am dying; there's no mistake. Lung cancer, that evil villain, is back. I had it nearly ten years ago. I had chemotherapy back then, quit smoking, and thought I had put an end to it, but it has returned. This time around, I decided I'm not doing chemo again. It was a horrendous ordeal, and I have no wish to repeat it."

She thought of the chemotherapy she'd endured the first time around. She'd never known a human being could feel so terrible and still survive. One night she was so weak, she'd crawled on her knees to the bathroom, vomited, then lain on the bathroom rug until morning, too exhausted to get up. The doctors said chemotherapy had improved since then, but she still told them she wasn't interested. Enough already. There was no use in prolonging the inevitable.

"The chemo bought me more time, but I'm older now and more tired. I just don't want to do it," she told Joe.

"Even if it means you won't live as long?"

She shrugged. "I don't want to die, but the truth is, we all die sooner or later."

His brow furrowed. "No, that's not right. I just met you. You and my father haven't spoken in how long?"

"Decades." Pearl took another sip of coffee. "Since he was about your age." She very clearly remembered the day Bill left. He'd grabbed only a few things and then was gone. He wouldn't listen to anything she had to say. "You're despicable," he'd said, right before the door shut behind him. She'd watched the taillights of his car as they got smaller in the distance. *He'll be back,* she'd thought, but she was wrong. He never came back.

At first, she knew that he'd gone to live with relatives on his father's side, but after that, there were years when she didn't know where he was. It wasn't until she hired a private investigator that she knew he'd put himself through college, started a career in finance, married, had a son, lost a wife, and then married again. He'd bought a house, gotten promotions, and gone on vacations, and she hadn't been a part of any of it. She knew about Joe but lost the trail again when he'd last moved, so she never knew about her granddaughter, Linda. Not until recently, when she'd hired another investigator and called their house. So many years without a family. One mistake, and look what was stolen from her. With Joe here, she might be able to make amends.

Joe gave her a serious look. "Don't you think you should patch things up with him, seeing as how your time is limited?"

Pearl regarded him thoughtfully. He was an adult in years, but in so many other ways, he was still so young. She'd made a few efforts to reach Bill, but he hadn't answered her letters or those of her attorney either. The phone call she'd made recently was the first time she'd telephoned. She'd had to pay a pretty penny to get his unlisted number and almost couldn't believe it when Linda had been so accommodating in answering her questions.

The boy was waiting for her answer, so she spoke carefully. "Patching things up would be ideal, of course, but life doesn't always work out the way you'd like it to." She kept going. "And here's something you should know. It's something you already know but probably don't quite believe. All of us have limited time. I'm ancient and have a terminal case of cancer. You're young and healthy. And guess what? You could get hit by a truck tomorrow, and I could live another three years. We aren't guaranteed even one more minute. Babies die, and so do young people. No one knows who's next. It's very unfair."

"I know that," he said somewhat impatiently. "But still, I'm here now, and I'd like to know more about you and my father's side of the family. If you're willing to tell me."

"Of course, and I'm very glad you're here. Let's start over. If we're going to have these heart-to-heart talks, we should figure out a few things. For instance, what would you like to call me?"

He exhaled and said tentatively, "Grandma?"

She didn't feel like a grandma, especially to a guy old enough to shave. Maybe it would be different if she'd known him from the beginning, but she'd missed his infancy and toddler years, had been kept away during his schoolboy days, and hadn't gotten to witness his teenage antics. Now he was man-size, and having him call her *Grandma* didn't fit.

She said, "How about you just call me Pearl?" Was it her imagination, or did he look relieved?

"You wouldn't mind?"

"No. I think it will make things easier. You don't know me as a grandmother. We're strangers, really. You call me Pearl, and I'll call you Joe. Does that work for you?"

"Yes, it does."

"Well, that's settled, then."

"So why don't you and my father talk? Why did he tell me you died?"

She shrugged. "Wishful thinking? Or maybe he says that because I'm dead to him, metaphorically speaking. As for the reason he cut me out of his life, this is it: I made a big mistake, and he's never been able to forgive me."

Joe leaned forward, his elbows on the table. "What was the mistake?"

Pearl paused for only a second. She was getting too old to sugarcoat things, so she just came out with it. "Your father believes that I killed someone."

The statement clearly took him by surprise. Joe appeared dumb-struck for a moment, and then he asked, "Did you?"

"Not on purpose."

CHAPTER TEN

1916

In the parlor, the younger girls clustered around John Lawrence in a way Pearl found irritating. Little Daisy parked herself right next to him, her arm draped over his elbow, and the twins took turns trying to impress him, first playing the piano and then telling him about the new kittens out in the barn. Helen and Emma sat nearby, twittering at everything he said. Pearl herself barely got a word in edgewise, and just when she began talking about the lake, trying to get a chance to tell him about the rowboat, Alice called her into the kitchen to help.

If Pearl didn't know better, she'd think Alice was trying to keep her from putting her mark on him. But that wasn't like Alice, and the truth of the matter was that getting a big Sunday dinner on the table was a lot of work. Why go to so much trouble? Pearl couldn't figure it out. Alice had worked up a sweat cooking all day in a hot kitchen, and in no time at all, the food would be eaten and there'd be dishes to do. Cooking was the work that created more work, and for what? The next meal would come around soon enough, and it would start all over again. Pearl had long ago decided that when she was famous and wealthy, she'd have servants to handle all the cooking, and all the housework too, for that matter. Unlike Alice, her nose would never get burned from weeding the garden, and her hands would stay soft and ladylike.

As dinnertime came closer, Alice pulled Emma and Helen into the kitchen as well and assigned all of them chores—putting food in serving dishes, setting the table, lighting candles, pouring milk for the children and water for adults. Pearl was glad to see she was included as an adult and given water instead of milk. Until recently, her father hadn't seen her that way. Pearl tried to stay in the dining room where she could keep an eye on John, her father, and the younger girls.

Howie and Mrs. Donohue arrived, Howie carrying a covered pan containing his mother's famous cobbler. "I had to use the apples I canned last year. I would have used fresh if they weren't out of season right now," Mrs. Donohue said apologetically as Howie carried the pan into the kitchen. On the other side of the swinging door, Pearl heard Alice exclaim over the treat. "I hope you don't mind."

"We don't mind," Emma said and then turned to John. "Mrs. Donohue makes the best cobbler. We all love it."

Mrs. Donohue looked over her glasses at him. "You must be John Lawrence, here to help at the mill this summer."

"Yes, ma'am."

"I'm Mrs. Donohue from down the road. My son, Howie, and I will most likely be seeing a lot of you."

"I certainly hope so, ma'am." He smiled. "I'm very pleased to meet you."

Later, after they were all seated around the dinner table and Alice had served the food, the questions from Mrs. Donohue to John began. Inwardly, Pearl groaned at the nosy way she kept probing at him, interrogating him under the guise of polite conversation. "So, Mr. Lawrence, you're from Gladly Falls, north of here, is that right?"

John's fork stopped halfway between his plate and his mouth. "Yes, ma'am."

Her father spoke up. "We're lucky John was able to come and help us, what with Wendall being laid up for the next few months." Wendall had worked for their father at the mill all Pearl's life. He was a good-hearted fellow but not all that swift in the head, and he had a fondness for the drink, far beyond what was usual for the men in their town. As of the week before last, he was laid up with a broken arm, a damaged shoulder, and a cracked pelvic bone, injuries that came from falling off the roof of his mother's house. The doctor said he was lucky to be alive. Pearl secretly wondered if he'd escaped death because he was so pickled that he'd tumbled down gently instead of crashing to the ground.

"So is there no work for a young man such as yourself in Gladly Falls, Mr. Lawrence, that you had to come all the way here?" Mrs. Donohue speared a piece of potato and examined it before putting it in her mouth. Her tone was accusatory, but John didn't seem to take it that way.

"Please call me John," he said. "Gladly Falls is a very small town." They all waited for him to say more, but he left it at that.

"I, for one, am very happy John is here to help," Father said. "He's a college man, Mrs. Donohue, and is set on becoming a doctor. I understand he saves every penny for tuition and his other expenses." Their father smiled in John's direction; he had a high regard for those who were thrifty and valued education.

Mrs. Donohue brightened at this. "Oh? A doctor! My Howie is quite the scholar himself. He will be heading off to the university after he finishes high school next year." Howie flushed in embarrassment and kept his head down. "Perhaps you can tell Howie what he can expect at the university. No one around here continues their education much past primary school. Where is it you attend classes, Mr. Lawrence?"

"The Marquette University School of Medicine in Milwaukee."

"I've heard good things about Marquette."

"All true, ma'am."

"Your parents must be very pleased." Mrs. Donohue herself swelled with pride, looking at Howie as she spoke. "A son who is to be a doctor! My word, that's quite an accomplishment."

John nodded thoughtfully. "My mother is very proud and will be prouder still once I graduate."

She frowned. "But is your father not proud as well?"

"It's just my mother and myself," John said, his head held high.

"A boy without a father. Such a shame."

Their father broke into the conversation. "You of all people must understand, Mrs. Donohue, seeing as how you've done such a wonderful job raising Howie. The loss of a father leaves a tremendous void, but life goes on."

"Of course," she said hurriedly. "I'm sorry to have broached the subject."

"No need to apologize," John said. Pearl got the impression this wasn't the first time he'd been asked about his father.

"It's just so surprising to see another young man at this table. It's usually just the Bennett girls and my Howie. Tell me," she said, leaning forward to speak to Pearl's father, "how is it that your family is related to young Mr. Lawrence?" The flame of the candle directly in front of her flickered.

Pearl found herself looking at Howie and rolling her eyes to signal that she thought his mother was a busybody. Despite his loyalty to his mother, his fondness for Pearl won out, and he grinned at her.

Their father said, "John's mother has worked for my cousin's family for a number of years. They consider John and his mother to be like family, and that is how we will think of John as well." He cocked his head to one side. "I have long been outnumbered in this household, so I welcome John as I'd welcome a son. I'm very glad he is here to be my right-hand man." He said it as if the subject was closed, but Mrs. Donohue couldn't resist one more comment.

"A welcome addition, but having a young man around does change things, does it not?" She raised her eyebrows and looked from Pearl to Alice and then around the table to the other girls. "There's so much to consider with so many young ladies in the household."

"That is true," their father agreed.

"You don't have to worry, Mrs. Donohue. John will be sleeping in the barn," Pearl said.

"Pearl!" Mrs. Donohue shrieked.

Their father sighed. "Pearl, where our guest will be staying is not appropriate dinnertime conversation."

"Especially in mixed company." Mrs. Donohue's eyebrows knit sternly together. "You should know that, Pearl. A lady's moral virtue is so important. If you want to be a respectable member of society, you need to think before you speak."

"I'm sorry," Pearl said meekly.

John just nodded and said, "Apology accepted. No harm done." He turned to Howie. "Since we'll be neighbors, perhaps you can show me how things are done around here."

"I'd be happy to," Howie said.

"Howie is always glad to serve," Mrs. Donohue declared. "He follows the path of Jesus in that way."

"Of course," their father said. "He's a fine young man and a credit to his mother."

Mrs. Donohue beamed with pride and turned back to her cobbler.

"This is delicious," Alice said, indicating her plate. "And I'm not the only one who thinks so. Daisy would lick the pan if I'd let her."

"Can I?" Daisy's little voice piped up. Normally, the younger girls didn't join the conversation unless spoken to first, but after their mother died, their father had become lackadaisical about the rules.

Alice smiled down on her. "No, you may not."

When the last bite was taken, the family adjourned to the parlor, all except the four oldest girls, who cleared the table and cleaned up the kitchen. Pearl found herself wandering back to the dining room to sneak peeks at John, who was talking animatedly with Howie while Mrs. Donohue looked on with satisfaction. It seemed the two young men, both destined for higher education, had found kindred spirits in each other. Their father and the younger girls sat quietly and listened.

By the time Alice had put the last dish away and Pearl had hung up the dish towels, the sun had started to lower in the sky and Mrs. Donohue was saying goodbye, eager to leave before it got too dark.

They were all out on the porch when Howie drove the wagon around to the front of the house, his mare stepping brightly, glad to be going home. Mr. Bennett helped Howie's mother up to her seat, and the girls waved goodbye.

The family and John Lawrence were still on the porch when they heard the roar of a motor coming down the road. Their heads turned collectively. They were amazed to see such a rare thing, an actual automobile, with Alice's admirer, Frank, at the wheel.

The black Model T came to a stop in front of them. Frank swung the door open and bellowed, "Will you take a look at this!" Mae and Maude ran forward to admire the new automobile while Daisy remained next to Alice, her hand clutching her older sister's skirt. Even their old dog, Shep, was curious. He came trotting out from behind the barn to check out the ruckus.

"Were you expecting Frank to come calling this evening?" Mr. Bennett asked his oldest daughter, his voice subdued compared to the hubbub in the front yard.

Alice shook her head. "No. In fact, I have asked him many times not to come." She folded her arms. "He never listens."

CHAPTER ELEVEN

1983

"Wait. Let me make sure I heard you right," Joe said, then repeated Pearl's words back to her. "You killed someone but not on purpose?"

"That's right," she said. The horrified look on his face made her sorry she'd even brought it up. Ancient history, that's what it was, and nothing she could take back at this point. Obviously, Joe was the type who would hold it against her. Maybe all Arneson men were the same.

"What does that mean?"

"It means there was a death, and your father thought I was responsible."

Joe mulled this over for a second. "*Were* you responsible?"

She sensed there was a lot riding on her answer. He could bolt out of here, just like his father did so many years ago. "I don't know. That's for the good Lord to decide. When I meet him—*if* I meet him—I'm sure he'll let me know." Mentioning God was a smart strategy, she thought. The association of a higher power was a good one. It made her look humble.

"So what happened?"

"If you don't mind, I'd rather not tell you just yet. I want you to get to know me first before you hear about the worst thing I've ever done.

I've long believed that no one should be judged on the worst thing they've ever done. And not on the best thing either, for that matter." She sighed. "Human beings are much more complex than one event that happened on one day in a very long life."

He nodded as if it made sense.

"I would guess your father is not worried about your safety here. If he really thought I was a murderer, I doubt he'd have let you stay."

"You're probably right."

"So we can assume I'm harmless enough." The comment made him smile. She was winning him over. "If you work for me this summer, and I hope you do, we'll have time to get to know each other."

"If I work for you this summer, would I be staying here, in this house?"

"Yes."

"Alone? No one else will be here?"

She choked out a laugh. "That's really up to you. I know I won't be here, and as far as I know, the place isn't haunted. Are you afraid to stay alone?"

"No, ma'am."

"You can drop the *ma'am*. *Pearl* is fine."

"No, I'm not afraid to stay alone. Just trying to figure it all out before I make a commitment."

"This sounds like I'll need another cup of coffee." She got up and poured herself another one, then sat back down. "Okay, shoot. Next question."

"What would I be doing? Specifically, I mean? I know you said to empty the house and get it ready to sell, but I'm not sure what's involved in doing all that."

Pearl leaned over to pick up her purse, pulled out a folder, and handed it to him. The outside of the folder was labeled with her name, the address of the house, and her contact information at Pine Ridge Hollow. Inside were forms giving him permission to hire others on her behalf and to conduct business with a resale shop in town called Secondhand Heaven. Another few pages had the contact information for a lawn service, gutter cleaning company, housecleaning business, pest control company, and painter. The last page detailed how much he would be paid. She saw his eyes widen when he got to that part. Fifteen dollars an hour for forty hours a week for a term of ten weeks. Double what he would have made in construction, and more than four times the minimum wage.

"You were pretty sure I'd do this," he said after a few minutes of reading through the paperwork. "My name is printed here." He tapped on one of the sheets.

"I wasn't entirely sure. Hoping is more like it, I guess," Pearl said. "I need this done, and I want to see it happen before I leave this big, bad world. I have a will, and my wishes for how my health should be handled at the end are very clear. This house, though—it's a sticking point. I'd like to see it cleaned out and sold. And if I can get acquainted with my grandson at the same time, all the better."

"Ten weeks seems like a long time to empty a house and clean it up." He looked around the kitchen. "What if I get it done sooner than that?"

"You won't," she said and took a sip of coffee. "There's an attic full of family items and a barn that hasn't been looked at in years. God knows what you'll find inside. You'll have to start off by inventorying everything in the place."

"Inventorying?"

"Yes, nothing fancy, just a list of each item, but you have to go through all of it. Every cupboard, closet, and storage area. It's a huge task. Then things will have to be sorted, packed, and moved. I've rented a large pickup truck to be delivered later today. It will be here for the duration of your stay."

"Again, you seem pretty sure that I'd be on board."

She continued, not addressing the comment. "You can move some of the things on your own. The bigger pieces you'll need help with, but I have all the details in the folder. The young woman who owns Secondhand Heaven is named Kathleen. I talked to her on the phone, and she's willing to take the furniture on consignment." She sighed. "At this point, though, it doesn't really matter if things sell or not. I'll be dead as dead soon enough, and all the money in the world won't help me then."

"That's a cheerful thought."

"It is what it is, and there's nothing to be done about it." She glanced back down the hallway. "If there's anything you want for yourself, feel free to take it. Just note it on the inventory sheet."

"Me? I can take what I want?"

"Of course—you're family. Who better to take family items than my own grandson? Keep your sister in mind too, and take anything you think she might like. I doubt I'll ever meet her. Not if that father of yours has anything to say about it."

Joe turned his attention back to the paperwork. "So I start off by taking inventory. Once I've done that, then what?"

"The inventory is for me. I'll go over the list and help you decide what to do with everything. The junk will get donated or tossed. I ordered a dumpster to be delivered as well. They'll park it on the driveway, and it will stay as long as you need it. Goodwill will get some of the household items, and the furniture and valuables that you don't want will be sold at Kathleen's shop."

"This Kathleen, you trust her?"

"I don't know her very well," Pearl said with a shrug. "She's a young woman, looks to be about your age. She inherited the shop from her great-aunt, Edna, who was a decent woman, known for being honest in her business dealings. A bit too tenderhearted, but she couldn't help that, I guess. And if you think I'm old, you should have seen Edna Clark. She wasn't much older than me, but she looked ancient! Even her wrinkles had wrinkles." Pearl tapped on the table with her fingertips and grinned. "Kathleen stepped up to the plate when Edna was at the end. I understand she came right away, driving up from Ohio when she heard she was ill, then helped her when she was in the hospital and kept the shop running. And this was before she knew she'd be inheriting the whole kit and caboodle. So I would guess she's not too bad."

Joe gathered up the papers and tucked them back into the folder. "I think I understand what I need to do."

"So you're taking the job?"

"Yes."

"Very good." She took another sip of her coffee. "Let me show you the rest of the property while I still have energy. I'm pretty good in the morning, but as the day goes on, I lose steam."

Joe walked ahead, pausing for her to catch up and holding the outside door open for her. When she headed for the stairs, he went to hold her elbow, but she waved him away. "I'll let you know if I need help." Pearl had never been opposed to accepting a gentleman's gallant offer, but at this stage in her life, having someone help her do something as simple as descend the porch steps made her feel old. Not as old as some of the people who lived at Pine Ridge Hollow. Those folks had one foot in the grave, their eyes cloudy and teeth barely holding on. She wasn't there yet.

It took a while, but she and Joe made the rounds of the property. She showed him two sheds and a chicken coop. "The chicken coop is only a shell of its former self," she said, giving the structure a push with her walker. "You can tear it down. Use the tools in the barn. If you can't find the right tools, go into town and buy what you need at the hardware store. Give them my name, and they can bill me."

She'd saved the barn for last, swinging the door open and standing in the doorway. Old bales of hay lined one wall. Dust motes swirled on a shaft of light. She inhaled something that tickled her throat, and she coughed loudly and then again. She gripped the handles of her walker and leaned to one side, hacking and wheezing, her whole body trying to expel the irritant. Finally, she spat out a wad of grayish saliva and cleared her throat. When she looked up at Joe, she expected disgust, but instead his face showed concern.

"Are you okay?" he asked.

She nodded, swallowing hard. "I could use a sip of water."

"Just a minute. I'll get some." He jogged off in the direction of the house.

By the time he'd returned holding a tall glass filled to the top with water, she was better but still grateful for the drink. Funny how a simple gesture made such a difference. She gulped it down. "Thank you."

"Maybe you should go back inside and sit down?" he said kindly. Pearl saw that Joe had a compassion that had been missing in his father. Was it because his mother died and he knew what it was like to have loss, or was this something a person was born with? She had a feeling people were born with it, and she knew herself well enough to know she'd never had it. Only recently had she started to realize all the damage she'd done in thinking only of herself.

"Not until you see the best part," she said. "The lake." She set the glass down on a bale of hay next to the barn door, then continued to the back of the property, with Joe trailing behind. The path down to the lake had never been paved, but a century of feet pounding its course had turned the dirt hard as asphalt. She was able to go about halfway, then stopped at the top of the incline. They could see the lake through the trees ahead; sunlight danced on the surface of the water. "The rest of this is rough sledding for an old lady like me. I'll wait here while you go take a look."

He hesitated. "Are you sure?"

"Yes, and then you can report back and tell me what you see. Let me know what shape the dock is in." From a distance it looked fine, but she knew that up close it could be another story.

He nodded. "I'll be right back."

As she watched him head toward the path, Pearl thought about the reliability of the lake. All of life was change, ongoing, never ceasing. Babies were born and grew up, seemingly overnight. And then, in the blink of an eye, those babies were married grown-ups announcing that they were expecting babies of their own. No one had warned her how fast it all would go.

The landscape, too, changed. Trees grew taller, saplings thickening and growing until they canopied overhead. Houses were built and over time fell into disrepair. Some were torn down and new ones built in their stead. Others took on additions or remodels, changing the look of the original house. Roads were widened and traffic lights updated. It was hard to keep track of it all.

Stores were the same for decades and then overnight became different kinds of stores. Tomlinson's Groceries was bought out by a national chain. Frederick's Pharmacy lost its soda fountain counter and candy display to focus solely on pharmaceuticals, snacks, and health-related items. She'd gotten her walker there, and Howard had gotten more than one cane. He had a tendency to misplace them. It was a shame to watch the world transform before one's eyes, powerless to stop it.

The lake, though, was timeless, looking almost exactly the way it had when she was a child. A spot of consistent tranquility in the midst of a fast-forward world.

She whispered, "The world is for the young." Pearl wasn't quite sure if she'd heard that expression somewhere or come up with it on her own, but she did know the truth of it. She was young once, with all sorts of wonderful possibilities ahead of her. Now the only thing she had left was this young man, her grandson. If she was going to make things right, it would fall to him. And it would have to happen soon, or it wouldn't be happening at all. So much depended on it.

CHAPTER TWELVE

1983

Kathleen stood at the front counter of Secondhand Heaven, the phone pressed to her ear. She listened as the old lady on the other end of the line rambled on, going over everything they'd discussed numerous times already. Kathleen absentmindedly looped the curly cord around one finger while commenting periodically to let Pearl know she understood. "Yes. Sure. Of course." She gazed around the room until she spotted her assistant, Marcia, then mouthed the words *Help me*, along with a roll of her eyes.

In response, Marcia sprang into action, opening the front door and letting it close so that the jangle of the bell could be clearly heard. "Excuse me!" she yelled. "Is there someone here who can give me the price of this dresser? Hello! Anyone?"

Kathleen said, "I'm sorry, Mrs. Arneson, but I'm alone in the store, and I have to attend to a customer." She unraveled the cord from her finger. "No, there's no need to call back. I understand perfectly. Yes, I will. Thank you, Mrs. Arneson. Goodbye." Kathleen set the receiver in its cradle and put her hand to her forehead.

"What was that all about?" Marcia asked with a grin.

"Pearl Arneson giving me more instructions. She must think I'm a complete idiot."

"What now?"

Kathleen's eyes went heavenward, resting on a crystal chandelier with the price tag twirling on a string off the bottom of the fixture. "She wanted to let me know her grandson, Joe, has agreed to take the job and will be staying in her house. She wanted confirmation that I will take all her furniture on consignment." She waved her hand. "And on and on. This is all stuff we've talked about before. Am I sure I'll take all the furniture? Do I have enough room in the store? It's going to be a lot of furniture, you know." She looked around the store. The stock hadn't been replenished in a while, so the floor space was thinning out. And there was the back room and a garage, now standing empty, ready for the overflow.

Marcia shook her head. "She's old. I'm sure she forgot you already talked about it. I heard she's dying."

"I heard that too. She told me so herself." Kathleen exhaled. She remembered how Pearl Arneson had come into the store two weeks earlier to set up the sale of her home's contents. At the same time, she'd announced her terminal status without a hint of emotion, making it sound more like a deadline than the end of her life. She was a hard woman to figure out, but Kathleen was not without compassion. "I'm sorry if I sounded impatient with her."

"Are you kidding me? You're as patient as they come. She's a really horrible woman. I mean, I'm sorry about her cancer coming back, but there's something about her that makes my teeth hurt. Before you took over the store, she would stop in and sort of make fun of your aunt Edna."

"No!" Kathleen had spent hundreds of hours at Aunt Edna's bedside at the hospital, and she'd never said a bad word about anyone, much less Pearl Arneson. "She made fun of her?" She couldn't imagine it. Aunt Edna was sweet as pie, thanking the nurses for all they did and apologizing for being so much trouble. And before that, when she was in good health, she was practically a saint, dropping off home-baked goods at the homes of people who were sick, not just friends or neighbors but also people she barely knew. Kathleen had heard story after story at the funeral. Her great-aunt Edna was known for giving money to those in need, sometimes anonymously. "It just showed up on my porch one day," one man said, explaining that he'd lost his job and then his baby had gotten sick. "An envelope full of fifties with a note saying it was from a friend and that she'd be praying for us. No signature, but my wife and I knew it was her. It couldn't have come at a better time, believe me. We were getting desperate. Your aunt was just an angel on earth."

"Pearl didn't make fun of her in an *obvious* way," Marcia clarified. She sat down on a stool and rested her feet on the rungs. "It was all disguised as being sickeningly sweet. She'd walk through the store and say how nice it was that some things never change, that Pullman was growing and changing and other people were traveling and coming and going, but you could always count on good ol' Edna Clark to be behind the counter at Secondhand Heaven, that she was practically a fixture of the store."

"That's not too bad," Kathleen said, mulling it over. She herself was becoming a fixture in the store, and it was working out fine for her. "Maybe she meant it in a nice way?"

Marcia shook her head. "Nope, she meant it like Edna had no life, and this store was outdated. But your aunt never rose to the bait. She was a true lady. Said she didn't pay much attention to what Pearl said, that Pearl had a tragic life, and if it made her feel better to put Edna down, so be it. She said some people are just who they are."

"Edna was wise and kind." Kathleen knew a thing or two about having a tragic life. She was twenty-six and already divorced. Against her parents' wishes, she'd married young and moved across the country with her new husband. It had been a mistake. A big mistake. She'd realized that on their honeymoon when her husband, who'd been doting, became controlling and jealous. Within months, her life became a constant attempt to keep him happy, to assure him that she wasn't looking at other men and that she loved only him. What she'd thought was passion became obsession, and what started as arguments escalated until she was defending herself from angry blows. Once he'd grabbed her upper arms so hard that later she saw finger-shaped bruises. He was always sorry. So sorry. He cried and vowed to change, and she always softened and gave him another chance.

One day Kathleen saw a couple at the grocery store in the produce aisle. From what they were saying, she surmised they were picking out a watermelon to take to a family picnic. The woman had a black eye visible from behind the side of her sunglasses, and the man was telling her to hurry up, that she was always making them late. His tone, neutral but with a threatening undercurrent, reminded her of her own husband's voice when he was just on the edge of exploding, and she saw herself in the woman, who was trying to please him so as not to raise his ire. As they walked away, she heard a female voice in her head, clear as a bell. The voice said: *He will never change*. It was either divine intervention, or she was losing her mind. Either way, she decided, it was time to make a break.

After that, she began squirreling away money until she had enough to take a Greyhound bus home to Ohio. Her parents helped her get a divorce, and she started her life anew, working as a bank teller in her hometown and saving her money. When her ex-husband started showing up everywhere she went, sometimes following her in his car, she was alarmed, and when the gifts and notes began arriving, it escalated.

The notes had started with pleading and over time became vaguely threatening. *I can't live without you. The thought of you with someone else is killing me. We are meant to be together. You'll never find someone who loves you like I do. I will spend the rest of my life convincing you that we need to be together. I'll do whatever it takes to keep you by my side.*

The police were no help. They didn't seem to understand the danger. "Ignore him, and he'll get bored and stop," one officer said.

Another suggested she might want to give her ex-husband another chance. "I talked to him, and he seems like a good guy," he said. "He admitted he made mistakes, but then we all make mistakes, am I right?" He patted Kathleen's shoulder as if she were a child, which made her fume. She tried to tell the cops of their history, that her ex had a violent temper and had been physically abusive, but she sensed that the polite nod of the police officer's head was all she'd be getting in the way of acknowledgment. No one took the threat seriously except her family.

One day her mother got off the phone after speaking to her great-aunt Edna and suggested she and Kathleen go up to Pullman to help take care of her. Kathleen jumped at the chance. She didn't tell anyone where she was going, so there would be no way for Ricky to find her.

After Edna died, Kathleen found out that everything—the house, the car, the business—had all been left to her. She stayed behind to sort things out and wound up stepping into her great-aunt's shoes. The business even came with Marcia, the assistant who was helpful in that she knew everything about the store but wasn't interested in running the place.

The stock in the store had been getting low, and Kathleen had been just about to hit the flea markets when she received the first call from Pearl. Marcia had said no one had been in her house for years aside from that old coot Howard Donohue, but the talk in town was that the house had a lot of nice furniture. Pearl's father reportedly had a knack for carpentry and had made some beautiful pieces. Soon her store would be filled from floor to ceiling.

Marcia broke into her thoughts. "So this Joe, Pearl's grandson—is he single?"

"I'm not sure. Why? Are you interested?"

"Not for me, silly, for you! You spend too much time alone. You need a boyfriend."

Romance was the last thing on Kathleen's mind. "That's sweet of you, Marcia, but I'm not looking for a boyfriend."

"Maybe you're not looking, per se, but if the right one happens to come along? It would be fate, right?"

Kathleen smiled. "I don't believe in fate, and I don't care if Joe Arneson is single. I'm not interested."

Marcia picked up the feather duster and took a swipe at a rolltop desk. "Don't say that! It would all be so perfect. You're new in town. Joe's new in town. You both came here to help elderly relatives. You'll meet, and sparks will fly! Think about what a great story it would make for your kids and grandkids."

Kathleen laughed. "Such an imagination. She didn't say how old he is. He's probably right out of high school."

"Nothing wrong with a younger man," Marcia said. "The heart doesn't know age, only love."

CHAPTER THIRTEEN

1983

After the divorce, Ricky had found it easy to keep track of Kathleen. He'd waited a respectable amount of time before moving across the country to be closer to her. He got a job and an apartment in an adjacent community, then spent most of his free time frequenting the spots she liked best, hoping she'd show up. Once patterns emerged—Saturday mornings at the library, Thursday lunches with a coworker at the same restaurant, grocery shopping on Tuesday evenings with her mom—he made a point to be in those places so he could watch for her. He knew that approaching her would be a big mistake, so he just quietly observed her movements, keeping track of the food she ordered and the books she preferred.

No one knew Kathleen the way he did. No one. And no one ever would. When Ricky listened to other guys talk about their wives and girlfriends, it was mostly griping about how long the women talked on the phone and how much time they spent getting ready in the morning. All of it so ordinary, he could have puked. None of them had a clue what it was like to find the perfect woman, the one a man couldn't live without. Kathleen was all that and more. She was made for him.

As soon as he met her, he'd known she was the one. Destiny. It wasn't just her looks or personality; it was how she made him feel. She brought out the chivalrous side of him. He found himself sending her flowers and calling her at work just because he missed hearing her voice.

True love.

When she'd said she didn't want to be married anymore, that had stung right to his core. How could she do that to him? Here she'd taken a vow to love, honor, and cherish him all the days of her life, and then she'd had the gall to walk away as if none of it mattered? It was infuriating. Ricky didn't understand it. He'd given her everything: all his time, love, and attention. He'd brought her flowers on a regular basis and helped her become more organized. Together they'd created a home of beauty and order. He'd planned that someday she was going to bear his children. They were going to grow old together.

And then, inexplicably, it was over.

Kathleen had single-handedly stomped on all his hopes and dreams. A lesser man would have moved on, given up on her for good, but that wasn't Ricky's way. He prided himself on his tenacity. His plan was simple. He'd ease his way back into her life. She was living in Ohio with her parents, two people he found tiresome, but he had tolerated them for Kathleen's sake. Her mother in particular was such a drag. Now residing in their home, Kathleen was reduced to the life of a teenager, walking their dog in the evening and taking their garbage down to the curb. One time he'd driven past and observed her helping her dad clean out the garage. Living with the old folks had to be a grind, which boded well for him. Soon enough, she'd be ready to be rescued.

He had noted a certain spring in her step on occasion, so he knew that even as a divorced woman, she was able to put on a brave front, giving the world her best smile and even joking around sometimes. Kathleen was never one to let her misery show.

Ricky began to send her greeting cards in a roundabout way—having a friend mail them from the town where he'd formerly lived so it didn't have a local postmark, and using the friend's return address. He kept his messages short and simple, saying he still missed her but was coping with the loss and had even started dating. He added that he'd love to hear how she was doing. Instinctively, he knew that a gentle approach was the way to go. Kathleen was so sensitive.

He'd hoped the reference to him dating would bother her. Certainly she'd realize over time what she'd given up. How could she not? Without him, her life had to be dreary. He waited and waited, but she never wrote back, and when he sent her flowers on her birthday, the florist called him to say she'd refused to accept them. He went and picked up the bouquet from the flower shop and then, the next day, gave them to one of the secretaries at work, the one he knew had a crush on him. She went gaga over them and over the next several days became even more solicitous toward him than usual, keeping his coffee mug topped up, complimenting his ties, and laughing at all his jokes. Now, that was a woman who knew how to act around men. Too bad she wasn't Kathleen.

One good thing—Kathleen wasn't dating anyone. That was in his favor. She had high standards and would never find someone who compared well to Ricky. That much he knew. The returned flowers were a setback, but he didn't take it to heart. She just needed time. Someday they'd tell the story of their breakup to their children and grandchildren. He'd describe it as a silly phase when Kathleen just needed to take a step back before realizing that Ricky really was the one for her. Getting married again would be necessary, but they'd still count the time in between when they celebrated their anniversary. In the scheme of things, it would make their lengthy, devoted marriage seem all the more precious. He pictured taking hold of her hand while telling the kids and grandkids, "I wasn't about to let this one get away."

In return, she'd beam at him, love in her eyes.

Kathleen was not making this easy, but nothing worth having ever came easily. He knew she was making him fight for their love, and he was up to the challenge. Ricky was a winner. Always had been; always would be.

CHAPTER FOURTEEN

1916

Attached to the side of the automobile was a bulb horn. Frank squeezed the bulb and laughed when the younger girls jumped at the noise. He did it twice more while making a point to grin at Alice as if she were in on the joke. Honk! Honk! It sounded loudly, making Mae cover her ears in alarm. Frank shouted, "Sounds like my granddad when he blows his nose!"

He turned off the engine, jumped out of the automobile, and bounded up the steps until he stood directly across from Alice, then pulled off his hat and held it to his chest. He wore a white shirt buttoned all the way to the top and breeches tucked into his boots. Pearl couldn't help but notice the way Frank's suspenders bulged over his muscular chest. So many times she'd tried to talk Frank up to Alice, citing his broad shoulders, sleek blond hair, deep voice, and baby-blue eyes, but Alice didn't care. She just didn't see him as a beau. Pearl thought Alice couldn't afford to rule anyone out, much less Frank, who came from a well-to-do farming family. And he so clearly adored her. That kind of devotion didn't come along every day.

Frank grinned broadly and said, "Whaddya think of my new chariot, Alice? It's a two-seater. Now I can drive you to the picture show on Saturday night." He spoke to her father. "With your permission, of course, sir. I can drive ahead of your wagon so you can keep an eye on us the whole time. I respect Alice. I wouldn't want to ruin her reputation."

Mr. Bennett put his arm around his daughter's shoulders. "I will be driving Alice and her sisters in the wagon as usual, Frank. I've seen enough of these automobiles stuck in the ditch spinning their wheels to have little faith in their ability. A horse-drawn wagon has always been good enough for the Bennett family."

"Yes, sir," Frank said. "Respectfully, might I ask you to make an exception, seeing as how I've been courting Alice for four and a half months now?"

Alice, who'd been leaning against Father's shoulder, took a step forward and spoke calmly. "I have told you many times, Frank, we are not courting. I am glad to consider you a friend, but I have no romantic interest at all."

"Aw, Alice, I know what you've said, but my mind is made up. There's no other girl for me. Someday I aim to propose marriage." He spoke confidently, then took a step back and smiled widely. Frank's own father had teeth that were stained yellow, but Frank himself had gleaming white teeth. He'd told Pearl that he'd never chew tobacco for that very reason. "Any wife of mine will be proud to be seen standing next to me," he'd said.

Alice shook her head, almost a little sadly, it seemed to Pearl. "I'm sorry to disappoint you, Frank, but my mind is made up as well. You need to find another girl to court if you're so eager to settle down." Her face flushed red with emotion. She hated to hurt anyone's feelings.

"What?" Frank's lips parted, as if he was about to make an objection. Then he seemed to collect himself and tried another tactic. "Are you teasing me, Miss Bennett?"

"No, I would never do that. I've tried to tell you before in a polite way, but you don't seem to understand, so I'll say it plainly. I don't think we're suited for one another."

Frank's face clouded. "You're making a mistake, Alice. Don't be so rash. Take a few days to think it through before you make such a final decision. I would hate to see you miss out and have regrets later."

John Lawrence came out of the shadows of the porch. Pearl had almost forgotten he was there. His voice rang out clearly. "I think the lady has made her decision in this matter very clear. A gentleman would defer to her wishes."

In the background, the younger girls watched with identical concerned expressions. They'd stopped gaping over the automobile and shifted their attention to the porch when their father had spoken out, telling Frank that Alice would not be accepting his invitation to ride in his new automobile. Now they all waited to see Frank's reaction to being corrected by John Lawrence.

Frank tilted his head to the side, like a dog sizing someone up. "I don't think we've been properly introduced." He stuck out his hand. "Name's Frank. My family owns the farm down the road. I've been friends of the Bennett family my whole life."

"John Lawrence." He grasped his hand. "I've just had the pleasure of meeting the Bennetts today."

The two men shook, but Frank wouldn't let go. He squeezed John's fingers and kept talking. "Are you the boy who's helping at the mill?"

"That would be me." John widened his stance and leaned in, matching Frank's grip in intensity. Pearl held her breath, hoping neither one would get broken fingers.

"Whereabouts you from, John?"

"Up north. Gladly Falls. I just came in on the train this afternoon."

"Gladly Falls?" Frank finally let go, pushing away John's hand. "I got an uncle who lives in Gladly Falls. Do you know the Thompsons? Edward Thompson?"

John hesitated. "Edward Thompson?" His fist went to his chin. "No, can't say that I know the name."

"That's hard to believe," Frank said, and now his voice was challenging. "Everybody knows my uncle. He's practically the mayor of Gladly Falls."

"If he's practically the mayor, that would mean he's not actually the mayor," John said.

"What are you saying?" Frank's face reddened as he pointed at John. "Are you saying I'm a liar?"

"Now, now, I'm sure that's not what he's saying," their father said mildly. "There will be no arguing on my front porch, Frank. John has only just arrived. We want him to feel welcome."

"He started it." Frank's gaze went straight to John, his eyes narrowing. Seeing him like this gave Pearl a little bit of a thrill. How could Alice not be impressed by a man who could become so impassioned so quickly? Their own father never raised his voice and seldom showed much emotion at all. How refreshing to see such a dramatic show of feeling.

Alice rested her fingertips on John's forearm. "Mr. Lawrence, would you mind helping me drain the cast-iron skillets into the grease pot? They're very heavy."

"Of course, I'd be happy to help, but please call me John." He looked to Mr. Bennett for approval and, upon getting a nod, followed Alice through the front door, followed by Daisy and the rest of the sisters. Only there a day, and already the younger girls were all agog. Pearl stayed on the porch next to her father, knowing that Frank would be sure to get in the last word.

When Frank opened his mouth again, the words came in an angry burst. "You know I offered to work at the mill while Wendall was out. You didn't have to bring some stranger into your house. I told you I'd do it."

He's spitting mad, Pearl thought, taking a step back. She'd often heard that expression but never fully understood what it meant. Until now. Rancor radiated off Frank in waves; it was palpable, and it struck her as exciting, like being close to a bear or a bobcat, dangerous in general, but safe in the knowledge she wasn't the one being targeted.

If her father was afraid, he didn't show it. "Frank, I know you offered, and I appreciate the thought, but I talked to your father, and he said he couldn't spare you what with his lumbago acting up and your ma feeling poorly. John needed the work and is willing to sleep in the barn. It's a fair deal all around."

"You could've told me before you hired someone else."

"I felt no need to consult you, young Frank. I've been making decisions on my own for a long time. Now I think it's time to bid you a good evening. Thank you for the visit."

Frank's eyes widened. He looked just about to say something but seemed to think better of it. "Good night, sir." He put his hat back on his head and bounded down the steps to his automobile. Opening the door, he said, "Pearl, you tell Alice I'll be watching for her on Saturday."

CHAPTER FIFTEEN

1916

In the barn that night, John was nearly asleep when he heard the barn door open and close. One of the horses whinnied, but none of the animals seemed alarmed. Whoever it was moved stealthily, their footsteps distinct but quiet. He rubbed his eyes, watching through the hanging fabric as the glow of a flame moved closer. The person who'd entered knew the layout of the barn, moving deftly around the horse and cow stalls. Who could it be? Mr. Bennett checking on his stock? Or maybe Frank, wanting to beat him to a pulp? The second was a distinct possibility.

John stood quietly, hearing whoever it was draw closer. His mattress was in one corner of the barn, the space cordoned off by two sheets hanging from lengths of rope. A rather ingenious way to create a private area. Alice had thought of it, according to her father. She had also sewn the cover for the horsehair mattress and made a pillow for him. All the comforts of home.

His eyes adjusted, and he looked around for something that could serve as a weapon, but there was nothing nearby, only the possessions he'd brought from home. Books, so he could study during his free time.

Paper, pen, and ink. Some clothing. A comb and his shaving kit. A letter his mother had snuck into his case saying how much she loved him and how proud she was to have him for a son. Nothing he could use to defend himself except the element of surprise.

He readied himself for a confrontation. He'd seen the kind of possessive anger Frank had displayed in other men. There was no reasoning with someone who had no reason. The best thing to do was to avoid such individuals and, if that couldn't be done, shut them down in a way that didn't hurt their pride. If men like that felt publicly shamed, they'd carry that grudge to the grave and spend every waking minute in the meantime seeking vengeance. An ugly way to live and hard to understand, but that's what he'd witnessed.

By the time the intruder was on the other side of the curtain, John was ready and waiting. He flexed his hand into a fist. When he heard the person's ragged breathing, he pulled the fabric aside in one quick movement, startled to see Pearl holding the handle of a kerosene lantern. It was a shock; he'd come close to hitting her.

"Oh, my word," she said, her hand to her heart. "Don't do that. You scared me!" She reached over and gave his arm a light slap, and he suddenly was aware of his lack of clothing. Wearing only pants, he felt shamefully bare. He turned his back on her and grabbed his shirt, then shook his arms into the sleeves while she watched.

When he turned back, she was still there, sizing him up with wide eyes. He said, "I'm surprised to see you here, Miss Bennett. Did your father send for me?"

"No," she said, smiling coquettishly. "This was all my own idea. I wanted to see if you're comfortable. Is there anything you need? A blanket? Some water?" She came closer and squeezed his biceps, and he stood woodenly, not wanting to encourage her.

"No, I think your sister Alice thought of everything."

"Oh, Alice." She rolled her eyes. "She's such an old mother hen."

"I found her to be very welcoming." Meeting the Bennett family was initially overwhelming—all those girls! But Alice was the calm in the center of the storm. Her father had sung her praises on the wagon ride home from the train, telling him about her cooking skills and how she loved to read and to sing. "My little Ally-bird," he'd called her. She had taken her mother's place in the household without complaint. John was already predisposed to like her, but it came to more than that once he actually met her.

He found her a little fascinating. She was soft-spoken but stood up for herself with Frank. John offered to help her wash the dishes, but she whisked him away with a snap of her dish towel, making him laugh. And then she flipped the towel over one shoulder and hummed her way to the sink, her hips swaying in a way he found mesmerizing.

And then there was the passionate way she played the piano after supper, her hands dancing on the keys and her singing voice sweet and pure. She'd pause and look up to encourage everyone to join in. He normally was not an enthusiast when it came to singing, but the occasion seemed to call for it. All of them added their voices to the song, some singing off-key and laughing when they fumbled the words. And Alice was at the center of it all.

Pearl was still standing there, so he added, "She created a comfortable place for me." He indicated the hanging sheets, mattress, and down pillow.

"Alice is good like that." The sentiment was favorable, but Pearl said it in a disapproving way. "She's very sensible." The words were spoken as if being sensible was not a positive trait.

"I don't think your father would approve of you being out here," John said. There was no question about it. Mr. Bennett would be horrified that his daughter was alone in a man's sleeping quarters without a chaperone. It was scandalous. John was likely to lose his job if her father found out. "Thank you for checking on me, but I'm fine."

"Are you dismissing me, Mr. Lawrence?" She tilted her head to one side and batted her eyelashes.

His mother had warned him about young women like her. "You have to watch out for those forward ones, the ones who come on to you shamelessly, flaunting themselves," she'd said. "If they act that way to you, they're doing it to other men as well. They're the kind that will get themselves in the family way, and then you'll be forced to marry them."

He'd been embarrassed that his mother felt the need to have this conversation with him, and he'd assured her he had common sense. She didn't have to worry about a shotgun wedding and an early baby where he was concerned.

"I think it's best if you go," he said to Pearl.

"Do you want to kiss me?" she asked, taking a step closer and tilting her face upward. Her blonde curls fell loosely to her shoulders, and he noticed that her nightgown draped closely to her body. Her arms were exposed, and so were her neck and collarbone. She was practically naked.

John had experienced bold women before, but their behavior usually consisted of winks and innuendo. And that was from the women who frequented taverns and consumed too much liquor. He'd never seen a girl from a good family act so familiar. If she continued conducting herself like this, she was setting herself up for a world of trouble. Most men, he knew, would take the bait. They'd take the bait and not stop until they were satiated. He knew to clamp down on this before it went any further.

"Pearl, there will be none of that with me. I am here for the summer to help your father at the mill. He needs the help, and I need to earn money for medical school. I decided a long time ago that I can't let romance interfere with my goal of becoming a doctor, so I have set any notion of that aside until I complete my education."

She pouted and tapped his arm. "Oh, John Lawrence, you're no fun at all. I didn't propose marriage, just a kiss."

"You need to leave before someone discovers you've been out here. You'll get both of us in trouble."

Pearl smiled. "I can keep a secret. No one will know."

She walked away, and he slid the curtain back over the clothesline so he was out of view. In the distance, she whispered loudly, "Good night, John. I'll be dreaming of you."

CHAPTER SIXTEEN

1983

It took three days for Joe to inventory the house. During that time, just as Pearl had promised, the dumpster arrived along with the rental truck. The truck came with a slide-out ramp, furniture dolly, and straps, as if someone had assumed he had the skills of a professional mover. He'd figure it out.

Pearl came by every day too, bringing him groceries and looking over the inventory sheets. She seemed pleased with his progress.

Each day, she made him stop working so they could sit at the kitchen table and talk. Sometimes he caught her intently staring at his face, and he wondered if she was noticing the resemblance between him and his father. Or maybe his grandfather? He had so many questions.

He took her visits as opportunities to ask her about the family history. For the most part, she was open to his questions. Joe kept them general at first, feeling his way forward. "We got electricity first," she said, answering his question about the house, "and then sometime later, indoor plumbing. By the late 1940s, most houses around here had both." She shook her head. "If you only knew how many hours we spent pumping and carrying water before then. Having it piped in was like a miracle. Of course, by then I was married, so I wasn't living in this house anymore."

"So how did you wind up owning it?"

"Dumb luck," she said, taking a sip of coffee. "I was the last one left in the area. Everyone else has died or moved. My father lived here right until the end." She smiled, thinking fondly. "People did that back then. No one sent people away just because they were old. You just stayed in your own home and died where you'd been planted. So he passed away, and his daughters inherited the house. I sold my place and bought out the others. I've been here ever since. My old house, the one I lived in as a married woman, had lost its charm for me by then. I'd been widowed, and your father had left. Lots of bad memories."

She told him about her sisters. "There were seven of us altogether, with me being the second oldest. Daisy was the baby, fourteen years younger than me. She was the only one besides me who had blonde curls like our mother." She tossed her head as if her hair were still blonde instead of white.

Joe and Pearl discovered they had something in common. They'd each lost their mother when they were young. "It was hard," she said, and he had to agree. "You lose a mother, there's an empty place that can't be filled."

"Did your father remarry?"

"No. He never did. Stayed right in this house all alone and had Sunday dinner with the family members who still lived in the area. We had dinner around that dining room table, and afterward we visited and caught up on the news. Once we had electricity and a radio, we'd gather around and listen. We thought that was the greatest. We had no idea television would be coming along. My father was a quiet man, but he enjoyed having us here. He'd listen to us talk while he bounced the grandchildren on his knee. He had a special fondness for my Bill."

It was odd for Joe to imagine his father as a little boy, perched on his grandfather's knee. "So my father came here for Sunday dinner when he was a kid?"

She nodded. "Nearly every week for years. My sister Mae lived down the road at the time, and so did her twin, Maude. They married local boys. Brothers. We saw the others on some holidays when they could make the trek in. Traveling used to be much harder. Cars weren't very reliable. It was a different world."

"Are any of your sisters alive?"

"Daisy lives in Hawaii, if you can imagine that. They never have winter there, and she says she doesn't miss the snow. Helen and her husband, Burt, live in Nebraska, and Mae and her husband retired to Florida. Everyone else is gone." By *gone*, she meant *dead*, Joe realized.

"I just feel kind of bad going through all this stuff, knowing it's going to be sold or tossed out, thinking maybe a relative might want it," Joe said.

"Like what kinds of things?"

"Family photos, for the most part."

"Don't feel bad. They all had their chance when our father passed away. The whole bunch of them came and went through every room. Copies of photos were made. Keepsakes were snatched up and put in their cars before I could even see what they took." She illustrated, pretending to grab something on the table. "It was like a swarm of locusts in here. No one is going to be mad at you, believe me."

"There are a few pictures that I'd like. If I show them to you, can you identify the people so I can write down their names?"

"Of course."

Joe pushed back his chair. "If you'll excuse me, I'll be right back." He went to the hallway, where he'd lined the framed photos on the floor along the wall, all the easier to organize and inventory. Most of them he planned to take out of the frame and keep, either for himself or Linda, but they wouldn't be worth much if he didn't know who was in the pictures. His father might know, but he couldn't count on his cooperation. And knowing that his grandmother had terminal cancer made the timing critical. Joe picked up three of the photos and returned to his seat in the kitchen.

"These are the three I'm most interested in," he said, setting the first one in front of her. It was the family portrait he'd spotted when he'd first arrived. "I'm assuming that's you and my dad and his father, your husband?"

"That's right. The Arneson family, in better days." She pointed to each one. "Me, William, Francis."

"What year was that?"

Her lips pressed together. "Your father would have been three and a half. You do the math. My noggin's not as sharp as it used to be."

The next photo was of a bride and groom. He sensed it was way before his father's time, and he was right. The couple turned out to be his great-grandparents. "Mary and George Bennett. Wasn't my mama pretty?" Pearl said, turning the image back to him.

"Very pretty."

"She died before she could get old, so in my memory, she's always young, although I didn't think so at the time. Bless her heart, she missed out on so much."

Joe wrote down the names. The year, luckily, was written on the back. When he was done, he pulled out the last one, a framed sepia-toned photograph of seven girls standing in a row like stairsteps, going from the tallest on down to a tiny little girl with curly light-colored hair. "This is you and your sisters, right?" He slid it across the table. "I recognized you, but if you'd let me know who is who, I can . . ."

Pearl gasped and put her hand to her mouth. She didn't say anything for a long time, and when she did, her voice was accusatory. "Where did you get this?"

"Is something wrong?"

"No, I . . . Where did you find this?"

"It was in a frame behind another photo." His grandmother nodded, her face softening, her eyes never leaving the picture. In the short time he'd known her, Pearl had displayed an array of emotions ranging from jubilation to irritation, but this expression was new to him. He couldn't quite identify it. Longing? Regret? Whatever it was, she appeared close to tears.

"Why? Is there something wrong?" he finally asked.

"No, I just didn't know a copy of this photo still existed. I hadn't seen it in, well, forever." She smiled ruefully. "When my father died, I burned a lot of photographs. Trying to erase some bad memories. Turns out you can't erase them, in case you were wondering. The past follows you around whether you want it to or not."

Joe pushed his chair closer and leaned in to look. "I'm guessing that's you with your sisters. Am I right?" He pointed to the one he thought was Pearl, second from the left, her chin tipped upward, a mysterious smile on her face.

She said, "This is the only photograph of all seven of us together."

He asked for their names, and she started with the littlest girl, Daisy, and worked her way across the photo ending with, "And Emma and Helen, and me, of course." There was a catch in her voice when she pointed to the last young woman. "And my older sister, Alice." Her lips pressed together as she looked beyond him at some point down the hall. Looking into the past, he thought. "Ally-bird, we called her, because she was always singing."

"I don't think you mentioned her name before."

She took a sharp intake of breath, and he saw it again. The expression he couldn't place, but now he recognized it as sorrow. "I'm sure I didn't mention her name. It's too difficult for me. I haven't been able to talk about her for a long time. She died young, too young. It was the biggest tragedy of my life."

CHAPTER SEVENTEEN

1983

With a job in sales, Ricky was able to set his own schedule, and he made sure it matched Kathleen's. He became bolder, showing up where he knew she would be. He didn't approach her, though, something that took all his willpower. She had to know that he now lived in the area. Whenever they were in the same place, he'd glance in her direction. Once he was sure he'd caught her eye, he'd pretend to be preoccupied. His strategy was to wait for her to approach him. This, he thought, was particularly generous on his part. Allowing her come to him in her own time would give her a sense of control. The ball was in her court. His devotion could not go unnoticed.

To grease the wheels, he began to send her small gifts—jewelry, books of poetry, candles—the kinds of things she used to go nuts over back when they were dating. He left them in her parents' mailbox or behind the screen door at their house. The notes he included were romantic and said things like: *We are meant to be together. You'll never find someone who loves you like I do. I will spend the rest of my life convincing you that we need to be together. I'll do whatever it takes to keep you by my side.*

Her routine outside work became his routine. Sometimes he'd boldly position himself close to her, overhearing conversations between her and the librarian or taking note of the cardigan sweater she'd purchased at Kohl's. She'd never have bought anything that shapeless when they were married. Without his advice, her taste in clothing had gotten sloppy.

At one point, a policeman had shown up at his door, saying Kathleen was uncomfortable with his gifts. Ricky had offered him a cold beer, which he'd turned down, and then a can of Coke, which he took, and they had a man-to-man talk about how difficult women could be. By the time the officer left, they'd nearly been buddies. After that, Ricky held back a little bit—not that he was giving up, just giving her some space.

And then, one day, she was gone. Nothing seemed to be out of the ordinary prior to her disappearance. She'd walked her parents' dog just the night before, as usual.

Where could she be? He went over the week's events in his head. She'd gone to work every day, returned her library books on Saturday, watched *Dynasty* on television with her parents in the living room the night before. Nothing odd. No signs of any new developments.

After much observation, he realized that her mother was gone as well, leaving Kathleen's father home alone. A girls' trip? It seemed unlikely. He called all of the area hospitals, thinking maybe they'd gotten in a car accident or something similar, but neither of the women were patients anywhere. When he finally called Kathleen's job, the woman who answered the phone said she no longer worked there. "Did she quit, or was she let go?" he asked, careful not to use the word *fired*. No one in their right mind would fire Kathleen, but the job market was tight, and positions were eliminated all the time. It happened even to people who were outstanding employees.

"I can't really speak to that," she answered, her voice guarded.

"Is it that you don't know, or that you won't tell me?" He tried not to let his impatience show, but it must have snuck out because the woman quickly bid him goodbye and hung up the phone. Rude. He was tempted to call back and ask to speak to management but thought better of it. He could figure this out on his own.

A month later, when Kathleen's mother returned home without her daughter, Ricky thought he'd go out of his mind from worry. Over the next few weeks, he watched from down the street as her parents came and went to work, church, and the grocery store and wondered where in the hell his mother-in-law had left her daughter. He followed them to their church twice, an excruciating experience of murmured prayers and boring songs, and listened as Kathleen's mother made small talk with other people after the service. At one point, an old biddy asked her, "How's Kathleen doing these days?" and his ears went on high alert, listening for the answer.

"Never better," his mother-in-law had answered. "She's really coming into her own."

Really coming into her own? What the hell was that supposed to mean?

And then the biddy had said to give Kathleen her love, as if she had any idea what it meant to love Kathleen. Only he was entitled to that privilege.

Ricky had swallowed his pride then and called her parents' house. When her mother answered, he greeted her warmly and asked if he could speak to Kathleen.

His mother-in-law's voice turned icy. "She doesn't want to talk to you, Ricky. Leave her be."

"Can you at least tell me where she is? Did she move?"

"Goodbye." The receiver slamming onto the base was an assault to his ear. How dare she! No one treated him that way.

He tossed and turned that night, running through all the possibilities. Had Kathleen joined the Peace Corps or the army? Gone back to school? Moved to work in another city? That last one seemed unlikely. All her friends and family were here in her hometown. Why randomly move? It would be so unlike her to do something on her own. She always needed guidance.

Eventually, Ricky fell asleep. When he woke up, he had an idea. His father-in-law's birthday the following week was a special occasion Kathleen would surely remember. Birthdays of loved ones and holidays were sacrosanct to her. She would never forget. If it were humanly possible, she would be coming home to celebrate in person, or if that wasn't doable, she'd certainly send a card or a package.

He called in sick that day and waited in his parked car on the street until he saw both Kathleen's mom and dad leave for work that morning. He followed her dad to make doubly sure he was heading to his job, then checked the parking lot of her mom's employer to verify her car was in her designated spot.

Going back to the house, he waited until the mail was delivered, then parked down the street until the truck was long gone. He walked down the sidewalk and then up to the house, striding casually as if it were no big deal. He made a show of knocking on the door in case any of the neighbors were watching, then lifted the mailbox flap and peered inside to see several cards. After taking them out and shuffling through them, he found one matching Kathleen's handwriting. There was no return address, but it was postmarked *Pullman, Wisconsin*.

So she was in Pullman, Wisconsin, then. Why? He shook his head, not knowing the answer. Why would anyone go live in Wisconsin, especially a beautiful young woman who could live anywhere? None of it made sense, but it didn't matter. He was getting closer to figuring out where she'd gone.

He stopped by the library and looked up Pullman, Wisconsin, in the reference section. Population 1,146. Once he realized what a podunk town it was, he went back to his apartment with a plan.

Calling the operator, he asked for the number of a restaurant in Pullman, Wisconsin. "I'm sorry, but I can't remember the name of it," he said. "The something family restaurant maybe?" Kathleen loved those kinds of eateries—little hole-in-the-wall places, family-owned and operated. If it had the words *Family Restaurant* or *Diner* in the name, she was sure to want to eat there. He himself never enjoyed eating in greasy spoons, but he begrudgingly had made an exception for her, and only for breakfast, a meal that was hard to mess up. He was willing to make that concession for a meal of eggs and toast, and he knew she was grateful for that. Marriage took compromise, and he was willing to give a little to make her happy.

"The Pine Cone Family Restaurant?" the operator asked.

"That's the one!"

She gave him the number, and he jotted it down, one step closer to finding his wife. When he called the Pine Cone Family Restaurant, he made up a convoluted story about trying to track down a classmate for an upcoming reunion. "Kathleen Dinsmore. Pretty girl in her twenties. Someone told me she moved to Pullman a few weeks ago. Do you know how I can reach her?"

"Edna Clark's great-niece? The one who runs Secondhand Heaven now?"

"I guess so. Is her last name Dinsmore?"

"I don't know, but it's gotta be her. She's the only Kathleen who's new in town."

"What's Secondhand Heaven?" In the background, he heard the bell of the cash register and a thunk of the drawer popping open. On the other end of the line, the girl's voice counted out change and wished someone a good day. "Sorry about that," she said hurriedly. "Super busy today. Secondhand Heaven is the resale shop here in town. Cute place. You can probably get the phone number from operator assistance. I don't know it offhand." And with that, she wrapped up the conversation, and the line went dead.

The decision to pack up and go to Pullman, Wisconsin, came easily to Ricky. He'd called the store first, and when he heard Kathleen's voice answer, "Secondhand Heaven, how may I help you?" he'd gruffly said, "Sorry, wrong number," and hung up. He smiled. She was there. He felt smug at having figured it out.

He told his boss his father had a brain tumor, and he'd be gone for at least a month. Luckily, he was well liked at the office and a good salesman, so they were willing to give him the time off. He would have gone with or without their permission, but it was better to keep his options open. He stopped shaving and grew a full beard, a look he'd never had before. It made him look so different, even he was shocked when he caught sight of his reflection.

Within days, he was ready to go. He left his apartment behind, taking only the possessions that would fit in his car. On the way out of town, he emptied his bank account, taking most of the money in fifties and twenties. Cash was king, and so was he.

Ricky had a plan, a good one. He would watch Kathleen and learn about her new life in Pullman, and then, when the time was right, he'd create a dangerous situation in which he could play the hero. She'd have to take him back. He remembered a time in their marriage when her car had broken down in a dicey part of town, and she'd called him from a pay phone, terrified because some teenagers had tried to shake her down for some money. He arranged to meet a tow truck there and found her locked in her car, overjoyed at his arrival. The look on her face made him feel invincible, and the warm feeling had lasted for days. Over the next few days, she'd curled up against him in bed in her sleep, as if he were her security blanket. Remembering all this now made him sure that his plan of action should include some crisis in which he could save her. Women loved that in a man, and Kathleen was no exception.

The closest motel Ricky could find was nearly an hour away from Pullman. That would never do. He had to find something more conveniently located. If nothing else, he could sleep in his car. The important thing was to be close to her.

When he first spotted Kathleen in Pullman, he was shocked to see her wearing a dress with a full skirt. The hemline fell to midcalf. In keeping with what had to be a 1950s theme, she wore short white socks and saddle shoes. Her hair, longer than he remembered, was pulled back into a high ponytail, a style he didn't care for at all. That day, he was sure she must be heading out to some costume party after work, but when she was similarly attired the next day, this time in 1940s garb, he figured it must be something to do with the store.

Within the first forty-eight hours, he'd figured out where she lived and her basic work schedule. Another woman worked at the store as well, a tomboyish sort who was always on the move, from what he could see through the front window. Asking around town, he learned that Kathleen's great-aunt Edna had left her both the store and a house. Ricky had never heard of Edna Clark, so it was puzzling that Kathleen would inherit the whole shebang, but who knew why old people did what they did? Most of them were senile anyway.

One evening when Kathleen had taken off in her car and he hadn't been able to follow, he made good use of the time by going to her house. He was on her porch, peering through the window next to the front door, when her busybody neighbor startled him by coming up from behind. "Can I help you, sir?"

Ricky, looking down on her from the stoop, turned and gave her a wide smile. He raised his sunglasses and perched them on top of his head. "Well, hello there." He proceeded to turn on the charm, something that worked on women old and young alike, and he could tell by the way the old woman's hand flew to her hair that it had the same effect now. "Maybe you can help me," he said, his voice a purr. Women loved to help; that was a fact. "I need a place to stay, and there don't seem to be any hotels around here. Someone told me that Edna Clark might want to rent out a room?"

"Oh dear," she said, her mouth downturned. "I'm not sure who you heard that from, but Edna Clark passed away. Her great-niece is living here now. I can't imagine a single young woman like her would be interested in renting out a room."

"Such a shame." He even managed to blink as if about to cry. "I was willing to pay top dollar. I'm really desperate." And then he spun a story explaining his urgent need to spend a few days in Pullman. He explained how he'd been driving home from the hospital up north after having had surgery and needed to rest a few days before continuing the trip home. "I thought I could do it," he said sadly. "But I'm weak as a kitten. I should have listened to the doctor and stayed a few more days to recover, but you know how we men are. Too proud."

She nodded thoughtfully, her hand resting under her chin. "I might be able to help you," she said finally, her head tilting in the direction of the house next door. "I have a guest bedroom that's sitting empty."

Ricky held back a grin. Sometimes the universe opened up and gave you a gift, and the best thing to do was not grab at it too quickly. "Oh no, I couldn't impose on you like that." He put out his hand and said, "I'm Richard, by the way. And you are?"

"Lorraine Whitt."

He gave her hand a gentle grasp and met her eyes. "I can't believe I got myself into this mess." He let go of her hand and clutched his abdomen as if in pain.

"What kind of surgery did you have?"

"Emergency appendectomy. I was lucky. They got it before it burst. Hurt like a son of a gun." He feigned a small smile.

"Oh, you poor thing."

"Not listening to doctor's orders was stupid on my part. I'm so tired now, I could sleep standing up."

She nodded in sympathy and offered her guest bedroom again, but he demurred, saying he didn't want to be any trouble. It seemed that the more he held back, the more insistent she was that he stay with her. "Well, maybe for a few days," he said. "You're so kind. I can't thank you enough."

Within minutes, he'd parked his car inside her garage, taken his suitcase into her house, and given her a stack of cash along with words of gratitude. "If only there were more people like you, the world would be a better place, Mrs. Whitt."

"It's actually Miss Whitt," she said. "I never married."

"A woman like you never married?" Ricky opened his mouth in mock astonishment. His mother said he could charm the birds out of the trees without half trying. "Hard to believe."

"Oh, but it's true."

"Well, then, there are a lot of men out there who missed out." He shook his head and made a tsk-tsking noise.

She giggled. "Just one thing," she said. "If anyone asks, I'm going to tell them you're my nephew. I wouldn't want people to get the wrong idea."

He winked at her. "Whatever you want, Aunt Lorraine."

CHAPTER EIGHTEEN

1983

Secondhand Heaven closed every night at six, which meant Kathleen could be back home by six thirty most nights, seven at the latest. Aunt Edna's house, now hers, was only a block away. An easy walk, even for someone who'd been on her feet all day. In the few months she'd lived there, the place felt more like home than the apartment she'd shared with her husband back in the days when she'd been married.

Ricky had preferred a modern look. Contemporary furniture with clean lines, uncluttered spaces. Nothing on the kitchen counters, very little on the walls. He didn't read, so he considered books to be no more than dust collectors. He didn't mind her *having* books; he just didn't want to look at them. She gave away most of her collection to the library book sale and kept her favorites in her bottom dresser drawer. At the time, it seemed a small price to pay for love.

He had all kinds of quirks. They could eat only at the kitchen table; otherwise, he said, falling crumbs would attract vermin. Vermin! She'd laughed at first, then realized he was dead serious. Dishes had to be done immediately, towels could be used only once, and their cars had to be kept impeccable, inside and out. Kathleen, trying to be accommodating, went along with whatever he wanted. She thought she was compromising, but in retrospect, it fit the cycle of abuse: his controlling nature and the need for him to make his mark. It was almost as if she'd been branded, along with the house. *Property of Ricky Dorsey.*

She came to detest the sound of his whistling as he walked about the house. Always some tune she didn't know, or maybe it wasn't a song at all. He said he did it without realizing it, but she believed otherwise. It was important for him to stand out, and a man who whistled as he walked up the path certainly did. It gave the neighbors the impression he was a happy and carefree person. If only that had been true.

When Kathleen took a stand and became less responsive to his needs, his moods darkened, and his anger overshadowed everything good in life. After that, the tidy, sparse apartment started to feel less like home and more like a prison cell.

Aunt Edna's house suited her much better. It was a small two-story brick house with a front porch large enough for two rocking chairs and a table in between. The place was spacious enough for one person and cozy too. Kathleen had arrived with only a suitcase, so the fact that the house was already furnished was a bonus. The house also came with linens and kitchenware and built-in bookcases filled with books. Everything from classics to Agatha Christie to paperback thrillers and the Bible too. Something for every mood. She didn't miss the fact that Aunt Edna didn't have a television. Maybe someday Kathleen might feel the urge to buy one, but for right now, she was fine.

The greatest draw of Pullman, Wisconsin, had been its usefulness as a refuge from her ex-husband, but now it was turning out to be her home. She planned on staying indefinitely. She had memories of visiting her great-aunt during her grade-school years. Her memories of Pullman had more to do with going with her parents to feed the ducks in the lake and a visit to the ice cream shop afterward than it did her great-aunt or Secondhand Heaven. On two different occasions, she and her mother had made the drive up when she was older. A girls' outing, her mother had called it. They'd rented a rowboat and spent the day on the lake, picnicking on a tiny island no bigger than her grade-school playground. They'd also spent time with Aunt Edna during those trips, but she couldn't recall much about those visits. She wished she'd paid more attention.

Pullman was a picture-postcard kind of town. Big enough to support shops and a movie theater, but small enough that everyone seemed to know everyone else. She got used to being greeted as she walked to work and tried to remember names so she could respond in kind. The mailman pushed a cart and delivered mail right to the house. Aunt Edna had a mail slot in her front door, and the letters dropped right onto the braided rug. The man driving the ice cream truck wore a white hat, and the town barbershop had a revolving red, white, and blue pole outside its front door.

The town was so quaint and old-fashioned that Kathleen felt like she'd gone back in time. No wonder Aunt Edna had led such a happy life here.

When her great-aunt was in hospice, they'd had time to connect on a personal level, talking as much as they could, considering her aunt's weakened state. Edna Clark was a simple woman in the best possible way. She'd lived a life of quiet contentment, doing good where she could, doling out kind words or smiles on a continuous basis. Even when she was near death, she'd been gracious to Kathleen and her mother and the nurses, thanking them for something as basic as a paper cup of ice chips, and saying how lucky she was to have family at her side.

She didn't seem to regret never having married or her lack of children. Aunt Edna's very being exuded acceptance and love. At her funeral, the local attorney cornered Kathleen and her mother, asking if they'd come to his office the next morning. That's when she discovered her inheritance. Her mother, the only other living relative, signed off on any claim to the estate, and it was all hers. It was a miracle. She'd needed a place to live that Ricky didn't know about, and Pullman, Wisconsin, dropped at her feet and welcomed her home.

The will had been dated one week after Kathleen and her mother had arrived in Pullman. They realized later that Aunt Edna must have had the attorney come to the hospital to do the paperwork. It had been witnessed by a doctor and a nurse.

Maybe Kathleen had said something that indicated her desperation? She didn't think so, but perhaps it was evident from things unsaid. When asked about her husband, Kathleen had simply said it didn't work out and that they weren't married anymore. Aunt Edna said she was sorry to hear that, which was what everybody said. Everyone was sympathetic, but not everybody followed up by giving her a house and a business.

So she stayed, slipping into Aunt Edna's life like putting on custom-made slippers. A perfect fit. Her parents called every week, and her mother wrote her letters too. They missed her and wanted to know if she was happy. The truth was, she was perfectly content.

"Content isn't the same thing as happy," her mother said.

"No, but it's close," she said. "Really close." At least the door to happiness was open, and she knew she'd get there eventually. Right now, she'd take contentment, along with satisfaction in her work and peace of mind. She needed time to refuel, for her mind and body to be restored.

That night Kathleen went into the kitchen, made herself a sandwich, and poured a glass of iced tea. She carried both into the living room, setting the plate and glass down on the end table and opening her latest book, chosen randomly from Aunt Edna's bookshelf. The woman hadn't let her down yet. Her taste in fiction was spot-on.

She was halfway through chapter 12 in a novel titled *Crooked House* when she heard the metallic flap of the mail slot lift and drop again. *What?* It was hours after mail delivery, already dark. If it was a neighbor dropping off mail they'd gotten by mistake, they'd probably have called out or rung the doorbell.

Setting down the book, she went to the entryway and flipped on the overhead light. On the rug at her feet was a single sheet of paper.

She picked it up, relieved to see it was just a business flyer, an ad for a cleaning service. Across the top it said: *Trouble keeping organized? Feeling like something is missing in your life? We can transform your cluttered rooms into spaces of peace and love. We're more than just a cleaning service: we'll teach you the proper methods to keep your life in order.* Bullet points down the center of the page listed all their services. Cleaning, organizing, decluttering. At the bottom, it said, *Don't say no. Call now!*

Kathleen crushed the sheet of paper into a little ball and tossed it onto the floor in a small show of defiance. *No, thanks,* she thought. She didn't need anyone teaching her how to organize her house or her life. She was in charge now.

CHAPTER NINETEEN

1983

As Joe drifted off to sleep, he thought about what his grandmother had said earlier about her older sister, Alice. *I haven't been able to talk about her for a long time. She died young, too young. It was the biggest tragedy of my life.* He thought he could envision how heartbreaking a sister's death would be, remembering the time Linda was hospitalized for meningitis. The whole family had been out of their minds with worry. Linda, of all people! The family baby, the girl whose entrance into the world had brought them all closer together. Linda, who looked up to him, bragging about him to all her friends. He didn't even want to think about how it would be if she hadn't pulled through and come home safe and sound. Losing his sister would have been devastating.

Still, the biggest tragedy of her life? Worse than the death of her husband? The decades-long estrangement from her only child? The deaths of other family members? What made this loss such an enormous tragedy? She didn't seem to want to elaborate, and he hadn't pressed the issue. Maybe, eventually, she'd tell him more. Or maybe it was just one of those things old people were fond of saying. *I remember it like it was yesterday! In a moment, my life changed forever. If I knew then what I know now.*

Just something to say. No need for him to attach too much importance to it.

The day had been busy. Once Pearl had looked over his inventory sheets and approved all his plans, he set to work. Anything he couldn't move himself using the wheeled dolly, Pearl had told him to leave behind. When the house was put up for sale, they'd list it as partially furnished. And she added, "Leave the kitchen and guest bedroom untouched until the end because you'll be using them while you stay." She also suggested he leave at least one comfortable chair so he'd have a place to sit and relax when the day was done. It wasn't a bad idea. He tried out every upholstered chair in the house until he found the one he'd be saving for last. It had a floral pattern with a doily draped across the top—not what he'd pick for himself, but it was as cushy as his father's easy chair back home and came with a padded footrest.

Cleaning the house and moving furniture was hot work. To make matters worse, the old place had no air-conditioning. The house itself was surrounded by tall trees, which helped, and there were plenty of fans, six different box fans that he could move as he worked, but they did nothing to help him as he went back and forth from the house to the outdoors. He worked up a sweat, cleaning and moving. He made countless trips to the dumpster, carrying moth-eaten linens and faded boxes. Old, musty books for the most part, but there were some other oddities as well. A tarnished birdcage. A carton containing nothing but scrub brushes. A hamper filled with fabric that had presumably once been clothing but now smelled and looked disgusting. Anything plastic that he came across in the attic had warped and faded, including Christmas decorations and food storage containers. All of it he threw over the side of the dumpster, waiting for the satisfying thud as it fell inside.

He'd decided to empty the house from the top down. As hot as it was outside, the temperatures were even higher in the space under the roof. He would have categorized it as oven-like with a touch of sauna. He consoled himself by thinking he was getting the most difficult part out of the way. It could only get better. After emptying the attic, he sorted and discarded the worst of it, keeping anything that looked of value, then followed up by loading the pickup truck with his first load. He parked it in the barn for the night, ready to drive into town first thing in the morning. He'd called Secondhand Heaven earlier and talked to the owner's assistant, some lady named Marcia. Marcia said both she and Kathleen would be there all day tomorrow to help him unload.

This was good news. After the last few days, Joe was ready to have some social interaction. Besides a quick run to the grocery store, he hadn't seen anyone but his grandmother. He'd taken to singing along with the radio and had started talking to himself. Funny how much he was looking forward to unloading a truck and conversing with other people. His grandmother had paid him for the first week in advance in cash, so he was ready to catch lunch in town and maybe poke around in some of the stores. If he identified himself as Bill Arneson's son, maybe someone would know the story behind the family rift.

He showered before going to bed, luxuriating in the coolness of the water. He stood for the longest time, eyes closed, his face tipped up to the showerhead. The temperature outside had dropped considerably since midday, and the open windows allowed for a cool breeze, helping him to relax. He was so tired from physical labor, sleep came quickly.

Before long, he'd drifted into the darkness of the unconscious and into another place and time. The Rowboat Dream. It was nighttime. A full yellow moon hung overhead, casting a glow onto the surface of the lake. He was seated on the middle slat of a wooden rowboat, hands gripping the oars, rowing in perfect rhythm. She sat across from him, their knees not quite touching. Like in the other dreams, he had only an impression of her. He could never see her face.

They rowed across the water, heading to a specific destination, one that his dream self knew, but Joe himself never found out. The destination didn't matter, though. It was just that he and the lovely young woman (and she *was* young, he knew that much) were alone at last. She laughed, and the sound of her mirth trilled across the water. He thought that if he could hear that laugh for the rest of his life, he'd be a happy man.

He kept rowing. Ahead of them came a little splash, startling him. She laughed again and said, "Don't be so jumpy. It's just a fish."

Their world closed in and became the boat, the lake, the moon, and each other. When they landed where they were heading, he knew one thing for certain. He would help her out of the boat first, of course, and as soon as the moment was right, he was going to tell her he loved her. When she said she loved him back, he would lean in for a kiss. The thought was intoxicating. The idea of kissing her filled him with an anticipation he'd never experienced before. If only she felt the same way.

He leaned back and swung the oars as far back as possible, then pulled deep, making the boat skim quickly across the water. "Show-off," she said, teasing. Her hand trailed into the water, her fingertips skimming the surface. He imagined her hands touching him, running the length of his body, then sheepishly brushed away the thought. There would be time for all that, if and when tonight went well. They'd have the rest of their lives.

The dream faded to black, the way it always did.

When Joe woke up, he felt like crying. He'd been there in the same way he was now in his own bed. He'd felt the resistance of the water against the pull of the oars. The sound of her voice still echoed in his ears. They had been so happy—*he*, the person he was in the dream, was so happy. That couple had thought the years stretched endlessly before them, but Joe knew better. It wouldn't end well. The events of the Death Dream would come soon enough, and this other self of his, the man in the dream, would never know the happiness of a lifetime with this beautiful young woman. Now that was a tragedy.

He fell back asleep soon enough and didn't dream again. When the morning sun glinted through the gap in his curtains, he groaned, then rolled over and closed his eyes again, trying for more sleep to make up for the time that had been stolen from him by another lifetime.

CHAPTER TWENTY

1916

As the days passed into weeks, John became part of the Bennett family—filling the big-brother role for the smaller girls and standing in as a son to their father. Each morning, he and Mr. Bennett harnessed the horses and rode the wagon to the mill. The mill was on the outskirts of town, a short ride by wagon, a half hour by foot. As an employee, John was more than satisfactory. Mr. Bennett never actually said as much, but his quiet nods of approval spoke volumes, and John once overheard his new boss tell one of the farmers at the mill that he would miss John's steady work habits once the younger man had gone back to school. The farmer had roared with laughter at hearing this. "Enjoy it while you can," he'd said, slapping his thigh. "You'll not get any such deal from Wendall."

John got the impression that Wendall was a bit of a mule who needed constant prodding to get the job done. John prided himself on working without need of supervision. His chores in the mill were physically demanding. It was hot and dirty, and the sacks of wheat flour were heavy, but he handled all of it, rarely even stopping to rest. He thought of each day as coming another step closer to paying his medical school fees and was pleased to be able to earn it among honest men who treated him well.

At the end of each day, he looked forward to returning to the Bennett house and relished the routine of washing up at the pump before eating one of Alice's delicious dinners. If he timed it right, he could sit at the kitchen table and sip cold water, watching as she bustled around putting the finishing touches on the evening's meal, oblivious to his watchful eyes. Pearl was the one he tried to avoid, a feat that proved to be harder all the time. She was a chatterbox, asking him countless questions about his life in Gladly Falls, none of which he wanted to answer. Most of which he *couldn't* answer, at least not honestly.

Alice, sensing his reluctance, had saved him more than once. "Pearl, you're being nosy to our guest. It's not polite to ask personal questions."

John sensed that Pearl resented Alice's interference, but she listened to her sister, switching the subject to popular music or the latest styles in the movie industry. "I read that one film director said the greatest beauties have eyes bigger than their mouths. Like Lillian Gish. He said that big eyes show more emotion on the big screen. Isn't that fascinating?" She batted her eyelashes at him, and he looked away, nodding as if what she'd said was of interest, even though he found the conversation excruciating.

Only once had John been upstairs, and that was to help Mr. Bennett carry Alice's hope chest to the upstairs bedroom she shared with Pearl. Once the chest was in place alongside one wall, they hadn't lingered, but he was there long enough to note the vanity table with its comb and hairbrush across from the tidily made bed. Being in the room where Alice slept felt very intimate.

Over time, he found that if he insisted on helping in the kitchen—mashing potatoes, chopping vegetables, or toting water—Pearl made herself scarce, and he'd have the kitchen alone with Alice and Daisy. He wasn't sure what it was about Alice that had captured his attention.

After giving it much thought, he decided it wasn't one thing but a thousand things. She said more in a few words than Pearl did in an endless stream of blather. She was prettier than her sister too, without even trying. Sometimes when Pearl rambled on about Hollywood or Daisy said something silly, Alice gifted John with a smile, as if they were in on a secret.

Alice was smart. She read the newspaper that her father brought home each night. She also did the books for her father's business and managed the household. She sewed all the girls' clothing as skillfully as a professional seamstress. It was a lot for anyone to do.

John rarely saw her idle, and yet hard as she worked, she didn't seem burdened. In fact, it was the opposite: she gave off an air of happiness that was contagious. She found joy in everyday things, celebrating the flowers Daisy picked for her and rejoicing when the cow produced more milk than usual. She sang as she worked and made silly jokes to make her sisters laugh. Alice anticipated what family members needed and had just that thing at the ready, whether it was a teaspoon of her homemade cough remedy, a cool wet cloth over a hot forehead, or a sympathetic ear. John didn't think it was unusual that he was falling a little in love with Alice. The unusual part was that everyone else overlooked her. They all took her for granted, unaware they were in the presence of someone exceptional.

The first few weeks John lived with the Bennetts, he stayed behind on Saturday nights while Mr. Bennett drove his whole brood into town to see the motion picture at the Victory Theater. Pearl had told him confidentially that once in a while Mr. Bennett escorted them into the theater, got them to their seats, and admonished them to behave, then left with the excuse that he had to go outside to talk business with one of his customers. The younger girls believed him, but Pearl saw right through the ruse.

"He actually goes to the tavern down the street. I know because I smell beer on his breath. He's always back by the time the picture is finished, though," she said, as if to offset any objections John might raise. "We scarcely know he's gone, and then before we know it, he returns, none the worse for wear." John was amused by Pearl's abashed explanation. Perhaps in Pullman a man having a beer counted as scandalous behavior? If that were so, the Bennetts would be shocked to know his secret.

On these prior Saturdays, John had not been invited but had watched them depart, Mr. Bennett and Alice in the raised front seat of the wagon, the other six girls sitting on a blanket in the open-air back, the same wagon he and Mr. Bennett used to transport supplies to and from the mill. He realized that first week that there would have been no room for him even if he had been asked, and so he didn't take it as a personal slight but listened with interest when the girls excitedly told him about the evening after returning home.

The first time, Daisy had come running in to share details about the evening, asking, "Do you know Charlie Chaplin?"

"No," John replied. "I can't say that I've had the pleasure of making his acquaintance." His answer made the girls laugh.

"He's not a *real* person," Daisy said, her eyes wide.

Helen said, "She's asking because his new picture is at our theater."

"It's not a new picture," Pearl said, exasperated. "We never get the new ones. It takes months and months for a new moving picture to get to Wisconsin, and then once they get here, they're not new anymore. And then they stay for weeks and weeks."

"Which is a very good thing," Alice interjected, "because it gives me time to improve my piano playing." She reached up and pulled a large pin out of her hat, a powder-blue number with a large brim and a fabric rose on the side. She lifted the hat off her head, revealing an elegant roll of hair pinned in place right above her shoulders. John had overheard Pearl say that this style, the Gibson tuck, was all the rage according to the fashion magazines, and Alice had taken to the idea, primarily for its ease, but he loved that this new hairstyle revealed the nape of her neck.

"Charlie Chaplin is so funny," Daisy said. "Whenever I see him in the picture show, I laugh and laugh. He walks like this." She illustrated a silly walk, almost falling over in the process.

"Someday I will have to see that for myself," John said with a smile. It was the polite thing to say, but he didn't actually think it would happen.

Just the next week, though, Mr. Bennett took him aside and asked if he would do him a favor. "Would you mind taking the girls to the motion picture?" he asked. "My back is giving me a bit of trouble, and it could use a rest."

"Of course. I'd be happy to."

Mr. Bennett said, "Alice can show you where the girls sit inside the theater. For propriety's sake, it would be best if you sat in the row in front of them." He added hurriedly, "It's not that I don't trust you, you understand, it's just . . ."

"That people talk?"

The older man nodded. "That they do."

John knew full well how small-minded people with time on their hands could make trouble for others. It was a shame, but that was the way of the world.

At the appropriate time, he hitched up the two horses and helped the girls into the wagon. Alice sat up front in her usual spot, the others in back. As Pearl began to climb up, she pretended to lose her balance and fell backward into his arms. "Excuse me," she cried out, arms flailing. "I don't know what's wrong with me."

John wordlessly guided her back into the wagon and then helped Helen, Emma, Mae, and Maude. He lifted Daisy last, handing her to the outstretched arms of Helen, Daisy's second-choice sister. Their father sternly told them to mind their manners that evening, and with a shake of the reins, off they went.

The drive to town went without incident, and John parked the wagon around back, following Alice's directions. Because Alice was the piano player, the family was allowed to enter from the alley, bypassing the ticket counter. Daisy pulled John along by one finger, eager to show him where they always sat. "What if someone is already sitting in your seats when you get here?" he asked, watching as people filtered in through the double doors.

"Everyone knows not to sit in those seats," Helen said. "The whole town knows this is where the Bennetts sit."

Emma pointed. "John, look, they have electric lights here." She pointed to the high ceiling. A large crystal chandelier hung from the center, and mounted directly above it was a bronze medallion decorated with a gold leaf pattern.

"Pretty fancy," he said with a smile.

"This whole building used to be a ballroom," Emma explained. "People would come here for weddings and elegant dances. The new owner converted it into a movie theater. It was quite exciting to finally have one right in town."

The theater was equipped with a raised stage, originally used for the orchestra when the building was a ballroom. A row of spotlights along the front had once been used for plays, or perhaps plays were still held there. The dark-colored stage curtains had been pulled back, revealing a large screen, and off to the left, below the screen, sat an upright piano, a small electric light aimed at the keys.

They sat and watched to see who else came through the doors. So many people. The whole town, by the looks of it. The sisters called out and waved to various friends, but not once did any of them leave their seats. The talk their father had given them had made an impression.

Over the din of the crowd, a male voice cried out, "Pearl, Pearl!" John looked to see Howie making his way toward them, followed by his mother and a young dark-haired woman in a floral-print dress.

To show good manners, John stood as they approached, but Pearl only glanced at the newcomers. "Hello, Howie." She nodded. "Mrs. Donohue, Edna." John sensed a tinge of irritation in her voice.

"I was hoping we'd see you here," Howie said. "I said, 'We should see if Pearl is here with her sisters.'"

"Of course we're here. We're here every week," Maude piped up. Or was it Mae? Even after hearing about the difference in their hairstyles, John could never tell them apart.

The young woman whom Pearl had identified as Edna said, "I think there are some better seats down in front, Howie." She tugged on the back of his jacket, then turned to his mother. "Don't you think that would be better, Mrs. Donohue?"

Mrs. Donohue straightened up and gave Edna a cool look. "Whatever Howie decides would be best."

"I want to sit with the Bennetts," Howie declared, nodding toward Pearl. He stood at the end of the sisters' row. If they had shifted a few seats down, there would have been room, but none of them made a move to do so.

John said, "I'd be happy to move to the end of my row. There's plenty of space."

Edna's face lit up. "Thank you, sir. That's very kind of you."

John introduced himself to Edna, and Howie explained that she was a neighbor who didn't get to town very often. "Edna is our town's seamstress. She reupholsters furniture and does alterations out of her home. Her mother is in ill health, and she takes care of her."

"That's a wonderful thing to do," John said, moving all the way down so that now he sat on the end of the row, next to the outside aisle. "I'm sure your mother appreciates your kindness."

"It's not a kindness, really," Edna said. "I don't mind at all." She sat next to John, with Howie and his mother on the other side. Howie leaned back to talk to Pearl, who regarded him with aloof politeness.

Edna pointed down the front of the theater and said, "Oh, there's Alice. Doesn't she look lovely in that blue dress? Alice is my best friend, you know. I don't know what I would have done without her when my mother had her attack. Alice came as soon as she heard." She turned to face John. "Apoplexy. It was horrible. Mother is better now, but the doctor says she will never be the same as she was before."

"I'm sorry to hear that," John said, aware of how insufficient the words were. He knew that apoplexy could strike a healthy person down in an instant, leaving their limbs paralyzed or their thinking affected. He had read of one patient who'd lost the ability to read. "Your mother is lucky to have you."

"And I'm lucky she is still with us today," Edna said. "So many who suffer in that way are not as fortunate. I could so easily have lost my sweet mother."

As they watched, Alice sat on the piano bench, and a man stepped into view. The crowd hushed in anticipation.

"Good evening, and welcome to the Victory Theater," the man announced grandly. "I'm Floyd Kramer, the owner of this establishment. I'm pleased to announce that our film tonight is *The Floorwalker* starring the very funny Charlie Chaplin. Ladies, please remove your hats." He looked off to one side. "Cut the lights, and we shall begin. I hope you enjoy the show."

As the audience clapped, the owner walked away, and Alice's fingers ran the length of the keyboard and back again, a warm-up for the event. The lights went down, and now the only lights in the theater came from the screen and the one small light over the piano. In other theaters, John had noticed the piano player working off sheet music with an assistant to turn the pages, but Alice worked alone, nothing to go by, just her hands dancing on the keys creating a swell of music, the backdrop for the moving pictures on the screen.

While everyone else concentrated on the movie, John had eyes only for Alice, the delicate way she swayed and leaned into the piano, her hands leaping and flying, brilliantly aligning the notes with the flickering images in front of them. He'd seen her play many times in the parlor of the Bennett home, but this was different. She was different.

John's mother often said the most successful people lived a life of passion and service to others, something he hadn't quite fully grasped until that moment. He'd always thought the two concepts were at odds. Following one's passion was self-serving. How could you do that *and* live a life of service to others? He saw now that Alice embodied both by bringing passion and service to everything she did. No task was too menial, no person too unimportant, no place too dreary for her enthusiasm and good cheer. She brought a handful of sunshine everywhere she went.

He sat, captivated by the sight of her at the piano, not paying any attention to the film on the screen. The rest of the audience laughed at Charlie Chaplin's tomfoolery, but John's grin was for the girl on the bench. She kept her face tilted up to the movie, making sure the music matched the action. Occasionally, when her face was angled that way, he thought he caught a glimpse of a smile, but it was fleeting. She took the accompaniment seriously. Her music gave the story sound and brought it to life.

As he watched, her handkerchief dropped out of her sleeve and fluttered to the floor behind her. John knew that his own mother kept a hankie on hand to dab her forehead when perspiring. She often said that ladies never sweat.

At some point, Alice would reach for her handkerchief and find it missing.

Without even a thought, he rose to his feet, stepped into the aisle, and made his way down the incline. When he got to the bench, he reached down to pick up the handkerchief and set it on the bench next to her. With a quick glance, she realized what he'd done, gave an appreciative nod, and continued playing.

An impulse overtook him. Silently, he slid onto the left side of the bench, his heart pounding. Why was he doing this, joining her without an invitation? It could all go wrong in a very public way, ruining everything. Part of him wondered at his own boldness, but it didn't matter what he thought. It was not up to him anymore; his body had moved of its own volition. His heart had taken over.

He was relieved to see her smile his way when there was a slight pause in the music. He didn't realize he'd been holding his breath until he exhaled. It was all right, then. She didn't mind that he was there. His arrival didn't affect her playing, so no one else would even notice, and if they did, no one could object that he'd done anything that could ruin her reputation. Anyone who was looking would see he was just sitting there out in the open. Harmless enough.

They were so close, he almost didn't know where to look. He was captivated by her hands, the confident way they went from caressing the keys to pressing boldly with wild abandon, her fingers flying. It was like a magic trick, one he could never do himself.

Her face too was mesmerizing. With her chin tipped upward, she kept her gaze on the screen, making the crescendos match the action, the music punctuating the downturns. She was improvising. The subject had come up before, during a conversation in the Bennett kitchen, and he'd asked, "If you don't have sheet music, how do you know what to play?"

Alice had laughed and answered, "I just know. I watch the motion picture first, silently, and then come up with the score. If it feels right to me, I know the audience will like it too."

She'd made it sound so easy.

Sitting next to her, it was apparent that she did indeed play by feel, pouring her entire self into making the music, arranging the sounds so they would both cue and surprise the audience. He noticed how gracefully her hair was swept back and pinned in place. He had a sudden urge to lean down and press his lips against the base of her neck and quelled the thought, knowing he didn't dare. As a compromise, he held his breath and eased a few inches closer.

He leaned in cautiously, wanting to inhale her, all of her, wondering if he could physically connect with her while everyone else was distracted by the antics on the screen. He'd wait for a surge of laughter and take a chance. All he wanted was one quick touch, and an innocent one at that—the brush of his hand on her arm or his knee brushing against hers. No one would have to know.

His heart pounding, he decided to take the chance. Just as he leaned in, someone grabbed the collar of his shirt and yanked him so hard, he was forcefully thrown backward, his head hitting the hardwood floor. The wind was knocked out of him, and he gasped for air. With the ceiling of the theater hazily swimming above him, the flickering lights outlined a looming figure leaning over him. A man's threatening voice said, "Keep your disgusting hands off her!"

A gasp came from the crowd. No one was watching Charlie Chaplin anymore. The moving picture played on, the images flickering silently on the screen. John blinked, and the threatening figure took shape. He knew who it was.

Frank.

Alice spoke. "Frank! What do you think you're doing?"

Sheepishly, John rose to his feet.

CHAPTER TWENTY-ONE

1983

When Joe pulled into the back alley behind Secondhand Heaven, he followed the instructions given to him over the phone and backed the truck up the ramp of the loading dock, then threw it in park. A small concrete staircase next to the ramp led to a metal door. He rang the doorbell, and when a short woman wearing denim coveralls and a red bandanna draped around her neck appeared, he said, "Kathleen?"

She barked out a short laugh as if he'd said something hilarious. When she smiled, he saw that she had a prominent gold canine tooth. "Wrong!" she said, almost gleefully. "I'm Marcia, Kathleen's right-hand man."

"Oh, sorry."

"She stepped out for minute but should be back soon." Her tone was cheerful. "Here to deliver some furniture?"

"Yes, I'm Joe Arneson. I've got the first load from Pearl Arneson's house."

Marcia was walking away before he'd even managed to finish the sentence. She called back over her shoulder, saying, "I'll raise the garage door."

Once the door was up, Joe started to carry out some of the smaller pieces, but soon Marcia joined him, helping with the larger pieces and taking over as if she were in charge of this project. Somehow he was fine with this. Maybe it was the lack of company for the last few days or the fact that she possessed an air of competency. Despite her small size, she was wiry and strong, and she knew how to use the straps and the wheeled cart that came with the truck. They'd just rolled in a large piece of furniture Marcia called a credenza when Joe spotted a slender young woman in an old-fashioned dress standing in the doorway, watching them work.

He turned to look, and a surge of recognition came over him. He knew her. The feeling of familiarity was so strong that without a second thought, he called out, "Hey!"

At the same time, her eyes widened with delight. "Hi there!"

He let go of his end of the cart to walk over to where she stood, his brain searching for how they would have met. School? A job? Mutual friends? He was far from home, so whatever the connection, it was quite a coincidence.

She tilted her head to one side, a puzzled look on her face, as if she were trying to parse out the connection as well. He saw her with surprising clarity, like watching a film where the camera went in for a close-up. She was exceptionally pretty and wore a sleeveless floral dress with a pleated skirt that flared outward and red shoes with a clunky heel and bows on the toes. Her arms were tanned, and her light-brown hair was pulled up into a high ponytail. As he drew closer, she said, "I don't know you, do I?" She crossed her arms.

"I'm not sure. You *seem* familiar." Now Joe felt like an idiot. It helped that she'd had the same reaction. "For a split second, I was certain I knew you, but maybe not. I'm Joe Arneson, by the way."

"Kathleen Dinsmore."

They compared notes, trying to figure out when they might have met. They covered where they'd lived, gone to school, and traveled. The only commonality was Pullman, but they'd never crossed paths there. Furthermore, Kathleen had visited Pullman only as a child, and Joe was new in town and had never been there before. Joe had never met her great-aunt, and Kathleen had only spoken to his grandmother on the phone. "Well, that's weird, then." Joe scratched his head. "I've never had this happen to me."

Marcia came up from behind Joe. "If you two are going to keep flapping your jaws, I might as well get in a smoke break." She pulled a pack of Winston Lights out of her front pocket and lit a cigarette with a Bic lighter. The end glowed when she inhaled, and Joe turned back to Kathleen.

"I've been going through my grandmother's old photos. Maybe your great-aunt was in one of them? If she looked like you when she was younger, that would explain why you're familiar to me." Maybe it was that simple.

"Maybe," she said, but she didn't sound convinced. A bell jangled from the front of the store. "I have a customer. I'll be back." She walked out with a swish of her skirt.

Joe turned to Marcia. "Is the 1950s look coming back in style?" He didn't know any women close to his age who wore skirts or dresses unless they were going to a dress-up event like a wedding. The norm, as far as he could tell, was stone-washed jeans, with the preferred brand being Guess. And the ponytail? Not a common sight. It wouldn't work with the layered haircuts that were currently popular.

"God, I hope not." Marcia shrugged. "It's called vintage clothing. We got four trunks and three racks full of it from an estate sale, and most of it fit Kathleen like a glove. You never saw a woman so excited about a bunch of old clothes. She took to it right away, and I haven't seen her wearing anything else since. She said it's a new look for a new life."

"She didn't like her old life?"

"I wouldn't know. She doesn't talk about it." They stood in silence for another moment while Marcia finished her cigarette. After she dropped the butt and stamped it with the toe of her Doc Martens boot, she snapped her fingers. "Party's over, pretty boy. Time to get back to work."

Kathleen returned to the back room just after they had finished emptying the truck. This time she had a dark-colored apron over the front of her skirt. She ran a hand over the credenza, then looked at her fingertips. "It's clean," she said incredulously.

Joe beamed. "I know. I used a lot of Murphy's Oil Soap and elbow grease to get it that way." A thought plagued him. "That's not going to lower the value, is it? I didn't ruin the finish or anything, I don't think."

She laughed, clearly amused. "No, cleanliness is generally considered a good thing. It's just that my aunt warned me that most people bring in things that are filthy. I mean, really disgustingly grungy. Cobwebs and ground-in dirt and grease. But your furniture looks like it's ready to go on the showroom floor."

"Well, thanks, I do my best."

"I really appreciate it."

Marcia coughed. "While you two are busy giving each other warm fuzzies, I'm going to cover the front of the store." She sauntered out, thumbs in her pockets.

"Friendly girl," Joe said. "Very sweet."

"She came with the place. I'd be lost without her."

"Ah, well, as long as she serves a purpose." Joe got out the inventory sheet, and they walked through the room, with Kathleen checking off each item as she identified it. She laughed at one of his entries. "Desk with mirror?" She raised her eyebrows. "That's what we're calling it?"

"That's not a desk with a mirror?"

"No."

"Antique furniture isn't my thing," he admitted. "What's it really called?"

"A vanity dresser with mirror," she said, pulling over a desk chair and sitting in front of it to demonstrate. "Say I'm a lady going out for the evening. I would sit here to do my hair, or have someone else do it for me." She twisted the ponytail into a bun, turned her head slightly to assess it, then let it go. "Also popular? Powdering one's nose, or adjusting a hat to get it angled just right before securing it with a hat pin." She looked up at him and winked. "Or, some ladies just liked to stare into the mirror and admire themselves." She leaned into the mirror. "Look at me! I'm so pretty." Her eyes were solemn, but her mouth twitched into a grin.

He couldn't help but smile at her reflection. "More than pretty. You're beautiful."

Kathleen's cheeks flushed pink. She stood and brushed off the front of her apron as if to deflect his words. "Trust me, I wasn't fishing for compliments." She gave him a wary sideways glance.

"I didn't think you were."

Kathleen got up, and they carried on, checking off two old trunks, each of them hinged on one side and secured by leather straps on the other. When Joe had first stumbled upon them, they'd reminded him of the kind that held pirate treasure. "And all this was in the attic?" she marveled. "I can't wait to see what you bring me from the rest of the house."

"There's a lot," Joe said. "I hope you'll have enough room."

Kathleen nodded. "What doesn't fit here can go in my garage. I can make it work."

They made their way through the list. Kathleen impressed Joe with her knowledge of antiques, although she claimed to know next to nothing. "I'm still learning. You should have seen my great-aunt. She was a walking encyclopedia. I have to look up most things. She left me these reference books, and I study them whenever I get a chance, but I could go my whole life and not know it all."

She paused, and her expression became serious. "Now this," she said. "This is interesting."

She knelt down in front of a large wooden box, admiring the carving on the top that had only become evident after Joe had cleaned it. Once the grime had been washed away, he was amazed as a two-dimensional image of two birds, a heart between them, came into view. The carving had been so painstakingly done that the feathers were shown in detail. Below the birds, a name had been carved: *Alice.* As soon as Joe saw the name, he knew it had belonged to Pearl's older sister, the one who'd died too young. The biggest tragedy of his grandmother's life.

Kathleen ran her finger over the top and flipped back the lid. "This is gorgeous," she said. "The craftsmanship is amazing."

"Is it from some famous manufacturer?"

"No, I don't think so. If I had to guess, I'd say this is a custom piece. A onetime labor of love." She looked up at him. "What was inside it?"

"It was full of what looked like junk. Yellowed fabric that I think were tablecloths and napkins, and some candlesticks that are still back at the house. They're tarnished."

"Real silver, then. My guess is that this was Alice's hope chest. Girls used to fill them with things they'd need when they got married and had a household of their own." She inspected the hinges and the latch, all the while talking. "It was clever the way it was constructed from solid oak and lined with cedar. The cedar was to keep the moths out. And the corners, here?" She pointed at the outside edges. "Dovetail joints. Tricky to do back then. This is one hope chest that was made for the ages. It was most likely built by Alice's father. I'd heard he was quite the carpenter. Such a sad thing that his daughter didn't live long enough to use all the things in this beautiful hope chest."

"How did you know that she died?" Joe asked, astounded.

"Alice Bennett was my aunt Edna's best friend. She mentioned her several times."

"My grandmother told me that her sister Alice died too young and that it was a tragedy, but she didn't want to say any more than that." Joe remembered the pained look on Pearl's face during this conversation. "Do you know how Alice died?"

Kathleen closed the lid of the chest. "It was an accident; that's all I heard. Aunt Edna didn't go into any details."

"How old was Alice when it happened?" Joe asked.

"Eighteen or nineteen, I think."

"Too young."

"Way too young," she agreed, sadly shaking her head. "Her whole life ahead of her, and she never got to see it happen."

CHAPTER TWENTY-TWO

1983

When Kathleen climbed into bed that night, Joe Arneson was still on her mind. She just couldn't get over her reaction to him. The second she saw him, there was a lightning bolt of familiarity. It was like watching a movie and seeing a favorite actor unexpectedly enter a scene. *Oh, there he is.*

There must have been a good reason for the instantaneous, powerful connection that went beyond a physical attraction. It was like her entire being said *yes* at the sight of him. She was at a loss to explain it. Perhaps he bore a resemblance to someone she knew, a former classmate or a television actor? Or maybe he looked like an adult she'd known as a child but had forgotten about as the years went past? There were only so many combinations of facial features in the world. She'd heard that everyone on the planet had a doppelgänger. The trouble was, Joe didn't just look or sound familiar. There was more to it than that. She sensed an intimacy that wasn't appropriate for a complete stranger. When they came face-to-face, she fought the urge to hug him, and it seemed like he was holding back too.

Marcia had a few things to say about it, of course. She wasn't one to mince words. After Joe left, Marcia said, "Whoa there, Nellie! What was going on between you two?"

Kathleen said, "What do you mean?"

"What do you mean, what do I mean? I got a D in chemistry in high school, and even I could tell the two of you together were combustible. From the minute you saw each other, it was like some kind of weird sexual tension started up. He couldn't take his eyes off you, and you—you were being all coy, sneaking glances at him, like you're shy." Marcia clutched the front of her chest and spoke in a high-pitched voice. "Joe, my darling, I know we've just met, but my loins are on fire, and I must make you mine."

"Oh, stop."

But Marcia wasn't going to let it go. "I had to leave just in case the clothes came off and the two of you went at it. No way I'd want to be a witness to that." She shuddered. "I'd have to boil my eyeballs afterward."

"I think you're making too much of this," Kathleen said. "I thought he looked familiar. That's all." Marcia didn't contradict her but just smiled smugly as she went about her work.

Lying in bed now, Kathleen could picture Joe with crystal clarity, astounding considering they'd just met. She fell asleep thinking about the way he'd held her gaze while she was describing details of different types of antique furniture. Every time she glanced up, he was nodding and looking at her, not the furniture. As if she were the most fascinating person in the world.

The pieces he'd brought were in excellent shape, with little wear considering their age, and as clean as could be. She found the hope chest particularly pleasing. It wasn't just lovely to look at, the wood polished to a high sheen. It was knowing (or speculating, really) that the chest had been made for Alice by her loving father. She wished her great-aunt was still alive so she could find out more about the Bennett family. She had so many questions and no one to ask besides Pearl, who struck her as a little testy.

Even with these thoughts crowding her head, sleep came quickly, the way it had ever since she'd arrived in Pullman. The bed was the only item of furniture she'd replaced in the house. She made sure to get a comfortable mattress, and every night she thanked herself for spending the extra money and getting the one she really wanted. Some things were worth the cost. As Kathleen drifted off, she found herself thinking about the hope chest, so painstakingly crafted. The addition of the lovebirds carved on the top added a unique touch. She might, she mused, just buy the hope chest for herself.

Something about it really spoke to her.

In the middle of the night, her brain woke her up, her mind reeling. She rubbed her eyes and turned her head to look at the time on her clock radio. Half past three. Too early, and yet the words inside her brain demanded to be acknowledged. She turned on her bedside lamp and pulled a pad of paper and pen from her nightstand, scrawling frantically before she forgot. When she was done, she'd written a poem:

> Little, little darling child
> Sweetest flower, small and wild
> Fill me with your love and light
> All my days' and nights' delight
> Nothing will keep us apart
> You're always there in my heart
> You are still my baby girl
> Dearest one in all the world

Where did that come from? She had no idea. It was like an ode to a future child, a baby girl. Reading it over a few more times, she found it impressive. As poetry went, it wasn't particularly outstanding, but considering she'd plucked it out of thin air, it was pretty good. In the back of her mind, a melody came, and she hummed along with the words. Was she composing music now? The idea was laughable. No, this had to be something she'd heard once, maybe as a child. Who knew what memory fragments lurked in her subconscious? The next time she called home, she'd ask her mother if the song sounded familiar. No doubt it was something she'd learned as a little kid.

Satisfied with having written it down, Kathleen set the notepad on the nightstand and turned off the lights, ready to get back to sleep, but now she felt wide awake. Inwardly, she groaned. It was way too early to start the day, and yet she knew from past experience that falling back asleep was unlikely. Inevitably, she'd lie awake for hours, biding the time, having to wait until morning. Her thoughts wandered to the events of the day, of the furniture Joe had brought to the store. Something about the construction of the hope chest jumped out at her. The base struck her as being almost separate from the rest of the chest. She'd have to take a closer look in the morning.

Or she could just get up and go to the store, check it out, then come back home and climb into the comfort of her bed.

She weighed each option, ultimately deciding curiosity won out. She dressed quickly, grabbed her key ring and purse, then headed out of the house, making sure the door was locked behind her.

The sidewalks were well lit in Pullman, and the summer air was warm and humid but not unbearably so. Aunt Edna knew what she was doing living a block away from her business. It was easy to go back and forth from home to work, which was also a drawback, of course. She never quite got away from the store; there was always some detail to attend to, not that she'd complain about it. Despite it being a small town, the lake visitors were good customers in the summer, sparing no expense if they liked what they saw. She made more than enough to keep the business afloat, give herself a fair salary, and pay Marcia as well. It helped that she owned the house and car free and clear. As long as she kept the store filled with new stock, she'd be fine, so in that regard,

Pearl Arneson's estate was a gift, hand-delivered, wrapped in fine paper, and tied with a bow.

The downtown consisted of one main street, and that stretch was now deserted. Even the tavern at the end of the block had closed and locked up for the night. She stood in front of Secondhand Heaven, the key in her hand, listening to the quiet hum of insects off in the distance. So peaceful.

After a moment, she let herself in, turning on the lights and surveying the store the way a customer would. Charming. That was the word she'd use. And quaint too. She was proud of her contributions to the place. She'd reorganized the stock, worked on creating better displays by grouping similar things together, and prided herself on learning the interests of repeat customers. Small changes had helped a great deal too. The antique light fixtures hanging from the ceiling had been largely ignored until she had the idea to post arrows at eye level marked, **LOOK UP!** Ever since then, they'd sold steadily. A simple thing made all the difference.

Kathleen walked to the back of the store and opened the door into the storeroom, flipping on the lights. The overhead fluorescent fixtures filled the space with white light, illuminating every corner. The room smelled faintly of linseed oil. She went back to Alice's hope chest and crouched down to take a good look at it. "What's your story?" she whispered, inspecting the chest. Her great-aunt had talked about antique pieces that carried a piece of history and emotion with them, but Kathleen had never experienced this until Joe brought in this hope chest. The previous owner's joy and hope for the future fairly emanated off it. So sad that Alice hadn't lived to take it to the home she'd share with a husband and, eventually, children.

She sat on the floor, giving the chest a good once-over. Just as she'd remembered from earlier, the hope chest rested on four short legs. Just above the legs sat the rectangular base, bigger than the rest of the chest. Lifting the lid, she peered down inside, trying to make sense of the space. The interior was just a cedar-lined cube that extended down to the top of the base. There was no reason for the base to be larger, except as a decorative element or—and this idea truly thrilled her—if there was a secret compartment inside of it.

Kathleen ran her hands over the sides of the base. The surface had been decorated with carved vertical lines, disguising the edges of what she realized had to be a shallow drawer on the left-hand side. If she hadn't read about this exact thing in one of her great-aunt's books, she never would have thought of it. Running her hand underneath, she found a latch the size of a wing nut. Turning the latch released the drawer. She pulled it out, and it resisted, squeaking slightly, the wood presumably having swollen with time. She managed to get it open only halfway and was reluctant to force it.

She knelt on the concrete floor, leaned over, and peered inside. There was something there that looked like fabric. With curious fingers, she eased the drawer all the way open. Inside was a drawstring bag made of some kind of coarse material, the kind she associated with feed bags. Her sense of anticipation heightened, she carefully widened the bag's opening and looked inside. At the bottom of the bag was one item, a small metal key. She took it out and held it in the palm of her hand. So tiny. Not the right size for a house or a car. The key to someone's diary, maybe? Or a very small cabinet? Her heart sank with disappointment. She'd been hoping for letters or documents or family jewelry. Something with meaning or value. This key could belong to anything. Chances were, she'd never find out what it was for.

She sighed, then closed the hope chest and walked out of the storage area, closing the door behind her. She put the key in the cash register drawer. Joe would be bringing in more items over the next week or two. With any luck, something he brought in would need this key. If that was the case, she'd be ready. Or maybe something in the house required this key, a curio cabinet or jewelry box. She'd ask Joe the next time they spoke if he had any ideas.

Kathleen turned off the lights, locked up the store, and headed down the sidewalk toward home. Now that she'd gotten that out of her system, the comfort of her bed sounded good. Going back to sleep was a real possibility. With any luck, she could get two to three hours before her alarm went off.

She was nearly home when a continuous reedy whistle pierced the night air. Pausing, she listened. There it was again, a whistle, more pronounced now. She'd never heard a bird that sounded like that, but living so close to the lake, she'd encountered all kinds of wildlife she'd never seen before. One evening shortly after her great-aunt had died, she'd sat on her porch, transfixed to see two cranes walk between her house and the neighbor's, pause at the curb, and then casually cross to the other side.

When the piercing whistle happened again, her stomach dropped, an old fear settling around her. She clutched her keys, ready to use them as a weapon, and hurried to her front door. Her hand shook as she fumbled the key into the lock, and she darted a glance over her shoulder. *Hurry, hurry, hurry.*

Finally, the key turned, and the door was open. In a moment, she was inside, the door locked, her back against the wall. She peered out through the small window at the top of the door, looking out to the street. No one was there, but she knew what she'd heard.

That whistling. It was a person, not a bird.

And she had an idea of whom it could be. She could picture him, his eyes hooded, whistling in that creepy way.

Ricky. He was here. In Pullman.

CHAPTER TWENTY-THREE

1983

Ricky found Miss Whitt to be the ideal landlady. From the moment he'd entered her front door, he made a point to call her "Aunt Lorraine," and she giggled every single time. Her guest bedroom was more than comfortable and had the added bonus of a patio door that led to the backyard, all the better to slip in and out without detection. He took inventory of everything he'd brought with him to Pullman. Clothing. Shaving kit. Money. Ski mask. Handgun. Without even trying, the universe had gifted him with all the components necessary to win Kathleen back. It was a sign, he thought. The two of them were destined to be together.

To Miss Whitt, her new guest, Richard, was a recovering surgical patient who slept day and night. He told her that if the door was shut, he was not to be disturbed. For added insurance, he wedged a chair underneath the doorknob. With the help of a baseball cap and sunglasses, he was able to go into town and keep an eye on everything Kathleen did. Once she was home, he was right next door, able to keep a close eye on her.

That night, Ricky was already awake when the light went on next door in Kathleen's upstairs bedroom. He watched the lights go on and off, following along as she moved through the house, ending with a lamp in the living room. He quickly got dressed to go outside and get a closer look. Was she expecting a middle-of-the-night visit from a lover? The thought momentarily filled him with fury, but then he calmed himself with the thought that this wouldn't be Kathleen's style. She was more the early-to-bed and early-to-rise type. Sometimes she didn't even make it through the ten-thirty news. The idea that she'd have a night-time rendezvous was unlikely. So it had to be something else. Maybe she just had a touch of insomnia and was going to drink some warm milk to settle herself. That was a trick his mother had taught her in the early days of their marriage.

He slipped out the patio door, sliding the door slowly so as not to wake Miss Whitt. Once he was outside, he watched the living room window to see Kathleen sling her purse over her shoulder and head to the front door. He glanced at his watch. Ten to four. There weren't any businesses open at this hour. Was she meeting someone?

She walked with purpose, striding down the sidewalk in the direction of downtown. He followed at a safe distance, keeping off the sidewalk and waiting as she turned the corner onto Main Street. What was she thinking, walking alone at this hour? It was still dark. No one was around. She could easily get assaulted or raped, and no one would hear her cries for help. Of course, he thought wryly, that would be his chance to save her. His plan could be executed without any manipulation on his part.

Ricky stood in the shadows as she let herself into her shop. She turned the lights on and went inside, then came back out about fifteen minutes later and headed back toward her house. Odd.

Again, he kept his distance. This time he was on the opposite side of the street, cutting through backyards and ducking behind bushes. When she reached her house, he couldn't resist letting out a whistle.

She stopped to look, and he paused, noting her look of surprise. His whistling had always been something that got her attention when they were married. He whistled again, and she continued on to the front door and hurried inside. The sound of the door closing and the lock clicking pierced the night air.

Did she know it was him? She would soon enough.

CHAPTER TWENTY-FOUR

1916

In the theater, Pearl watched John and Alice at the piano with rapt attention but didn't notice Frank until he'd actually yanked John off the bench. By the time John got to his feet, Floyd Kramer had rushed in to intervene. Frank had his hands clenched into fists, and Alice had stopped playing the piano and now stood next to John.

"Frank, really!" she said, mortified. "What's gotten into you?"

Floyd had a similar question. "What's going on here?" The motion picture was now only a backdrop. No one in the audience was paying attention to it anymore. All eyes were on the small-town drama now unfolding in front of the screen.

"I'll tell you what's going on," Frank said angrily. "This hired hand, this *stranger*, had his hands all over Alice."

"That's not true," Alice protested. "John was just sitting next to me watching me play. He didn't touch me. I will vouch for him."

"Sure, you'd vouch for *him*." Frank spat out the words.

John said, "I would never do anything to hurt Alice's reputation. I swear to you that my interest was in her piano playing. I was not even sitting close enough to touch her."

"Maybe he didn't touch her, but he wanted to! He was moving in to kiss my girlfriend. I'm not standing for it, I tell you. I'll kill any man who lays a hand on her."

Alice said, "I'm not your girlfriend, Frank. I never was and never will be."

Floyd sighed heavily. "You're changing your story, Frank. A second ago, you said you saw him do something. Now you say it didn't happen yet. Seems like you're just causing trouble."

"It would have happened if I hadn't stopped him," Frank argued, a finger poking at John. "He's the one causing all the trouble."

"This is absurd." John shook his head. "Nothing happened."

A boy's voice rang out in the darkness. "Fight, fight, fight!" Someone shushed him.

Floyd said, "I'm going to ask you two gentlemen to take it outside, and don't come back. I can't have this kind of thing going on during a show." Neither of them moved, and he added, "Don't make this difficult for me, Frank. I'd hate to tell your father. Out you go." He pointed up the aisle to the exit doors.

John led the way, with Frank on his heels. When they were nearly to the last row, Frank shoved John's back, making him stumble, but John quickly regained his balance and stepped nimbly aside. "After you," he said, gesturing with a grin. Frank grumbled but took the lead.

Alice returned to the piano and began playing, seamlessly joining the story in progress. Her head drooped, though, and her posture showed a decided lack of enthusiasm.

Pearl leaned over and whispered to Helen, "I'll be back in a few minutes. You're in charge of the younger girls until I return." She didn't wait for a response but slipped out of her seat and hurried after Frank and John, eager to see what would happen.

She found them facing off in the street in front of the theater, Frank with fists raised, John holding up his hands in surrender. "This whole conversation is preposterous," John said. "I'm not going to fight you, Frank." His arms dropped to his sides. "Can we just agree that this was a misunderstanding and walk away in peace?"

If anything, this incensed Frank even more. "A misunderstanding? Do you think I'm stupid? I know what I saw, and what I saw was you moving closer to Alice, practically drooling over her." He noticed Pearl standing on the sidewalk. "You saw it too, didn't you, Pearl?"

She hadn't counted on being drawn into the conflict. There was no good way to answer his question without fanning the flames of his anger. If she disagreed, he'd be furious, and if she agreed, he'd turn on John. She didn't want that to happen. Yes, she'd seen John move closer and closer to Alice, but he hadn't actually touched her, and he *did* seem impressed by her piano playing, so perhaps that part was true.

John had said the conversation was preposterous, but what Pearl found preposterous was the notion of two young men fighting over Alice. Alice, of all people! Alice, who canned all their vegetables; Alice, who scrubbed the floors, cooked their meals, and mended their clothing. She was a drudge, caring nothing for her own appearance, putting everyone else first. Her hands were calloused and her skin tanned from hanging laundry and weeding the garden. She had little interest in the newest fashions and dressed the same way their mother had. Reading the newspaper was what she did for fun. Alice was already an old maid; she just hadn't reached the right age yet.

"Pearl?" Frank shouted. "You saw him making eyes at Alice, trying to romance her, didn't you?"

She shook her head. "I was watching the show. I didn't see anything."

"I will not fight you," John said. "I'm sorry you misunderstood, but your anger, sir, is misplaced. And if Alice was not offended, I don't think it's your place to take umbrage on her behalf."

"Umbrage?" Frank mocked with a sneer. "College boy. You with your big words. You think you're better than everyone else."

"Well, not *everyone* else," John said pleasantly. "Look, Frank, getting better acquainted with you has been a delight, but I'm not going to fight with you, so there's no point in furthering this discussion."

He turned and walked away, presumably heading to the back alley to wait by the wagon.

"You're a chicken!" Frank yelled. "You come back here right now, or I'll tell everyone you were too afraid to fight for Alice."

John didn't turn around. "Good evening, Frank." He threw up one arm as if to say farewell.

Frank took a running start and slammed into John's back, throwing his arms around the other man's upper body. As Pearl watched, John tried unsuccessfully to shake him off. She ran into the street, yelling, "Stop it, Frank! Leave him alone."

John spun in a circle, and Frank held tighter, saying, "Fight me like a man, you coward!"

"Stop it, both of you. Just stop it!" Pearl was ready to pummel Frank with her fists, but before she could, a hand reached out and held her back. Howie.

"Come back inside, Pearl," Howie said, his voice in her ear. "Let them settle this on their own."

"Leave me alone, Howie." She struggled to get free of him.

Down the street, the two men grappled, Frank not letting go. Round and round they went until John, realizing he couldn't break free from Frank's grip, bent his knees and leaned forward. Thrown off-balance, Frank flipped over John's head and landed on his back in the street. John stood over him. "I didn't want to hurt you, Frank, but you left me with no choice. Now let's be gentlemen and part on friendly terms."

Frank sat up, rubbing the back of his head. John held out a hand to help him up, but Frank smacked it away, speaking through gritted teeth, his words a snarl. "You bastard."

"Good evening, Frank." John stepped away and went down the street, turning the corner and disappearing from sight.

Howie went to Frank, extended a hand, and helped him to his feet. Frank brushed off the front of his shirt. "I'm going to get him," he said. "No one makes a fool out of me." From the sidewalk, Pearl watched, enthralled by his show of manly rage. Her own father never raised his voice and rarely appeared to be angry.

"What would that solve?" Howie asked. "Better to turn a blind eye."

"Ha!" Frank leaned over and spat onto the street. "I believe in an eye for an eye."

"That's Old Testament, Frank," Howie said. "The New Testament says to turn the other cheek."

"I don't know so much about the Bible," Frank said. "But I know right from wrong, and it's wrong for him to be trying things with another man's girl. I don't know how they do things in Gladly Falls, but here, it's a big mistake."

Howie didn't have anything to say about that.

Later, at home, after the younger girls had excitedly told their father about the incident, John explained and apologized for the trouble. He spoke in measured tones to their father, his hat in his hand. "Sir, I hope this doesn't cause any problems for you in town. I respect all your daughters and would never do anything to hurt them."

Alice, standing nearby, said, "Nothing happened. He was just watching me play, the same as at home."

Their father listened, and when all of them had spoken their piece, he said, "It sounds as if a misunderstanding has occurred. I trust there will be no more misunderstandings in the future?"

"No, sir," John said.

"Very good." He nodded. "I will speak to Frank myself and put this to rest. I can't afford to lose a good employee because of a young man's hot-tempered ways."

Later, after John had left to sleep in the barn and Alice was getting Daisy and the other girls off to bed, Pearl took the opportunity to talk to their father in private, approaching him while he was smoking his pipe on the front porch. "Father? Can I tell you what I saw at the theater with Frank and John?"

"Was it different than what Alice and John told me? Was there some form of impropriety?" He gave her an inquiring look.

"No, sir. It happened just as they said. It's just that . . ." She paused, thinking how best to express it. "I think there's more to it. I think that John is sweet on Alice." Her father was so quiet, she wasn't sure he fully understood. "He seems to go out of his way to help her in the kitchen, and he's always looking at her too."

He blew out a puff of sweet tobacco smoke and looked at her, his eyes perceptive and knowing. "I too have noticed that the young man seems smitten with my eldest daughter."

"You have?" she asked, astounded. If their father had noticed, it was worse than she suspected. The good news was that it hadn't gone too far yet. There was still time for John to become disenchanted with Alice, and when that happened, she, Pearl, could step in and be there for him. "Why haven't you said anything to him? You need to stop this. We don't even know John's family. If people start gossiping, it would be the talk of the town."

He shifted his body toward her, his mouth set in a firm line. "Alice does so much for all of us and asks for nothing in return. Sometimes I forget she's still a young woman. She works for the betterment of this household from sunup to sundown with nary a complaint. I cannot lighten her load, but I see no harm in letting her enjoy some attention from a gentleman for the summer. Can you begrudge your sister such a small thing?"

She squirmed. "Well, no, of course not. It's just that people talk."

"Yes, they do," he agreed. "Foolish people with nothing better to do always talk. You might learn to ignore them, Pearl."

"I'm just thinking of Alice and her prospects."

Her father carried on. "As for us not knowing John's family, while that is true, his conduct and habit of diligent work speak well for him and for them. And soon enough, John will be back to school, and this will be over. We can let Alice have her day in the sun, can't we, Pearl?"

"I guess so."

He sighed. "Winter will be here soon enough, and all of this will be behind us."

CHAPTER TWENTY-FIVE

1983

Joe woke in the middle of the night to the sound of an owl hooting in the distance. The dream he'd just awakened from had featured a hooting owl as well, which was disconcerting to his sense of reality.

The Owl Dream was a pleasant enough one, although it was tinged with longing. He always woke from the experience feeling like he'd lost something valuable.

In the dream, he was the same man as before. He'd sensed that this man had his physical build, not overly tall but tall enough, slim and fairly muscular. Young too, at least in his twenties. He remembered Dr. Jensen saying that of course his dream self would match him physically; it was an extension of Joe himself. Joe hadn't agreed. The dream man was a whole separate entity. It was like he'd climbed into this man's body and saw the world through his eyes.

This particular dream always began with a nighttime walk. He sensed that a building was behind him, but he never looked back. His focus was on the letter in his hand, a letter he'd written and was now going to deliver. He walked over dirt and patches of grass, heading straight to his destination. A house was nearby, but it was dark, every light long having been extinguished, every occupant sound asleep in their beds. No one would know what he'd done, and this idea pleased him. The letter was trifolded, light in his hand but heavy with meaning. He was eager for her to read it.

He found the tree, a mature hardwood with a trunk so thick he couldn't have wrapped his arms around it. A small hollow slightly larger than a basketball had naturally formed in the trunk, and this was where his journey had led. He reached up and placed the letter inside the hollow, anchoring it with something metal already inside.

Dr. Jensen had asked him, "Who is the letter for?"

"It's for her." There was no need to explain. His dreams always centered on this woman, the one this man loved but whose face Joe himself never saw.

"What was in the letter?"

Joe had shaken his head. "I don't know for sure, but I have the idea it's important. He's revealing something he would never tell anyone else."

Dr. Jensen had tapped on the arm of his chair. "The man in the dream is you, Joe, your subconscious self. Next time you have the dream, tell yourself to read the letter, and maybe when you wake up, you'll know what secret you're holding back."

Joe was skeptical but took his advice anyway. It didn't help. The dreams were constant, the images and feelings always occurring in the same order, like rewinding a VHS tape and watching the same segment of a movie over and over again. He had no power over the dreams. If anything, it was the other way around.

CHAPTER TWENTY-SIX

1983

The next morning, Kathleen decided her reaction to the nighttime whistling had been overly dramatic. The idea that Ricky could have tracked her down, traveled to Pullman, and then lurked near her house just waiting for her to come out was ludicrous. Add that to the middle-of-the-night timing, and it became even more far-fetched. Who would go to all that trouble and then hide in the bushes for hours just to whistle? The light of day put that silly idea to rest. Being able to attribute it to her own paranoia was a relief. In all honesty, she wasn't sure what she'd heard. It could easily have been a bird. She didn't know of one that made that particular sound, but that didn't mean anything. Pullman was proving to be full of surprises.

Marcia had taken the morning off to go to the dentist, so when Joe arrived with another load from Pearl's house, Kathleen was alone in the store. She put a sign on the front counter near the bell, asking customers to ring if they needed help, then went to help unload.

When he jumped out of the truck, his appearance rendered her speechless—jeans, a button-up shirt, suspenders, and a newsboy cap.

Like he'd traveled to 1983 from some bygone era. "Good morning," he called out, grinning. "I brought you some treasures."

She stared, knowing she should answer but unable to form words. Good-looking men were considered handsome, and Joe was good-looking, but there was more to it than that. Without Marcia there to make her feel self-conscious, she was able to give him a more thorough once-over, now taking note of his tall, athletic build, friendly steel-gray eyes, and brilliant smile. He was unshaven, which only accentuated his strong jaw, and his hair, though not as long as that of many guys his age, covered his collar, waving slightly at the ends.

"Something wrong?" he asked.

His question brought her back to the moment. "What? I'm sorry. I'm just preoccupied." She gestured. "Is this a new look for you?"

"Why, yes, it is." He plucked the cap off his head and held it to his chest. "You were my inspiration, if you want to know the truth."

She tried not to blush but felt the color rise to her cheeks anyway. "How so?"

"Your vintage clothing. I needed a hat to keep the sun off my face, and instead of buying one, I found this in one of the dressers in the house." He thumbed the suspenders. "These were in there as well. The shirt, however, is mine. I never cared for it much before, but it seems to fit with the suspenders."

"The whole thing suits you."

"Thanks. It feels right," he said, donning the cap once again.

"That's how dressing this way makes me feel too," she confided, smoothing down the front of her full skirt. "Like I stepped out of my old life and became someone else. Though still me, underneath it all, if that makes any sense."

"It does. Sometimes you just need a change." He gave her a friendly smile. "I brought you something."

"I'd say you brought me a truckload of somethings, Joe."

"No, something just for you. Wait." He went back into the cab of the truck and came out with a bouquet of flowers, which he presented to her. "For you, m'lady."

"For me? Why?" She brought the flowers up to her nose to take in their fragrance.

"I've been thinking," he said, pushing the cap up from his forehead. "You must seem familiar because our families knew each other. I had to have come across photos of you or your great-aunt, which means, of course, that we are officially friends from way back. A very good thing, because I have no friends in Pullman, and it's getting kind of lonely being in that big old house by myself. But I don't want to be presumptuous, so I'm asking you, Kathleen, will you be my friend?"

The gesture took her breath away. From Ricky, flowers were a bribe or an apology, but from Joe, they seemed the nicest possible gesture. "I would love to be your friend, Joe Arneson," she said, flashing him a smile. Thank goodness Marcia wasn't there. With one snide remark, she'd turn this lovely exchange into something sordid.

"That went well," he said, almost to himself, and then to her, "Don't worry, I'm not a demanding friend. The relationship won't take up much of your time."

"I'm not worried about that at all." And now he was the one smiling. Sheepishly, she excused herself to put the flowers in water. Luckily, the store had no shortage of vases. She found a particularly pretty one made of carnival glass and unwrapped the cellophane from around the flowers, noting that they came from the local florist down the street. *Great.* She almost laughed aloud thinking about how all of Pullman would know that Pearl Arneson's grandson had bought Edna Clark's grand-niece flowers. The whole town would have them married off by the time the gossip died down.

After she'd arranged the flowers, she returned to the back room to help Joe, but he was nearly finished unloading. "I didn't have a whole truckful," he said, hoisting an upholstered chair with ease. Obligingly, she stepped out of the way as he brought in the last few items. Having finished the task successfully, he brushed his hands together.

"So now you have the rest of the day off?" Kathleen asked.

"Believe me, there's plenty of work waiting for me," Joe said. "But I do have time to take my new friend out to lunch, if she's agreeable."

"You mean me?" Kathleen asked, and immediately wanted to bite her tongue. Of course he meant her.

"If you can spare the time. There's a pretty cool-looking restaurant about two blocks down the street. The Pine Cone Family Restaurant. Rumor has it that the pie is to die for. Don't worry, just because they call it a family restaurant, you're not obligated to bring your family. Friends are allowed. I checked."

"That's good to know," she replied good-naturedly. "I can't leave just yet, but Marcia should be here soon. How about I meet you there at twelve thirty?"

"Works for me," he said. "Do you need directions for the Pine Cone?" His tone was teasing. "I can map it if you want."

"Trust me, I can find it."

At twelve twenty, Kathleen was out the door, heading down the sidewalk. She felt her mood lighten with every step and fought to keep from grinning. The words *I have a friend* came to mind, and the thought made her ridiculously happy. She'd had friends before, of course. Most of them had fallen by the wayside once Ricky came into the picture. He liked having her to himself, and when they'd moved away from her hometown, keeping up with other people became troublesome. Writing letters was unsatisfying, and Ricky blew a gasket when he saw long-distance calls on the phone bill, so she rarely made them and kept it short when she did. Eventually, her friendships tapered off until all she had left was a handful of cards at Christmastime and occasional gossip passed on by her mother.

So many of her friends had moved on in their lives, their connections dwindling over time. Once she arrived in Pullman, she deliberately cut ties, not wanting to leave a trail that Ricky could follow. Did she have any friends at all? She and Marcia were friendly, but that was the extent of it. She wouldn't say they were friends, exactly. Her interactions with others in town—her customers, neighbors, fellow store owners—were all warm and accessible. There were any number of people she could call in an emergency, but no one she could call just to go to lunch.

Maybe she was making too much of it. If she'd even made an effort, if she'd actually opened herself up to other people, perhaps she'd have friends already. It was just hard to do because once you opened the door, you never knew who might walk in. That was the scary part. Once bitten, twice shy.

She had a good feeling about Joe, though, and she definitely could use a friend, even if it was just for the summer. And if he tried to step over the friend line, she was prepared to push him right back.

Walking through the door at the restaurant, she spotted Joe sitting in one of the booths alongside the front window, his cap on the table in front of him. He waved, his face lighting up at the sight of her. She slid into the seat opposite him. "Am I late?"

He glanced at his watch. "You are right on time, but even if you were late, it would have been fine, because I've been reading about the history of the Pine Cone." He tapped the back of the shiny menu as his eyes met hers. "Fascinating."

"You enjoy reading, then?"

"I've become quite the reader lately. You see, I have no choice. My grandmother's house does not have a television."

"Wow, such a hardship," she said, her tone mocking. "How can you stand it?"

He inclined his head as if thinking. "Sometimes I act out the shows I can remember. Yesterday I was both Laverne and Shirley. If you want to stop by sometime, I would let you be Squiggy."

"This friendship with you just gives and gives and gives, doesn't it?"

"Oh, believe me, we're just getting started."

The waitress came with her pad at the ready. Luckily, Kathleen was familiar with the menu and could order on the spot. Joe too was able to rattle off his order. She was struck by how easy it was to spend time with him. They quickly filled each other in on the basics of their lives—hometown, siblings, school years—almost as if to get that out of the way so they could begin really talking. There were no awkward pauses, no intrusive questions; she didn't get the sense that he was pushing for anything beyond her comfort zone. He teased her as if they'd been friends their whole lives. The two of them together were a fit. Right as rain, Aunt Edna would have said.

Joe made her laugh, which was no small thing. She couldn't remember the last time she'd laughed that way, continuous mirth, making it hard to breathe. He was especially fascinated by the waitress, a serious battleship of a woman named Doris. He said his new personal goal was to make her smile. "There's gotta be a way."

"Believe me, it's not going to happen," Kathleen said. She'd eaten at the Pine Cone several times and knew Doris was not to be trifled with. She didn't own the place but thought she did, barking out orders to the cooks and keeping unruly teenage customers in line. Running a restaurant was no joke, and smiling was fine for other people, but not for Doris. "It may not actually be possible for her lips to move upward. I'm just saying you might be setting your sights too high."

"We'll see about that," Joe said. "I've got the rest of the summer to wear her down."

The conversation shifted to Pearl's house and the lakefront part of the property.

"The lake is big business here in the summer," Kathleen said. "It used to be that most of the people on the lake lived here year-round, but now a lot of it is summer rentals. And those vacationers shop at my store, eat at the restaurants, and buy live bait at the hardware store. It gives Pullman a big financial boost."

"You can buy live bait at the hardware store?" He raised his eyebrows.

"As much as you want, city boy," she said, her tone teasing. "When you buy the earthworms, they come in mud in a Styrofoam cup. If you keep the cup in your fridge, they live longer."

"Worms in a Styrofoam cup that you can refrigerate. How barbaric."

"I know it seems like it, but when my mom was here, we rented a boat and fed worms to some turtles out by the island. It made the turtles very happy."

"There's an island?"

She nodded. "If you can call it that. It's not much of an island. You can't build a house on it or anything. Nowadays, it's mostly used by teenagers for partying."

"I'd like to see the island," Joe said, his voice suddenly serious. "Would you take me there someday?"

Kathleen nodded. "Sure. I'd be happy to." Because, she reflected, that's what friends were for.

"Good." He sat back. "Then it's a date."

The word *date* jarred her. She hoped he meant it as a general expression and not that their friendship, only in its infancy, had already progressed to something more. She was not ready for a romance and couldn't imagine that she ever would be.

Before she could delve into it, Doris brought their sandwiches, setting them down with brisk efficiency and saying, "Here ya go. Eat up."

"Thank you, Doris. You're the best," Joe said, but Doris had already left to greet some incoming customers. He turned his attention to

Kathleen. "Do you suppose when Doris is sick, they just shut down the whole restaurant?"

"Doris is never sick," she said. "She wouldn't allow it."

And just like that, the conversation was back on track, flowing as easily as if she were talking to her best friend from high school, the one she'd known since the first day of junior high. If Joe thought they had plans to go on a date, she'd deal with it later. Right now, they were having too much fun to complicate matters.

When there were only crumbs left on their plates, she remembered about the key. She took it out of her purse and slid it across the table. "I found this in a secret drawer in Alice's hope chest. Do you have any idea what it's for?"

Joe picked it up and examined it carefully before ruefully shaking his head. "Sorry." His eyes met hers. "You found a secret drawer? Was there anything else in it?"

"Just the key." She took it back and put it away. "If you come across something in the house that might fit the key, let me know. Otherwise, I'd like to hang on to it."

"Of course. Whatever you want." And then more seriously: "I'd love to see the secret drawer, if you don't mind. I don't remember noticing anything like that, and trust me, I spent a lot of time cleaning that chest. How did you come to find it?" Joe asked, taking a sip from his glass of water.

"The way the base of the chest was constructed reminded me of a photo I saw in one of my great-aunt's antique reference books," Kathleen said. "I noticed it when you first brought it in, but I didn't quite put it together until later that night . . ." She found herself caught up in the telling, all the more because Joe listened intently, seemingly impressed by her ingenuity.

When she got to the part about discovering the fabric bag, she became distracted, her attention drawn to the window by the sight of a man standing on the sidewalk directly across the street from the restaurant. A single glance turned into a startled stare as the man on the opposite side of the street came into focus for her. He was facing her, wearing sunglasses, khaki shorts, a plain white T-shirt, and blue-and-white high-top Reeboks. A baseball cap was pulled low over his forehead, and he had a full beard, but his build, shoes, and stance were identical to Ricky's. Even more chilling was the possessive way he stared at her. She knew that look.

Kathleen froze in midsentence.

"What's wrong?" Joe asked, leaning over to cover her hand with his. "Kathleen?"

A white delivery truck, black smoke coming out of its tailpipe, drove by, blocking her view of the man. It went by in a flash, and once it was past, the man wasn't there anymore. He'd simply vanished. She squinted, looking at the businesses on that side of the street. She couldn't imagine where he might have gone.

"Kathleen? Are you okay?" He gave her fingers a gentle squeeze. "You look like you've seen a ghost."

His voice broke the spell, and his touch calmed her pounding heart. She shook her head. "I'm sorry. I thought I saw someone I knew."

"Out there? Where?" He craned his neck to look.

"Never mind. He's not there anymore." She forced a smile that she hoped was reassuring. "There's no way it could have been him. There was a resemblance, that's all. It caught me off guard."

He let go of her hand but still looked concerned. "Has someone been bothering you at the store?"

"No, nothing like that."

Doris interrupted the conversation, stopping to whisk away their plates in one swift motion. "You'll be having pie, then?" she said, as if it were a given.

"Cherry for me, please," Kathleen said, glad to let the discussion rest.

Joe said, "I'll have banana cream."

"And then we'll have separate checks," Kathleen added.

"Not a problem."

Doris's head bobbed for just a moment before she left the table to get their dessert. Something about her approving gesture lifted the weight from Kathleen's chest. There was nothing menacing here. She was out to lunch with her new friend, Joe Arneson, in the Pine Cone Family Restaurant in Pullman, Wisconsin. It was a beautiful sunny day. Her past was behind her. Knowing Ricky and his need to be in the spotlight, he'd probably moved on by now and was wrapped in the arms of another woman.

He had no reason to seek her out. There was no reason to be afraid.

CHAPTER TWENTY-SEVEN

1916

Was there any smell better than sun-dried laundry? Alice thought it was worth the work just to be able to take in the freshness once it was dry. She lifted a damp sheet and pinned it on the line, still clutching the other end with her free hand. Sheets could be tricky. One slip, and the sheet would fall to the ground, and then the whole washing process would have to be done over again. That was a mistake no one was apt to make twice.

Laundry day was her least favorite day of the week, but when the weather was nice, it more than made up for it. Alice sang as she worked, glad for the gentle breeze and the feel of the sun on her face.

The apron tied around her middle held a pocketful of wooden clothespins, the same pins that doubled as little people when Daisy wanted to create whole towns on the kitchen floor while Alice cooked dinner. Pearl always tried to shoo their youngest sister away, saying she was underfoot and might cause someone to trip, but Alice had the last word in the kitchen, and so Daisy stayed. She liked having her little one close by. Knowing where Daisy was and seeing her happily occupied was reassuring.

As if Alice's thoughts had conjured her, Daisy's face popped up over the other side of the clothesline. "Alice, look at me! I'm a giant," she said, giggling madly. The sun illuminated her crazy curls, making a halo effect.

"Daisy!" Alice shrieked in mock surprise. "How did you get up so high? Did you grow when I wasn't looking?" She opened her mouth and pressed her hands to her cheeks in pretend amazement.

"No, Alice. I didn't growed any bigger. John is holding me up!" Daisy yelled.

John's face suddenly came up alongside Daisy's. "My apologies if we scared you. I was just following Miss Daisy's plan."

Alice ducked through the gap in the sheets to join them on the other side. John lowered Daisy to the ground. "I do not scare that easily," she said with a smile. She handed the empty wicker basket to Daisy. "If you would please put this on the front porch for me, I'd be ever so grateful."

Daisy smiled up at her. The child loved to help. "Can I play boat captain?"

"Yes, you may."

The basket was nearly as big as Daisy, but the little girl managed to keep it off the ground as she headed toward the porch. John took a step toward the child, but Alice put out an arm to stop him. "Don't help her," she said. "I know the temptation to step in and offer assistance, but she needs to learn to do things on her own."

"I'm sorry."

She faced him, her eyes kind. "You don't have to be sorry. You didn't know. I just have to teach her all the lessons my mother taught me, and it begins with learning to do for herself. Not a day goes by that I don't think about my mother and everything I learned from her. I'm glad she taught me well so I can pass it on to the younger ones."

"So much has fallen on your shoulders. You seem to do everything around here."

She shrugged. "God has given me two good hands and a strong back and the will to be of service. My father provides well for us, but someone has to take care of the house and my sisters, and as the oldest, it has fallen to me."

A thoughtful expression came over his face. "You've a fine disposition, considering your circumstances. Your father and sisters are fortunate to have you."

"And I am fortunate to have them."

"I'm not family, so perhaps this isn't my place, but . . ." He shook his head. "Never mind. You will think I'm rude."

"No, please share your thoughts. I hope you know you can speak your mind with me." Her eyes searched his face. "Just tell me. I promise I won't think badly of you."

"It's just . . . could Pearl not be doing more to help you? She also has two hands and a strong back. I see you work so hard while she does so little. Could someone speak to her and ask her to spend more time doing housework and help share the load? Your father, maybe?"

Alice hesitated a moment before answering. "Pearl has the hands and the back, but sadly for her, she wasn't given the gift of wanting to be of service. Any attempts to press her into work would be met with resentment and resistance, so there's no use forcing the issue. I would rather work joyfully on my own than work side by side with my sister when she is in a foul mood."

"It just doesn't seem fair," he said softly. "But then life isn't fair, is it?"

"No, it is not." She looked down, fiddling with the wooden clothespins in her front pocket. "If it were fair, my mother would be here alive and well. Instead, she left a husband with a broken heart and seven daughters without a mother to love and guide them." She looked up. "But there's no point in dwelling on it. I have learned that we all have our heartaches. Even those who seem to be the most privileged have some secret trouble, something in their lives that causes them grief."

"But what about you? When do you get to live your own life? Don't you want to fall in love, get married, and have a family of your own?"

"I want all that and more," she said evenly. "As any young woman would. It will have to be later, though, if it happens at all."

"I see." His eyes tender, John reached over and tucked a loose strand of hair behind her ear. He thought she might pull away at his forwardness, but she didn't move, just regarded him with wide eyes. "You are wise beyond your years, Alice Bennett."

She blushed with pleasure. "Not so wise at all. I just know how life plays out for many people. My friend Edna Clark is my age and cares for her ailing mother, so she is also living a life of service. Family duty comes before pleasure." A strong breeze came through, making the hanging sheets billow and snap. Lifting her head, she said, "Would you like to know a secret?"

"Need you ask?" He leaned in close. "Of course I'd like to know a secret, especially if it's yours."

Her eyes danced. "Even if it means that you must share a secret with me? There must be trust between us."

He hesitated for only a second. "I'm not quite sure what you mean, but I do trust you, and I know you are true to your word."

"This is how it will work," she said, suddenly emboldened. "Each of us will tell the other a secret, something of great personal importance. That way, we have an assurance that our secret is safe. By doing it this way, I will know that you won't divulge my secret, because if you do, I'll be free to reveal yours. Do you agree?"

"I would never betray a confidence regardless, Miss Bennett." He grinned.

"Those are my terms. Take it or leave it."

"I will take it, and I would be happy to go first," he said.

"No namby-pamby secrets either. You must tell me something important, something that you don't want anyone else to know."

"Understood." He glanced around the yard, checking to make sure no one was in sight. When he confirmed the only one around was Daisy, who was now sitting in the wicker basket on the porch, he took in a deep breath and said, "I am here under somewhat false pretenses. Lawrence is not my last name."

She frowned. "Your name is not John Lawrence?"

"My actual name is John Lawrence Robinson. I am not using my last name because I am trying to distance myself from a scandal. In my hometown of Gladly Falls, my family name is held in disgrace."

"But why?" She tilted her head to one side, her brow furrowed. "Why is it held in disgrace?"

"My father is in prison for murder." He toed the ground and was quiet for a moment before continuing.

"But surely he didn't do it?" Her eyes grew soft.

He shook his head. "I wish I could say that he was innocent, but he did indeed kill someone. A man with a grudge against my family broke into our house and threatened my mother. In defending her, my father got out his gun. There was a struggle, the gun went off, and the man was killed. My father was convicted of murder. It didn't matter that it was in his own home or that he was defending his wife. The jury didn't care."

"Oh no," Alice said softly.

John nodded. "This happened when I was a little boy, so young I was just beginning to walk. I don't remember it. After my father went to prison . . ." He faltered, the words hard to say. "The relatives abandoned us, and my mother was forced to get work as a live-in housekeeper for your father's cousin. As I got older, I began to work for her employers as well." He exhaled again and kept on talking, as if wanting to get it all out. "They are a nice family, but they are not my family, and it is not our house. Anytime we leave the grounds, people in town snicker behind our backs. Frank's uncle, Edward Thompson, the one he mentioned who lives in Gladly Falls? I know the man well. Very wealthy and influential but cruel. I didn't know how to answer Frank's question asking if I knew his uncle and found myself trapped in my own lie." John searched her face, eager for a reaction. "I am not proud of this, but I cannot think of any other way to shake off my family's disgrace. I'm not ashamed of my father. I just see no need to carry the stain of his past with me. Please don't tell anyone this."

"I would never tell a soul," she promised, making a cross over her heart. "With God as my witness, I won't speak a word of it. How terrible for you to lose your father under such a circumstance. Your mother must be a very strong woman."

"She is wonderful. I couldn't have asked for a better mother. Someday, when I'm a doctor, I'll move to another city and buy a house of my own and bring her there to live with me." He glanced at Daisy, who was now dragging an unwilling cat into the laundry basket. "I love my mother, and I miss her, but it is nice to be in Pullman, where people judge me only on my work and my character."

"I can imagine that would be true." She looked into his eyes and sighed. "Well, now my secret pales in comparison. You will think it childish, I'm afraid."

"I'm sure I won't," he said, his eyes smiling.

She felt a flush of color come back to her face. "You're just being kind."

"Not at all, and now that you have my attention, you have to tell me."

She regarded him for an instant, then beckoned with one crooked finger, leading him away from the clothesline and into a patch of trees fifteen feet away. "I have a secret place," she said, "where I hide the things that are most valuable to me."

He followed her into a thicket of old trees and watched as she went to one tree in particular, a tree with a hollow the size of a dinner platter. Standing on her tiptoes, she reached up, stuck her hand inside the hollow, and pulled out a metal box. She produced a small key from her pocket and unlocked it, then lifted the lid.

"See?" she said, pulling out a piece of wrapped leather and unrolling it to show what was inside. "This is where I keep all my mementos. My mother's engagement ring and wedding ring and two of her brooches, a seashell given to me by my favorite teacher, and a book of poems my aunt gave to me. Also, a porcelain frog I won at the fair one year."

"I see."

She closed the lid shut in sudden embarrassment. "I can tell by the look on your face that you think it's foolishness."

"No, not at all," he said. "I'm just wondering why you feel the need to have it out here. Wouldn't it be safer in the house?"

She laughed, a surprisingly happy lilt. "You clearly have no sisters, John. There is nothing private in my house. And Pearl would love to get her hands on my mother's jewelry. She is of the impression that my father has them locked in his safe at the mill."

"But he's given them to you?"

"Yes. He knows I will treat her jewelry with great care. Pearl loses everything. She cherishes things for about a day and a half, and then she's on to the next thing." The words were dismissive, but her tone was affectionate. "That's just how she is."

John reached up into the hollow and placed his hand on the bottom, feeling nothing but a solid resting spot. "I'd think your treasures would get wet being outside all the time. Aren't you worried about your things getting ruined?"

"Not at all. The box lid fits snugly, and everything inside is wrapped in leather. The hollow is deep, and I push the box as far back as I can. Nothing has ever gotten wet." She grinned. "I found this hiding spot on my own. No one knows about it but me."

"And now me," he said.

"And I know you won't tell," she said, wrapping up her mementos and tucking them back into the box. "Because we have confided in each other."

He held the box while she secured the lock. Looking into his eyes, she asked, "Would you mind returning it to its place?" He set it inside the hollow, pushing it as far back as possible.

"What if," he asked thoughtfully, "you were to come to your secret hiding spot one day and find a letter from an admirer? Would it please you to come across such a letter?"

"It would depend on the letter, and also on the admirer," she said, "but I believe finding a letter like that would be a most welcome surprise."

CHAPTER TWENTY-EIGHT

1916

Pearl had gone upstairs on the pretense of doing some dusting and mopping, and she did *start* to do just that, at least at first, but household chores were so tedious and never-ending that she paused to leaf through a magazine, which made her lethargic, and the next thing she knew, she'd stretched out on her bed for a very short nap.

When she woke up, some time had passed, and she felt refreshed, despite the heat of the day. She stretched like a cat and then got to her feet, smoothing out the bedspread to hide the evidence of her indolence. She went to the dresser and picked up a hand mirror, fixed her hair, and rubbed the creases out of her face. Considering she'd just gotten up, her appearance wasn't too bad. It was hard to know how long she'd dozed. None of her sisters had come looking for her, which was a good sign.

Going to the window, Pearl held back the curtains that had been closed to block the midday sun. From this height, she could see the yard, the hanging laundry swaying in the breeze, the barn and the lake off in the distance. Their dog, Shep, was taking a leisurely trot around the chicken coop, pretending to be a guard dog. The sun glinted off the lake, waterfowl bobbing and dipping on the surface. It was the same view she'd seen her entire life, and she was so tired of it. Someday she'd be living in the thick of a big city, where every day she'd come across someone new instead of having to look at the same old faces she'd known ever since she was a child.

She was just about to drop the curtain when she spotted Alice and John stepping out from a cluster of trees just beyond the hanging laundry. John still wore his tweed cap, but he'd taken off his jacket. He was wearing his work clothes: button-down shirt and suspenders, along with his patched trousers and boots. Alice, clad in a gray dress, still wore the apron she used to hold the clothespins when she hung the wash. Normally, this combination made Pearl think of the word *dowdy*, but today Alice looked uncharacteristically attractive: her step was carefree, and the sun made her hair gleam. John and Alice weren't touching, but there was no mistaking there was something between them. Alice's face radiated pure joy, and John had a sly look, as if he had a secret. Their hands hung at their sides as they walked, but Pearl suspected those hands had been clasped together at some point. She watched as John leaned over and said something to make her sister laugh. Pearl had seen enough motion pictures to know when a couple looked completely head over heels in love, and she recognized it now, right in front of her.

Alice and John in love? A raw, ugly feeling rose from within her, and she found herself seething. Unfair. It was so unfair! How could it be that Alice was the one he chose, when Alice didn't even care about such things?

Pearl had yearned for a love affair of her own for years: she'd pored over movie magazines, envying the pictured couples, lain in bed imagining herself in the arms of a handsome beau as he declared his love, and mentally put herself in the place of actresses in the romantic scenes. She'd been sure that out of the two oldest sisters, she would be the first to fall in love—so sure, in fact, that she'd already planned the words she'd use to console Alice.

Don't worry, Alice, it will be your turn soon enough.

You'll meet someone soon.

Any man would be lucky to have you on his arm.

She knew Alice would understand that Pearl was the prettier sister, and more lively too. That men were just drawn to her like moths to a flame. This, she knew, was true. So why didn't John realize it as well?

Not that John was such a catch. He was a student, his family had no property or money, and he took so long to answer a question that she often wondered if he had a brain in his head. No, her father was wrong. John wasn't the one for Alice, not even for the summer.

If anyone else had seen them coming out of the woods, Alice with that foolish grin, John looking like the cat that swallowed the canary, it would be scandalous. They were fortunate Pearl was the one who spotted them and no one else. Next time they might not be so lucky.

She dropped the curtain, unsure what to do next but certain that she couldn't, *wouldn't* let this romance between John and Alice go any further. It just wasn't right.

CHAPTER TWENTY-NINE

1916

My dearest Alice (if I may),

I am glad you have entrusted me with your secret hiding spot. I hope that by tucking this letter underneath your box you find it in good shape and entirely legible.

When I knew I was going to be spending the summer months in Pullman, Wisconsin, working in a feed mill, my greatest hope was that I would earn enough money to cover my tuition for the year. I knew the work would be tiring, and that the accommodations would not be luxurious, but it didn't matter. I am no stranger to hardship.

What I did not anticipate, what I never could have anticipated, even in my wildest dreams, was that I would meet a girl like you. There have been so many things I have longed to say to you these past few weeks, but your busy household made it difficult to find a quiet moment when I could speak only to you.

I was also a little hesitant to speak of matters of the heart, for fear you would find me too bold and not share my feelings. I have discovered that I find it easier to write such things than to speak them aloud, and so I am glad to be able to write this all down in a letter.

I do not know how best to say how important you have become to me. Seeing your beautiful face each day has become my greatest pleasure. Hearing you sing is all the music I will ever need. Your laughter is tonic for my soul. You have a keen intelligence, and I enjoy hearing your opinions after reading the newspaper.

I just read what I wrote above, and it all sounds insufficient. None of it quite conveys the sentiment of my heart. I think what I mean to say is that I think I am growing in love with you a little more each day.

Forever yours,

John

CHAPTER THIRTY

1916

Dear John,

Rest assured that when I retrieved your letter, it was just as you had left it and quite readable.

You said that you think you are growing in love with me a little more each day. Your use of the word "think" troubles me, as I do not want to have this kind of conversation with a man who is not entirely sure. When you know for certain that you are growing in love with me, we can continue this discourse.

Sincerely,

Alice

CHAPTER THIRTY-ONE

1916

The next day when no one else was in sight, John strode out to Alice's hiding place in the trees, reached up, and pulled out a sheet of paper anchored by the metal box. His hands shook with anticipation as he unfolded her letter, and then, upon reading her words, he burst out laughing.

She was clever, so clever. What other girl in the entire world would have caught the ambiguity in his sentence? Alice was unlike anyone else he'd ever met, smart as a whip but also caring, always happy, and ultimately surprising.

As for his letter, he'd only phrased it that way so as not to overwhelm her. He smiled, thinking how she'd turned the words back at him. Never mind. It was easy enough to set things straight.

He went back to the barn and got his writing things out of his trunk. Dipping the nub of his pen in his inkwell, he added his correction below her words.

Dearest Alice,
I am certain I am growing in love with you more each passing day. Please tell me you feel the same way.

Yours forever,

John

CHAPTER THIRTY-TWO

1983

Joe and Kathleen began spending more time together in the evenings after the store closed and at lunchtime after his conveniently timed deliveries to the store. She'd made it known, however, that she had no interest in dating him. Upon hearing this, he pulled a sad face and said, "And here I thought Doris was going to be my biggest challenge this summer."

She gave his shoulder a gentle push. "Just for the record, I talked to Doris, and she doesn't want to date you either."

He mimed a stab to the heart and followed it up by wiping away a nonexistent tear. "Poor me. Destined to die old and alone."

"But not friendless," she pointed out.

"Never friendless," he agreed.

Joe good-naturedly accepted her terms, which simplified things greatly. She had the pleasure of spending time with him without worrying about the location of his hands or if things were moving too quickly. They were just friends. Marcia refused to acknowledge this friendship, or maybe she just didn't understand it. Every time she saw Joe's truck arrive, she'd announce, "Your boyfriend's here."

Kathleen's standard response was, "He's not my boyfriend," which made Marcia smirk.

One time Marcia had answered by saying, "Anyone can see that Joe's a fox. I mean, he's not my type, but he's really got the hots for you. I think you should just admit it and go with it."

"There's nothing to admit," Kathleen said.

After that Marcia started singing the refrain from the Elvis song "Burning Love" every time Joe made a delivery.

If Joe noticed, he didn't say anything.

The people in town, seeing them together so often, assumed they were dating as well. In conversations with others, Kathleen made a point of calling Joe her friend, not that it helped. Thinking about it made her sigh. Oh well, you couldn't keep people from talking. Soon enough, the residents of Pullman would find something else to gossip about.

This evening, for the first time, they were going to a movie at the Victory Theater. After Kathleen locked up the shop, she set off down the sidewalk to the theater, where she found Joe waiting for her, his back against the brick exterior of the building, one knee bent with his foot flat against the wall. He had his trademark newsboy cap on along with the suspenders over a button-down shirt and the tan work pants he'd begun wearing instead of blue jeans. "Hey there," she called out as she approached.

He doffed his cap. "Evening, ma'am." He held up the tickets. "Took care of this ahead of time. Tickets for two to see *Trading Places*, the new smash film starring Eddie Murphy and Dan Aykroyd."

"How much do I owe you?" she asked, taking her purse off her shoulder.

"Forget it. I've got it covered."

She grinned. "Then I'm buying dinner."

"You are one suspicious person, Kathleen Dinsmore. Just because I paid for the tickets does not mean it's a date."

"Just making sure that there's no misunderstanding."

Joe handed the tickets to the man at the door, who ripped them in two and handed half back. The theater was a third full, but they found two seats on the left-hand side. Kathleen went in first, and Joe took the seat on the aisle.

Once they were situated, Joe glanced upward, his eyebrows lifting. "This is the first time I've ever seen an elegant chandelier in a movie theater. It's enormous."

"That's a leftover from when this used to be the Victory Ballroom, a million years ago. Pretty, isn't it?"

"Yes," he said, his attention still focused on the ceiling. "What do you call that fancy disc on the ceiling, the big round thing that the chandelier is mounted on?"

"That," Kathleen said, her head tilted upward, "is a decorative ceiling medallion."

"Lots of places have them? Would you say they're pretty common?"

"This particular one isn't common at all; in fact, it's one of a kind. See the pattern? Gilded. Done in gold leaf. The owner hired an artist from Chicago to create it just for the ballroom."

Joe didn't say anything for an uncomfortably long time, just peered upward, his forehead creased. His mouth twisted, as if he was puzzling through something difficult.

"Joe? Is something wrong?"

"No." He shook his head with a bit of a shudder. "I was just thinking." He turned to her and smiled. "It's very impressive."

The lights went down then, and Joe finally pulled his gaze away from the ceiling to look at the screen. Kathleen had been concerned that if Joe was going to break their friends-only rule, the movie theater might be the place. Sitting next to each other in the dark was the perfect setup for deliberate, casual touching—the press of one arm against another, the brush of fingertips, the bump of a knee. A whispered comment during a movie could be done in a flirtatious way, his lips brushing against her ear. She knew from experience that guys knew how to start something casual, then delve further while still making it look innocent enough. And if she allowed that to happen, it might lure her in, and she'd find herself responding, leaving the door open for more.

Kathleen knew she could weaken and find herself receptive to overtures of love. She wasn't immune to romance, even if her marriage had been a disaster. It was safer, though, to leave things as they were. She wasn't looking forward to having to rebuff any overtures from Joe. She only had the one friend, after all.

But she needn't have worried. Joe didn't do any of that. She might not have been there for all the attention he paid to her. He fidgeted, one knee jiggling, seemingly preoccupied during the previews and only relaxing a bit once the movie had started.

Kathleen was engrossed in the movie, delighted to see Jamie Lee Curtis come on the screen, when Joe abruptly got to his feet and walked down the aisle toward the front of the theater. She craned her neck to see what he was doing. There was no exit door in that direction.

Joe reached the end of the aisle, close to the screen, and stopped, just standing there, looking at nothing at all. His back was to the crowd, and since he wasn't blocking the screen, no one objected. She could barely make out his form in the dim light, but he appeared to look up at the ceiling and back down at a spot on the floor. Then he took a few steps back and did the same thing again. What in the world was he doing?

She got up and went to join him, touching his shoulder. "Joe?" she whispered. Startled, he turned around, a stricken look on his face. "Is something wrong?" she asked softly.

"No, I just . . ." He shook his head, like he couldn't figure it out.

"The lobby is that way."

"No, that's not it. I just remembered something."

Someone in the audience yelled out, "Hey, quiet down in front! Take it outside."

Kathleen took Joe by the arm and led him back up the aisle. Instead of stopping at their row, Joe kept going, so she grabbed his cap off the seat and joined him as he went through the swinging doors.

Out in the lobby, she presented him with his cap, which he took from her and held loosely at his side. "I'm sorry," he said. "I think I have to cut the evening short."

"You don't look so good," she said kindly. "Why don't we get some air?"

Wordlessly, he followed her outside. Leading the way to a bench facing the street, she indicated he should sit, then took the spot beside him. "Do you want to tell me what's going on?"

He took in a deep breath, his chest swelling. "I feel a little unsteady, like I just lived through an earthquake."

"You look like you've lived through an earthquake. What happened in there?"

He turned to her. "You mentioned dinner. Would you mind going now?"

"The Pine Cone?"

Joe shook his head. "No. Somewhere with a bar. I need a drink."

Kathleen knew of a steak house a few blocks down the street, and they were able to walk there. They arrived in a matter of minutes. The sign outside read **Marjorie's Supper Club—Food and Drinks.**

"From the name, I thought it was a private club," he said, sliding into his side of the booth. "Like a country club. I didn't know it was open to anyone."

"A supper club isn't really a club. It's a type of restaurant. A Wisconsin thing," Kathleen said. The hostess set menus down in front of them, assuring them their waitress would be with them shortly, then walked away.

"So what makes a restaurant a supper club?" Joe asked.

"I'm not entirely sure, but they all seem to have relish trays on the table." She pointed to a cut-glass serving tray holding pats of butter, crackers, carrots, pickles, and celery. "And the decor is sort of old-fashioned posh." She indicated the dark paneling and framed oil paintings of landscapes, each with its own spotlight. "Supper clubs usually feature prime rib and steaks. And you'll see a lot of old people drinking a cocktail called a Brandy Old Fashioned Sweet."

The waitress came for their drink order. Joe said, "I'll have a Brandy Old Fashioned Sweet." He grinned at Kathleen. "When in Rome."

Kathleen said, "I'll have the same."

After they'd been served their drinks and ordered the prime rib special, she finally broached the subject of Joe's behavior at the movie theater. "So you felt like you lived through an earthquake?" she asked carefully. "Literally, or was that a metaphor?"

"Not literally." Joe looked pensive. "I just had a strong physical response to being there. I think . . ." He paused, taking a sip from his drink. "I think I'm losing my mind."

She chuckled but stopped upon seeing his expression. "I'm sorry. I thought you were kidding."

"I wish. I was hoping this wouldn't come up. Did my grandmother happen to tell you where I was before I came here to Pullman to help her with the house?"

Kathleen shook her head.

"I was in a mental health facility. I was what they call a full-time resident, which meant I lived there. An inpatient. For months." He studied her face, then kept going. "You don't have to worry. I'm not dangerous."

"I didn't think you were." She pulled the fruit skewer off the rim of her drink glass and inspected the orange slice and cherry. "So why were you there?"

"It wasn't my idea, believe me. I'd been living with my folks and having really vivid, troubling dreams. I'd call out in my sleep or wake up shaking, feeling absolutely devastated. My parents were worried. I thought I was going for a consultation at a place called Trendale Psychiatric Treatment Center, and the next thing I knew, I was talked into being admitted for a short stay so I could"—here he made finger quotes—"be *assessed.*"

"And what was their assessment?"

"I don't know that there ever was an official diagnosis. All I know is that they couldn't help me. They were going down the wrong path. The doctors were sure it was tied to something in my childhood, but I'm telling you"—he leaned over the table—"these dreams have nothing to do with me or my life. In the dreams, I'm this other man, and I'm reliving the same things over and over again. It's like I'm living his life or something. I tried to tell them, but no one believed me. One of the docs kept saying they were creations of my own mind. But today, at the theater, I now have proof that it's not just my imagination at work. In one of the dreams, this man was knocked to the floor, and when he looked up, he saw a chandelier exactly like that one, with that same decorative medallion. You said it was one of a kind."

"As far as I know, it is."

"I've seen that chandelier and medallion in one of the dreams, dozens of times. It's the same exact one. So what that means," he said, "is that at least one of the dreams took place here, in Pullman, a place I'd never been before. There's a reason I'm here, and I feel like I'm getting closer to figuring it out."

She nodded thoughtfully, then pulled the fruit off the skewer and ate the cherry. "So tell me about the dreams. Do you remember them?"

"Remember them? I can't forget them." He told her every detail of every dream, starting with the Piano Dream, the one that took place in the Victory Theater. "That's what the flickering lights in the background were," he said, suddenly realizing. "There was a movie playing."

"So this was after it was converted from the ballroom to a theater," Kathleen said.

"I would think so."

"If there was a piano player, this was probably during the era of silent films."

"That would make sense." He went on to tell more, making sure to include everything he could remember, including how he felt during the dreams and his mental state when he awoke. By the time he was done explaining it all, they were done with the salad course and the prime rib had arrived.

"You know what we should do?" she said. "Write down every detail of every dream and see if we can figure out when and where they took place. If you're dreaming of being the same man, and one of the dreams took place in Pullman, there's a good chance all of it happened around here. Maybe that will help us figure it all out." She tapped the table. "I can try to find out when the Victory had silent films. Maybe they'll have records telling who they hired to play the piano. We might be able to track down your mystery girl."

"So you believe me, then? You don't think I'm crazy?" Relief washed over his face.

"Of course I believe you. Why would you lie about it?"

He exhaled. "I'm so glad. I wanted to tell you about being at Trendale, but there was some small part of me that didn't want to look like a head case." He smiled. "You've become really important to me, Kathleen. You're such an open, honest person and my only friend in Pullman. I didn't want there to be this big secret between us, but I wasn't sure how to bring it up."

"I'm glad you did."

"I'm glad I told you. Thank you for taking it so well."

He was so clearly relieved; she could almost see the tension lift off his shoulders. How would that feel? she wondered. To say the thing you didn't want to say, to announce something that wanted to stay hidden? She felt the shame of the truth about Ricky and their marriage, the ugliness that emerged out of what had been, she'd thought, real love. But it hadn't been real love at all, just the illusion of love. She'd not been a good judge of who he was and what they were together, and so it felt like a failure on her part, although logically she knew that wasn't true.

"We all have something in our past that we're not eager for people to know," she finally said, drawing the words out. "For instance, no one in Pullman knows I'm divorced."

His fork came down with a clang; his eyes widened. "You're divorced?" he said, clearly astounded. "How old are you?"

"Twenty-six."

"I didn't think you were that old."

"Hey!" Her eyes crinkled in amusement.

"Not that twenty-six is old. I just thought you were closer to my age."

Closer to my age. So he was younger? Kathleen had assumed he was her age or maybe even a year or two older. Not that he looked all that much older; he just had a mature vibe. An old soul. "And what age would that be?"

"Twenty-three as of last week. Old enough." He studied her face. "If you don't mind my asking, who in their right mind would want to divorce you?"

She was surprised and touched by his words. Most people wanted to know who was at fault or who had initiated filing the paperwork. That always made her feel like she'd attempted something and failed, but Joe's question put the blame squarely in Ricky's camp. *Who in their right mind would want to divorce you?* As if only a fool would let her go.

"It was my fault," she said, after a pause. "The man I married, his name is Ricky—I saw glimpses of his true colors right from the start, but I brushed it off because I thought I was in love with him. I found out who he really was after we got married, when it got ugly. He was possessive and jealous and controlling." She sighed. "And cheap too. He was a terrible tipper. I was always so embarrassed when we went out to eat. I used to pretend I'd left something behind and go back and leave more money on the table. So he had all these not-very-nice personality traits, but he was also charming and smart, and he loved his mother. I thought the jealousy was sweet when we dated, that it meant he was passionate about me. He kept it in check in the early days, but after we married, his temper emerged. He'd fly into rages over nothing. If he saw me smile at the teenage bag boy at the grocery store, he was convinced I was flirting with him, and when we got home, he would viciously berate me. It didn't matter what I said. I would apologize and everything, but it never helped. It would continue to escalate and build until he was out of control. It was terrifying. Believe me, I didn't want a failed marriage, but I had to get out. It was the only way for me to live a peaceful, happy, safe life."

"A safe life?" His voice trailed off, and then he looked deep into her eyes. "Did he *hit* you?" His tone was indignant.

"It was a long time ago," she said. "I'd rather just put it behind me. Let's just say we're not keeping in touch, and I hope I never see him again."

"Does this Ricky know you're in Pullman?"

She shook her head. "No. I made sure of that. No one knows except my parents, and they would never tell."

CHAPTER THIRTY-THREE

1983

Most nights, Ricky stood in her backyard behind a thick tree trunk and peered into the closest window, rewarded by the view of her moving around the house, oblivious to his presence. He watched her sing to herself as she washed the dishes and discovered she had a penchant for curling up on the oversize chair closest to the bay window to read. He imagined those same hands, the ones squeezing the soapy sponge, washing his back in the shower like she had when they were newlyweds. Once she was back home with him, he'd allow her to read novels in the evening, but the picture wouldn't be complete unless he was in the same room, watching sports on television. He could see it now, very clearly. So very soon, their life would be restored, back to the way it had been, back to the way it was supposed to be.

The one glitch in the whole plan was the obnoxious deliveryman—well, boy, really—who brought truckloads of old furniture and crap to the back loading dock on a regular basis. Kathleen and the other woman who worked in the store had an easy camaraderie with this guy, something that didn't alarm him too much at first. Kathleen had a weakness for the underdog. Always holding the door for old folks and cripples, making small talk with the help at hotels. She even used to give money to panhandlers until he put an end to that on principle alone. Ricky felt that if she was going to be kind to anyone, it should be her own husband. Every moment spent talking to other people was time that she should have been paying attention to him.

When she went to lunch with the delivery guy, the easy back-and-forth between them as they walked down the sidewalk infuriated him. Kathleen had never laughed like that at anything Ricky had ever said, and he was her own husband.

He'd overheard the troll-doll employee address the delivery guy as Joe, a workingman's name if ever there was one. Another point against this Joe? The outlandish way he dressed, with suspenders and a newsboy's cap, as if he were a child whose mother had dressed him for a visit to the JCPenney portrait studio. The guy looked like a complete butthead. No competition there.

Ricky didn't give him another thought until the night Kathleen and this Joe went to the movies. He waited until they were safely inside and stepped up to the ticket counter. "One, please." Once inside the theater, he took a seat where he could watch them closely.

Joe wandered down the aisle like he was brain-dead, and then both he and Kathleen suddenly left, throwing a monkey wrench in his plan. He had to sneak out carefully behind them. Ricky witnessed them talking intently on a bench outside and followed them to Marjorie's Supper Club, a place that looked a little too fancy for just friends. Ricky stood outside for a moment, infuriated. Was she dating this maggot?

He stormed off, intending to go back to Miss Whitt's and think through his plan, the one in which he would play the hero, but when he arrived in the neighborhood, he changed his mind. Going to Kathleen's backyard, he took an edging stone from a planting bed and broke one of the panes of glass in her back door. He held his breath, waiting to see if anyone nearby had heard the noise, but when he was greeted with silence, he reached inside and let himself in.

A feeling of power washed over him as he walked through her house. She couldn't keep him out of her life. Not now. Not ever.

Ricky noted the dishes in the sink with disgust. Had she learned nothing from their time together? If these kinds of chores were done right away, a person would always return to a clean kitchen. This was something he'd learned from his mother. Kathleen had balked at this initially but eventually saw the wisdom of his ways. She'd obviously backslid since their marriage ended. "This is just disgusting," he said aloud. He briefly considered washing them himself before deciding against it. He'd already moved across the country for her and gotten a new job. He was supposed to provide maid service too? Not happening.

He went from room to room, checking drawers and closets. Most of them weren't too bad. He used the toilet while he was in the bathroom, almost laughing at the way he'd made himself at home.

When he'd thoroughly investigated the entire house, he did a final walk-through, flipping on every light switch as he went. Kathleen would find out that her house had been broken into, but she'd never suspect him, not in a million years. He was adamant about turning off lights in unoccupied rooms. Keeping them on was wasteful.

Yes, she'd know someone had been in her house, and that would make her fearful. Just what he wanted.

CHAPTER THIRTY-FOUR

1916

Dear John,

I was very happy to get your letter, and happier still to read of your certainty in your feelings for me. As for me, I have felt myself drawn to you from the start. Is it possible to feel like you already know someone from the moment you've first met? If so, that is what I have found in you.

I find myself thinking about you during the day as I go about my work. You are the last thing I think of before I fall asleep. I count the hours until I can see you again. I thought I was happy before, and I was, but having you in my life has made me happier still in a way I never could have imagined. If this is love, then yes, I feel it too.

Yesterday, in the kitchen, you asked about the title and words of the song I was singing, but we were interrupted before I could explain. The song does not have a title. It is just a little ditty I made up to sing to Daisy. I often write little poems and put them to music. The words to this one go like this:

Little, little darling child
Sweetest flower, small and wild
Fill me with your love and light
All my days' and nights' delight
Nothing will keep us apart
You're always there in my heart
You are still my baby girl
Dearest one in all the world

It is silly, I know, but it pleases her and gives me something new to sing.

Father said that Frank came to the mill and caused quite a ruckus, saying he should fire you, but that they had a talk, and all is resolved now. Pearl is upset that Frank can't come to the house to visit until after you have gone away, but that is not my concern.

I am already thinking about summer's end, when you will go away. I do not think I can bear it. The days will seem so empty without you here. I hope you will be willing to write to me when you are away at school. I know you'll be very busy, but hearing about your days would help to fill the loneliness of my own.

Yours,
Alice

CHAPTER THIRTY-FIVE

1916

Dearest Alice,

There was a time when I had wished this summer would go quickly, but now I would be content to have it last until the end of my days. Before I go to sleep at night, I take out my stack of letters from you and read them over and over again by the light of the kerosene lamp. So many letters, full of your ideas and thoughts, your hopes for the future, and your concerns about the war on the other side of the world, which I assure you will never reach the United States, so you need not worry any longer. The war cannot touch anyone here.

Please believe me when I say you are never dull, my dearest, and each word is etched into my memory. Your letters are what sustains me.

You asked a few weeks ago if we could continue writing after I am back at school. That was only a few weeks ago, but so much has changed in that time. It was then I had confessed my feelings to you, and you told me you felt the same way. I did not think it could get better than that, but now, to hear you call me sweetheart, your voice whispering the word in my ear when no one else is nearby, I know true happiness.

Yours forever,

John

CHAPTER THIRTY-SIX

1916

In the Bennett kitchen one evening, John was mashing the potatoes on the counter next to the stove. Alice, who'd just finished basting the roast chicken, closed the oven door and began singing to Daisy, who sat in the corner, rocking her dolly. Her voice sang out, sweet and clear, "Little, little darling child, sweetest flower, small and wild."

John smiled and opened his mouth, his baritone voice joining hers. Together they sang, "Fill me with your love and light. All my days' and nights' delight. Nothing will keep us apart. You're always there in my heart."

And Alice finished the last two lines: "You are still my baby girl. Dearest one in all the world."

Daisy beamed the way she did every time Alice sang to her. She set down her dolly to clap when they were done, and John took a slight bow.

Mae and Maude sat at the kitchen table, snapping the ends off fresh green beans from the garden. Mae said, "I have never seen a man do women's work like you do, John Lawrence. Pearl says men working in the kitchen is for sissy boys."

John's laugh filled the room. He said, "You can tell Pearl I don't believe there's women's work and men's work. Work is work. It needs to be done, and if everyone helps, it's easier all around."

Maude held up a green bean. "But you and Father have worked all day already."

"And so has Alice. Why should I sit idle when I can help?"

"Alice doesn't mind cooking dinner by herself, do you, Alice?" Maude gnawed on the end of the bean.

"I don't mind hard work, but I am always happy to have help," Alice said. "John is setting a fine example for the rest of you. I never have to ask him. He always offers." She looked around the room, hoping her words would plant a seed of willingness in her younger sisters. Having them come to her with offers of assistance would be very welcome. She did not mind the work, but she grew weary of serving as taskmaster. Barking orders was not in her nature, and her gentle nudges sometimes went unheeded.

John continued with his chore, pushing the potato masher up and down into a large pot. "I have a selfish reason for helping too. I get to listen to Alice's lovely singing and learn how she cooks such delicious food." He turned in the direction of the twins. "You had better be careful. I am growing quite fond of your sister. When I leave, I'm tempted to steal her away and take her with me." He raised his eyebrows, and the twins reacted with indignant expressions.

Alice sucked in a breath, shocked at his boldness. In their letters, both of them had expressed a yearning to be together. Perhaps he thought that since it was so close to the end of the summer, her father would not mind John's declarations of love toward his eldest daughter, but he was wrong. Her father was, she knew, allowing their stolen glances and John's flattery because he was sure it would not lead to more. Alice had no idea what he'd do if he discovered their letters and the subtle ways they showed their love: the knowing looks; the way they brushed against each other when they moved about the kitchen;

the way John helped her in and out of the wagon, one hand grasping hers, the other firmly against her back. Even the smallest touch filled her with a thrill.

"You can't take Alice away from us," Mae said, outraged. "Who will take care of us if she's not here?"

"John is teasing you, Mae," Alice said, but no one paid any attention.

"Oh, but you see, I have thought this through. All of you can play a part in filling Alice's role when she is gone." John grinned wickedly. "There are five of you sisters, plus Daisy. You can take turns filling the job, each of you doing it for a year or two. First Pearl and then Helen, then Emma, then the two of you. It could go right down the line. If you've been paying attention to Alice's teachings, you'll be able to do everything just as she does, and the household will run smoothly."

"No one can cook like Alice," Maude objected. "Besides, girls can't leave home until they're married. It's a rule."

Alice saw the twinkle in John's eyes and felt a wellspring of dread at his response. She gave him a warning look, but he wasn't watching her, too busy giving his attention to the twins.

"If that's the case . . . ," he said.

She knew how this sentence would end. To stop him, she reached out to grab his arm, but instead of making contact with him, her fingertips smacked against the still-hot mashed potato pan.

"Perhaps I will marry her," John said. "If Alice will have me."

The words had no sooner left his mouth than Alice gasped and cried out in pain, clutching her burned fingers with the other hand. She rushed to the sink and plunged her hand into a pot of soapy water. The twins pushed their chairs back and went to her side. From her spot in the corner, Daisy began to cry. "I don't want Alice to go away!"

"Don't cry, Daisy. No one's going anywhere," Alice said through gritted teeth. She grabbed the pitcher of water and poured some into the washbasin in the dry sink, then dipped her fingers into the water.

Now the twins and John were clustered around Alice, trying to get a good look at her injured fingers. "Is it bad?" Maude said, craning her neck.

"It's nothing." Alice winced.

"Let me see." John eased his way past the girls and took Alice's hand, carefully examining it. "It doesn't look too serious. We should wrap it in a cold, wet compress."

"We could put some butter on it," Mae said.

"No, not butter." John turned her hand over, caressing her wrist. "That's proven to be wrong. Butter isn't the best thing for a burn."

A moment earlier, Alice had been upset with his shocking candor in front of her sisters, but now, despite the pain, she felt a rush of love and gratitude toward John. She could forgive him his lack of discretion.

John turned to her younger sisters. "Honey is better. Do you have any?"

"Down in the root cellar," Alice said, speaking to the twins. "Could one of you please go down and get a jar of honey?"

"I'll do it!"

"No, I'll do it!"

Both girls ran out of the room, determined to beat the other one down the stairs to the cellar.

Alice took the opportunity to speak to John alone. She whispered, "You mustn't talk like that in front of the girls. They are such chatterboxes that my father is sure to hear of it. And if Pearl finds out, she would certainly make trouble for us."

He dampened a dish towel and pressed it against her fingers. "I'm not afraid of Pearl. I would love to tell the whole world how I feel about you, Alice Louise Bennett. What are your worries? Your father likes me, and my time here is coming to a close. There is not much he could do to me at this point."

"You have mistaken his kindness for weakness," she said. "Something you don't want to do. My father is very protective of all his daughters. If he thinks there are improprieties between us, he would send you packing tonight." Her large eyes implored him. "Please promise you won't do anything more to put us at risk. We have so little time together."

"I promise," he said. "I'm sorry for upsetting you. And I apologize for speaking out of turn. It won't happen again."

CHAPTER THIRTY-SEVEN

1916

My dearest Alice,

I want to apologize again, this time in writing, for having misspoken in front of your sisters. You are right, of course, in saying that I went too far and that my boldness could jeopardize our time together. If your father found out and took issue with the two of us, I would never forgive myself for putting you in the position of having to defend our deceptive ways.

I can tell you only that my emotion got the better of me. You are my heart, Alice, and I would love for everyone to know that you are mine. I hate that we are doing this behind your father's back. I understand why you want it this way, but I would like something more for the both of us.

For that reason, I feel the need to tell the truth about me and my life before I met you. I told you that my father is in prison, and the reason he was convicted, but I did not tell you the full story behind the crime. My mother once cautioned me against sharing what I am about to tell you, in the hopes of sparing me the pain she and my father faced. I did, in fact, promise her that I would never tell anyone, a promise I am breaking in order to be honest with you. I am not exaggerating when I say that the thought of breaking a promise to my mother has been a moral dilemma for me, but after giving it much thought, I am pressing forward.

I fear your reaction to this news, even as I don't want there to be any secrets between us.

The truth of it is that my great-grandfather on my father's side was a Negro, which means that I have Negro blood as well. This is why my parents were attacked in their own home, which led to my father shooting and killing a man.

My heart is pounding as I'm writing this, fearing your reaction. I will be in agony awaiting your reply. I wonder, can you ever forgive me for keeping this from you? Could you love a man whose family is such as mine? I hope that you do not feel that I deliberately led you astray in presenting myself as someone I am not.

I would not cast off my family heritage even if I could. It's part of who I am. I will understand if this changes things between us. I am praying it does not.

I hold you in high regard and am hoping you will answer this letter and tell me what you think.

Yours truly,

John

CHAPTER THIRTY-EIGHT

1916

The next day, Mr. Bennett was eager to get to work early, so John didn't get a chance to speak to Alice alone. When he returned from the mill that evening, he checked the tree hollow and found that his letter was no longer where he'd left it. She'd retrieved it and by now would know the contents. He hoped to read something in her eyes at dinnertime, some small clue of her reaction, but she wasn't home.

"Where's Alice?" He tried to act nonchalant as he looked around the kitchen, but still his heart sped up as he wondered if his letter was the cause of her absence.

"She took food over to the Clarks' house," Maude said, making a face. "Edna sent for her. Her mother is feeling poorly, and Alice is going to stay all evening to help, so we have to eat cold chicken and leftover biscuits for dinner."

John felt his heart sink. She'd never been absent in the evening before. Could she have made up an excuse to go to the Clarks' in order not to face him? He didn't think she would do such a thing, even though his news must have been horrifying to her. Maybe she wouldn't be able to look him in the eye ever again.

He'd made a big mistake in telling her. His mother had been right. And in a letter too, which meant it could be read by others. What had he been thinking? He had a sinking feeling that he'd live to regret his disclosure.

"Now, Maude," said Helen, "no complaints about the food. You get what you get, and you're lucky to get it. Others are not as fortunate." Of all the sisters, Helen, after Alice, was the most maternal. John could see a day when she'd be taking over the household, leaving Alice free to marry. In his imaginings, he was the one she would marry, but now that idea seemed impossible.

At dinner John ate a few bites of cold chicken and a biscuit, the food feeling like a brick dropping into his stomach. He excused himself and went to the barn for the night, not even staying to help with the dishes.

He tried to read, lighting a kerosene lamp when the sun lowered in the sky, but found that the words refused to go from his eyes to his brain. He had gotten through several chapters, none of it sticking. He closed the book and turned off the lamp.

The sun was almost below the horizon when he heard the arrival of a wagon, the clip-clop of the horse's hooves accompanying the sound of female voices, one of them Alice's. He sat up and listened but was unable to make out any words. Now the women were laughing as he heard the wagon come to a stop. Getting to his feet and crossing the barn, he passed the cow, who lowed in her stall, a mournful, deep-throated cry. "Hush," he said, making his way to the door and peering out through the crack. He saw Alice hop down from the wagon and exchange goodbyes with her friend. Listening carefully, he could make out what was being said.

"I don't know what I'd do without you, Alice," Edna said. "You are a true-blue friend."

"It's my pleasure," Alice said. "I hope your mother feels better soon." Alice waved as Edna drove off, then stepped lightly into the house. She didn't appear distraught or upset, but it was hard to tell.

Miserable, John went back to his mattress and settled down, cradling his head in his hands. A dozen thoughts whirled through his brain. Maybe she hated him and was disgusted by the memory of the times they'd touched, brief and fleeting though they had been. Or perhaps she couldn't love a man who hadn't been truthful from the start. Alice herself was so good, he couldn't imagine her deliberately lying. He wouldn't blame her if she held others to the same high standards. She deserved that and more.

The more he thought about it, the odder he found the timing of her visit to the Clarks. A coincidence? Unlikely, he thought.

Despite his best efforts, he never did fall asleep. He shifted position, then considered trying to read but dismissed the idea. The animals in the barn, sensing his fidgeting, were themselves restless, mooing and whinnying in their stalls.

When he heard the barn door open, his breath caught in his chest. Could it be Pearl again? After her visit to the barn earlier in the summer, she hadn't approached him in such a forward way again, perhaps embarrassed at being turned down. This time around, it was more likely to be Mr. Bennett, coming to take him to task after having heard about his talk of marrying Alice.

He stood up and pulled the curtain back, stunned to see Alice walking toward him, a kerosene lantern in her hand lighting the way. She was dressed for sleep, a cotton dressing gown wrapped around her front and tied in the middle. One long braid fell over her shoulder.

"Alice," he said, her name coming out like a breath.

"Shhh." She put a finger to her lips. "I can't stay long, but I had to see you." She was close now, so close he could have leaned over and kissed her with one small movement, but he held back.

"My letter," he said. "I'm sorry I didn't tell you before . . ."

She put a finger up to his lips and shook her head. "I came because I knew you would worry, but you needn't. It doesn't matter to me. None of it matters."

He clutched her hand in his and pressed his lips to her palm. "It matters a lot to the rest of the world. There are doors that will be closed to me, to us, if I'm found out."

"It doesn't matter to me," she repeated. "There will always be ignorant people spouting nonsense and causing trouble. I wouldn't care about any of that if we were together. You're you, and I love you."

Could a heart swell with joy? He knew from having studied the anatomy of the human body that it didn't work that way, but he could have sworn that was exactly what happened.

"I have to go back to the house before my sisters wonder why I'm gone so long. They think I'm making a nighttime visit," she said, her head making a quick tilt toward the direction of the outhouse. She reached over and patted his cheek. "I'll see you in the morning at breakfast."

He watched as she floated across the barn floor and let herself out. The morning couldn't come soon enough. He went to his trunk and unpacked his writing things, then sat down to write her a letter.

CHAPTER THIRTY-NINE

1916

My dearest Alice,

Your visit in the barn, albeit brief, was a cure for my worried heart. Hearing you say that none of it matters, that you love me for who I am, is more than I could have hoped for. I promise that from now on, I will always tell you everything. There will be no secrets between us.

I wanted to let you know I have written to my mother, telling her I met a wonderful girl named Alice and that I hope that someday she can meet you. I did not tell her we are in love, but she will know, I am sure. When you finally get a chance to meet her, I know you will love her as much as I do. I know she will love you.

I wish we could tell everyone how we feel, but I respect your wishes to keep it between us for now. And now, my dearest Alice, I have saved the best news for last. At work a few days ago, I took the liberty of asking your father if I could accompany you to the Barn Dance in three weeks, and yesterday he said yes. I hope you are smiling right now, as hearing this made me smile as well. Your father said Mrs. Donohue has agreed to chaperone both you and Pearl at the dance, because she will already be there chaperoning Edna and Howard. Furthermore, he gave me permission to drive the wagon to take both of you there. He said that he hoped I would treat his daughter with the respect she deserved, and I assured him I would.

Yours forever,
John

John waited for the ink to dry, then folded up the letter and left the barn, making his way to Alice's special tree in the dark. After so many trips, he knew every inch between the barn door and his destination. He made his way around troublesome tree roots and stayed in the shadows as much as possible. Anyone watching from the house would lose sight of him once he passed the tree line, but he took precautions all the same.

He put the letter in his usual spot, knowing that Alice would find it the next day. Ending their time together with a social event like the Barn Dance was ideal, and he looked forward to holding her in his arms, even if it was in public on a crowded dance floor.

John had other plans for that evening as well. He wasn't going to leave Pullman without asking Alice if she'd be his wife. He was willing to have a long engagement, if need be. The wait would kill him, and the separation would be torturous, but a man did not come across a woman like Alice and let her slip away.

He was ready to end the secrecy and tell the whole world he was in love with Alice Bennett.

CHAPTER FORTY

1983

Joe and Kathleen wound up closing Marjorie's Supper Club. Once again, she marveled at how effortless it was to talk to him. With Ricky, conversation had been a land mine. Seemingly innocent questions were actually attempts on his part to ferret out information. What sounded like throwaway comments were often invitations for her to give him compliments, to assure him that other men didn't match up to him in any area. Even that could be tricky. He homed in on her tone and facial expressions, accusing her of insincerity if she didn't phrase things just right. They'd once had a three-week dispute where he claimed that her apology didn't count because she only said it to end the argument.

Exhausting was what it was. The longer she lived with him, the more turned around she became until she didn't know what to think anymore. The truth of it was that she *had* just apologized to restore the peace. So he was right about that, which clouded things in her mind. By the time she left, she wasn't sure who she was anymore. It took the divorce and moving away to make her feel like herself again. Her life was completely different now, and yet she felt more herself than she had in years.

Tonight, for instance.

Ricky hated it when she drank, claimed it made her mean. She guessed that it wasn't meanness exactly but a loosening of her tongue, making her more inclined to speak her mind. Regardless, over the course of the marriage, she'd quit drinking alcohol in his presence and eventually altogether, and her status as a teetotaler had carried over even after she'd moved to Pullman. The fact that she'd imbibed and had three Brandy Old Fashioned Sweets at the restaurant was a radical departure for her. The liquor gave her a warm feeling, both physically and toward Joe, so when he took the bill and paid, she let him, and when he offered to walk her home, she allowed it as well, slipping her hand into the crook of his elbow.

"Tell the truth," Joe said, as they walked down the sidewalk. "Are you a little drunk, Miss Kathleen? I ask because it's starting to look like we're dating, and I know how you feel about that."

She didn't answer but laughed. He really was very charming. She was starting to forget about their age difference and her fear of men and relationships in general. Joe didn't have any of the annoying attributes she associated with men in their early twenties. No stories of partying, no bragging, no trying to impress her with his strength or cleverness. He was just Joe. Smart, funny, kind. The friendship between them had come quickly and was uncomplicated.

She finally answered, "No, we're not dating, but if I *was* open to dating, it would start with you."

"And hopefully end with me as well."

She found herself laughing again, giggling as they passed dark houses, the streetlights illuminating the way. Maybe she *was* a little drunk. A little punchy anyway. Three drinks weren't much, but she hadn't had anything alcoholic in a long time. Certainly, her tolerance wasn't what it used to be.

He made her laugh all the way home, assigning names to garden gnomes in one family's front yard and doing riffs on the street names they passed. "Why is it called Park Place when there's no park and it's not much of a place?" he asked.

"I have no idea," she admitted.

"If it were up to me, it would be called Street Street. Far more accurate."

She hung on to his arm, along for the ride, having such a delightful time that turning the corner to her street felt like a letdown, the end of the evening. "Thank you for walking me home," she said. "I—" She stopped, noticing her house all lit up like a beacon. It appeared as if every light in the place was on, as well as the porch light in front.

"What's wrong?"

"My house," she said, pointing. "The lights are all on. I never leave them on." A sense of dread came over her. Someone had been in her house while she was gone, and might still be there.

"Okay, let's think this through," Joe said calmly. "You're sure you couldn't have left them on by mistake? It was daylight when you left for work. Maybe they were on, but you didn't realize it?"

"No." She shook her head. "I'm really careful about not leaving lights on, and I always double-check before I leave. I'm a little compulsive about it, actually. I wouldn't just forget. I never have before."

"So you didn't leave them on." Joe's voice was a balm for the knot in her stomach. "Does anyone else have the key? Maybe a neighbor who stopped in to drop off tomatoes from their garden or something?"

"The only spare key I have is at work hidden in my desk. No one else knows about it." She gripped Joe's arm more tightly.

He said, "Why don't you wait here, and I'll go take a look?"

"No!" she said frantically, not even caring if she sounded childish. "I don't want to be alone out here. And what if you get attacked inside, and I'm out here and can't help you? Don't leave me."

"I won't leave you," Joe said, and she almost fell to her knees on the sidewalk in gratitude. He made a suggestion: "Let's just walk around the outside of the house together. We can check the windows and doors to see if anyone broke in."

"And then we'll call the police?"

"We'll do whatever it is you want to do."

The front door looked the same as always, as did the side of the house next to the driveway. When they got to the back door, they saw that one of the panes of glass in the door had been broken, making it easy for someone to reach in and unlock the door. Pieces of broken glass were on the stoop, but the door was closed shut.

"There's our answer," Joe said. "I'm sorry, Kathleen, but it looks like you've had a break-in, and it's possible whoever did it might still be there. Let me go in and check it out."

"No, no, don't go in. Let's call the police." She was breathless and afraid, clutching his arm tightly, holding him in place.

"Okay, don't panic. We'll do whatever you want."

"Just don't leave me."

"I'm not going anywhere until we know it's safe. How about this? We can walk back to the main street and use a pay phone, or else we can wake up one of your neighbors and ask them to call the police."

"Miss Whitt next door. She was a friend of my aunt Edna's."

They knocked on Miss Whitt's door. After a long wait, the older woman answered in her housecoat, her hair in curlers. Initially Miss Whitt was confused, but once Kathleen explained what had happened, she was accommodating, going back inside to make the phone call for them.

Two officers, both middle-aged men, came fairly quickly. They asked Kathleen a series of questions before going into the house. Joe and Kathleen waited on the driveway.

When the officers came back out, Kathleen let out a sigh of relief. "What did you find?"

"We went through the whole house from the basement to the attic. Checked every cabinet and closet too. Whoever it was is gone," Officer

Rank said. "Besides the broken window, nothing looks disturbed, but only you can tell us if anything is missing, Miss Dinsmore."

The officers suggested that they all go inside, and so Kathleen followed them, staying close to Joe's side. The buzz of the alcohol was long gone, and now she had a sick feeling from the violation of someone having been in her home.

They walked through each room, with Kathleen doing a quick check to see if anything was moved or missing, but it was all just as she'd left it that morning. Her jewelry, Aunt Edna's silver candlesticks, and other antiques—nothing of value had been touched.

"Why would someone break in and not take anything?" Joe wondered aloud.

Officer Rank said, "It could have been kids on a dare. Or someone who was going to rob you but was spooked and left."

"Spooked?"

"We've seen it happen," his partner said. "Maybe they heard a dog barking outside or a car go past."

"Have you seen it happen where every light in the house is on?" Joe asked. "That seems odd to me."

"No, that's a new one," the officer admitted. "It almost seems like someone is trying to scare you. Miss Dinsmore, has anyone given you trouble lately? Threatened you in any way?"

"No trouble, no threats," she said. "Everyone in Pullman has been very welcoming."

"Any disgruntled customers at the store? Any old boyfriends with a grudge?"

"No. I mean, my ex-husband had a terrible temper, but I haven't seen or talked to him in over a year. And he lives hundreds of miles away and doesn't know where I am."

The officer frowned. "Is there some way he could find you? Is your phone number unlisted?"

"It's still listed under Aunt Edna's name in the phone book. I didn't have the post office forward my mail or anything. The only ones who know I moved here are my parents, and they know not to tell anyone."

Officer Rank said, "It sounds like it's not likely to be him, but we'll keep an eye out anyway. Can you give me a description of your ex and the kind of car he's most likely driving?"

Kathleen filled him in, and Joe's eyebrows rose when she mentioned Ricky's massive size—six foot four and built like a football player. Was he jealous or just surprised that a woman as petite as she would wind up marrying such a large man? Well, it didn't make a difference. She wasn't dating Joe, and even if she were, or did so in the future, it was unlikely the two men would ever meet.

After the officer left, Joe suggested they cover the broken windowpane with cardboard. She found a box she hadn't yet unpacked. Joe cut out a square, and they secured it with masking tape.

"I can go to the hardware store in the morning and get a piece of glass cut to size and fix it for you," he offered.

"But if that person comes back tonight, they'll still be able to get in," she pointed out, putting the roll of tape on her wrist like a bracelet and nervously twisting it.

"The chances of them coming back are slim," Joe said. "We can put a chair under the knob. That should help."

"There's something else, something I didn't tell Officer Rank because I wasn't sure, and I didn't want to sound paranoid." She took a moment to breathe, noticing how patiently Joe waited for her to finish her thought. "It's about Ricky. I thought I saw him the other day, across from the Pine Cone when you and I were having lunch. Then a truck went by, and the man was gone. Just for a second, it looked just like him."

"That was when you said you thought you saw someone you knew."

"Yeah." She nodded, her gaze dropping to the floor. How was it that Ricky, even just the thought of Ricky, still had power over her?

She'd been so sure she'd moved beyond this. "I mean, it's silly because I'm sure it wasn't him . . ."

There was silence between them, and he finally said, "Why don't I stay for the night? I can sleep on the couch. Would that help?"

"Yes, I would like that." His offer, Kathleen knew, came from the spirit of wanting to be helpful rather than an opportunity to make a move on her. With a start, she realized she trusted Joe. Trusted him more than she had ever trusted Ricky, and she had been married to Ricky. Oh, what a mess she'd made of her life. Thank God her aunt had given her the opportunity for a fresh start.

"Then it's settled."

She gave him a hug. "Thank you, Joe. You're a very good friend."

He shrugged. "It's not a big deal. I'm glad to help."

Curled up on the couch, with his head on a borrowed pillow, a lightweight blanket covering him, Joe was certain he wouldn't be able to sleep, which was good. If the intruder came back, Ricky or whoever, he wanted to be prepared to jump him. He was irate on Kathleen's behalf. How dare someone shake her sense of safety and the sanctity of her home? Was it someone who knew she lived alone? He thought about installing dead bolts the next day when he was repairing the glass. He'd have to get her permission to do so first, but she would probably think it was a good idea.

When sleep finally came, he fought against it, but it was beyond his control. His eyelids grew heavy, and although he struggled, his breathing slowed, and he sank further and further until he was deep in sleep and having a dream.

One of those dreams.

When he was awake, he referred to this one as the Death Dream, the most troubling, awful dream of them all. Joe was no longer Joe but had become the mystery man, helping the woman, the piano woman, out of a rowboat and onto dry land. It was nighttime, and the moon hung low in the sky. He saw the scene through the other man's eyes and noted the slight flare of her skirt, the hem of which fell so low, he could see only a flash of ankle covered by a stocking. Despite the fact that she was more modestly attired than women in 1983, Joe could tell the man thought she was a knockout, absolutely gorgeous, the most beautiful woman in the world. He loved her.

The man said something, and she turned her head and smiled at him, both of them giddy at getting a chance to be alone. The anticipation the man felt was palpable. There was something he wanted to tell her, something that would be life-changing.

Joe couldn't get a good look at her face, just an impression. Her light-brown hair was styled in a more formal way than he'd seen in the Piano Dream.

The dream continued. Joe was carried away by the next sequence of events, an unwilling passenger on a train that went off course in a horrible way each and every time. The man led the woman farther away from the water, and they kissed passionately. This part always made Joe a little sad. Although he was no stranger to intimacy with past girlfriends, he'd never been flooded with unmitigated joy the way this man was. The couple whispered to each other things Joe couldn't quite make out, although he knew they were words of endearment.

Through a blur, Joe sensed that the two had been interrupted by another man. He clearly heard the other man's angry voice saying, "What the hell do you think you're doing? I know what you are."

I know what you are.

Those words struck home with the man, and a negative feeling washed over him. Shame? Regret? Joe could never quite identify the feeling because the emotion was fleeting and overshadowed by what happened next. The angry man pulled out a gun and waved it in the air. The two men exchanged words Joe couldn't quite make out, and the situation escalated, with the angry man pointing the gun straight at him.

In the blink of an eye, the man's sweetheart, the love of his life, stepped in front of him, and the gun went off, a boom accompanied by a flash of light in the dark.

The woman, the most beautiful woman in the world, fell back against him, and he caught her, both of them falling to the ground. He cradled her in his arms while a pool of blood on the front of her dress widened and spread. She whispered something, and he cried out, "No, no!" His voice caught in his throat, and he began to sob.

When Joe awoke from this dream, he was always heartbroken and crying, his pillow damp with tears. This time was different only because for the first time, right at the end of the dream, he was finally able to see the woman's face.

It was Kathleen.

CHAPTER FORTY-ONE

1916

Dearest John,

Your news about the Barn Dance made me smile, and I haven't stopped smiling since. I am remaking one of my mother's dresses for the occasion and might even wear one of her brooches. It is not the fanciest affair, but those attending do usually wear their Sunday best.

You may not know this, but the Barn Dance has been a Pullman tradition since my father was a little boy. He and my mother went when they were courting, and so did most of the married couples in this town. I am so happy that my father is allowing us to go together. To have a whole evening to ourselves, away from the prying eyes and ears of the younger Bennett girls, is a gift. Time spent with you this way is something I've been dreaming of.

John, you said there should be no secrets between us, so I am also going to share something with you.

Edna told me something in strictest confidence and said I could confide in you as well. It has happened that she has fallen in love with Howie, and now her heart is a little broken because Howie seems more interested in Pearl. Pearl, of course, does not see Howie as a suitor. Howie is accompanying Edna to the dance only because Mrs. Donohue does not care for Pearl and encouraged him to ask Edna.

Might I ask a favor of you? If you speak to Howie, man-to-man, could you put in a good word for Edna? She is my dearest friend and truly a fine young woman. She has a giving spirit and is as good as the day is long. Howie does not realize this, but he would be fortunate to have her affections. I cannot help but feel that Howie is being influenced by outward appearances and as a result is missing out on what really matters.

I am counting down the minutes until I see you again.

Yours forever,

Alice

CHAPTER FORTY-TWO

1983

Late the next morning, Joe walked into Secondhand Heaven, keys in hand. He'd spent the morning fixing the broken window and installing dead bolts on both the front and back doors at Kathleen's house.

From behind the register, she smiled when he slid the keys across the counter. "Your house is now officially secure," he said. "I've changed the locks, fixed the glass, and added dead bolts to both entrances. I also took the liberty of buying you a very large, very mean dog named Junker. If he doesn't let you into the house, I'm sorry, but you're just going to have to move. It's the only way."

He was glad to see her laugh. Even that morning as they drank coffee at her kitchen table, she seemed worried about the intruder returning, darting glances at the taped cardboard. In the light of day, it looked even less effective as a barrier than it had the night before. A paltry defense, good only against insects.

"I can't thank you enough, Joe." She picked up the keys and slipped them in her pocket, then opened the cash register. "How much do I owe you?"

He waved her money aside with a shake of his head. "No charge. Just one of the many fine benefits of my friendship."

From across the way came Marcia's audible scoff. They followed the sound to see her, feather duster in hand, no longer dusting but watching their exchange. "Heard you spent the night over at Kathleen's," she said with a knowing grin.

"On the couch," Joe said. "Solely as a precaution in case the criminal returned."

She turned back to her dusting, but they both heard what she muttered under her breath. "That's how it starts."

Kathleen turned back to Joe. "How about I buy you lunch as a thank-you?"

"Sure. Our usual?"

"Our usual," Marcia echoed, lightly mocking, her back to them.

Kathleen asked, "Can you handle things here while I go out to lunch, Marcia?"

Marcia looked around the completely empty store. "I think I can handle it. You two go off and have fun doing whatever it is you do that's not dating." She winked broadly.

Kathleen grabbed her purse, and they headed out the door together. Joe asked, "What's with Marcia and the winking?"

"You caught that, huh?"

"It would be hard to miss."

"She's convinced there's something going on between us." Kathleen gestured back and forth between them. "Between you and me, I mean."

"Well, there is, right? A crazy sexual attraction that neither of us is acting on because we have such high moral standards?" He held up a palm. "At least, that's how I see it. I've been holding strong, but I can tell you're slipping, Kathleen. Honestly, I'm not sure how long I'll be able to fend you off. I'm trying my best, but I'll be the first to admit, I'm not a saint."

She laughed. "Believe me, I never thought you were."

When they arrived at the Pine Cone, the booths were full, so the hostess seated them at a table. When Doris came to take their order, Joe said, "Doris, you look particularly beautiful today."

Doris wasn't buying it. "What'll you have?" she asked sternly, pen poised above her pad.

Acknowledging defeat, Joe gestured to Kathleen, who ordered her usual BLT. He followed, saying he'd take a Reuben sandwich. After Doris walked away, Kathleen said, "Still thinking you can make her smile?"

"Oh, it's going to happen," he said. "No doubt about that. Right now I'm just ruling out everything that doesn't work. I know now that she won't smile for baseless flattery, lame jokes, grade-school magic tricks, or an outright request for a smile. This is all important information."

"Have you tried sticking straws in your nose walrus-style?"

"No, I haven't. Do you think that would work?" Joe held his straw between two fingers, considering the idea.

"No. I just wondered how far you'd go."

"Please, Kathleen. Let me have my dignity."

Just as their sandwiches were being delivered, the outside door swung open, and in walked Joe's grandmother, her walker leading the way. Behind her, her friend Howard held the door, his cane holding him steady. Joe glanced up and said to Kathleen, "It's my grandmother. You'll finally get a chance to meet her."

He stood and waved them over. Over the last few weeks, Joe had gotten to see Pearl's softer side. He'd realized that so much of her bluster was a cover for fear. She was afraid that Howard was the only one at Pine Ridge Hollow who liked her. She mourned the lost years with her son. She was terrified of dying, both the pain of it and the lack of knowing what was on the other side. Joe was aware that her life had not gone as she'd wanted and that much of it was her own fault, but that was behind her. He tried to help, sharing his thoughts on the afterlife and heaven, and although she didn't look entirely convinced, she'd murmured, "I hope you're right, Joe."

It seemed to take forever for them to get to the table. When they did, Howard solicitously pulled out a chair for Pearl, then folded up her walker and leaned it against an adjacent wall before taking a seat himself. Joe did the introductions, and Kathleen explained that she and Howard had already met. "Mr. Donohue came to visit my aunt when she was in hospice," she explained. "You were old friends, right?"

He nodded. "I knew Edna back when we were all younger than the two of you. Back before she had the store, even. She used to do upholstery and seamstress work out of her home while she took care of her mother, who'd suffered a stroke. Apoplexy is what they called it back then. She was quite a gal, your aunt."

"Yes, she was," Kathleen said, and went on to explain how she hadn't expected to inherit Edna's entire estate. "I really didn't know her very well until the end of her life, but when my mother and I came up here to help, we just hit it off. She was a dear; even when she was in pain, she always had a kind word for everyone. All the nurses loved her. Aunt Edna was one of a kind, as good as the day is long."

Pearl, who'd seemed engrossed in the menu, perked up. "Did you say 'as good as the day is long'?"

"I guess I did."

"That's an odd phrase for a young person to use. I haven't heard that in a long time." Pearl's brows knit together.

Kathleen gave an apologetic shrug. "It's not something I usually say. I must have picked it up somewhere."

"Probably from working around all the antiques," Joe suggested. "You're absorbing things from yesteryear. Pretty soon you'll be talking about darning socks and churning butter."

Doris paused at the table, long enough for Pearl and Howard to give her their orders, and then she was gone again. Joe brought up the break-in at Kathleen's house the night before, telling them that nothing was taken.

"I bet it was teenagers," Howard said.

Pearl nodded in agreement. "Looking for money for drugs. That's what kids these days are after."

Kathleen changed the subject. "Mr. Donohue, Mrs. Arneson, as long as both of you are here, can I ask you some questions about the history of Pullman? Specifically, the movie theater?"

"The Victory, right here in town?" Howard asked.

"That's the one. Do you remember if they once showed silent films?"

His head bobbed up and down. "That's all they showed at the start. Charlie Chaplin, Mary Pickford, Douglas Fairbanks. We saw 'em all. I went nearly every week, even if the show hadn't changed from the week before. This was before television. Seeing those picture shows moving on the screen was like magic."

"And did the Victory have someone playing the piano during the movie?"

"Of course. All different ones, people from town," Howard said. He turned to Pearl. "Remember how on Saturday nights when Alice played, all of you Bennett girls would get in for free?" He spoke to Joe. "You should have seen all those sisters sitting in a row in the back, one right next to the other. Pearl the prettiest of them all."

"Oh, Howard," Pearl said, looking pleased. "They don't want to hear about that. It was a long time ago."

"So your sister Alice used to play the piano during the movies?" Joe asked.

"Just on Saturdays," Howard said. "Women didn't usually work outside the home back then, but her father allowed Alice to do it because he was friends with Floyd, the owner of the theater. Right, Pearl?"

Pearl nodded.

"Oh, Alice could play piano like nobody else. I can still see her on that piano bench, her back straight, arms out, graceful as can be, her fingers flying back and forth. She was really something." His eyes lit up at the memory.

Kathleen spoke softly. "What happened to Alice? My aunt said there was some kind of accident, and she died young?"

Pearl and Howard exchanged an uneasy glance before Howard said, "It was tragic, and it's hard to speak of it even now, but we lost Alice when she was only nineteen."

"What happened?" Joe asked.

"A freak accident. A gun went off, and she was shot. Just at the wrong place at the wrong time."

"How awful," Kathleen said. "I'm so sorry."

Howard continued. "It happened the night of the Barn Dance. I saw her at the dance, laughing and dancing, and then later heard she was gone. Her funeral was the saddest thing I ever saw in this town. She was so young."

"The Barn Dance?" Kathleen said. "Like the one they're having next week? Is it the same thing?"

Howard nodded. "It's a Pullman tradition, held on the same weekend every year. I haven't gone since Alice died, so I don't know if it's like it used to be, but it's held in the same barn. They charge admission. There's a band, and they serve refreshments."

"I don't want to talk about this anymore," Pearl said abruptly. "I'm going to the bathroom." She reached for her walker, fumbled it open, and made her way down the aisle.

Kathleen leaned across the table. "I'm sorry to have brought it up."

Howard said, "You didn't know. How could you have? She's sensitive about the subject. She and Alice were only a year apart. They weren't two peas in a pod, that's for sure, but they were very close. They'd already lost their mother a few years before, and then when Alice died, it just crushed the whole family." He looked around to make sure he couldn't be heard and then spoke conspiratorially. "Pearl was there when it happened. She's never gotten over it."

Kathleen said, "I won't mention it again, then. I do have another question for you, though, and it's about the piano playing at the movies."

"Yes?"

From across the restaurant, there came a burst of laughter from a group of young women sitting in a booth by the front door. Kathleen had noticed them when they'd walked in and recognized them as tellers from the local bank. She said, "When Alice was playing the piano, was there ever a disruption that made her stop playing?"

"A disruption?" he asked. "There was a power outage once during a storm. The whole place went dark, and everyone panicked. Almost caused a stampede."

"No, I'm talking about something different," Kathleen said. "A disruption like someone causing a scene, or a man sitting next to Alice when she was playing, and someone else, another guy, an angry man, coming along and knocking him off the bench?"

Howard's face scrunched up, and he looked past her as if trying to recall. "Something like that did happen, now that you mention it. It didn't stop the movie for very long, though. The owner made them take their fight outside, and the whole thing was over lickety-split." He gave her an intense look. "I haven't thought of that in years. Did Edna tell you that story?"

Before Kathleen could answer, Joe jumped in to ask, "What was the name of the man sitting on the piano bench next to Alice, the one who got knocked to the floor?" He had both hands flat on the table, as if trying to keep himself grounded.

"Why, that was John Lawrence. New guy who came to town to work at the mill that summer."

The door to the bathroom slammed open, and Pearl came trudging back, faster than Kathleen would have thought possible, given her age and the walker. "Howard, we have to go," she called out from eight feet away. "I don't feel well. My stomach's upset."

CHAPTER FORTY-THREE

1916

Pearl walked into Trapp's General Store with Alice's list clutched in her hand and her younger sister Emma on her heels. Flour, sugar, salt, and other foodstuffs were written neatly on the piece of paper going from top to bottom. Pearl had no interest in baking or cooking, but she had a definite interest in leaving the house and going to town, and so she, along with Emma, had volunteered for this errand. Pearl was glad to have Emma come along. At eleven, she was old enough to be helpful in carrying the bags and young enough to see Pearl as an authority figure. Of all her younger sisters, Emma was the one most likely to agree to wander aimlessly through the town, window-shopping at other stores and looking over hair ribbons and fabric at the dry goods store. She would also be agreeable to making stops along the way home if the notion struck them. Furthermore, she could be trusted to keep her mouth shut about such things.

Helen would have balked at the idea of straying from an assigned task. She was way too serious-minded, thinking it frivolous to look at things they couldn't afford. The twins weren't a good choice either, as they never wanted to be separated. Too, the twins were apt to tell Alice of how they'd intentionally dawdled. Not that Alice would get angry or do anything exactly, unless one counted her wide-eyed look of disappointment upon their return.

That morning, as they'd left in the wagon with their father and John, Alice had called out to them, "Come right home afterward. I want to start baking the bread right away."

"Goodbye, Alice!" Emma had called out.

Pearl held up the list. "I'll make sure to get everything you want," she added. Neither one promised to return home immediately, she'd thought with a small grin.

Now at Trapp's General Store, Emma wandered off to look at the jars of candy while Pearl went straight to the front counter. "Good morning, Mrs. Trapp," she said, pushing the list toward her. "Alice has sent me for supplies."

Mrs. Trapp inspected Pearl over her glasses. "Good morning. And how is Alice these days? She almost never comes into the store anymore. I can only guess she's very busy taking care of your large family." This was the kind of conversation Pearl had no patience for: the inquiries of the health of family members, chitchat about the weather, and if the family planned to attend church functions. And why was Alice so often the focus of these tedious questions? It wasn't as if she could be doing anything of interest. She cleaned the house, made the food, read the paper, and darned the socks, as well as doing countless other tedious chores. All while singing joyfully, as if she was oblivious to the fact that she was stuck in the middle of nowhere doing thankless work.

But Pearl knew enough to respond in a polite way. "Alice is fine, thank you. She sends her regards and hopes you and your family are well." From there, Mrs. Trapp went down the line, asking about her father and the rest of her sisters. Pearl assured her all was fine with the Bennett family.

When Mrs. Trapp left with the list, heading to the back room to fill their order, Pearl tapped her fingers on the counter. Once they had the grocery order fulfilled and in the wagon, they'd be free to walk along the storefronts of Merchants' Row. If they didn't linger too long, their father wouldn't get word of their digressions, and Alice would be none the wiser.

She'd been mentally planning their next course of action when the door swung open and Frank walked in, dressed in work clothes. She hadn't imagined running into him during this outing, as his mother usually did the shopping. "Why, Frank!" she said, giving him her widest smile. "What a pleasant surprise. Are you doing the shopping today?"

He strode quickly to her side, then took her elbow and pulled her away from the counter, leaning in to whisper, "I saw you through the window and came in to speak with you."

Pearl glanced over at Emma, who was daydreaming over maple hard candy and peppermint sticks. Mrs. Trapp was still in the back, out of earshot. "You wanted to talk to me?" Her first thought was that Frank, having been spurned by Alice, now had his sights set on her. This was not entirely a bad thing. Frank's family had money, and Frank had shown himself to be a serious and generous beau. Alice hadn't even acknowledged him as a suitor and he'd left her gifts of flowers and, knowing of her love of knitting, skeins of soft yarn in sky blue, her favorite color. She'd returned all the gifts, and in response he'd written her poetry, begging her to reconsider. Frank might be fun for a short while, even if he was Alice's castoff.

"Yes," Frank said, keeping his voice low. "It's about John Lawrence. He's not who he says he is. His real name is John Lawrence Robinson."

Pearl didn't really see the distinction. "So he doesn't use his last name?"

"No, and this is why he hides behind a different name . . ." Frank leaned in so close, she could smell coffee on his breath. "His father is a murderer—killed a man in cold blood. He's in prison for life and will never get out. Everyone in Gladly Falls knows about it."

"No!" Her hand flew to her mouth. *How scandalous!* Pearl didn't know of anyone who'd committed a major crime, and killing someone was the worst of all. "His father is a murderer? Are you sure?"

Frank nodded. "I got a letter from my uncle who lives there. I wrote him and asked what he knew about John Lawrence, and when he wrote back, boy, did I find out a lot of dirt. John's father killed a man when he was just a baby, and ever since, John and his mother have been working as servants. And here he's acting all high and mighty, like he's better than me."

"I just can't believe it." Pearl wondered if her father knew. Would he have hired him if he did? Maybe. Her father didn't believe in casting judgment, and John wasn't guilty of murder just because his father had killed someone. Her father was always willing to give people a chance.

"It gets worse," Frank said, his face clouding. "John is a damn Negro."

"No."

"Yes, he is. My uncle said so. If I see him go anywhere near Alice, I'm going to beat him so hard, he won't be able to walk. I can't believe he's been passing himself off as one of us. The nerve!"

"That can't be true," protested Pearl. "His skin is as light as yours or mine."

"Sometimes they come out that way. It was his father's granddad who was a darkie, and you know what they say. No matter what you do, that stain never comes out."

"That's just talk," Pearl said. "People say things all the time. That doesn't mean it's true. Someone probably just made the whole thing up." She knew herself how stories grew from the smallest of things. How many times had it been gossiped that she was a bit loose with the boys when she hadn't done much of anything yet?

"No." He squeezed her elbow. "It's true, and I'll prove it. Let's go to the mill right now and ask him. I'll ask him right to his face and make him tell the truth. He's going to have to confess, and once that gets out, your father will send him on his way. We don't want that kind of garbage in our town."

Pearl shook her head. "No, don't do it now." The timing was all wrong. John was supposed to drive her and Alice to the Barn Dance, something she was looking forward to. For the first time, they'd be at a social event unaccompanied by their father. She'd heard, of course, that Mrs. Donohue would be keeping an eye on them, which was perfect, because Mrs. Donohue didn't have the best eyesight. Even more than that, most of her attention would be on her own son, Howie. It would be easy enough to slip away from her watchful eye, almost as if they weren't chaperoned at all. If Frank ran John out of town now, it would ruin everything. "Do it at the Barn Dance in front of Alice. That's the only way she'll believe it."

"That's days away," Frank said with a frown. "What if he gets his paws on Alice before then? The idea makes me sick."

"Oh, Frank," Pearl said, her tone matter-of-fact and reassuring. "You know how Alice is. She can't help herself. She's such a lady. She's not about to do a single thing with any man unless she's engaged, and you know that's not going to happen. My father would never allow it. Alice will be fine until the Barn Dance. You have my word."

"I'm not sure I can wait."

Pearl was good at making men wait. "You can and you will, Frank." She leaned in close and gestured for him to lower his face to hers. When he did, she brushed her lips against his cheek and softly said, "I promise I will keep Alice away from John, and you need to promise me that you'll wait. It will make a better impression if you do it in front of the crowd at the Barn Dance. Doing it now at the mill, you'll only have old men as witnesses."

He hesitated, and she added an enticement. "It will be more of a scene if you bring your revolver and wave it at him. You can run him out of town." She knew Frank was proud of the .44 Colt that had once belonged to his grandfather.

"I can do a lot more than wave it at him. I'm a crack shot. Best of anyone around here."

"I know that," she said soothingly. "But it will hardly be necessary. Everyone knows you *could* do it. The sight of the gun alone will cause a stir."

Frank gazed down at her as if seeing her for the first time. He sighed. "If you think it's best, Pearl, we'll do it your way."

"I think it's best to wait until the Barn Dance. Do you promise to wait?"

"I promise," he said. "But it's not going to be easy."

"I know," Pearl said. "But do it for me, Frank." She ran a hand over his shirtsleeve and felt the muscles of his arm loosen under her touch. He would wait. They always did.

CHAPTER FORTY-FOUR

1983

That night, lying in bed on the second floor of his grandmother's house, Joe had a lot to think about. Sleep wasn't going to come anytime soon, not with the way the wind whipped outside, howling like some kind of beastly ghost. This was the kind of weather that had spooked Linda when she was little, but it had never scared Joe, not even when he was a kid. Tonight, his biggest concern was the noise level keeping him awake and the fear that he'd lose power. It was bad enough without air-conditioning, but not having the fan would make it even worse.

He and Kathleen had stayed at their table at the Pine Cone and talked long after Pearl and Howard had bolted from the restaurant. Kathleen felt terrible for having asked about Alice. "I should have known that talking about her sister's death would be upsetting," she said. "It's been so long that I thought it would be okay, but from her reaction . . ." She sighed. "I guess you never really get over losing someone so close to you."

"You didn't mean to upset her," Joe reassured her. "And who knows? Maybe her stomach was just upset. I wouldn't worry about it."

"Easy for you to say," she said. "I just hate knowing when I've caused someone else pain. I'll probably lie in bed all night replaying the conversation and wishing I hadn't brought it up at all."

"And I'll be thinking about it, glad you brought it up," Joe added. "Because now we have a name for my mystery man. John Lawrence. And the woman at the piano bench had to be Alice Bennett. Weird that my dreams are of someone I'm related to."

Doris came and delivered their pies, setting a fork next to each plate. Kathleen broke from the conversation to look up. "Thanks, Doris. This looks delicious."

As usual, Doris had walked away from the table before the compliment was complete. The woman was nothing if not efficient.

She dug her fork into her slice of pie. "There has to be an explanation. You probably heard family stories about Alice at some point in time. Even though you don't remember, maybe you overheard a relative talk about her when you were a small child? People internalize things without even realizing it." She gave him a look up and down. "I took psychology in college and remember a thing or two."

"Maybe," Joe said dubiously. "But the dreams are so vivid. It's like I'm there, experiencing it. Where would that much detail come from?"

"I don't know," she admitted.

They continued eating their pie in silence, while all around them conversations abounded. From the kitchen, they heard a bell ring and a man's voice call out, "Food's up for table six."

"It's not just my imagination," Joe said after a moment.

"Clearly not just your imagination. You dreamed things that actually happened, kind of like being psychic in reverse. Maybe . . ." Here, she looked thoughtful. "Maybe it's true what some say about all the experiences of our ancestors being wired into us. Our predisposition toward certain foods, our temperaments, our metabolisms—some people believe that all that stuff is inherited. It's not that far-fetched that our psyches would be stamped with the experiences of the ones who came before us, is it?"

"I guess not," he said. That idea, along with the realization that the events in his dreams were real, made him feel better. The dreams didn't come from his mother's death or a mental illness. There was nothing wrong with him. He was just replaying events from the past over and over again at night in his dreams. But why? That was the real question. Alice's death was terrible, but it had happened long ago. It's not like he could prevent it, and he couldn't heal his grandmother's pain.

"Maybe all of us unknowingly carry those kinds of memories, and you, for some reason, are just unconsciously replaying them."

He suddenly remembered how the dream had been altered the night he spent on Kathleen's couch. "That's a good theory," he said, "except that I had the Death Dream again this morning at your house, and for the first time, it changed. This time, it ended differently."

"Oh?" She waited.

"This time, when I was holding the dying woman in my arms, heartbroken, I could finally see her face."

"Yes?"

"And it was you."

She studied his face, checking for signs he was kidding. Seeing none, she said, "Joe, you're giving me the chills."

"Yeah. I know. I'm sorry. It's weird. I'm not sure what to make of it." He took a sip of his water.

"Why didn't you tell me this before?"

"I don't know. It was odd waking up at your place, and then you were getting ready for work and it felt awkward, so I just left. Also, I had to let it sink in, think about what it could mean that I saw your face in this sad, sad dream."

"And what do you think it means?"

"That I'd be heartbroken if you died?"

"Oh, that's so nice." Her smile was dazzling.

"I'm not being nice. That's really how I feel." As she sat across the table from him, all he could see was how extraordinary she was. She was so stunningly attractive, so clever, so kindhearted that he didn't know why everyone in the restaurant wasn't looking at her. Instead, they were dipping their fries in ketchup and talking about the weather. It was as if there was a movie star in their midst and all of them were unaware, while he, on the other hand, couldn't keep his eyes off her.

He'd memorized all her gestures and mannerisms. How she stopped midsentence to thank the restaurant staff, whether it was the hostess seating them or a busboy clearing away plates or Doris taking their order. The way she tried to hold back from laughing until it came out in one delightful burst. And that laugh? It was like a melody. He would do the most ridiculous things just to hear it. He was shameless, really, the way he went out of his way to get her to smile. When that happened, her joy reflected back at him, and over time he longed for more. Luckily, she gave freely of her happiness.

"Well, hopefully, I won't die," she said finally. "At least, not anytime soon."

"I wouldn't let that happen," he'd assured her.

That night, with the storm raging outside, Joe wondered if she was awake at that moment as well. When the rumble of thunder came, he decided that no one could be sleeping through this. He got out of bed and pulled the curtain back to look out. It was dark, far darker than it would be at Kathleen's house, where the streetlights lit the way. When flashes of lightning lit up the sky, he could clearly see, for a split second, the trees whipping in the wind. There would be limbs down in the morning, no doubt about that. He could add yard cleanup to his list of things to do. The thunder came in surges, building and ebbing as the rain came down in sheets. He felt sorry for anyone out in this weather. Even driving would be a challenge. A person would definitely need to have their windshield wipers on high.

He pulled the curtains aside and dragged a chair to the window, positioning himself to watch the storm's light show. This was one of those times it would be nice to have someone there with him to share the experience. The rain softened to a gentle patter, and in the distance, he could now see rolling waves on the surface of the lake.

Lightning flashed lower in the sky and then zigzagged downward, striking a tree. Crack! Joe's jaw dropped as the top half of the tree broke off, and limbs flew in every direction, like a bomb had detonated.

He leaned forward, peering downward, thinking the lightning strike might have started a fire, but there was no sign of flames. Still, he mused, it could be smoldering unseen. Unlikely, but did he really want to take a chance? He exhaled in frustration; he wouldn't be able to fall back asleep until he checked.

He pulled on his jeans and a T-shirt, knowing they'd be soaked by the time he returned. At the bottom of the stairs were some work boots, an ancient pair he'd found in the barn and had used a few times already. He slid his feet into the boots, grabbed a flashlight, and went out to inspect the damage.

He went into the cluster of trees, moving instinctively until he came to where the lightning had struck. Just as he'd seen from the window, the branches and limbs of the tree were scattered in every direction. Walking around the tree trunk, he saw that it had broken off at shoulder level. From the scorch marks, it looked as if the lightning had hit the trunk on one side. The rain fell steadily, and he walked around the tree, shining a beam of light from every angle, glad that he wasn't seeing any burning embers. He had the rain to thank for that, he guessed. The tree looked half-dead, the wood too damp to burn. Tomorrow, he'd gather up the mess and saw down the remaining part of the tree.

Satisfied that there was no fire hazard, Joe had turned away from the tree to go back to the house when the toe of his boot hit something. He swung the light beam and landed on a section of the tree trunk with a hollow in its center. Nestled in the hollow was something rectangular. He leaned over to get a closer look and discovered a container the size of a small shoebox. He bent over and picked it up, jogging to the porch to get a closer look out of the rain.

Once he was under the overhang, he noticed that although the exterior of the box was rimmed with rust along the edges, it was intact. He put the flashlight under his arm and tried to open it but found it locked tight. Aiming the light at the latch, he spotted an opening designed for a key. So it was locked, but it wasn't Fort Knox. Nothing that a crowbar couldn't pop open.

Then he remembered the dream he'd named the Owl Dream. In the dream, he was the one who'd put the metal box in the hollow of the tree. It was both a dream and a memory. He'd put the box in that spot decades ago, before he, Joe, was even born, and there it had sat until just now. The idea boggled his mind.

He was halfway to the house when he remembered the key Kathleen had found in the hope chest.

CHAPTER FORTY-FIVE

1983

Kathleen had just shut off her alarm clock and gotten out of bed when the phone rang. She ran down the stairs two at a time and plucked the phone out of its receiver. "Hello?" She clutched it to her ear and tried to catch her breath.

"Kathleen, it's Joe. It's not too early to call, is it?"

"No, it's fine. I was awake."

"Good."

"Is something wrong?" She rubbed the sleep out of her eyes and stifled a yawn. She was usually staggering into the kitchen to make coffee at this hour. The store didn't open until later on Saturdays, but she liked to get an early start at home.

"No, nothing's wrong. I just wondered if you still have the key you found in Alice's hope chest. I found a locked metal box that I'm thinking might be a fit."

Kathleen perked up at hearing this. "Really?"

"Yes, really." The grin in Joe's voice came over the telephone line. "If I'm wrong, I can always pry it open, but I wanted to try the key first."

She leaned against the wall. "Where did you find this box?"

"That's the really interesting part. It was inside the hollow of a tree that got struck by lightning last night. I went out to check on the damage, and it was right there, waiting for me."

"Inside the hollow of the tree? Like in your dream?"

"Yeah. This is all pretty weird, right?"

"Incredible."

"It was just there. If it wasn't for the storm, it would still be there."

"I can't wait to see what's in it."

"Should I meet you at the store, or come to your house?"

"I'll come to you," she said.

When Kathleen pulled into the driveway, she was relieved to see Joe sitting in one of a pair of rocking chairs on the covered porch, waiting for her, the box in his lap. Walking up to join him, she held the key aloft. "Brought it."

"Knew you would." He put the box on the table between the chairs, stood, and extended a hand. "Be careful of the steps. They're slippery from the rain."

Somehow, Kathleen knew it wasn't that slippery. He was using it as an excuse to take her hand, which was fine with her. She took a seat in the other rocking chair and set the key down on the table. "Let me look at this box for a minute." She held it and examined it closely from every angle. "I don't think the box itself is anything out of the ordinary. Just a standard metal lockbox." She turned the key in the lock. "It's definitely a fit." Twisting, she heard a slight click and then pried open the lid. She pulled out a piece of wrapped leather, held together with a cord. She removed the cord and opened it up to see what was inside.

"What is it?" he asked.

"A lot of different things." One by one, she pulled out the items and placed them on the table. Two brooches, a wedding band, an engagement ring, a book, a seashell, a ceramic frog, and a bundle wrapped in cloth and tied with a ribbon. "Someone's treasures." She examined the rings with interest. They needed a good cleaning, but otherwise, they were in perfect shape. Not that she'd advise Joe to sell them. Obviously, they'd belonged to someone in the family and as such were heirlooms.

She removed the ribbon and unwrapped the cloth to reveal a stack of yellowed paper. Setting the ribbon and fabric aside, she unfolded it. Her brow furrowed as she studied the pages.

"What is it?"

Kathleen glanced up at Joe. "This is probably the most exciting thing you've come across yet, Joe Arneson." She smiled. "This box must have belonged to Alice, and these letters are to Alice from someone named John. It must have been your mystery man, John Lawrence, the one Howard said worked at the mill that summer." She unfolded each one and smoothed them out carefully, keeping them in order.

"But why was it in a tree? Was that a usual hiding place back then?"

"Not that I know of."

With the letters resting on her lap, she said, "The print is faded. Do you have a magnifying glass?"

When Joe returned, glass in hand, he found her already reading.

"I'm sorry. I couldn't help myself." She held the letters up. "Did you want to be the one to read them first?"

"No, you go ahead." He leaned against the railing and watched as Kathleen returned to the letters, this time using the magnifying glass.

She looked up and caught his eye. "Just so you know, in the first letter, John refers to the box being in Alice's secret hiding spot, so I'm guessing that would be the hollow in the tree you mentioned."

"Odd that she kept it outdoors." Joe folded his arms.

"She had six sisters. It was probably safer in a tree than in her room."

Joe nodded. He'd caught Linda snooping through his stuff more than once. He didn't own anything incriminating or valuable, but that wasn't the point. A person deserved a little privacy.

Kathleen kept reading, and Joe kept his eyes on her. She ran a finger above each page, not even touching the paper, just as a guide. After about fifteen minutes, she sighed, putting a hand over her heart, and straightened the pile. She was finished.

Joe waited for her to hand the letters over, but when she didn't, he asked, "So?"

"In the first letter, he talks about being able to write of matters of the heart and says . . ." Her gaze dropped back down to the page, and she began to read. "'I do not know how best to say how important you have become to me. Seeing your beautiful face each day has become my greatest pleasure. Hearing you sing is all the music I will ever need. Your laughter is tonic for my soul. You have a keen intelligence, and I enjoy hearing your opinions after reading the newspaper. I just read what I wrote above, and it all sounds insufficient. None of it quite conveys the sentiment of my heart. I think what I mean to say is that I think I am growing in love with you a little more each day.'"

"Oh, that's nice," Joe said.

"That's *nice*? I think you're understating it by a lot. It's more than nice. It's the most beautiful thing I've ever heard." She shuffled the papers and continued. "He talks about reading her letters over and over again." She looked up. "Later, he tells her that she's his heart and that he wishes they could make their love public but understands why she wants to keep it quiet."

"Why would they need to keep it quiet?"

She shook her head. "I don't know. Maybe her father wouldn't approve?"

Joe nodded.

"He talks about working for her father at the mill, and they mention the war overseas and the weather and various things about their day-to-day life, but the really fascinating part is that toward the end, he confides in her. He tells Alice that he wants to share a secret with her, something his mother cautioned him never to tell anyone." Her voice rose with emotion. "John says his father is in prison for murder and goes on to say that his great-grandfather was a Negro. He says . . ." She rifled through the papers, stopping when she located the right one. "'Could you love a man whose family is such as mine?' John says he'll be in agony awaiting her reply."

Joe leaned in. "So what happened then?"

"In the last letter, John talks about Alice coming to visit him in the barn to reassure him that none of it matters, that she loves him for who he is. And he's so relieved. He loves her back and says there will be no more secrets between them. He says he has good news, that her father has given him permission to escort her to the Barn Dance, and that he will be driving the wagon to take both Alice and her sister Pearl to the dance that night."

He nodded. "So odd to hear my grandmother's name as part of this."

Kathleen looked up at him and nodded, tears slowly running down her cheeks. She wiped them away with the back of her hand. "John says he hopes the news about the dance will make her smile because he is smiling as well. The last letter is signed, 'Yours forever.' He was so happy. You can tell."

Her voice caught in her throat. She set the pages on the table and covered her face with her hands, her shoulders beginning to shake. "I'm sorry, I don't know what's wrong with me. I can't help it," she stammered.

Her crying startled Joe. When she'd first begun to read the letters, she'd seemed merely intrigued. Now she sobbed as if there had been a death in her family. He crouched down beside her chair. "Kathleen, are you okay?"

"No, I'm not okay. I can't help it. I'm just . . . I'm . . . I don't know why, but I feel absolutely devastated. This wave of emotion just came over me. They were so in love, and we know the night of the Barn Dance was her last night, and it's just not fair, is it?" She looked up at him, her eyes brimming with tears.

"No, it's not fair."

"There's nothing we can do to stop it either," she said, sounding a little bitter.

"Because it already happened," Joe said. "Believe me, I've been there." It came back to him—the helpless feeling of holding the dying woman in his arms, the horror at the sight of her blood, frantic in the knowledge she was slipping away from him. All this time, he hadn't known that the man he'd been dreaming about had been John and the woman that he as John had loved was Alice. Attaching names didn't lessen the intensity of the feeling. If anything, it made it more real and more terrible.

"She was so young. She'd barely had a chance to live, and then she died. It's just so tragic."

"I know."

Kathleen got to her feet, and he rose as well. She surprised him by wrapping her arms around his neck and then holding tight. With her head nestled against his shoulder, she said, "I know this sounds crazy, but I feel like Alice wants me to find out the truth of what happened to the two of them."

"I don't think it sounds crazy at all."

"Thank you," she murmured. "Will you help me figure out what happened?"

He brushed the top of her head with his lips. "Of course I will."

CHAPTER FORTY-SIX

1983

After Kathleen left, Joe went to the kitchen to phone his father. He hadn't called home since the night he'd arrived, but his father had called him several times over the last few weeks. Their conversations had been pleasant but guarded.

His parents still hoped he'd go back to Trendale. He tried to reassure them, saying that the dreams had subsided and he was feeling much better. "I've been sleeping really well," he told his mom.

"And are you eating well too? Regular meals? Nutritious food?" She'd always been a bit of a worrier, something that had seemed grating when he'd lived at home. Now, given the distance and the time apart, he heard the love behind the worry and found it touching.

"Really well. Vegetables and everything." That particular call had ended on a good note because he'd finished by talking to Linda, the only one in the family who'd never thought he was losing his mind. She just missed her brother.

And he missed her too. Funny how he'd taken the people in his life for granted.

During these phone calls, his dad would never elaborate on the reason he'd cut Pearl out of his life. If Joe broached the subject, his father would abruptly steer the conversation elsewhere. It wasn't hard to read between the lines. The man didn't want to talk about it.

Today, though, Joe was determined to find answers. He dialed his family's number, nervously wrapping the cord around his finger while it rang. When Linda answered, he spent a few minutes listening to her excitedly chatter on about her baton lessons before asking to speak to their dad.

The initial greeting gave way to small talk about the weather. Joe waited for the first pause in the conversation before telling his dad everything that had transpired since they'd last talked. He started with his discovery after the thunderstorm. "Inside the metal box there was jewelry, a book of poetry, and love letters from a guy named John to your aunt Alice. It mentions them going to the Barn Dance here in town. Pearl's friend said Alice died the night of the Barn Dance and that she was shot. It was an accident, he said. Do you know anything about that?"

His father sighed. "Joe, this all happened before I was born. Honestly, I never heard that Alice was shot. I knew she died young, and I assumed she died of some illness. My mother never talked about her. I sensed it was a sore spot, so I never brought it up."

Joe couldn't help himself. "It seems like not wanting to talk about things runs in the family." He braced himself for some backlash; his dad didn't take well to anything resembling criticism. Instead of being irritated, his father chuckled.

"We're not the best communicators—that much is true," he said. "That's probably something I should work on."

"Probably. And as long as you mentioned wanting to work on it, how about you start with this? What exactly happened that made you cut your mother out of your life?"

"This again." His father's voice had a tone of resignation.

"Yeah, this again. Neither of you will tell me, and since she's dying of cancer, I'm thinking it has to come from you."

Maybe it was the reference to dying, but Joe sensed a shift in his father. "I can give you my take on it, but you know that she'll probably have a different version of events?"

"Sure."

"She can say what she wants, but I was there. I saw it." He exhaled. "My father, your grandfather, was a troubled man. He fought in the First World War and came back missing a leg. He was in pain much of the time from that and other injuries, and he started drinking. A lot. And when he got drunk, which was all the time, he was morose, feeling sorry for himself, for how his life turned out. His family had owned a prosperous farm, but he wasn't coping well, so his younger brother took over managing it. After he and my mother got married, they moved into town, and he took a job in an office, which he hated. My mother wasn't helpful, what with her nagging all the time. She wanted to travel and to dress in all the latest fashions, but they couldn't afford it. Whatever she wanted in a husband, it wasn't him. Frankly, I don't know why those two ever got married. There was no love there that I saw. But you know, I didn't really know the difference when I was a kid. It was just my life, you know?"

"Yeah."

"So one Saturday when I was seventeen, almost eighteen, my dad and I leave for the day to go target shooting out in the country. No sooner do we get all the way out there than he says he feels sick, and we have to go back home. When we get there, we notice a car pulling out of the driveway, and at the wheel is Howard Donohue, a friend of my folks. My dad gets really mad and says to wait in the car, and I did at first, but it seemed like he was gone a really long time, and I got tired of waiting."

Joe clutched the phone to his ear, not knowing what to say.

"So I finally go inside, and my father is crying, sobbing, and my mother is in her bathrobe, screaming at him that he should mind his own business. And he's saying that she is his business, that she's his wife, and he can't believe she just cheated on him with Howard, of all people. And she says that she and Howard are just friends, that my dad was blowing the whole thing out of proportion as usual. And then she says no one would fault her if she *was* cheating on him because he was barely half a man, and he'd ruined her life."

He paused. Joe waited a minute before saying, "Then what happened?"

"My mother said she wished she'd never married him, that the only reason she did was because she felt sorry for him. That no one else would want him. And he straightens up and says kind of quietly, 'It was your idea that we get married. I did it for you. I've done everything for you.'"

"What was he talking about?"

"I don't know," his father said. "And then she just goes off, telling him things like her life would have been better without him, and she never loved him, not even for a minute. That he just made everyone miserable, and that she'd have been better off if he'd died in the war."

"That's terrible." Joe could imagine it. His father as a teenager finding out his mother had been with another man and then watching his parents fight, his mother so cruel, his father falling apart emotionally.

"And then he said if anyone made a sacrifice, it was him, and she laughed and laughed like she was mocking him. And right after that, he put a gun to his head."

That last sentence took Joe by shocked surprise. All he could manage to utter was, "What?"

"I didn't see him take the handgun into the house with him. The first I noticed it was when he raised it to the side of his head. My mother stops laughing and goes, 'We both know you don't have the balls to do it.'" There was a long pause on the other end of the line.

Joe said, "He shot himself?"

"No." His father's voice got quieter. "He handed her the gun and asked her to shoot him and put him out of his pain, and she said, 'You aren't worth the bullet.' Then they noticed me standing there. My mother told me to go to my room, and my dad went outside to the garage. An hour later, my mom told me to go tell my dad it was time for dinner. That was how she operated. Pretend like nothing happened. So I go out to get him and . . ." He choked back the words. "And he was hanging from the rafters. I got the ladder and cut him down, but it was too late."

"Oh my God. I'm sorry, Dad." Joe felt a wave of sympathy for what his father had endured. He couldn't even imagine it.

"You never get over a thing like that. At least, I didn't."

"No, I wouldn't think so." Even as the words came out of his mouth, he was aware of how inadequate they were.

"I've felt guilty about his death my whole life."

"You didn't know."

"So many times, I've thought that I should have run into the room and made them stop fighting. Maybe if I'd gotten between them, I could have calmed things down, and it wouldn't have gotten to that point . . ."

"It wasn't your fault."

He cleared his throat. "I know that, but some part of me doesn't believe it. I was there, and I didn't do anything to stop her viciousness. That's a tough thing to live with. And you want to know the kicker?"

"What's that?"

"My mother played the grieving widow at the funeral. She cried and carried on like you wouldn't believe, and then once everyone was gone, she turned it off like it was a faucet. I asked if she even felt bad for how my dad died, and she said it didn't matter how she felt. He was already gone, and nothing was going to bring him back. She was so cold, it made me sick. As soon as I turned eighteen, I moved in with my grandparents at the farm. They paid for my college, and that was it. I never saw her again. I didn't take her calls, never answered her letters. I didn't want to have anything to do with her. As far as I was concerned, she'd killed him."

CHAPTER FORTY-SEVEN

1983

Driving the truck from his grandmother's house to Pine Ridge Hollow, Joe couldn't help but think about his father's words. *As far as I was concerned, she'd killed him.*

Mentally, he made a comparison to what his grandmother had told him about the reason her son wasn't in her life. *Your father believes that I killed someone.* And when Joe asked if she had, she'd answered, *Not on purpose.*

He hadn't picked up on any remorse on her part. Cutting a family member out of your life forever was pretty extreme, but now that he'd heard his father's take on it, he understood. Still, Pearl was old and dying and seemed to want to make amends. And she hadn't actually killed him; his grandfather had taken his own life. The fact that they'd had a vicious argument was beside the point, he thought. Would it hurt his dad to talk to her? One short conversation, just to put this behind them before she passed away? Because once she was gone, the opportunity to talk it through would be over as well. He knew this, and yet somehow he knew his father's mind was made up. Joe shook his head. Why did family relationships have to be so complicated?

Joe found an open parking spot close to the front door of his grandmother's building. He checked in at the front desk and was directed to a hallway that led to his grandmother's apartment.

Her face lit up at the sight of him. "Joe! What a pleasant surprise." She ushered him into her small apartment and indicated he should sit in the plaid recliner in the corner. He took a seat, Alice's metal box resting on his lap. Pearl sat down on a plump upholstered chair. The end table between them held a *TV Guide* magazine and a remote control.

He said, "I'm sorry I didn't call first."

"No need to call. I'm always glad to see you."

"I came across this box recently." He held it up. "Does it look familiar?"

She shook her head. "No. If it was in the barn, it was probably my father's."

"Actually, it belonged to your sister Alice." He opened the lid and proceeded to tell her about the storm and the way a bolt of lightning had struck the tree, freeing the metal box from its hiding place of more than sixty years.

"I'm almost afraid to ask," she said quietly, "but what's in it?"

"Nothing bad," he assured her, pulling out the contents and putting each item on the table next to him. He kept the stack of letters in the box, saving them for last, while his grandmother exclaimed over the jewelry. "All these years, my mother's jewelry was in a box in a tree." She pursed her lips. "My sisters and I wondered where it went. We asked my father, but he said he didn't know and wouldn't say any more about it. He was devastated after . . . well, after Alice was gone, he was shattered, as were the rest of us. First my mother, and then my sister. I suppose he knew she had it but didn't know her hiding place." She put the engagement ring on her finger and held out her hand. "They didn't have big diamonds like they do now. Getting betrothed was an event. The ring wasn't for status. It showed the world that you'd found your true love and were going to be together forever."

"Do you know why she kept these other things?" Joe pointed to the seashell, book of poetry, and the tiny china frog.

"I haven't a clue. Just keepsakes, I guess. It's been so long, Joe."

He pulled out the stack of letters and set them alongside the book of poetry. "There were also these love letters from that John Lawrence who worked at your father's mill. Did you know he and your sister were secretly meeting and writing back and forth?"

She sighed and didn't answer, her gaze dropping to her hands resting on her lap. He was about to repeat the question when she whispered, "Yes, I knew. I was the one who found the letters Alice wrote to him." She looked up, and her voice got stronger. "I found them in his trunk in the barn, and I burned them."

Joe was jolted by her words and the bitterness in her tone. "You burned them? Why?"

"By then she was gone, and I didn't want my younger sisters to know what she'd done. It would have been shameful. They all thought the best of Alice, and that's how I wanted to leave it."

What she'd done? None of John's letters indicated that he or Alice had done anything even remotely shameful. There had to be more to the story. "So what happened? How did Alice wind up getting shot?"

"It was an accident," Pearl said, sounding pained. "No one intended for anyone to get hurt." She met his eyes. "I don't like to talk about it. Now tell me about your progress on the house. What have you been up to lately?"

This was, Joe realized, how both his father and his grandmother operated. When anyone came close to discussing something painful or sensitive, they locked the door and veered away. Changed the subject and never went back. He'd been raised to respect his elders, and the fact that his grandmother was terminally ill made pressing the issue even more difficult, but he had to know what happened. He'd experienced

Alice's death in his dreams countless times and felt the pain of losing her. His grandmother had been the one to bring him to Pullman. They hadn't met until recently, but her life and his were now irrevocably bound together. She might be stubborn, but he could be too. Dangling these vague hints in front of him but not giving him answers to his questions was wrong. She owed him the truth.

"What have I been up to lately?" He repeated the words back and decided to answer before returning to the subject of Alice. "I was talking to my dad on the phone earlier. He told me the story of his dad dying and why you aren't on speaking terms."

A look crossed her face. Relief? Surprise? He wasn't entirely sure.

"Then you know what happened," she said.

"I know what *he* said happened." Joe kept his voice neutral. "I'm sure you have your own take on it."

"Did he tell you that we had a huge argument? That he caught me being unfaithful, and that afterward he committed suicide? Hung himself from the rafters of the garage?" Her voice was quiet. She kept her gaze on the floor; suddenly, she looked so beaten down and sad that he wanted to drop the whole subject, walk away, and let the family secrets stay secret. But he'd come to Pullman for a reason. The dreams that had tormented him had been real events, and it looked like those events had tormented his grandmother as well. Kathleen felt that Alice wanted the truth to be known. Joe wasn't so sure about that, but it was as good a theory as any to explain everything that had happened to him in the last year. Things had been buried for way too long.

He nodded. "That's the gist of it."

"There's always two sides to every story, Joe. Always." She sighed wearily. "Not that I want to discuss this with my grandson, but to set the record straight, that was the only time I strayed from my marriage. Believe me, I regretted it immediately. Such a mistake."

Joe nodded. One mistake that set off so much misery. He said, "I'm sorry."

She looked up at him, tears glinting in her eyes. "There was far more to the story, Joe, not that I want to elaborate. Just believe me when I say I haven't lived a good life. I am truly sorry for all the pain I've caused, but I can't go back and do things differently. If I could, I would."

"You could call my dad, tell him that."

"He won't even talk to me, so I don't think that's an option." She shook her head sadly.

Her softening gave him an opening. "Howard said Alice died from a gunshot wound. I know John Lawrence was with her when she died. You said it was an accident. What happened? Who shot her?"

Pearl wilted, her body hunched over, her hands clutching her forehead. "Alice . . . ," she said, her voice cracking. "You have to understand. I loved my sister Alice. I still do. She was good, so good. I never wanted anything bad to happen to her." She lifted her head, and Joe saw the gleam of tears in her eyes.

He got up and knelt down in front of her. "Do you know what happened? Do you know who killed Alice?" He fought the instinct to give her a reassuring hug. The feeling of loss that accompanied the dream of holding the dying Alice was still fresh. He still felt the rawness, the pain, the grief that a man felt losing the love of his life.

"Yes, I know who killed her." A sob escaped her. "It was me. God help me—Alice would still be alive if it wasn't for me."

"You shot her?"

"It's haunted me for years. I'm afraid that when I die, I'll go straight to hell."

CHAPTER FORTY-EIGHT

1983

Joe made plans to meet Kathleen at the Pine Cone. It wasn't even lunchtime yet, but there was no way he could wait until noon to talk to her. He used the pay phone in the lobby before he left his grandmother's building, putting the coin in the slot with shaky fingers. First he'd heard the details of his grandfather's death; then his grandmother had admitted she'd been responsible for Alice's shooting. Good grief, his family had this horrible history of tragedy. He'd gone from childhood to adulthood and never had a clue.

When Marcia answered the phone at the store, he asked to speak to Kathleen. Once she got on the line, he blurted out, "You have to meet me at the restaurant. I need you. I mean, I need to talk to you."

She answered, "Of course," without questioning him at all. "Ten minutes?"

"That will work. Thanks."

He drove down the country road, reeling with what he'd just heard. None of it would make sense until he spoke to Kathleen. She would know what to do with this information. He himself didn't have a clue.

By the time she got to the restaurant, he was already sitting in a booth, waiting. "Sorry it took so long. I got caught up with a customer," Kathleen said when she finally reached the table. She gave him a thoughtful look. "Are you okay?"

"I've been better."

Doris came with her pad and pen. "What'll you have?" Neither of them was hungry, but they ordered eggs and toast anyway. Doris would have booted them to the counter if they tried to get away with just having coffee. They'd seen it happen.

After she walked away, Kathleen said, "Spill."

Joe began with the conversation with his father, not even pausing when Doris brought their coffee and juice. Kathleen listened, rapt. "I went to see my grandmother and finally confronted her about everything, starting with her rift with my father. She agreed with what he told me, more or less, and seemed to feel terrible about it." He continued, relating the entire conversation with his grandmother.

When he finished, Kathleen said, "She admitted killing Alice? That's unbelievable."

"Yes, but it's also not true," he said as Doris came with their plates. After she walked away, he added, "I've been there. I've seen Alice die dozens of times, and I can tell you without a doubt that Pearl wasn't the one who pulled the trigger. I told her I knew she was lying and that it was a man who killed Alice. I asked her again to please tell me the truth, but she just claimed not to know what I was talking about. And then I asked her whatever happened to John Lawrence, and she totally clammed up and changed the subject. Told me to call the front desk and have them send the nurse because she had low blood sugar and was having an episode."

"An episode? Is this something that's happened before?"

Joe shrugged. "Not that I know of. I called the front desk, and they sent a nurse's aide down to check on her, at which point she told me I should go." He raised his eyebrows. "I was dismissed."

"Wow." She sounded incredulous.

"I know. She did tell me I could keep the contents of the box. She said it's family jewelry, and she wanted to keep it in the family. She had zero interest in reading John's love letters to Alice. She said that after Alice died, she found the ones Alice wrote to him, and she burned them."

"No!" Kathleen sounded shocked. "Why would she do that?"

"I don't know. She said something about not wanting the younger sisters to see the letters."

"None of this makes sense. So many years have passed. Why lie about it now? And why take the blame for something she didn't do? Especially killing her own sister?"

"I was hoping you could talk me through this. Seriously, Kathleen, I was just starting to feel like I wasn't losing my mind after all. Now talking to my grandmother, I feel like I'm losing it again."

"Again?" She gave him a kindly smile. "You were never losing it, Joe. We can figure it out. We'll get through this."

We'll get through this. Hearing those words helped Joe breathe more easily. They would do it together. He said, "It's just that I feel that if I could get to the bottom of this, the dreams would stop completely, you know? I'm having them less frequently. In fact . . ." He stopped, something occurring to him.

"What?" Kathleen nibbled at her toast, her eyes on him.

"Two of the dreams I haven't had at all. Not in a long time." His forehead furrowed. "The one I used to call the Piano Dream."

"The one we figured must have taken place in the theater."

"Yeah, that one. And the second one was the dream where I was putting a metal box in the hollow of a tree."

"The box you discovered the night of the storm."

"Yes. Exactly."

"Maybe," she said thoughtfully, "once you've lived the dream in this life, you no longer experience it anymore."

"Huh." He grew quiet, parsing it out. "Okay. That makes sense."

"So that means you have two dreams left, right? The Rowboat Dream and the Death Dream. We know that the Death Dream took place the evening of the Barn Dance." Doris came with her coffeepot and gestured toward Kathleen's cup. "Thanks, Doris. I'll take a touch more." She turned her attention back to Joe. "Maybe we should go to the Barn Dance this weekend?"

Joe looked up. "What do you think, Doris? Is the Barn Dance a good idea?"

Doris shrugged as she poured the coffee. "Suit yourself."

"Would you go as my date, Doris? I would be honored if you'd accompany me. I can pick you up in my truck."

"Ha!" Doris said with the slightest twitch of her lips. "You wish. I already got me a date, so you might as well stop yanking my chain and take your girlfriend here."

"You already have a date? And it's not me?" Joe called out with fake anguish as she turned and walked away. "Doris, how could you?" He met Kathleen's eyes and shook his head. "Did you see her smile? I finally did it, Kathleen. I made Doris smile. And you said it couldn't be done." He folded his arms in satisfaction.

"Nope. It doesn't count," Kathleen said firmly. "It wasn't a real smile, just an amused look."

"I saw her lips move upward. It was a definite smile. I agree that it was quick, but it was there."

"Nice try. I know what a smile looks like, and I didn't see one on Doris. You'll have to keep trying."

He sighed. "Want to go to the Barn Dance with me?"

"I would love to go to the Barn Dance with you, Joe Arneson. Thank you very much." And she gave him a smile, a real smile. This time he could clearly see the difference.

CHAPTER FORTY-NINE

1983

The night of the Barn Dance, Joe picked Kathleen up at her house. On the way out, he apologized for having to take her in a truck. "I know it's not the best vehicle for a date," he said, emphasizing the word *date* and then waiting for her reaction.

"It's not a problem," she assured him as he opened the door and helped her inside.

Joe shut the door with a smile. *Well, well, well.* So he'd graduated from friend to someone she'd date. One more step, and there was a good possibility he could be upgraded to boyfriend, something that had definite appeal, but he knew enough not to push the subject. All in good time.

Joe drove around to the other side of the lake, following the makeshift signs directing them to the dance. Even without the signs, he could have found it. All traffic was going in that direction. He kept glancing her way, distracted by her appearance.

"What are you looking at?"

"You, Miss Dinsmore. You are looking pretty fine. What era is that dress, if I can ask?"

She laughed. "I'm not entirely sure. Maybe 1920s, or even earlier? It's an antique. I think at some point someone took the sleeves off and shortened it, but otherwise, it's all original. Do you like it?" It was gorgeous, cream and blue with a cinched waist and flowing skirt. The back was cut provocatively low, considering the time period. Her hair was pulled away from her face, falling in curls in the back. The combination of a modern woman in an old-fashioned dress was bewitching.

He gave her a slow grin. "Most definitely. You look stunning."

"Thank you." She smiled. "You're not too bad yourself."

He was glad to have found some fancy vintage clothing of his own. Kathleen had helped him select the whole outfit from the store. The clothing she'd set aside for him—high-collared shirt and pleated trousers with leather suspenders—fit perfectly.

When they reached the barn, a volunteer wearing an orange vest waved them off the road and into a parking lot. Another volunteer directed them to a space under an oak tree.

At the entrance, Joe paid, and they each got their hand stamped with the image of a purple star. Judging from the size of the crowd, most of the town was in attendance.

The dance floor was in the center of the barn's open space below a large disco ball. On one side was a table with snacks and coolers filled with cans of soda, and next to that table, a bar was set up with wine and beer. Behind each table stood an attendant with a cash box, ready to make change.

On the opposite side of the hall, chairs were lined up, most of them empty. According to the signs, soda was a quarter, beer was seventy-five cents, and a glass of wine was a buck. A DJ stood over a record player while Duran Duran's "Hungry Like the Wolf" blared from the speakers. The dance floor was crowded.

"Do you suppose this is what the barn looked like when Alice and John were here?" Kathleen asked, talking over the music.

He shook his head. "It's hard to say, but it must have been at least somewhat different. The disco ball is a fairly recent invention, and I'm guessing that pay phone wasn't here then."

"I know it's different, and yet they were here. They walked through the same door we did and came to socialize and dance. They were so looking forward to this evening. But Alice never made it home." She looked about to cry. "It's so sad."

"It is sad."

"I'm sorry. I can't seem to help myself."

"You don't need to apologize." Joe leaned close. "Do you want to dance?"

She shook her head. "Not just yet. Let's get something to drink and watch for a bit."

After they got their clear plastic cups of wine, they found a table. Kathleen set down her purse and they sipped their wine, surveying the crowd. Even with air-conditioning, it was warm inside, not nearly as conducive for romance as Joe had hoped, but the organizers had really tried. He'd give them that much. The hall was adorned with white twinkly Christmas lights, and banners hung above the refreshments urging the crowd to "Party On" and "Get Down Tonight."

He and Kathleen were dressed conspicuously different from the rest of the crowd, most of whom wore more casual clothing. Some of the young women wore halters or crop tops. The guys all wore T-shirts, and nearly all of them wore shorts or jeans.

Kathleen pointed out some small children spinning in circles and then gestured toward a teenage girl in leg warmers with her shirt open over one shoulder. "She's got the *Flashdance* look down pat."

Joe puzzled it out for a second before answering. "I have no idea what that means."

"Like Jennifer Beals in the movie *Flashdance*? She's got that look. The leg warmers and the ripped neckline?" Seeing his bemused expression, she said, "I take it you didn't see the movie?"

"Never heard of it."

"You never heard of *Flashdance*? Really? It was a big deal. Came out this spring."

"Well, that explains it. I was an inpatient at Trendale at the time."

As they were finishing their wine, the opening notes of Lionel Richie's "Truly" came over the speakers. Joe took Kathleen's hand and led her out to the dance floor with a confidence he didn't even know he had. "Pretty smooth, Arneson," she said as they began to sway back and forth. "I can tell you've done this before."

He said, "I've imagined dancing with you a million times."

CHAPTER FIFTY

1983

Ricky parked down the street from Kathleen's house and hunched down in the front seat, watching and waiting and eventually being rewarded when Joe and Kathleen came out the front door. He noticed the weird clothing that pansy-ass Joe wore and snickered. Kathleen had on some odd old-timey dress too, but at least she looked good in it.

While he waited for them to get into Joe's truck, he double-checked the glove compartment to make sure his black ski mask and handgun were right where he'd left them.

They pulled away from the curb, and he followed at a respectable distance. Once they'd arrived and entered the Barn Dance, he reached over to the passenger-side floor mat and grabbed the plastic bottle he'd filled with water before leaving Lorraine Whitt's house.

Ricky casually got out of the car, bottle in hand, and nodded to a couple walking past. Nonchalantly, he strode over to Joe's truck, unscrewed the gas cap, and poured the water into the tank. Afterward, he quickly screwed the cap back on, tossing the bottle into the weeds and heading toward the barn, smiling. Joe's truck wasn't going to get too far, and once they were stuck, he could enact the plan in which he was Kathleen's savior. He'd thought it through, and it went like this: either

Joe would leave her in the truck and walk for help, or both of them would leave the truck and walk together. Either way, Joe was going to come to a bad end when a masked gunman robbed and attacked him, coming out of the woods, seemingly from nowhere.

And who would reconnect with Kathleen once Joe was dead or in the hospital? He would. He'd show up just when she needed him most, sans beard, of course. After what happened to Joe, she'd be traumatized and in need of a protector, and Ricky was good at that. His size alone made women feel safe. He'd say that he'd tracked her down through one of her friends and had a dream that she was in danger, drove across the country nonstop to get to her side. Kathleen was trusting. She'd believe him.

He thought of every possible scenario and decided that unless some interfering Good Samaritan came along, his plan was a sure thing.

Just to play it safe, Ricky waited another fifteen minutes in the parking lot before going inside. The entrance fee was ridiculous. Three dollars, and for what? A joke of a DJ and decorations that looked like they'd been designed by high school students. The beverages cost extra too. At least the snacks were free.

Ricky got himself a can of Schlitz and a handful of pretzels. He stood with his back to the wall and surveyed the room, looking for Kathleen. He'd purposely worn his gray-tinted sunglasses. The lenses were light enough not to look too odd worn indoors but dark enough to obscure his identity. Between the sunglasses, beard, and the baseball cap, he was fairly certain Kathleen wouldn't recognize him.

When he finally caught sight of Kathleen, she was slow dancing with Joe, her body pressed right up against his, cheek resting on his shoulder, eyes closed. He watched, feeling anger build until rage threatened to overtake his body. Ricky dropped the remaining pretzel, and his fingers tightened at his side. He could almost envision the sound of his fist as it slammed against Joe's jaw. That wuss would be no match for a real man. Ricky could pulverize him in no time at all.

He wanted to take those cheesy suspenders and wrap them around Joe's throat, tightening and tightening until Joe couldn't breathe, and then, once the loser had passed out, he'd finish him off by grabbing his jaw and snapping his neck.

But if he did that right now, he'd look like a monster to Kathleen.

Ricky took a deep breath and willed himself to look elsewhere, glancing around the barn and finally settling on a woman pushing a boy in a wheelchair around the perimeter of the crowd. One of the wheels was askew, and she had to keep shifting it constantly to get it to work smoothly. The boy's head lolled to one side. Why the woman even bothered to bring him Ricky didn't know. If it were up to him, he'd leave the kid at home. She was probably one of those martyr types who thought her good deeds would earn her a crown in heaven.

Ha. She wished.

The truth of it was that there was nothing after death but a black void. That was the reason Ricky went for what he wanted every single time. This life, this moment, was all there was. Grab and get it while the getting is good. The idea of a heavenly reward was a myth for the stupid and gullible.

Watching the woman and her boy distracted him for the better. His anger subsided; his heart rate slowed.

A young woman came up to him. "Hello there." Her hair was feathered and curled, her white T-shirt sheer enough that he could see the black lace bra underneath. When he glanced down, he noticed her mouth was shiny with lip gloss. She said, "Are you here by yourself?"

"What?" he asked. Normally, she'd be as tempting as cheese spread on a cracker, but he had no time or patience for her right now. "Oh, yeah, I'm here by myself." He kept his eyes on the swaying crowd. The disco ball overhead cast beams of light in kaleidoscopic patterns around the room.

"Want to dance?"

"No. I don't want to dance."

"Okay," she said, an edge to her voice. "Be that way. I'll just leave you alone, then."

He watched her walk away, her hips purposefully swaying. Man, that was one fine piece of ass. Downright bodacious in a way Kathleen never could be. He faltered for an instant, considered going after the young woman, and then held himself back. Girls like that were side dishes. There would be time for that down the road. Tonight, he had to focus. He was there for one reason and one reason only. To get his wife back.

If only Kathleen knew all the sacrifices he'd made for her. Someday she would. He'd tell her how heroic he'd been once they were back together. He'd gone above and beyond what the average man would do, that much was sure. His story would go down the line to future generations. A family legend of undying love and devotion.

He peered around the hall and got Kathleen and Joe back in his sights, watching as they talked from the sideline chairs for what seemed like forever. Eventually, they got up and danced again, then sat and talked some more. When the wheelchair duo came rolling in front of them, Joe jumped up and said something to the woman, then knelt and made some adjustment to the wheels, all the while talking to the boy in the chair. In response, the kid flapped his hands excitedly. Standing up, Joe brushed his hands against his pants and made a gesture as if to say that was as good as it got. The woman nodded and continued on.

Idiot. What a do-gooder.

When Joe and Kathleen got up an hour later and headed for the exit, Ricky followed, slipping through the door only minutes behind them.

CHAPTER FIFTY-ONE

1916

John steered the buckboard down the drive toward the barn. Mr. Wilson, one of the men who brought his grain to the mill, was there to greet them. He grabbed the horse's halter and pulled, lining the wagon up alongside some others, then told John, who was helping Alice and Pearl down off the seat, "I will handle this, John." He nodded toward a paddock where a few other horses grazed while their owners socialized. "Just take the ladies inside and have a good time. I'll make sure your mare joins the others."

"Thank you, Mr. Wilson." He doffed his brimmed hat toward the older man.

"We came too early, John," Pearl grumbled as she walked across the gravel, clutching John's arm. She'd noticed John crooking an elbow for Alice and took it upon herself to take hold of his other side. "There's hardly anyone here." Pearl kicked at the gravel in annoyance.

"It was my idea to leave so early," Alice reminded her. "I wanted to have a full evening, with not a minute wasted."

"I know, but I just hate being one of the first to arrive. It makes me look too eager."

Alice laughed. "You are such a funny girl, Pearl. I'm so glad you're my sister."

Pearl frowned. "And I do wish we had long white gloves, and I would give anything to have a fan like real ladies do when they go to dances."

"We will have a grand time even without gloves and fans," Alice said cheerfully. "Besides, this is the Barn Dance, not some high-society event. No one expects us to be dressed to the nines."

At the door, a plump elderly woman sold John their tickets and laid out the rules for the evening. "No liquor is allowed on the premises, and young people will be expected to conduct themselves as ladies and gentlemen. Couples who are dancing must have a respectable space between them. Scandalous behavior will not be tolerated, and young ladies will be escorted home if there is even a hint of impropriety."

"Yes, ma'am," John said.

Once inside, all of them paused to survey the room. From the outside, the barn had looked like any other barn, but inside, it had been transformed into a place of wonder. Tables arranged around the edge of the room were covered with linen tablecloths and adorned with flowers in glass vases. Kerosene lanterns sat on shelves along the outside walls and hung overhead between large swaths of sheer, colorful fabric. On one side of the room, a long table held several punch bowls and plates of desserts: cakes and pies and cookies of every kind. A band was busily setting up chairs and music stands on a low stage at the far end. The hardwood floor had been polished to a high sheen. A few other early arrivals—including Edna, Mrs. Donohue, and Howie—stood clustered near one of the punch bowls.

"The decorations are so pretty. This is even better than last year," Pearl said, forgetting to be crabby.

"I have a feeling it's going to be the best Barn Dance yet," Alice said, looking up at John with a shy smile. She'd let go of his arm, self-conscious at the sight of Mrs. Donohue, who stared at them over her glasses. Alice stood tall, doing her best to look proper. She knew even one minor mistake could lead to the evening being cut short. *Young ladies will be escorted home if there is even a hint of impropriety.*

This, she knew, was not just talk. Being sent home would be scandalous and the talk of the town for years to come. The residents of Pullman had long memories and not much else to talk about.

"Let's go join Howie and Edna," she suggested to Pearl, who begrudgingly followed her and John across the room.

"Pearl. Alice. Mr. Lawrence." Mrs. Donohue looked each of them in the eye. "Since I am responsible for you, I'm glad to see you have arrived safely."

"Oh, you don't have to worry about me, Mrs. Donohue," Pearl said, her voice assured. "I know how to behave at a dance."

"Don't tell me who I need to worry about, Pearl. If the truth be told, you're the one I'm most concerned about." Mrs. Donohue rested her hand on Howie's arm. "I see right through you, Pearl Bennett. If your father and Alice didn't watch over you, there's no telling what you'd do."

Pearl laughed. "Alice does watch over me, ma'am, but I would be fine on my own. I wouldn't do anything too bad, although I have always wanted to dance on a tabletop." She mischievously eyed a nearby table. "And I just might before the night is through."

Alice cringed, knowing that Pearl's brashness could be taken the wrong way, but luckily, Edna—dear, sweet Edna—stepped forward with a grin. "This is one of the things I've always admired about you, Pearl. I never know what you might say. You make merry at every opportunity, and your teasing lifts my spirits."

Howie joined in with a chuckle. "You can't take Pearl too seriously, Mother. She likes to have a little fun, but she never overdoes it. I have never seen her be anything but a perfect lady."

"Well, she'd best be a lady tonight." Mrs. Donohue caught sight of a neighbor's arrival and excused herself to greet them. "I'll be watching all of you," she cautioned before walking off.

"Yes, ma'am," a chorus of voices answered.

Edna explained that the three of them had helped set up the hall. "Howie climbed the ladder to hang the decorations," Edna said. "I brought a cake and helped light the lanterns."

As they talked, more people poured into the place, and the murmur of voices echoed off the ceiling. One of the chaperones kept a careful eye on the punch bowls to prevent them from being spiked. The band began to play, and the music muffled conversations around the room.

"I'm bored," Pearl announced. "Howie, will you dance with me?"

Howie's face fell. "My mother made me promise I would dance only with Edna."

"Then John!" She patted his arm. "You're staying in our barn. A dance with me is small payment for the privilege."

Alice could not suppress a grin. Pearl, poor thing, was never content. She always had to shine a light on herself because she didn't understand how to light herself from within.

John looked awkwardly at Alice and then said, "I asked your father if I could accompany Alice, and it would be rude of me to—"

Alice broke in. "I don't mind, John, if you don't."

"See?" Pearl said, lifting her chin. "Alice doesn't mind at all!"

"I see," John said, uncertainty in his voice.

"On one condition, Pearl." Alice waited until she had her sister's full attention. "Since you get to dance with John first, I am claiming him for the rest of the night. One dance is all you will get, and I don't want to hear another word about it."

"But this dance is mine!" Pearl triumphantly pulled John onto the dance floor. Once they'd stopped in the middle of the crowd, he held her as far away as possible, shooting a miserable expression back at Alice as they swayed back and forth.

"That's not like you to be mean, Alice," Edna said, sidling up to her. "Poor John looks like he'd rather be slaughtering hogs."

"There was no way around it," Alice said with a slight shake of her head. "Once Pearl gets an idea in her head, there is no stopping her. She would have been hanging on John all night and crowding in on my time with him. Better to give her what she wants and put an end to it before it even begins."

When the music ended, everyone clapped politely, and Pearl and John returned. "That's hardly fair," Pearl said grumpily. "The song had already started, so I didn't get a full dance. Don't you think I deserve another to make up for it?" She batted her eyes at John.

He answered before Alice could say a word. "I'm sorry, Pearl, but your sister was very clear, and I intend to respect her wishes." He held his arm out. "Alice, would you honor me with this dance?"

"I'd be delighted."

He twirled her around the dance floor, mindful not to hold her too close. Alice felt a wellspring of emotion fill the space between them: it was no longer air alone but a connection of love and longing. Whoever had invented dancing had known the yearning of a young lady's heart. She was transformed, no longer the same Alice she was at home, the one who wiped noses and hung laundry and solved the family's problems.

"What are you thinking?" he asked.

"I was thinking how lucky it was that of all the places you could have worked this summer, you came to me."

He nodded and leaned in a bit to talk quietly. "I have had that same thought myself. I have thanked God every night ever since you said you loved me. And when you said it didn't matter about my family background, I knew you were an angel."

"I cannot believe my father gave you permission to accompany me this evening," she said. "He is so protective of all of us and rarely lets us out of his sight."

John said, "We had a long talk one day at the mill between customers. He had guessed we are in love, Alice."

She looked up at him, shocked. "No."

John laughed, his eyes twinkling. "Yes. And he did not run me out of town, as you had feared. We discussed my life and my future at length. I told him about my father. He already knew he was in prison for murder, if you can imagine that, and he still hired me for the summer. He said he would judge me based only on my actions and deeds, not by those who came before me. Your father is an uncommon man, Alice."

Out of the corner of Alice's eye, she spotted Mrs. Donohue looking their way, so they hurriedly resumed dancing. She fought the urge to pull him close and rest her head on his shoulder. Doing so would be paradise, but the few moments of joy were not worth the cost. For now, she would take what she could get.

They danced six songs in a row before taking a break for refreshments. Walking off the dance floor, Alice became suddenly aware of her surroundings. She'd been so wrapped up in enjoying John's company that she barely noticed that the barn had filled to capacity, the crowd growing while the music played. She ignored the room's mugginess and the ache of her heels from rubbing against the backs of her shoes. In the morning, her feet might be blistered and bleeding, but tonight she was dancing on air.

They found an empty table and were sipping their punch when the music stopped. They noticed Edna, up on the stage, talking to the bandleader. "The fiddle player is Edna's cousin, so she knows all the men in the band," Alice explained. No doubt Edna was requesting a favorite song or letting the band know they should announce a birthday or anniversary of someone in the crowd. She was always thinking of others.

The middle-aged bandleader helped Edna step off the stage, then had the drummer tap several times in succession to get the crowd's attention. "Good evening, everyone," he called out. "Welcome to Pullman's annual Barn Dance. I am Chester Larson, and this is my band." A smattering of applause rose up from the crowd. "Miss Edna Clark has just informed me that we have a songbird in our midst, and that if we hear her sing, we will know heaven here on earth. I am talking about Miss Alice Bennett. Are you out there, Alice?" He shielded his eyes with the flat of his hand.

"Oh no," Alice whispered, her heart sinking. She and Edna sang the night away when they were together doing kitchen chores at Edna's house, but the idea of singing in front of other people was unthinkable.

"Alice, would you come up and grace us with a song? Please?"

Voices rang out:

"Come on, Alice."

"Sing for us, Alice!"

And then Pearl's voice, above all the others. "She won't do it. Alice is a scaredy-cat."

John leaned toward her. "If you don't want to . . ."

"No, I will," she said, suddenly pushing back her chair and walking defiantly up to the stage. The sound of clapping spurred her on.

Chester helped her onto the stage and asked, "What would you like to sing, Miss Bennett?"

"I don't know." She wrung her hands and glanced out at the crowd. In the softness of the kerosene glow, the mass of people looked less intimidating, their faces encouraging and friendly. Members of the audience yelled out suggestions:

"Alexander's Ragtime Band!"

"By the Light of the Silvery Moon!"

"Alice, sing 'Steamboat Bill'!"

"I don't know the words to any of those songs," she told Chester apologetically. "I only know church music and little ditties that I sing to my baby sister."

"Church music." He looked thoughtful. "How about 'In the Sweet By-and-By'?"

She nodded. With only the violin to accompany her, she began to sing. To her surprise, she settled easily into the song, singing loudly enough to be heard throughout the barn. She kept her gaze on John, who stood at her feet, staring up with admiration in his eyes.

It helped that it was such a beautiful song and one that she'd sung since she was a little girl. She especially loved the refrain:

In the sweet by-and-by,
We shall meet on that beautiful shore

And when she got to the end, she sang the words right to John.

For the glorious gift of His love
And the blessings that hallow our days.

When the song was over, the inside of the barn filled with the roar of applause. Sheepishly, Alice gave the crowd a wave of thanks before John helped her down. When the band started up again, her time was over, and dancers streamed back onto the floor.

"Are you having a good time?" John asked when they'd resumed dancing.

"I am having the loveliest evening." Alice looked up at him, eyes sparkling. "I can't remember ever having such a good time."

"And this is only the beginning. Just wait."

She gave him an inquiring look, but when she asked him to explain, he only repeated himself. "Just wait." And then he added, "You'll see."

John didn't mean to let the cat out of the bag by telling Alice there was more to come. He just couldn't help himself. He'd already kept the secret for more than a week and was bursting with the knowledge. Without intending to, he hinted at it when he told Alice that he'd had a long talk with her father at the mill. He'd said, "We discussed my life and my future at length," but there was so much more to it than that.

There had been a lull between customers that day, and John, seeing his opportunity, had asked if he could accompany Alice to the dance. When he was granted permission, he summoned up all his courage and told Mr. Bennett, "I pride myself on being honest and forthright, so I need to tell you that I have fallen in love with Alice."

If he'd expected the older man to pummel him or toss him out the door with a kick in the pants, he would have been wrong. Mr. Bennett just nodded and said, "I thought as much. The two of you have that look. I know it well." A slow smile came across his face.

With that bit of encouragement, John felt free to say more. He told him about his father's imprisonment and was relieved to hear that the older man already knew of it and didn't seem unduly alarmed. Swallowing his trepidation, John continued, telling him the family secret, that his great-grandfather had been a Negro.

"I knew that piece of information as well," Mr. Bennett said. "And I also know that your family name is Robinson." There was a long pause, during which John's insides curled in fear as he waited for the judgment that never came. Instead, Mr. Bennett said, "None of this changes my opinion of you. I judge a man by his actions and words, and over this summer, you have proved yourself to have a fine character."

John nodded, letting out a sigh of relief.

"Besides," he said, leaning in conspiratorially, "in my own family, there's some Indian blood, so I'm not one to talk." He waved a finger. "Now don't go repeating that to anyone."

"No, sir, of course not." John cleared his throat, tapping his toe nervously.

"Was there something else?" He studied John quizzically.

"There is one more thing. I would like to have your permission to propose to Alice."

"You'd like to marry my daughter?"

"Yes, sir. I love her and want her for my wife." He held his breath, knowing it was one thing for Mr. Bennett to accept John as an employee, another for John to ask for his daughter's hand in marriage.

Mr. Bennett nodded thoughtfully. "I would be proud to welcome you into the family, John, but I am sad to say I can't spare Alice, so my answer is no. I know that sounds harsh, but the two of you have known each other only a short while. It might make you feel better to know that first love is often fleeting, and you are both young. In time, you will meet another girl and find love again."

"With all due respect, Mr. Bennett, I am not that young. Many men my age are already married, and I can say with certainty I will never love another girl the way I love Alice. She is unlike any other." Wanting to convince the older man, John said, "If you would reconsider, and Alice will have me, I have planned for a long engagement while I finish medical school. I would write to her every single day and visit when I could. By the time we marry, some of the younger girls will be capable of running the household in her stead."

Mr. Bennett nodded. "It sounds like you've thought this through, young man." He stared into space, his mind elsewhere. "Oh, how I envy you, John. You're in the prime of your life, just starting out, with so many years lying ahead. These are glorious days for you." The older man's eyes got misty, presumably thinking of his own youth.

"Are you saying I may propose to Alice after all? I would like to ask her the night of the Barn Dance."

Mr. Bennett gave John his full attention. "You seem determined, and I give you credit for thinking this through. Yes, you have my blessing."

John had replayed this conversation in his head so many times since then. Getting the approval of Alice's father had seemed unlikely, so having Mr. Bennett's blessing had been a gift dropped at his feet. It only got better from there.

When a customer had arrived at the mill, John had quickly added a last thought. "If she'll have me, I promise to spend the rest of my days making Alice happy."

In response, his future father-in-law said, "I have no doubt you will."

Now, tonight, at the dance, John bided his time, waiting for the right opportunity to broach the subject. He'd imagined the dance to be a romantic place, and while dancing with Alice was wonderful, the hall was crowded and humid. Too many people and so much noise. He wanted to ask her to marry him when he had her undivided attention and there were no distractions. So far, he hadn't encountered any such conditions.

If Pearl was not around, and if it were just the two of them, he could pull the wagon aside on the way home and ask her to marry him under the starry night sky, but of course, Alice's father would not have allowed her to ride alone with a man unchaperoned. Maybe it would be different when they were engaged.

The evening wore on, the minutes building to hours, and John despaired of finding the perfect moment to propose. To make matters worse, while he and Alice stopped to rest and drink punch, some kind of fight broke out on one side of the hall, a young woman wailing and carrying on something terrible while other people clustered around. "Whatever is going on?" Alice asked, craning her neck to see.

"I don't know, but it looks like Mrs. Donohue is involved somehow." John could see the plump lady, hands on her hips, taking charge of the situation.

A few minutes later, Pearl wove her way across the hall to find John and Alice. She blurted out, "You won't believe what just happened!

Mrs. Donohue caught Lorraine Whitt kissing one of the Farber twins. Lorraine claimed she was just whispering in his ear, but there were other witnesses besides Mrs. Donohue who saw it plain as day. Lorraine can deny it all she wants, but everyone knows she did it."

"Lorraine Whitt? But she's Helen's age," Alice said, shocked. "Barely thirteen!"

Pearl's eyes widened. "I know. Isn't it outrageous? Kissing a boy she hardly knows. Right out in public too!"

"Poor Lorraine," Alice said, watching as people left the dance floor to go witness the scene unfolding. Lorraine was still wailing as if she'd broken a leg; others were now chiming in to offer their opinions.

"Poor Lorraine?" Pearl spoke incredulously. "I don't feel one bit sorry for her. She brought it upon herself." She craned her neck to get a better look. "I can't see much of anything from here. I'm going back." Hastily, she turned and headed toward the turmoil.

Alice switched her attention to John, and a sudden look came across her face. "I've just had a thought," she said, setting her punch glass down on the table. "Come with me."

Without a word, he set his glass down as well and kept her in his sights as she worked her way toward the door. Because the ticket taker had left her station to see what the racket was all about, they were able to slip outside unnoticed.

The cooler air was a welcome relief after being in the stuffy barn for so long. "What are we doing out here?" John asked.

Smiling, Alice took his hand and led him down a path around the barn, away from where the wagons were parked. "I got tired of talking over the noise," she said to him, calling back over her shoulder. "I wanted to have time with you before our evening is over."

Once his eyes adapted to the dark, John realized she was leading him toward the lakefront. When they got closer to the water, a cloud moved, revealing a nearly full moon above the lake. Half a dozen rowboats tied up to the pier shimmied and bumped while silvery moonlight glistened on the surface of the water.

"Let's go for a boat ride," she said, turning with a grin. Behind her the boats bobbed, tantalizingly empty.

"You want to go for a ride in someone else's boat and leave the dance? Aren't you afraid of getting into trouble?"

"Perhaps a little afraid," she admitted. "But my thinking is that with all the commotion with Lorraine Whitt, we have at least an hour before anyone notices we're gone. And if they do, I can say I felt ill, so you took me outside to catch my breath."

"But that would be a lie," John said. "And I don't believe you are someone who lies, Alice Bennett."

"Normally that is true, but I am willing to make a onetime exception so I can spend time with you."

Under different circumstances, Alice's reputation risked being ruined, but John had to believe that coming back an engaged woman would smooth out any rumors that might arise from their absence. Oh, he couldn't wait to ask her to be his wife. He had not felt this joyful since he was a child. Back then, when he hadn't known so much, the world was a simpler, kinder place. With Alice by his side, he was starting to think it could be again.

He helped her into the boat and then climbed in, taking the seat opposite her before untying the rope that anchored them to the pier. "We are lucky that whoever owns these boats left the oars behind," he said.

"It was not luck. Chances are, the boat belongs to someone who lives on the lake, and they are now at the dance."

She sounded cheerfully self-assured. This was a side of Alice he'd only glimpsed before, but he liked it. He asked, "And what if they come out and find their boat gone? What then?"

"We'll be back soon enough. I want to show you the island. It's only a few minutes from here." She moved forward so their knees touched, and John felt his breath catch in his throat at the intimacy. They were alone now, really alone, floating along on a sparkling lake. In the distance, he heard the band playing and the bleat of an automobile horn, but the noises were far away, as if in a dream.

Alice pointed. "It's right over there. See it?" He turned his head and saw a simple patch of ground thick with trees rising above the water in the middle of the lake. The island was not much larger in area than the barn they'd just come from. It would be the perfect place for him to propose to Alice, creating a memory only the two of them would share.

He dipped the oars into the water and pulled with ease, creating a rhythm. Ahead of them came a little splash, startling him. She laughed and said, "Don't be so jumpy. It's just a fish." Leaning back, he swung the oars as far as possible, then pulled deep, making the boat skim quickly across the water. "Show-off," she said, teasing. Her hand trailed into the water, her fingertips skimming the surface.

John gave her a smile. "You know, you really do look exceptionally beautiful tonight, Alice," he said, not taking his eyes off her.

"Oh, John," she said, her eyes cast downward. "I don't know what to say."

"When someone pays you a compliment, a simple 'thank you' will usually suffice."

She laughed. "I'm sorry. I know you have paid me many compliments in your letters, but I am not used to hearing it said aloud. Truly, I almost never hear such kind words about my looks. Pearl is the pretty one. I am the one who gets praised for cooking or running an orderly household."

"There is something wrong with the men in Pullman, Wisconsin, if they cannot see you the way I do." John leaned back to pull on the oars, and the boat moved smoothly through the water. "I am glad, of course, that they are such dolts since they don't deserve you, but I do find it puzzling. I noticed how lovely you are the minute I met you, and if I could look at your beautiful face every day for the rest of my life, I'd be a happy man indeed."

"Every day for the rest of your life? Oh, John, I do believe we want the same things." She smiled dolefully. "If only we could make it so."

"Perhaps we can."

"No." She shook her head sadly. "Too soon you'll be gone. And then I will go back to my duties at home, and all of this will be just a beautiful memory."

CHAPTER FIFTY-TWO

1916

The ladies tending the punch bowls had gasped upon seeing Pearl climb onto a chair to get a better view of the ruckus at the Barn Dance. Pearl watched, fascinated at the sight of so many people, normally polite and reserved, carrying on like they'd lost their minds. Lorraine was now curled up on the floor, sobbing like a big baby. Mrs. Donohue tried to pull on her arms to bring her to her feet, but Lorraine resisted, kicking and flailing at every turn.

Pearl had to shake her head. What was Lorraine hoping to accomplish?

Next, Lorraine's mother spoke up on her behalf, telling everyone who would listen that her daughter was a good girl and, as an only child, a special gift from God. "I don't know what you think you saw," she said, confronting Mrs. Donohue directly, "but my Lorraine is a lady and would never succumb to the charms of a boy, especially"—she looked at the Farber twin with disdain—"not the likes of him."

Their father, Mr. Farber, took issue with this statement. "What in tarnation is that supposed to mean?" he roared. The band, sensing the onslaught of complete pandemonium, began to play a slow song.

"Language, Mr. Farber!" Mrs. Donohue said, clearly shocked. "There are ladies and children here."

Mr. Farber poked a finger in Mrs. Whitt's direction. "Who do you think you are, calling my son names?" He was a beefy farmer, towering over Mrs. Whitt by a foot, but his size didn't intimidate Mrs. Whitt at all.

"I didn't call him a name," she said. "He's just not the sort of young man Lorraine would be interested in."

On the floor, Lorraine let out one long wail, and her mother called out, "Hush now, Lorraine. That's enough. Let's go home, and I'll fix you a nice cup of tea to calm your nerves."

"I don't want to go home," Lorraine said, lifting her head and coming to a sitting position. She was, Pearl noticed, in complete disarray, her hair tangled and face red. She might as well go home. Nothing good was going to happen to a girl who looked like that.

Pearl felt a tugging on her dress and looked down to see Frank standing next to her.

"Pearlie," he said. "Whatcha doing up there?"

"Frank!" she said, taking his hand to jump off the chair. "Where have you been? I've been waiting and waiting. I was beginning to think you weren't coming at all."

"My father wouldn't let me leave," he said bitterly. "There were chores to do. I told him I was a grown man and should be able to do as I like, but he said as long as I live in his house, his word was law. I told him about the dance, but he didn't care." He puffed out his chest. "I could have left if I wanted to, but I let the old man have his way." Pearl noticed his throat pulse as he swallowed. "This time, I let him have his way."

Pearl said, "Well, you missed all the excitement. Lorraine Whitt was caught kissing one of the Farber boys, and the whole place is atwitter."

"I don't care about that." Frank frowned. "Where's Alice?"

"Why, she's—" Pearl turned to show him and stopped, bewildered. "They were right there a minute ago." She gave the room a once-over. "I just saw Alice and John. They were drinking punch. They have to be around here somewhere."

"You were supposed to watch them."

"I was watching them, but it was so boring, Frank, and then you weren't even here."

"We need to find them. I've waited long enough. Tonight I put an end to this and let everyone know the truth of John Robinson. Time to send that darkie back to his hole, away from decent folk." He took hold of her arm.

"Ow, you're hurting me!" He released his grip, and she rubbed her upper arm. "Have you been drinking, Frank? You smell like hard liquor."

"Just a little bit of whiskey, not that it's any of your business. Now help me find your sister."

"We'll find them, Frank. You'll see."

Together they walked around the room, but they couldn't find Alice and John anywhere. "He's done something with her," Frank said. "She wouldn't leave on her own. He dragged her out of here, and you didn't even notice."

"John wouldn't do that," Pearl objected. "There has to be a good reason why they're not here. They must have stepped out for a minute."

"I just got here, and I didn't see them outside."

"Maybe they're checking on the horse?"

There was nothing left to do but go see for themselves. Frank left the dance hall first, and a few minutes later, when Pearl was sure no one would notice, she slipped out as well. She found Frank standing next to the Bennetts' buckboard. "The old man watching the horses says he hasn't seen them." Frank growled. "I can tell you one thing. When I do find John, he's a dead man." He raised his arm from his side, and Pearl recoiled at the sight of the gun in his hand.

"You brought your gun?"

"Of course. It was your idea." Frank smirked. "You wanted me to scare him, right?"

"Scare him, yes, but not do anything to him."

"Pearl, you're talking like a girl. Men like me take care of our women. Getting shot will run him out of town faster than any threats."

"You can't shoot him," Pearl said. "You'll get in trouble. You'll go to jail."

"I won't get in trouble if I catch him attacking Alice. I'd get an award for saving her."

"Well, now you're just being silly. John would never attack Alice. You don't need to shoot him."

He shrugged. "I'd let him off easy. If I can shoot a squirrel in the eye at a hundred yards, I can aim at Robinson and hit him somewhere it won't kill him. A warning shot. Just a graze."

Pearl crossed her arms. "And what if you miss and it's more than that?"

"I'm not gonna miss, Pearl. I'm a crack shot."

"What if you shoot near him, just to scare him? That would send the message, I think."

"Just scare him?"

"Fire it in the air or at the ground. The noise alone would scare a city boy like that and send him packing."

"If you say so, Pearl." Frank shrugged and stuck the gun in his waistband. "Let's keep searching. We can start by walking around the barn."

He strode away so quickly she was barely able to keep pace with him. After they'd rounded the barn, she was relieved to see that Alice and John weren't romancing in the dark in the back of the building, something that would have set Frank off and made Alice the talk of the town if word got out. She said, "Let's go back inside. Maybe they've returned by now."

Frank waved a dismissive hand. "You do what you want. I'm heading down to the lake. That's where all the lovers go. That's where he'd take her."

She couldn't really leave now. Frank had a gun and was going to confront Alice and John, maybe even shoot John and wound him. The idea struck Pearl as unthinkably awful and also oddly thrilling. Things like this only happened in motion pictures. She'd never dreamed she'd see it happen in real life.

Pearl stumbled down the path after him, silently cursing the dirt that must be covering her good shoes. She'd be a wreck by the time this was all over. Not as bad as Lorraine Whitt, though. There was no way she'd ever look that bad. The thought brought her some comfort.

When they got to the edge of the water, Frank pointed and said, "Right there. In the boat."

By the light of the moon, Pearl could barely make out the two people rowing toward the island. She squinted. "Are you sure it's them?"

"Looks like."

As they watched, the boat reached the island. The man got out first and pulled the bow onto shore before helping the lady out of her seat and onto dry ground. He actually lifted her by the waist and swung her around. Across the water skipped the unmistakable sound of Alice's laughter.

"Come on," Frank said, gripping her sleeve and pulling her toward one of the other rowboats.

"Where are we going?"

"To the island, of course. We need to save Alice from that bastard."

Frank helped Pearl into the rowboat and climbed in himself. In a minute, he'd unknotted the boat from its moorings, pushed off, and they were on their way.

CHAPTER FIFTY-THREE

1983

Standing outside the barn, Kathleen took a deep breath. "It was so crowded in there," she said, lifting her hair off the back of her neck. "I don't know about you, but I imagined it differently."

"Me too." Joe glanced back at the door. "I thought it would be more elegant. It reminded me of a high school dance." His dreams, he knew, had influenced his expectations. Even though none of his dreams were set at the Barn Dance, he'd inhabited John's skin often enough to sense the man's world and form an idea of what might have been. As John, Joe had seen Alice's upswept hair as she sat at the piano at the Victory Theater. He'd felt the styles of the day, the way things were back then. Going to the Barn Dance in 1983 was like experiencing a broken promise. The music, the clothes, the decorations—all of it just seemed wrong.

"So John and Alice went to the dance," Kathleen said. "We know that much. And then she was shot and died. But where did this happen?"

"Somewhere outdoors. The same evening as the dance," Joe said thoughtfully. "The dreams were separate, but I always got the feeling that the Death Dream happened after the Rowboat Dream."

A car turned into the parking lot and pulled into a space, the headlights veering as it turned. The laughter of giddy teenagers accompanied the sound of the car doors opening and closing. "The Rowboat Dream." Kathleen mulled over the words. "You know we're close to the lake?"

Five minutes later, they were at the metal pier, looking at rowboats dipping and bumping against each other in rhythm with the soft waves. "Was the rowboat in your dream like these?" she asked.

He shook his head. "My boat had a different kind of thing where the oars were attached. And inside the bottom of the boat were support pieces that looked like a rib cage." He spread out his fingers and touched his fingertips together to illustrate.

"A wooden one, then."

"I guess."

"That would make sense, given the time period." She gestured toward the boat at her feet. "Want to go for a ride? It might make your nightmares end completely."

"Doesn't it belong to someone?"

"No doubt, but we'll just take it out and be back in no time at all. I can finally show you the island. It's not too far."

"And if the owners of the boat come here in the meantime?"

"We can leave a note on the pier if you want." Kathleen snapped open her purse and pulled out a small spiral-bound pad of paper and a pen. She flipped back the cover and wrote:

BORROWED YOUR ROWBOAT. WILL BE BACK SOON.

KATHLEEN DINSMORE

With a flourish, she dropped the pad onto the pier and stuck the pen back in her bag.

"If you're willing to put your name to the crime, I'm okay with it," Joe said with a smile.

"If I get prosecuted, you can visit me in prison."

"I'll bake you a cake with a file in it."

"I never got that. What would I do with a file?" She reached down and pulled the rowboat parallel to the pier, then sat down and swung her legs over. Joe held the boat steady while she climbed in, then got in and sat opposite her.

"File the bars in your cell?"

"Ha! Do my nails is more like it," she said. "A file would be worthless. I'll tell you what: if you're going to the trouble, you might as well bake me a cake with some dynamite inside it, or a shovel. Something useful."

"I'll do my best." Joe gestured to the oars. "You do know you're in the seat to row? You want to switch?"

"No, I'll do it for a while, and then we can trade off," she said, lifting the oars and lowering them into the water.

She never stopped surprising him, in a good way. He nodded and sat back, admiring the capable way she eased the oars back, then dipped and pulled them forward, propelling the boat farther and farther away from the Barn Dance. The strains of the song "Crazy Little Thing Called Love" drifted across the surface of the water, a musical backdrop just for them. Joe tapped his palm on the side of the boat in time to the music and studied Kathleen as she happily rowed them toward the island. The Barn Dance had been a letdown, but this evening was turning into a good night after all.

Ricky stood on the shore and watched as the couple in the boat receded into the distance, disgust rising from his gut. Kathleen was really on a date with that guy, complete with slow dancing and a romantic boat ride. That guy. Unbelievable. He couldn't believe the pansy-ass was making her row. What kind of man would do such a thing?

In his opinion, Joe wasn't a man at all but a skinny kid aiming higher than his reach. She had to be dating him out of pity. The idea of this man-child touching Kathleen—kissing her, putting his filthy hands on her—made him want to puke. The rage that welled up in him made him all the more convinced that he was doing the right thing by maneuvering to take back what belonged to him.

If she didn't know it already, Kathleen would see Joe's true colors by the time the night was through. Ricky knew he would shine by comparison. He still remembered her saying how safe she felt in his presence in their early dating days. And while they were together, she'd often comment on his height and broad shoulders. He couldn't help but draw the conclusion that his strength, size, and confidence had been a draw for her.

And now she was out with Barney Fife? She was so mixed up, it wasn't even funny. The girl didn't know what she wanted.

He walked onto the pier and saw the notepad; her words made him smile. Proper Kathleen. So polite, she would have made a good librarian. He picked it up and flipped through the pages. Finding them all blank, he dropped the pad in the water, watching as it momentarily lingered on the surface. He gave it a shove with the toe of his shoe, and it sank, the words lost to the water.

He heard Kathleen's voice float over the water and Joe's in response, although he couldn't make out the words. He kept his eyes on the boat, noticing that they were heading toward a plot of land that seemed to be growing right up out of the lake. An island or a peninsula? Hard to tell. Within a few minutes, they were there. Joe hopped out and pulled the boat up on land, then helped Kathleen out.

Ricky mentally reconfigured his next course of action. His original scheme had counted on Joe's truck breaking down and Ricky, the masked assailant, beating the hell out of him by the side of the road. This plan was brilliant in a way, but risky. Some nosy parker could come upon the scene at the wrong time and ruin everything. If his identity was revealed, it would wreck his chance of reconciliation with his wife.

This boat outing changed things, possibly for the better. If they could rewrite the script, he could too. Ricky was not about to be outmaneuvered.

Among the rowboats, there was one canoe and a boat with an outboard motor. He unmoored the motorboat and started the engine, which roared to life. As he steered the boat away from the pier, he smiled, knowing he'd catch up to them in no time.

CHAPTER FIFTY-FOUR

1916

When John lifted Alice by the waist and swung her out of the boat and onto the shore, she laughed, carefree as a child. After so much time in service to her family at home, she now had an entire evening to devote entirely to herself. It was selfish on her part, she knew, but also long overdue. It had been risky to leave the dance without a chaperone, but she was able to justify her actions. Other people were impetuous all the time, and no one gave it a second thought. Wasn't she entitled to one evening of foolhardy behavior? Soon enough, John would be gone, and she'd be back to the stove and the washboard, once again mending clothing and weeding the garden. She didn't mind the work, at least not all that much. Someone had to do it, and she was more than adequate to the task, but one evening away from her chores was not too much to ask.

In the back of the boat, John found a box of matches along with a square privy lantern holding a fat candle. He opened the glass door on one side, lit the candle, and held the lantern aloft. "The owners of this boat are quite generous."

"And right now they're dancing the night away, unaware of their good deeds." She took the lantern from him and beckoned, knowing he'd follow her anywhere.

"So this is the island," John said as she led the way down a narrow path. "Are we going to run into any buccaneers?"

Alice turned and said, "No buccaneers. No buried treasure either. But I do want to show you something." She continued onward, her eyes adjusting as they ventured farther. When they came to a large clearing, empty except for four wooden tables with attached benches, she stretched her arm out with a flourish. "Look! It's a place for picnicking! Isn't it charming?" She set the lantern on one of the tables.

"Very charming. This is just for picnics?"

She nodded. "Just for picnics and celebrations. The eighth-grade class had only six graduates last year, so they had their ceremony here. When I was a little girl, I used to love to come here with my family. Pearl and I would pretend that we were shipwrecked on this island and had to make it our home."

"So you have happy memories from being here?" he asked, pulling her into his arms.

"Very happy memories." She felt her heart flutter as she nestled against him, resting her head against his shoulder. She'd never kissed a man on the lips, but she hoped John would kiss her that way tonight. He wouldn't think less of her for giving in to such a thing, she knew that much. He really cared for her. A kiss would be a promise between them, a memory in the making.

More important, she just yearned for a kiss, the touch of intimacy between them. She ached to feel his mouth on hers, to know what it was like to be a woman in love, to take that first step. She'd heard older women in Pullman brag that they'd never kissed anyone until the marriage ceremony had been completed. "I was at the altar with a ring on my finger," Mrs. Donohue had said more than once. When Alice was younger, she'd thought that was the only way, the righteous way. It wasn't until her father had let it slip that he and her mother had kissed before they'd wedded that she'd reconsidered the matter completely. During the times she'd imagined doing such a thing, she'd worried that if she did kiss a man, her ineptitude would be evident. That was before she'd met John.

She said, "So many happy memories. And now I have one more."

"Being here with me?"

"Of course."

He pulled away from her and whispered, "Alice, you have become everything to me. I've never felt this way before. I didn't know I *could* feel this way. I love you, and every day I fall even more in love with you."

"I love you too."

He dropped to one knee and took her hand. "Alice, dear Alice, would you do me the honor of becoming my wife?"

She heard the words, but it took a moment for her to take the meaning. "John, you know that I'd love nothing better . . ."

He stood up, a grin across his face. "I've already asked your father, and he's granted us permission. Say yes. Please say yes."

"My father agreed to this?" She sounded skeptical, but hopeful.

"Yes, he did. I even told him about my great-grandfather, and he still approved the match. I told him our engagement can last until I finish school. I know it's a long time to wait, sweetheart, but I will write to you every day and visit whenever I can."

"My father said yes." She shook her head incredulously. "I can't believe it."

"I don't have a ring for you yet, but I have money saved and will get one for you soon."

"I don't care about a ring. I only care about us." Alice couldn't believe it. She'd been so happy at the dance, happier still when they'd arrived on the island. She would not have thought it possible to surpass that feeling, but now the joy in her heart swelled beyond anything she could have envisioned. John wanted to marry her, and her father had given his permission.

"You have not answered my question. Will you marry me, Alice?"

"Yes. Oh yes."

He lifted her off her feet and swung her around in a circle, making her laugh, then gently set her down, holding her in a firm embrace. Putting his lips next to her ear, he breathed a question. "May I kiss you, Alice Louise Bennett?"

It was a good thing he was holding her close, because now she felt her knees weaken. "Yes, you may," she said, and then his mouth was against hers, his lips warm and tender. It was everything she'd ever dreamed it would be and yet not nearly enough. She marveled at how natural it seemed and felt elated to realize that this was just the beginning. They could kiss like this for the rest of their lives. The other part, the married intimacy, was something she was not entirely clear on, but with John, it could be only an expression of love. And then someday, besides having each other to count on, they'd have a family and a home. A few minutes ago, she'd dreaded her life after John left for school. Now she saw the years ahead unfolding in beauty like rose petals come to bloom.

She was still kissing John when they heard the sounds of a boat scraping onto the shore. They pulled apart, and she froze, listening. She was alarmed to hear footsteps on the path coming in their direction. She whispered to John, "We'll be discovered together."

"Don't worry, Alice," he said, not even lowering his voice. "We are engaged to be married, and we have your father's consent."

Alice stepped back even farther and smoothed her hair. If they left right now, darting through the trees away from the path, they might be able to avoid whoever was coming. It was no doubt another couple wanting privacy for lovemaking, which would not put them in a position to judge Alice and John, but still, she worried for her reputation. Until now, it had been completely untarnished.

"Maybe we should go," she said, motioning to one side. "We could circle around to the path and go unnoticed."

"I am not scurrying in the grass like a rat being hunted," John said, taking her hand. "We will leave the same way we arrived. There's no cause for alarm, Alice. We've done nothing wrong."

Alice listened as the rustling got louder, a feeling of dread building. When Pearl and Frank came into the clearing, she gave a sigh of relief. *Oh, thank goodness it was them and not one of the chaperones.* A second later, when Frank angrily opened his mouth, her sense of ease drained away, replaced by alarm.

"What the hell do you think you're doing?" Frank yelled, pointing a finger at John. "I know what you are."

Alice caught the slight slur in his words. Frank had been drinking. Pearl held a finger up to Frank to indicate he should wait.

"We've been looking for you," Pearl said, her eyes darting nervously from Frank to Alice and John. "I can't believe you left the dance. Father will not be pleased to hear this."

Alice had spent years smoothing over arguments between her sisters and was very good at it. Distraction was often the key. She let go of John's hand. "Frank! Pearl! You've come just in time to hear the good news. John has proposed, and I have accepted. We are engaged to be married."

"Engaged?" Pearl sounded more irate than congratulatory. She folded her arms. "No. You can't be engaged. Father is not going to allow such a thing. And where is your ring if you are engaged?"

John straightened up. "Alice does not have a ring yet, but I will be getting one for her soon."

"Soon?" Frank laughed in a mean way. "I have a ring at home I was ready to give you, and this fellow offers you nothing, and you think that's better than me?"

"Father will not be pleased," Pearl said. "You sneaking off like this and agreeing to marry John. He's not even from Pullman."

"Father has already given his permission," Alice assured her. "John asked him earlier."

John spoke up. "I spoke to him one day at the mill, and he gave us his blessing."

"His blessing?" Frank said, becoming enraged. "He'll take it back after he finds out who you really are." He turned to Alice. "Did you know he's a Negro, Alice? And that his father is in prison for killing a man? I bet he didn't tell you that. I've known your family my whole life, and I know your father. He would never let you marry a man beneath you, especially one with Negro blood and a murderer for a father."

"Frank!" Alice said, shocked. "I don't want to hear you say such things."

"It's true," Frank said. "All true." He reached behind him, and when his arm swung forward, Alice shivered at the sight of the gun, now aimed right at John. "My uncle in Gladly Falls told me all about you, John Lawrence Robinson. You got yourself a grandpappy black as coal. There's no use denying it."

Alice said, "Frank, put the gun down."

But Frank kept going. "Your daddy is a jailbird, and you and your mother are servants in some rich person's house. You aren't fit to lick my boots, and you think you can have Alice?"

John took a step forward. "Frank, I think you need to face facts, my friend. It's a hard truth, but Alice is not interested in your affections. She and I are in love, and we're going to get married. When you sober up, you'll see your way clear in all this."

Frank staggered forward, but his outstretched arm still had the gun aimed at John. "Sober up? You use big words, college boy, like you think you're better than me, but you're nothin'."

John held his hands out. "I never said I was better than you."

Alice spoke through gritted teeth. "Put the gun down, Frank, before someone gets hurt."

"Oh, I'm counting on someone getting hurt. And his name is John Lawrence Robinson. You don't believe me, Alice? You don't think I know what I'm talking about? I can prove all of it." Frank's words came out in a bellow.

"You don't need to prove anything to me," she said. "John told me all of this already. It doesn't matter about his father or his great-grandfather. He's the one I love."

"You love him? Him?" He waved the gun back and forth. "That's an insult to all decent men."

"Frank," John said, "can you put down the gun and shake my hand? We can solve this like gentlemen and talk it through. And if you don't want to shake my hand, you can punch me if it will make you feel better. Just put down the gun."

He was, Alice realized, trying to jolly Frank out of his anger, but she knew Frank well enough to know he would not be swayed that easily.

She pulled on John's arm. "Let's go," she said. "It's getting late. We can row back, and you can drive Pearl and me home. We can talk tomorrow if you want, Frank. I'm getting tired, and I want to go home."

Both men were locked in a stare and didn't waver. "Put away the gun, Frank," John said, stepping forward with his hand outstretched. "You're scaring Alice."

"Looks like I'm scaring you too." He waved the gun again.

Pearl went up to Alice and slipped her hand through the crook of her elbow. "Let's take the boat back to the dance and let the gentlemen settle this themselves. It's getting late."

Alice wasn't going anywhere without John. "This has to stop, Frank. I am in love with John, and we are going to get married. There is nothing you can do about it."

Frank shook with anger. "Nothing I can do about it? That's where you're wrong, Alice." He cocked the gun. "You will never marry him."

"That's enough, Frank." John kept his voice even.

"Not enough for me," Frank said. "You aren't gonna be fit for pigs to eat by the time I'm through with you."

Alice wrenched her arm away from Pearl and rushed forward, putting herself between Frank and John and grabbing at the barrel of the gun. The word *no* was barely past her lips when the gun went off. The deafening bang overshadowed everything else, and she fell back into John's arms, setting off a profusion of sounds.

Screams from Pearl.

An utterance of profanity from Frank.

A cry from John.

There was despair on John's face as he held her, sitting on the ground, frantically pressing on the front of her dress to try to stop the flow of blood. "Stay with me, Alice. Just keep breathing," he said. "You're going to be fine. Just stay here."

The last thing she wanted was to leave him, but she felt herself weakening, her grip on this world slipping as she was pulled into the next.

"I love you, Alice," he said, his eyes filling with tears. "Don't leave me."

She tried to tell him she loved him too, but her lips wouldn't cooperate, and the light called to her with a pull stronger than her own will. She began to shake, and now, despite the sticky night air, she felt cold, so cold.

One second she was there lying on the ground, her eyelids flickering, breath ragged, and love in her heart.

The next second her body was limp and lifeless.

She was gone.

CHAPTER FIFTY-FIVE

1916

And then it was quiet, so quiet, only the chirping of insects to interrupt the silence.

"She's dead," John said, sobbing. "You killed her."

"No," Pearl said in shock. How could that be? Alice had been fine only a minute ago, and now she was dead? No. It was unfathomable. She stared down at John, who held Alice in his arms, blood everywhere. "Someone has to do something." She knelt next to her sister and frantically said, "Alice? Can you hear me?" She looked up at Frank. "We have to get her to the doctor. Right away."

Tears streamed down John's face; he pressed his lips against Alice's head and rocked her in his arms. "It's too late. She's gone."

A few feet away, Frank turned his back and dropped to a crouch, cradling his head in his hands. "I didn't mean to hurt anyone. She shouldn't have stepped in front of me and grabbed the gun."

"You didn't have to shoot her!" Pearl cried out. "Why'd you pull the trigger?"

Frank said, "Dammit, Pearl, this was your idea. I'm not going to jail for this. I'm telling them it was you."

"Me? Shoot my own sister with *your* gun? You bastard. No one will believe you." She began to wail, tears streaming from her eyes.

John interrupted. "I'm taking her home." He scooped Alice up and started to stand, then staggered back. "I think . . ." He looked down at the front of his white shirt, now stained bright with blood. "I think it got me too."

CHAPTER FIFTY-SIX

1983

Impressively enough, Kathleen rowed all the way to the island. Joe watched her elegant strokes, perfectly in rhythm.

"Quite the biceps you've got there, Miss Dinsmore," Joe said as they approached the opposite shore. "I could get used to this." He leaned over one side of the boat, a hand trailing in the cool water while he admired her determination.

"Moving furniture at the store does more for me than Jane Fonda's *Workout*. I do a lot of heavy lifting. I'm strong." To his amusement, she paused to flex, then went back to rowing. "I'll let you row on the way back, though."

"Fair enough." He watched the reflection of the moon on the lake. "I'm looking forward to seeing those turtles you mentioned, unless you don't think they'll be out at night."

She stared at him in amazement. "You remember me talking about the turtles?"

"Of course. You and your mom fed them worms from a Styrofoam cup. You told me about it the first time we ate lunch at the Pine Cone."

"I can't believe you remember that."

"Well, of course. I remember everything you tell me. That day was notable because it was the day you agreed to be my friend. Quite a score for me. I like to think of it as my lucky day."

"Really?" It was just the one word, but she sounded pleased.

As the boat banged against the rocky shoreline, Joe hopped out and dragged one end to ground it, then helped Kathleen out of the boat. She held up a red plastic flashlight. "Nice of the boat's owners to leave this for us."

"So we're exploring?" he said, glancing back.

"There's not much to explore, but we might as well look around as long as we're here," she said. They followed the cone of light down a wood-chipped path and came to a clearing with a firepit in the middle of it. Kathleen shone the light in an arc, revealing two picnic tables and a large metal garbage bin. On the ground was assorted trash: plastic bags, beer cans, and scraps of paper.

"Looks like the aftermath of a raccoon convention," Joe said.

"More like a visit from some slobs. It was never like this when I came here as a kid. Honestly, how hard is it to pick up after yourself?" She moved the light around, stopping on what looked like a deflated balloon. "Is that . . . ?"

Joe got closer and inspected it. "Yup, it's a used rubber." He shook his head. "Kids today. We teach them about abstinence, but they don't listen."

"Gross. I was thinking of picking up some of this trash, but now I'm not touching anything."

"Smart decision."

"I hate to leave it like this, though. It makes me sad to see all this garbage. When I used to come out here with my mom, it was so lovely."

Joe sensed the wistfulness in her voice. "If it really bothers you, we can come back tomorrow with gloves and work on cleaning this place up together."

"You'd do that?"

"Sure, why not? I mean, if it's important to you. It wouldn't take long."

"You know what I like about you, Joe?" Without waiting for an answer, she continued. "You really care about other people. When my house was broken into, you slept on the couch and fixed the door. At restaurants, you leave good tips. You hold doors open for people and are polite to everyone. You pay people compliments, even Marcia, who gives you a hard time. You've been a good friend to me."

"Well, thanks. It's easy to be your friend, Kathleen."

"It's not just me, though. When we saw Doris at the dance, you didn't make any jokey comments to her. You just offered to fix her son's wheelchair, and then you did it."

"Yeah, about that. Did you know she has a child?"

"I did. His name is Randy."

"I didn't know. I feel kind of bad now for razzing her all the time."

Kathleen said, "I think she gets a kick out of you. When I go to the restaurant without you, she always asks where you are."

"You go to the Pine Cone without me?" he asked in mock indignation, hands pressed against both sides of his face.

"Just to pick up carryout."

"Well, that's okay, then." Joe was thoughtful. "That wheelchair is a total wreck. She's got it all duct-taped up. I got the wheel back in alignment, but it needs a lot more than that. If I had a few days and some replacement parts I could fix it, but I'm guessing Randy couldn't go without it for that long."

"Probably not."

Joe looked beyond the clearing. "What's the rest of the island like?"

"Trees and dirt."

"You make it sound so enticing. You should be a tour director." He deepened his voice. "And here on your left, you can see trees and dirt. On the right, more trees and dirt."

"I call it like I see it."

The sound of a motorboat cut into the conversation, and both of them stopped to listen. It grew louder and louder until it was apparent the boat was headed toward them. When the engine cut, Kathleen said, "I think we've got company. Some kids wanting to party, maybe?"

"Or a couple wanting to have sex on the picnic table?"

"Yuck. My mom and I used to eat at these tables. We'd bring a bag lunch, and I'd eat my chips and lemonade and peanut butter sandwich right here."

"You're not going to do that anymore."

"You got that right."

"We should go," Joe said. "Give the new people their privacy."

They were halfway down the path when they heard a rustling in the woods that eclipsed the sound of the breeze in the trees. Joe held out an arm to stop her. "Did you hear that?" When she nodded, he called out, "Who's out there?"

They listened, but it was quiet once again. When they resumed walking, the rustling started again. Joe heard Kathleen's breathing beside him; she'd moved next to him. She whispered, "I don't like this."

"Probably just a squirrel," Joe said loudly, more to assuage Kathleen's fears than anything else. He whispered into her ear, "Or some teenagers trying to freak us out. Let's keep going."

Her fingers trembling, she took his hand and kept the flashlight ahead of them. They went more slowly this time but kept a steady pace. Joe breathed easier upon seeing the rowboat at the end of the path. They were nearly there when they heard the stomping of heavy boots in the underbrush and the crash of someone coming out of the trees. The intruder came running at full speed and slammed into Joe, who was knocked to the ground with a force that took his breath away.

Kathleen screamed, and the attacker turned and went after her, smacking the flashlight out of her hand and pushing her down. The man was somewhat visible now—a large guy in dark clothing wearing a black ski mask. Joe was halfway to standing when the man returned, pulling him to his feet. From behind, the masked man put him in a choke hold, his arm tight around Joe's neck. Joe felt something metal and cylindrical pressed against his temple. A gun. It had to be.

Overcome by terror, he forced out the words: "What is it that you want? Money? In my back pocket . . ."

The man spoke quietly. "Shut up."

Kathleen got up and held her hands in the surrender position. With the flashlight on the ground, she was only a dim outline, but it was clear she saw the gun pressed against Joe's head. "Don't hurt him. Please don't hurt him. I have jewelry. My earrings are antique. Real pearls. I have money too. I'm going to slowly open my purse and get my money out for you." Kathleen opened her purse and began to rifle through it.

Joe heard a growl in his ear and the man's voice saying, "Tell her to take the boat and leave. If she stays, I'll kill you first and then rape her."

His heart knocking, Joe found his voice. "Kathleen, listen to me. You need to get in the rowboat and go back to the dance. I'll be fine."

"I'm not leaving."

The gun pressed tighter against Joe's head, making him wince in pain. "Kathleen, believe me, you need to go, or he's going to kill me." Joe felt strangely detached, as if he were watching all this happen to someone else. It was confusing and crazy and horrible. He was in this vise grip, held prisoner by a complete stranger for no reason he could discern. On occasion, he'd considered how it was he might die, but he'd never imagined it would be like this.

She hesitated. "But if I go . . ."

"Please, Kathleen, I'm begging you. I'll be fine. Please go."

Without a word, she ran down the path, and a minute or so later, he heard the scrape of the boat being pushed away from the shore and the splash of the oars in the water. As soon as Joe knew she was safe, he began to struggle, trying to break free. Death was a foregone conclusion, whether he objected or not. He wasn't giving up without a fight.

The way this man appeared out of nowhere, his frightening strength, and the presence of a gun brought back the terror of the Death Dream, with the added horror of having it happen in real life. Perhaps only a minute or so had passed since Kathleen had left—it was hard to say—but the gun was pressed so hard against his head, it felt like it was boring a hole in his skull. "Stop it," Joe said, twisting his body. His voice seemed to remind the man of his existence, and he suddenly dragged Joe down the path.

When they got to the clearing, he threw Joe down on the ground and stomped on his chest. Pain shot through him as he heard the sickening crack of his breaking ribs. Looking up, Joe saw the man in outline standing over him, the gun pointed straight at him. The man mocked him with his own words. "'Please, Kathleen, I'm begging you.' You are pathetic."

Joe forced words out through the pain. "What do you want?"

"You think you're so great. You're nothing. You're scum."

In agony, he clutched his front and said, "If I agree, can we end this?"

"Shut up!" He kicked at Joe's legs. "You don't talk unless I say you can."

Joe's mind raced, calculating how long it would take for Kathleen to get back to the other side of the lake and return with help. Half an hour? That was wishful thinking. It would certainly take longer than that. And who would she bring back with her? Any of the young men at the dance might be able to help. But against a madman with a gun?

Every time he tried to get up, the attacker knocked him back down. Desperate, he began to crawl, something that infuriated the man, who pistol-whipped him across the back of his skull. Joe's hands flew up to protect his head, and the man said, "By the time I'm through with you, you aren't gonna be fit for pigs to eat."

The man stomped on Joe's arm, and Joe cried out in pain, collapsing on the ground. Vertigo overcame him, and the world became a kaleidoscope of dim images. Though his vision was blurry, he was able to make out the man's form, a large blot blocking the stars of the night sky, his gun pointed right at Joe. "You are nothin' but a pansy-ass." He heard the sharp click of the gun being cocked.

The stabbing pain in Joe's chest was worse when he breathed, so he inhaled carefully. As his eyes adjusted, Joe noticed movement. Behind the man, someone else had crept into the clearing. Joe watched as something long and thin rose up in the air over the man's head. Then the man spun around, and Joe saw Kathleen, brandishing the oar like a weapon. The man lurched forward, and as he and Kathleen grappled, the oar tumbled sideways to the ground. Joe heard the rumble of the man's voice and Kathleen responding, "No, no, no."

Joe fought to get to his feet, ignoring the ice-pick agony of his rib cage. Kathleen and the man struggled, the man grabbing her hair and making her cry out. "Let go!" she wailed. The sound of her voice keening in pain made him forget about his own. He rushed at the man and slammed his fist into his shoulder, getting an elbow to the chest in return.

In a slow-motion moment, he saw Kathleen and the intruder grapple for the gun and heard the man yell, "But I love you, Kathleen!"

Kathleen cried out, "I don't love you. I never will!" He had her by one arm, and as she struggled, the gun was between them. There was a spark of light and a loud crack, the sound reverberating off the lake.

The man crumpled to the ground, and Kathleen screamed. In the pale light, Joe saw the blood splattered across the front of her dress and the lifeless form of the man on the ground. He went to Kathleen, and she nearly collapsed in his arms, tears beginning to flow.

"Are you okay?" Joe asked. "Are you hurt?"

She looked up at him, her eyes wet, and shook her head. Just a few feet from where they stood lay the body of the man, arms sprawled and blood pouring from a gaping wound in his chest.

Joe wrapped his arms around her, feeling her body tremble as she clung to him, and said, "It's okay. You're safe. Everything's going to be fine."

When she could finally manage to talk, she blurted out, "It's Ricky."

CHAPTER FIFTY-SEVEN

1983

Grimacing through the pain, Joe leaned over and pulled the ski mask off Ricky. He was dead—that would have been clear enough even without the lack of a pulse. Kathleen found the gun nearby. Joe emptied it, and they carried it with them.

Taking the motorboat back was an easy decision. Along the way, Kathleen managed to fill him in on what had happened after she'd fled. She'd circled the island in the rowboat, looking for a way to sneak back to him, when she'd encountered the motorboat tied to a tree. She left the rowboat there as well and took an oar to come to his rescue. She realized it was Ricky when she recognized his voice taunting Joe. "It all made sense then. It *was* him that day when I thought I saw him standing across the street. He was the one who broke into my house, and he followed us across the lake."

"You took a big risk coming back. You could have gotten hurt or killed," Joe said, holding his injured arm to his side. He winced as the boat crested and dropped.

"I couldn't leave you," she said. "I had no choice."

Once they reached the other side of the lake, she told Joe to stay put while she scrambled out of the boat to get help at the Barn Dance. A rush of assistance arrived in the form of several young men who helped Joe onto the pier. A local doctor was in attendance, as was a police officer and a sheriff's deputy. Kathleen hovered over Joe while filling them all in on what had happened on the island.

The doctor drove them to the closest hospital, where Joe was immediately seen in the emergency room. Joe's severest injuries were cracked ribs and a broken arm, a displaced fracture that required surgery. As they wheeled him down the hall to the operating room, he felt awful that he was leaving Kathleen to be interviewed by a police officer, but he didn't have a choice.

Coming out of the anesthesia after the surgery, he found himself mentally drifting along a river of memories—not his own, but those of John Lawrence Robinson. The fragmented dreams he'd had for months were gone, replaced by more complete memories: John carrying Daisy on his shoulders while Alice hung the wash; the feeling of dancing with Alice in his arms; the joy in discovering a new love letter and then keeping it safe so he could read it over and over again. All these and so many more.

And finally, the memory of John's marriage proposal to Alice and the joy of hearing her say yes. At that moment, John's entire life made sense. Knowing she would become his wife gave meaning to all his struggles.

The swirl of memories ended with the confrontation with Pearl and Frank at the island. Now Joe saw more than just a glimpse of what had happened. He felt as if he had lived the experience, with details to accompany the emotions. As John, he registered a pang of guilt; he should have taken Frank more seriously. He'd made the mistake of pegging Frank as a simple farm boy, hotheaded but unlikely to pull the trigger. He'd misjudged him, and Alice had paid the price when she stepped between them.

When John realized all was lost and that she was slipping away, he held her tightly and begged her not to go. He'd had only a few minutes to grieve her death before he realized the bullet that had killed Alice had pierced him as well.

Joe felt John's anguish because it was his own. And then, a new memory, which felt like a dream within a dream. John's own injury was not nearly as bad as Alice's, but without medical attention, the blood loss was devastating. John felt himself get light-headed and weak. Pearl and Frank were useless, not knowing what to do. He didn't fault them. It was too late to get help. It was dark, and they'd had no medical training. He remembered thinking he was dying, and he felt the sorrow of knowing he was leaving his mother behind.

And then, a sense of utter tranquility. John closed his eyes in the earthly world and opened them in a different, better world. There was pure white light and beautiful music, and best of all, Alice aglow, standing there to meet him, her hand extended.

Joe was jolted awake, confused to find himself in a hospital bed. The room smelled like disinfectant, and although his room was quiet, he heard beeping and talking and the rattle of carts in the hallway being pushed to their destinations. His chest was securely bandaged, and his left arm was in a cast. His head felt like it had been compressed by a trash compactor. He was fully conscious now but still foggy.

When he turned his head to one side, he spotted Kathleen, reading. He watched her for what seemed like a long time before she noticed he was awake. She closed the magazine. "Hey there, Joe. Ready to join the world?" She gave him a soft smile.

He blinked. "You're still here."

"Of course I'm still here. Where would I go?"

"I don't know." He looked around the room, letting it all come into focus. "You're a good friend, Kathleen."

"Well, I certainly hope I'm more than that," she said, allowing herself a small grin.

Before he could address that statement, she went on to explain that the police officer wanted to question Joe, but based on Kathleen's statement and Joe's injuries, it seemed certain that Ricky's death would be categorized as accidental self-defense, and no charges would be filed against her. "It was a good thing I filed a police report for abuse when we were married. At the time, it didn't seem to do much, but having it on record established a pattern of violence that's now in my favor. Not that any of this is in my favor," she added ruefully.

"I'm sorry," Joe said.

"Why are you sorry? You didn't do anything wrong. If anything, I should be apologizing to you for what you've gone through. I look at you and want to cry."

"That bad, huh?"

"Temporarily."

A long pause. "What time is it? What day is it?"

"It's about eight thirty on Sunday morning. The Barn Dance was last night."

He let that one sink in. He'd been out a long time after the surgery. "Did anyone call my parents?"

"I called your grandmother, and she called your family. They're on their way."

"Did my dad actually talk to Pearl?"

She nodded. "That's what she told me. She said it was like a miracle to hear his voice. They had a pretty good talk, according to your grandmother."

Joe suddenly missed his family and wanted to see them. Best yet would be if he could see them all together—all the important people in his life in one place. Kathleen, his dad and mom, Linda, Pearl, and even Marcia and Howard, everybody in one room, and all of them getting along. He wanted Linda to see their grandmother's house and the old family photos. He wanted to take the whole lot of them to the Pine

Cone and say something to make Doris smile. The fact that his dad and Pearl had spoken to each other was a good sign, a start.

But before he did any of that, he wanted to talk to Pearl and tell her he knew the truth of what happened to Alice. He sensed that underneath that tough exterior, she yearned for forgiveness, and he believed he might be able to help in that department. She had been waiting a long time to find some peace of mind.

He said to Kathleen, "I know what happened to John and Alice after they left the Barn Dance."

"You do?"

"Yes. I've had a dream of what happened that night."

"Recently?"

"Since I've been here. I guess it was the anesthesia."

She sucked in a breath and exhaled in disappointment. "Oh no. Another dream?"

"This time felt different," he said, struggling to explain. "It felt like the end, like this has run its course, and it's over now. I don't think I'll have any more dreams." He'd so badly wanted to stop having the dreams, but now that they were over, there was a sadness to it. A finality. Like saying goodbye to old friends.

"I hope you're right."

"I've been thinking about it, and I believe," he said thoughtfully, "that you and I have been re-creating their time together. Our own version of it anyway. That night at the Barn Dance, we sort of relived their last night, but for us, it turned out differently because of you. You changed the ending."

She tilted her head to one side. "*I* changed the ending. What do you mean?"

"Let me tell you." And then, to her wide-eyed amazement, he told her the whole story.

CHAPTER FIFTY-EIGHT

1983

Joe heard Linda's voice in the hallway just outside his hospital room, so he was ready when she burst through the door. His mom and dad followed, both of them with concerned expressions on their faces. "Hey, Joe!" Linda said. "Guess what? We have a new grandmother."

"I know! Isn't that something?" He grinned at her, amazed to see that her earlobes were adorned with tiny studs. Linda had long wanted pierced ears, but their mom had sworn she would have to wait until she was fifteen. Linda had an adorable way of wheedling to get what she wanted. Apparently, she'd worn their mother down.

"How are you, Joe?" His mom looked down on him in concern and then noticed Kathleen, who stood from her bedside chair and introduced herself.

"Are you Joe's girlfriend?" Linda asked.

"Yes, she is," Joe answered before Kathleen could say a word. "Be nice to her. I don't want her scared away."

They made small talk, discussing Joe's injuries and the drive up to Pullman. Chicago traffic had been particularly bad, his father said.

Eventually, when the nurse came in to take his blood pressure, Kathleen excused herself and slipped out of the room.

"Your girlfriend's pretty," Linda said, watching her go.

"I think so too."

His dad said, "So it was a jealous ex-husband who did this to you?" His forehead creased with concern.

Joe nodded as the nurse slipped the blood pressure cuff over his arm. "That's right." He waited for his father to expand on this, to say that Kathleen was trouble, or that he should really date someone closer to his own age, but he only said, "What's wrong with people?"

They stayed to visit until Joe was too tired to keep his eyes open, then decided to leave to visit Pearl. His father made a face and said, "We made the trip here. We might as well see her while we're in town."

His mom smoothed the cover on Joe's bed while talking to his dad. "Just be pleasant, Bill. She's an old lady. It doesn't cost anything to be kind." She leaned over and gave Joe a kiss on the cheek. "We've missed you, Joe. I hope you feel better soon."

Linda gave him a hug and a loud smooch. "We'll be back tomorrow." And then she leaned in and whispered, "I'll tell you how it goes."

Even his usually undemonstrative father leaned in for a hug and a pat on the arm. "Follow the doctor's orders, son, and you'll be healed in no time."

When Joe was preparing to leave the hospital the next day, his family suggested he drive back with them. His dad said, "Joe, I really think it would be best if you come home to finish recovering. We'd love to have you with us. You shouldn't be here all alone."

Joe appreciated the offer and knew it was made with love, but he also knew he wasn't finished with Pullman and all it had to offer. Also, his dad had gotten it wrong. He wasn't alone.

After he was discharged from the hospital, Kathleen drove him back to his grandmother's house. As they pulled up to the porch, he was surprised to see the truck he'd driven to the Barn Dance now parked next to the house. He gave Kathleen a curious look. "How did the truck find its way home?"

"Marcia and I did it. It turned out that someone had added water to the fuel line, so it stalled out halfway down the road. Luckily, she was driving right behind me at the time. We had to get it towed. The mechanic fixed it. Don't ask me how."

"Thanks for taking care of it."

She flexed. "You will find that not only am I strong, I am also resourceful."

He grinned. She was really something. Their relationship had evolved from just friends to more than friends without even a discussion. "Smartest, strongest woman I know. Thank you."

"I have another surprise for you as well. In the kitchen."

If Joe expected a gourmet feast or an apple pie, he would have been disappointed. Instead of delicious food, he found Pearl sitting at the table, her big purse in her lap, her walker positioned next to her like a loyal dog.

"Joe!" she said, her face lighting up. "I'm so glad to see you!"

"It's good to see you too."

She'd called him at the hospital but hadn't visited. It was a long drive that required asking someone to take her, and she'd been too tired for an outing. "This old body is betraying me," she'd said during the call. "It doesn't cooperate at all anymore."

"I'm sorry."

"Nothing to be sorry about. I just got old and got cancer." There was a long pause, and then she said, "Funny, but I never thought it would happen to me."

Talking to his grandmother alone had been first on his list of things to do once he'd returned from the hospital. Knowing this, Kathleen had made it happen.

Now his grandmother was here, ready and waiting. "Do you feel better?" she asked.

"A ton better," Joe assured her. "Once the arm heals, I'll be good as new." He pulled out a chair and sat across from her.

Without a word, Kathleen got out two glasses and took a pitcher of lemonade from the refrigerator. After she'd set the lemonade and a napkin in front of each of them, she said, "If you'll excuse me, I have to run a quick errand. I'll be back in about an hour."

After she left the room, Pearl said, "That girl is sweet on you."

"I hope you're right." He took a sip of his drink. "The feeling is mutual."

She leaned over and put her hand over his. Her skin was warm and transparent as tissue paper, the veins showing through the skin. "I want to thank you for bringing your father to me. We had a nice talk."

Joe nodded. At the hospital, Linda had surreptitiously filled him in while his parents were in the hallway, talking to the doctor. All three of them had gone to visit Pearl at Pine Ridge Hollow after leaving the hospital the day before. Pearl, knowing they were coming, was waiting. When she opened the door to her apartment, she greeted them, then asked their father, "Bill, can you give an old lady a hug?" Linda said he'd hesitated for only a second before he walked into her outstretched arms. It was a short hug, Linda said, but still, after so many decades, Joe considered it a minor miracle. "Dad told her that they'll never be able to agree on things, but that he was willing to move forward if she was. And then she said all she wanted was his forgiveness, and he said, 'Life is too short to hold on to grudges. I can't forget what happened in the past, but I can forgive you.'" Linda's eyes widened in amazement. "I think he did it because Mom told him to, but later in the car, he said just saying the words made him feel better."

Just saying the words and knowing you were heard. Sometimes that was all it took. Joe said, "I didn't really bring him to you, but you're welcome."

"Oh, but you did," she said. "When you got into the car at Trendale, you took a leap of faith that brought him here. If not for you, I would have died without seeing my only son one more time or meeting my grandchildren." Joe noticed that his grandmother looked changed since the last time he'd seen her. Softer, more fragile. It seemed to him that she had less fight in her, and for a moment, he considered letting it go, not bringing up the subject of Alice's death at all. But if he did that, he'd be robbing her of closure.

"I'm glad you and my dad were able to work things out, but the reason Kathleen asked you here was because she knew I wanted to talk to you."

She squeezed his fingers and then let go. "Well, don't be shy. Just spit it out, then."

"It's about Alice's death." He let the sentence lie there for a second.

"I'm not going to talk about it, if it's all the same to you. She's gone, and there's nothing I can do about it. Talking endlessly about the way she died isn't going to change anything." She sat back in her chair and clutched her purse.

"I don't need you to talk about it. I already know how it happened. I just want to understand why it happened. Why did you say you shot Alice when it was Frank who pulled the trigger? Why would you take the blame for something you didn't do?"

The silence between them was thick. Her lower lip began to tremble, and suddenly she reminded Joe of a younger, more vulnerable woman. Just when he thought she was at a complete loss for words, she said, "I took the blame because I was to blame." Tears filled her eyes. "It was all my fault. If I had insisted that Frank leave the gun behind, he would have listened to me, but I egged him on. I wanted to scare John."

Joe sorted through her words. "Because you didn't want John to take Alice away?"

"No." She shook her head. "Worse than that. I didn't want her to have something I didn't. I was jealous. And then when Frank told me that John's great-grandfather was a black man and his father was in prison, well, that was pretty scandalous back then. I was all for exposing him to everyone."

"You were young. You didn't mean for it to happen."

She dabbed her eyes with the napkin. "I meant for something to happen. I remember that day like it was yesterday. Frank told me he was going to shoot John, not to kill him, just to wound him, and secretly, I found the idea thrilling. Can you believe that? It was like a big game to me." Her gaze dropped to her lap. "Because of my stupidity, two innocent people died."

"I'm sorry."

When she finally looked up, Joe saw sorrow reflected in her eyes. "Oh, she was special, my sister Alice. One in a million, although I didn't realize it at the time." Pearl drew a quiet breath. "I wish you could have known her, Joe. She was the best of us all."

And then, for someone who'd initially said she wasn't going to talk about it, it seemed all Pearl could do was talk about it. She told Joe that everything bad in her life that happened after that came about as a result of that evening. "My unhappy marriage, my husband's drinking, my son cutting me out of his life—it all followed." Her finger traced the edge of the table. "One thing leading to another. A chain linked by shame and unhappiness."

"What did your husband's drinking have to do with Alice's death?"

"Frank was never the same after that night. He lost a leg in the war, and he came home angry and depressed. He married me out of guilt, I guess."

"Wait a minute!" Joe sat up straight. "Frank was your husband? My dad's father was Frank?"

"Of course." Her brow furrowed. "How did you not know that?"

"No one told me. I mean, my dad never mentioned his name, and neither did you."

"Then how did you know what happened that day?"

Joe recalled all the dreams given to him, presented like a gift for him to pass on to his grandmother. He sensed that it was important for him to share the feeling of peace that Alice and John had given him at the end. It could only bring her comfort. But how to explain without sounding crazy? It struck him that neither of them had drunk very much of their lemonade. Kathleen had left only a few minutes ago, so there was plenty of time to fill.

Finally, he said, "I know exactly what happened because I experienced it. I was there."

"I don't understand."

"I have a lot to tell you. Please keep an open mind. What I'm going to tell you will sound crazy, but I assure you it's the truth."

CHAPTER FIFTY-NINE

PEARL ~ 1983

Time has a way of evening things out. I was beautiful once, turning heads and garnering admiring glances. Now I can see how little this matters.

You see, I am dying.

I had regrets, so many regrets. One night, while lying in bed, I realized that I'd broken each of the Ten Commandments at least once. It was a horrifying thought, made all the worse by realizing there's nothing I could do about it. What's done is done. You can't unring the bell. I surely would, if given a chance.

I found myself praying every day, something I never did much of before. Fear is what drove me. I did not want to go to hell. And I knew I was not a shoo-in for heaven; this had worried me.

If I did one thing right, it was seeking out my grandson, even if it was for selfish reasons.

After my son, Bill, told me he forgave me, I began to forgive myself. And when Joe told me his vision of John—the sense of utter tranquility, the pure white light and beautiful music, and best of all, Alice, all aglow, standing there to meet him, her hand extended—I felt my fear melt away.

Alice had a heart of gold. My father called her Ally-bird because she sang like a nightingale. She loved everyone in our family, but I always thought I was her favorite. She was the best of us all.

After she left this earth, nothing was ever the same.

I cannot wait to see her again.

CHAPTER SIXTY

1983

There was only one funeral home in Pullman: Mueller & Sons. Their brochure said the business had been in the family for five generations, and judging from the style of the furniture and drapes, the decor was just as old. Joe had dreaded Pearl's funeral, most of all because she'd left him in charge, but as it turned out, she'd preplanned and prepaid for all of it, taking away most of the burden.

He had help. Kathleen had gone through this when her great-aunt Edna died, so she was familiar with funeral protocol. She was by his side when he sorted through the family photos and arranged them on poster boards to display on the easels provided by the funeral home.

She also was the one who went to the historical society and found the 1916 newspaper articles reporting what had happened on the island that day. When questioned by the police, Frank and Pearl had told the same story. They'd followed Alice and John to the island because it looked like she was taken against her will and they feared for her safety. Once there, they got confused in the dark, and Frank had discharged the gun by mistake. The bullet had struck Alice, causing a fatal injury, and then passed through her chest, hitting John, who bled to death. The incident was deemed an unfortunate accident, and there were no criminal charges. The article said that Alice Bennett's sister was devastated and not available for comment.

"No wonder they married each other," Joe had said. "They had to keep each other's secret."

"I for one am glad they got married," Kathleen said, "or you would never have been born."

Kathleen had helped line up the chaplain from Pine Ridge Hollow to speak at the service, and she also assisted in writing the obituary. Joe's family would be coming, and some of Pearl's out-of-town relatives were going to be there as well. They hired the Pine Cone to provide sandwiches, side dishes, and beverages for a buffet lunch after the service.

Joe and Kathleen stood in the parlor of the funeral home, waiting for guests to arrive. To their right, Pearl lay serenely in a mahogany casket, hands folded one atop the other. Floral arrangements ringed either side of the casket, so many that Joe had been shocked when he first arrived. "I didn't know she had so many friends," he'd said to Kathleen.

"It's not just friends," she said. "It's everyone who knew her or who knew anyone in her family. It's a way for people to recognize her life and her passing. To be there for the people who were there for her. It's a show of community."

He nodded and then, because he didn't know what else to say, said, "She looks really peaceful."

"Like she's sleeping." Kathleen had chosen the dress Pearl wore and picked out the earrings. There were so many details that Joe had never considered before this.

He said, "I know it sounds stupid, but it's hard for me to believe she's dead. I mean, I just talked to her, and I was starting to feel like we had a connection. When they called and said she'd passed away, I was stunned."

During their last conversation, that day in the kitchen, when he'd told her about the dreams, she'd listened to him talk and didn't say a word until he'd finished. He expected her to contradict him in some way, to tell him that he'd imagined it, but instead she just nodded.

"So you believe me?" he asked.

"Of course. How else would you have known so many details?"

"I really felt like Alice wants you to know she's at peace."

Pearl patted his hand, then grabbed a napkin to wipe her tears. "That would be like Alice too. She hated for anyone to feel bad. And she was always making the best of things. I want to thank you, Joe, for telling me this. I've been dreading the end, but if Alice can forgive me, I have hope." And then, in a sudden rush of emotion, she said, "I love you, Joe."

And he said, "I love you too, Grandma."

Now, standing next to her casket, he was glad he'd said it back, even though at the time he wasn't sure he truly felt that way. In the short period of time that he'd known her, he'd become totally immersed in her life, past and present. He cared about Pearl, but saying he loved her may have been a stretch. But really, did it matter to what extent he loved her? The important thing was that he'd wanted her to feel loved. In the end, that was all that mattered.

Joe's parents and Linda arrived first, wearing their Sunday best. Joe was relieved they were there, especially when the residents of Pullman began to pour through the door, all of them presumably to pay their respects to Joe, and also to his father, Bill. As his father began working the crowd, Joe realized with a shock that of course his father knew people. Pullman had been his hometown; this was where his father had grown up. He seemed beloved. One man called out "Bill!" from across the room and ran up to clutch him in a bear hug. Several people told Joe they'd known his dad in high school, and one of the older women said she had been a neighbor from down the block.

Linda, overwhelmed by all the attention, attached herself to Kathleen, who didn't mind at all. "I just love your little sister," Kathleen said to Joe, and he nodded. It was clear the feeling was mutual.

And when a group of people, three generations, walked in, Joe caught his breath at the sight of the youngest of them, a curly-haired girl no older than four. The spitting image of little Daisy. When the eldest woman in the group approached Joe, he said, "You must be Pearl's sister Daisy."

Her hand flew to her chest in amazement. "How did you know?"

He smiled. "The little one looks just like you when you were a little girl. I'm Bill's son, Joe."

His great-aunt Daisy gave him a big hug. She apologized for her sisters Helen and Mae, who weren't able to make the trip for the funeral but sent their condolences. Daisy introduced him to her family—her husband, two children, their spouses and children. In turn, he introduced Linda and Kathleen. "This is Kathleen, my girlfriend. She's also Edna Clark's great-niece."

"Well, isn't that nice," Daisy said. "I always liked Edna. She was my sister Alice's best friend."

"I know," Kathleen said. "Edna told me about Alice. She sounded like a lovely person."

"Oh, she was. I was very young when she died, and I remember not quite understanding why she wasn't around anymore. She used to make up little songs just for me, and for a long time I thought if I sang them at night in my bed, she would come back to tuck me in." Her eyes got misty and her expression reflective. "I still remember one of them, all these years later. Isn't that something? I sing it to my granddaughter Julia." Her hand rested on the little girl's head.

"What do you sing to me, Grammy?" Julia asked, her chin tipped upward.

"Our special song. You know, the one I call the Alice song," Daisy said, and she began to sing softly: "Little, little darling child / Sweetest flower, small and wild / Fill me with your love and light / All my days' and nights' delight."

Kathleen listened, incredulous. As the little girl joined her grandmother in song, Kathleen mouthed the last few lines along with them.

"Nothing will keep us apart / You're always there in my heart / You are still my baby girl / Dearest one in all the world."

Somehow, Kathleen thought, Alice had made her presence known right then and there. Alice had been there for her little sister Daisy at the beginning of her life, and through her song, she'd stayed with her all the way through. She'd been only nineteen when she died, but her life had made such a difference. And, Kathleen reflected with a smile, Alice had ultimately brought her Joe, which was no small thing.

No small thing at all.

CHAPTER SIXTY-ONE

1983

When Kathleen walked into the Pine Cone during the lunch hour, Joe was in their usual booth, her drink waiting. On her way in, she paused to say hello to Miss Whitt, who was sitting at the counter. Ever since it came out that Miss Whitt had let Ricky stay at her house, Kathleen had gone out of her way to assure the old lady there were no hard feelings. "You had no way of knowing," Kathleen had said when Miss Whitt had tearfully confessed. Today she and Miss Whitt had a brief exchange. From where Joe sat, it looked like it concerned the soup of the day.

After leaving Miss Whitt, Kathleen came to join him, sliding into the other side of the booth with a smile. Her hair was down, soft and curled, and she wore narrow pants and a cashmere sweater, like Laura Petrie on *The Dick Van Dyke Show*. Her wardrobe was vast and varied but never boring.

"I like those skinny pants," he said. "They look good on you."

"They're called cigarette pants." She rested her hand on the menu. Neither of them needed to look at a menu anymore, but the staff provided them anyway. "Now that I'm wearing them, I'm required to take up smoking." She made her fingers into a *V* and feigned bringing a cigarette to her lips and blowing out a smoke ring.

He laughed at her silliness, and she reached over to take his hand. They no longer told people they were just friends. Now that they'd admitted they were dating, the townspeople had begun asking when they would be getting married. It was impossible to keep a low profile in Pullman.

After Pearl's death, Joe had discovered that he and Linda had inherited their grandmother's estate. He was staying behind in Pullman, ostensibly just to settle the estate and sell the house, but he knew he wasn't leaving after that. If Kathleen was in Pullman, that was where he was going to be. He had no reason to go and every reason to stay.

Doris came to take their order. "What'll it be?"

"The usual for me," Kathleen said.

"The usual for me as well." Joe gathered up the laminated menus and handed them over. After Doris walked away, he said to Kathleen, "You know what today is?"

"September fifth, 1983."

"Remember that date, because history is going to be made today at exactly one thirty this afternoon."

"One thirty? What are you talking about? What history?"

"Wait and watch the front door, and all will be revealed." He grinned, glad that most of the lunch crowd had already left. Doris brought their drinks and then later the sandwiches; the entire time Joe kept his eyes on his watch, waiting as the minute hand made its way to the bottom. Every now and then, he snuck a look behind him, worried he might miss it.

"I wish I knew what I was waiting for." Kathleen's gaze was aimed at the front of the restaurant. "Is a marching band going to come in or something?"

"Better than that. I'll give you a hint. Keep your eyes on Doris. She's the key to this whole thing."

When the door swung open, Joe allowed himself a glance back, relieved to see the boy he'd paid earlier coming in with a white envelope in his hand. The kid yelled, "Special delivery! I got something here for someone named Doris?"

Kathleen stared, mesmerized, and narrated for Joe's benefit. "Okay, the kid's holding up an envelope. Doris must have heard because she's coming out of the kitchen and going straight for him."

Doris's voice could be heard saying, "My name's Doris."

"Then this is for you." The kid's voice floated over the heads of the restaurant patrons.

Kathleen leaned forward and said, "He handed her the envelope and took off out the door. She's opening it now."

"Watch her face," Joe said. "Don't look away for even a second." They'd both forgotten their sandwiches, now half-eaten on their plates. "What do you see?"

"She's opened the envelope and looks puzzled. Now she's pulled out a note and is reading it."

"Keep looking," Joe said, barely able to contain his excitement. "What is she doing now?"

"She's smiling." A look of wonder came over Kathleen's face. "Really smiling, and she looks like she might cry."

"She's smiling, huh?" He rested his elbows on the table and tented his fingers. "But I thought that you said making her smile would be impossible." Joe couldn't stop grinning.

Kathleen tossed him a knowing look. "Joe Arneson, what did you do?" She reached over and nudged his arm.

"After I figured out that I was trying too hard and doing all the wrong things, I changed my strategy. I realized that I needed to give her a reason to smile. After a lot of thought, I came up with a plan. I filled an envelope with five hundred dollars in cash and put in an anonymous note saying she should use the money to buy Randy a new wheelchair and whatever else he needed."

"Nice," she said approvingly. "Where did you get the kid who delivered it?"

"Just a random child riding his bike on the street."

"And you just handed over an envelope with that much cash? What if he took off with the envelope?"

Joe shrugged. "I wasn't too worried about it. I paid him ten bucks and made a big deal about him coming in right at one thirty. Told him it was a secret mission. He seemed like a good kid."

"Wow, five hundred dollars. That's a lot of money. Nice of you."

"I had it, and she needed it. It was an easy thing to do."

Kathleen gave him an appreciative nod. "Well, you know what they say: God gives people money to see what they do with it."

"Who says that?"

She thought a second and said, "I'm not sure. It just popped into my head."

"I like it," he said approvingly. "God gives people money to see what they do with it. Words to live by."

CHAPTER SIXTY-TWO

Spring 1984

When Joe suggested a rowboat ride out to the island the first warm day of spring might be romantic, Kathleen was more than agreeable. This time around, Joe had rented a rowboat and arranged for her to meet him at the pier. When she arrived, he helped her into the boat and settled in to row, giving her the luxury of being a passenger. The lake rippled with small waves, and the air was warm and fresh, smelling like sunshine. Kathleen took a deep breath and opened her arms.

"What a glorious day," she said. "There's something so calming about being on the water."

Kathleen watched Joe happily rowing and took note of the way the surface of the water shimmered and sparkled, undulating before her eyes. She smoothed out the front of her skirt and lifted her chin to watch birds fly overhead. It had taken a lot for her to shake the guilt of being responsible for Ricky's death. Now, after so many months, some sadness still lingered, but she was working to put it behind her.

When they reached the island, Joe hopped out and pulled the boat onto shore, then helped her out. The island had a different feeling during the day, she reflected. Peaceful. Joe reached back into the boat and pulled a towel off a picnic basket, then grabbed the handle.

"I was wondering what that was," she said. "Aren't you the tricky one?"

"You haven't seen anything yet." Joe took her hand and led her down the path. When they reached the clearing, Kathleen stared in wonder, taking it all in. The site had been cleared of trash, and a linen tablecloth covered one of the picnic tables.

The trash barrel had been replaced with a shiny new one, and the metal sign hanging on it said **Keep Nature the Way God Intended. Pick Up after Yourself.**

Joe opened the picnic basket and took out an ice bucket and a bottle of champagne, along with two champagne flutes, and set them on the table.

"Champagne. Why the champagne?" she asked.

"To celebrate afterward."

"Afterward?" She felt a flutter of anticipation.

Joe took a small jeweler's box out of the picnic basket and said, "Kathleen, you've become everything to me. I've never felt this way before. I didn't know I *could* feel this way. I love you, and every day I fall even more in love with you."

"I love you too."

He dropped to one knee and took her hand. "Kathleen, would you do me the honor of becoming my wife?" He opened the box and revealed the engagement ring that had belonged to his great-grandmother. "If this ring isn't what you want, we can get something different."

Speechless, she motioned for him to get up, and he did, still holding the box. She took the offered ring and put it on her left ring finger. "It's beautiful. I love it."

"Kathleen, you didn't actually answer my question. Will you marry me?"

"Yes. Oh yes."

He lifted her off her feet and swung her around in a circle, making her laugh, then gently set her down, holding her in a firm embrace. Putting his lips next to her ear, he breathed a question. "May I kiss you, Kathleen Dinsmore?"

It was a good thing he was holding her close, because now she felt her knees weaken. "Yes, you may," she said, and then his mouth was against hers, his lips warm and tender, and it was everything she'd ever dreamed it would be and yet not nearly enough. She marveled at how natural it seemed and felt elated to realize that this was just the beginning. They could kiss like this for the rest of their lives. And then someday, besides having each other to count on, they'd have a family and a home.

When she'd first moved to Pullman, life was something to be gotten through, each day leading to the next, nothing remarkable about any of them. Now she saw the years ahead unfolding in beauty like rose petals come to bloom.

ACKNOWLEDGMENTS

A heartfelt thank-you to the Lake Union Publishing team at Amazon—Danielle Marshall, Gabe Dumpit, Kristin King, Erin Calligan Mooney, Nicole Pomeroy, Mikyla Bruder, Jeff Belle, and many others. You make writing and publishing books one of the greatest joys of my life.

To my family: Greg, Charlie, Rachel, Maria, and Jack McQuestion, you give my life love and purpose, and I appreciate you more than I can say.

What would I do without my early readers? Make a lot more mistakes would be my guess. Shout-outs go to Kristy Barrett, Kay Bratt, Tonni Callan, Kay Ehlers, Michelle San Juan, Barbara Taylor Sissel, and Cyndy Salamati for all their thoughtful comments and suggestions. Michelle San Juan gets an extra high five for really knowing her cocktail garnishes and generously sharing that knowledge with me.

I was lucky to have multiple people read over these pages in order to make corrections and suggest improvements. Sincere thanks go to Jessica Fogleman, Robin O'Dell, Karin Silver, Penina Lopez, Danielle Marshall, and Emma Reh. Copy editor Valerie Kalfrin gets a special thank-you for her astounding attention to detail.

A huge debt of gratitude to Alice L. Kent, who let me bestow two of her names on what is now my favorite character. Thank you, Alice.

To the other founding members of our reader Facebook group, My Book Tribe, thank you for including me in your inner circle. I love our drama-free, book-loving community. (If you're reading this and aren't part of our group, go join now. You won't be sorry.)

And last but never least, thanks to the readers who make it all possible. I cherish your reviews and messages and am glad you enjoy my stories. As long as you keep reading, I'll keep writing. Thank you for giving me that privilege.

ABOUT THE AUTHOR

Photo © 2016 Greg McQuestion

Karen McQuestion, the bestselling author of *Good Man, Dalton* and *Hello Love*, writes the books she would love to read—not only for adults but also for kids and teens. Her publishing story has been covered by the *Wall Street Journal*, *Entertainment Weekly*, and NPR. Karen has also appeared on ABC's *World News Now* and *America This Morning*. She lives with her family in Hartland, Wisconsin. To find out more about Karen and her books, visit www.KarenMcQuestion.com.